THE RADICAL NOVEL RECONSIDERED

A series of paperback reissues of mid-twentieth-century
U.S. left-wing fiction, with new biographical and critical
introductions by contemporary scholars.

Series Editor
Alan Wald, University of Michigan

THE WORLD ABOVE

The World Above

ABRAHAM POLONSKY

Introduction by Paul Buhle and Dave Wagner

UNIVERSITY OF ILLINOIS PRESS
Urbana and Chicago

Library of Congress Cataloging-in-Publication Data
Polonsky, Abraham.
The world above / Abraham Polonsky ;
introduction by Paul Buhle
and Dave Wagner.
p. cm. — (Radical novel reconsidered)
Includes bibliographical references (p.).
ISBN 0-252-06806-8 (pbk. : alk. paper)
1. German Americans—Fiction. I. Title. II. Series.
PS3531.0377W67   1999
813'.54—DC21   98-45490
CIP

For Sylvia

The Filmmaker as Novelist

Paul Buhle and Dave Wagner

Abraham Lincoln Polonsky's fame and stature rest primarily on his interrupted film career as a screenwriter and occasional director. Had he not written a single novel or short story, he would be remembered as a significant film artist in the estimation of many critics (including the director Martin Scorsese, an admirer and colleague) and one of the most significant scriptwriters of early television drama. *Body and Soul* and *Force of Evil*, the two masterpieces Polonsky co-created in 1947 and 1948, forcefully presented the promise of an independent film art in the United States, a promise cut off by the blacklisting that silenced him as a filmmaker for nearly twenty years. Those early efforts and television's "You Are There" (1953–55), along with the films *I Can Get It for You Wholesale* (released in 1951, on the eve of his blacklisting), his "comeback" feature *Tell Them Willie Boy Is Here* (1969), as well as *Odds against Tomorrow* (1958), *Madigan* (1968), *Romance of a Horse Thief* (1971), and several lesser efforts might well be considered enough for one career. But Polonsky began his artistic aspirations as a novelist and returned to the form again as circumstances changed. If less remembered than his film work, his novels have their own unique interest and importance, especially his personal favorite, *The World Above*.[1]

Over the course of his career, Polonsky published five novels. *The*

Goose Is Cooked (1940), devised for Simon and Schuster's series Inner Sanctum Mystery and written collaboratively with the scientist Mitchell Wilson under the joint nom de plume "Emmett Hogarth," is a playful jab at the whodunit genre of the day. Published as a magazine serial and reprinted in book form, *The Enemy Sea* (1943), an adventure novel about a Nazi plot to steal the contents of American oil tankers, afforded Polonsky the opportunity to analyze fascist personalities. *Season of Fear* (1956) is arguably the outstanding effort to make psychological sense out of the phenomenon of the Friendly Witness, the erstwhile friend and collaborator who testifies for the government against his own past and against the futures of those who made his success possible. *Zenia's Way* (1980), deeply autobiographical, traces a precocious boy's development in a left-wing environment of the 1910s and 1920s and two survivors' experiences in the terror-torn Middle East after they have outlived the historic moment of twentieth-century revolutionary dreams. *The World Above*, originally published in 1951, is Polonsky's second completed novel. An unusual work for any time, it might be best described as a combination of a bildungsroman-inflected life story, a Marxist-Freudian philosophical treatise with strong feminist overtones, and a reflection on the inner life of the New Deal/Popular Front intelligentsia, all moving in tandem across a wide swath of modern American history.

The World Above was written at a crucial juncture of left-wing (and American literary) history, and its importance rests in no small degree on the revelations that it makes directly and indirectly about that experience. Indeed, not unlike Polonsky's key films, this novel is conditioned by the sense that an era has passed and the time has come for reflection on its inner qualities.

The growing wave of repression long urged by political conservatives swept through intellectual and cultural life like a firestorm. Up to 1945, the Roosevelt administration's quiet embrace of progressives, and the wartime alliance with Soviet Russia, had for the most part protected those who dreamed of socialism but accepted New Deal liberalism as the best possible reality of the present. The new

Truman administration, however, turned the emerging cold war into a test of domestic politics. Determined to root out opponents of post–New Deal foreign policy, and threatened politically by the baiting of Republican conservatives, Truman directed his attorney general to compose a list of hundreds of proscribed cultural, social, and political organizations, announced dramatically in 1947.

Not only current participants but all individuals *ever* associated with these organizations were considered tainted, a taint removed by confession of past sins and the naming of associated sinners. Resistors were subjected to many penalties, including jail sentences but most often being banned from employment in their chosen fields. Within a half-dozen years, as the so-called blacklist swept through entertainment and education, many of the leading figures of the previous twenty years were swept aside, their reputations ruined, their careers finished. Blacklistees like Abraham Polonsky naturally pondered the larger narrative of heroic 1930s reformism, the defeat of fascism, the postwar era, and what it had meant after all.[2]

The Left around Abraham Polonsky was in crisis on other grounds as well. After the great victories of the Red Army and Marshall Tito against fascism came the dark years of revelations about Stalinist wrongdoing, including repression within the Soviet Union and its new satellite states. Jews and artists were among the obviously persecuted, and the rationalizations formerly employed (fascism's threat and the newness of the Soviet Union) no longer applied. These realities immeasurably diminished the American Left's appeal—even as Communists and their extended allies courageously led the postwar struggles for labor, civil rights, and civil liberties within the United States. The old certainties were gone here, too, and a time arrived for reflection on the irrational impulses that lay deeper than economic need.

Artistically speaking, the large Depression motifs of stylistic naturalism and politically labeled class conflict were receding amid the postwar prosperity. Radical novelists, like radical playwrights and filmmakers, devoted considerable effort to reconstructing the recollections of earlier days. They also turned to themes of racism and anti-Semitism in more focused ways than before, when class had seemed to crowd out other issues. But the mass psychology of a troubled society, suffering anomie and alienation despite the return of prosperity, now occupied a central status previously present only within the recesses of the artist's inwardness and self-conscious literary experimentation.

The contemporary popularity of psychology and psychoanalysis, especially but not only of the Freudian variety, played heavily on these themes. The war had dramatized the role of the irrational, most obviously in nazism and the Holocaust, while bringing many of the distinguished interpreters of irrationality to U.S. shores as intellectual exiles. The unsettling effects of wartime changes in American society excited fears just as deep, and more lasting.

These fears had a wide variety of conservative applications. The high rates of mental problems among draftees, and the public anxiety about the implications of women working in factories with their own wages and lives, prompted critics to declare a major crisis in sex roles. For liberals leaning rightward, the purported loss of masculinity even explained the African-American poverty that the Communists and other Marxists continued to interpret as the consequence of exploitation and racism. In the liberal (and conservative) view later popularized by Daniel P. Moynihan, a history of matrilineal families had deprived blacks of strong father figures, causing severe character deformation. *The Lost Sex* (1947), by Frederick Lundberg and Marnya Farnham, and *The Psychological Frontiers of Society* (1945), by the distinguished anthropologist Abram Kardiner, fairly set these dual theories into place as cold war truisms. Mainstream novels less than popular plays and films like *Lady in the Dark* (1946) prescribed a return to traditional sex roles as the answer—along with sturdy anticommunism and patience for gradual racial adjustments—to the contemporary restlessness.[3]

Left-wing artists had their own interpretations of the malaise. Another novel in the University of Illinois series The Radical Novel Reconsidered, Ira Wolfert's *Tucker's People* (on which Polonsky's classic film noir *Force of Evil* is based), explores blue-collar gambling and suggests themes of universal corruption that Polonsky renders with such vividness. Hollywood offered a wide arena for such explorations generally, at that immediate postwar moment, because of the wartime commercial success of left-wing scriptwriters (also a few directors) and because of public hunger for expressions of the widely perceived sensibility rarely permitted in the mainstream politics of the time. Between 1945 and 1951, when America's Iron Curtain fell definitively on the arts, dozens of left-influenced films noir drew out their themes of psychological despair with deep social roots. *Detour* (1945), *They Live by Night* (1948), *Thieves' Highway* (1949), *The Big Clock* (1948), *Framed* (1947), *Kiss the Blood Off My Hands* (1948), *Naked City* (1948), *Night in the City* (1950), *Raw Deal* (1948), and *The Strange Loves of Martha Ivers* (1946) are only a few of the more memorable entries in what was arguably American cinema's artistic apex.

Left-wing filmmakers had a curiously wider scope in some respects than politically like-minded novelists to explore the psychological byways of social themes. Given commercial film's presumed political limits (and given the considerable prestige and finances that the Beverly Hills faithful provided the Communist party), Hollywood radicals felt less need for realist (or naturalist) subjects and treatments as well as enjoying fewer opportunities to undertake them. The notorious "Hollywood ending," although perhaps scarcely less unrealistic than the class struggle conclusion of the standard 1930s proletarian novel, guaranteed a different and more "personal" framing. The relatively fixed character of the film genre (detective, musical comedy, "women's film," etc.) usually set the tone in any case. Rarely under intense scrutiny of the Left critics for the films they helped to create, Hollywoodites managed artistic-political experimentation of many kinds, albeit within some apparently unlikely venues like the family film or the slapstick comedy.[4]

The party's staunch ideologues did intermittently object to Freudianism, a perceived competitor to Marxism for intellectuals' loyalties and perhaps (via the probing psychoanalyst) even a security risk to the status of nonpublic members. Nevertheless, elements of the Hollywood Left did make efforts to bridge the gaps between the two encompassing theoretical schools of the day. Just as Polonsky arrived in Hollywood in 1946, a series of intended engagements between prominent psychoanalysts (some of them personally strong supporters of the Left) and scriptwriters ended in desultory fashion. The gaps were too large for either side to cross.[5] Much experimentation with psychological themes nevertheless continued in artistic practice, especially in those quarters where new, independent film companies sprang up, free of some of the constraints of the giants. Efforts like Enterprise Studios, whose atmosphere made possible Polonsky's best films, would presumably have grown by leaps and bounds if not for the Hollywood blacklist. Meanwhile, experimentation also languished in formal theory, victim of the cold war climate that included the rightward turn of psychoanalytical theorists and Communist intellectual rigidity.[6] This circumstance alone might explain Polonsky's use of the novel to unfold his simultaneously materialist and psychological observations about society, sex, and the natural world.

There were ample other reasons to do so. Given the political and legal pressures on the American Left after the crushing defeat of the Progressive party presidential candidate Henry Wallace in 1948, most radical novelists and screenwriters drifted away from the party or found their local political groups in such a desultory state that critical dialogue had lapsed into a private conversation among friends. In Europe, especially in the high-powered French milieu of Jean-Paul Sartre and *Les Tempes Moderne*, which Polonsky followed carefully, the literary-philosophical controversies swirling around the Left reached new heights. In the United States, left-wing writers were by 1950 mainly individuals on their own, struggling to make a living and to find a practical means—often enough, the novel—to put their ideas forward.

As Alan Wald has argued, these writers achieved more in sheer literary terms than anyone might have expected, and certainly more than any critics until the last few years have given them credit for accomplishing. Fellow Hollywood blacklistees Albert Maltz, Alvah Bessie, Philip Stevenson, Edward Huebsch, John Sanford, Samuel Ornitz, and Gordon Kahn stood among a large field of nearly forgotten writers who worked in almost every genre (except the anti-Communist novel), wrote high and low, gaining little attention at the time.[7] Nearly all deserved better than obscurity, but only Polonsky managed to return to the center of controversy via films (with *Tell Them Willie Boy Is Here*, in 1969, at once celebrated and bitterly attacked by critics) and to survive long enough to become a late-life celebrity of National Public Radio and the film festival circuit. To explain why his work should take a particular shape, and more precisely why *The World Above* deserves a more serious look today than it could gain in the blacklist era, we need to know a great deal more about Abraham Polonsky.

In brief, Polonsky is the son of educated, left-wing Jewish immigrants, has been successively a law student and sometime lawyer, college English professor, dramatic and comedy radio writer, union educator, military intelligence operative, filmmaker, novelist, television writer, and film teacher. Nearly all the while, Polonsky saw himself as an avid revolutionary—as much in the artistic sense as in the political sense.

A story like this holds more than one mystery. Perhaps the best point of initial entry is the novel Polonsky has described as the closest to autobiography that he will ever choose to put down: *Zenia's Way*. The world of the boy "Ram" is—as Polonsky now admits—more or less transparently his childhood world of East 180th Street in the Bronx, close to the Bronx Zoo, Bronx Lake, the Bronx River, and the Botanical Gardens. During the late 1910s and early 1920s, the area was on the verge of becoming a vast housing tract. Yet "miles and miles of empty lots where once there had been farms" remained empty, still close to real farms and wild fields by way of trolleys.[8]

Polonsky's father, a trained pharmacist who dreamed of becoming a physician, was diabetic and scarcely secure enough to maintain an independent business (the boy dutifully worked in the drugstore before and after school). Yet he kept a good political library and considered himself a socialist, even if not drawn to political activity in the thoroughly bourgeois United States. His legacy went to the boy whom he named, with pride and expectation, Abraham Lincoln.

His mother's mother, an avid storyteller, read to Polonsky endlessly from the fiction in the Yiddish-language *Jewish Daily Forward*, transposing historical characters rather than translating language. For her (and for the credulous boy), Huck and Tom in that most

xv

famous of all American adventure stories were actually Jewish boys rafting the Volga, and "Nigger Jim" was a muzhik, an escaped serf whom they assisted. When Polonsky testifies that his grandmother gave him all the stories he would ever need, we can take him at his metaphorical word: she bestowed on him a literary way of looking at the world. He would become many things, but he would never stop being a storyteller.[9]

Polonsky's family moved from the Bronx to Manhattan after his early years, and upon graduation from the famous DeWitt Clinton High School, he enrolled at the City College of New York. There he quickly became bored and restless, despite participating in a literary society with his friends Paul Goodman and Leonard Boudin, helping to revive a defunct college literary publication called *Lavendar*, and himself writing a witty column for the school newspaper. He spent a season on the track team and lost interest in classes, escaping middle-class life for a few months by following the fictional footprints of Melville's Ishmael (with "October in his soul"), shipping out to sea on a Morgan Line commercial vessel from New York to Galveston, Texas. He came back to finish at City College, by now more interested in writing novels than in a profession or in the radical politics then increasingly current during the early years of the Depression.

As the Depression continued, Polonsky adapted both practically and politically. He enrolled in Columbia Law School, paying his way by teaching night classes in English literature and writing at CCNY. In 1936, he joined the Communist party. He had instinctively voted in 1932 for Franklin Roosevelt and seen in the New Deal a way forward for the Left as well as the nation. With the Popular Front emerging, Polonsky formalized the relationship already established among his colleagues on pressing issues in and around the campus, from freedom of speech to the status of instructors. For him, the Communist party always represented at once a collection of free individuals (especially at the local base) and a distant bureaucracy. To be a Communist but to take as few orders as possible (either as artist or activist) was problematic at best. But then so was the idea of being a revolutionary in the United States—even during the Depression.

Polonsky always seemed to mix fatalism and idealism, as his films and novels reveal.

By 1935, law degree in hand, Polonsky was working in a New York law firm that had as one of its clients Gertrude Berg, the producer, writer, and star of the enormously popular radio show "The Goldbergs." When Berg herself appeared at the doorstep of the firm one day seeking help in writing a courtroom scene, the task was passed on to Polonsky, who drew on his writing background to dash off several pages of dialogue. Berg was so taken with his skill in scripting subsequent episodes that she invited the young lawyer to join her in 1937 on a trip to Hollywood, where she had been offered a screenwriting assignment. He discovered an unexpected taste: "As soon as I saw this magnificent nonsense going on, I said, 'This is the work for me.' I not only became an inmate, I wanted to run the asylum."[10]

Like dozens of other writers who finally ended up in films, Polonsky began writing dramatic pieces for network radio of the later 1930s. The media moment that first made Orson Welles famous (or notorious) on radio—the later New Deal years—saw the rise of quality drama, including audio versions of many serious contemporary films and a striking amount of original material. After returning to New York, Polonsky quit the law firm and made a living by balancing CCNY teaching assignments and writing briefly for "The Goldbergs," "The Columbia Workshop Theater," and Orson Welles's famous radio series "The Mercury Theater of the Air." He also collaborated with a close friend to produce his first novel, *The Goose Is Cooked*.[11]

By 1939–40, Polonsky might well have taken a chance and shifted his talents, as others did at the time, to California and films. That he did not do so reveals the claims that political commitments had already made on him. The industrially based, left-led CIO, reaching outward into territories previously hoarded by the conservative, craft-based AFL, needed someone to man the intellectual ramparts in Westchester County, New York, which despite its future as a wealthy suburbanites' haven was still largely a combination of countryside and industrial villages. For two years, Polonsky doubled as education director and editor of the district newspaper, *The Home*

Front, while continuing to teach at CCNY. His experience in the labor movement contributed to his comparative fearlessness in the days of the blacklist, because unlike other screenwriters (or directors) he had seen the struggle up close and violent.

Polonsky used his spare time to begin to write an occasional play. One fascinating script of the early 1940s focuses on a materially successful but spiritually desiccated Jewish family ripped apart by investigatory hearings targeted at "subversives."[12] Never produced—perhaps because the hearings and persecutions ended with the German invasion of the Soviet Union—the drama delves into family loyalty, also a central issue for the film *Force of Evil*, and freedom of speech, which Polonsky would treat repeatedly in his television years. He spent further available hours writing his second novel, the thriller *The Enemy Sea*, which was serialized in *American Magazine* and which barely surfaced in hard cover but got him a preliminary screenwriting contract.[13] Once again his destination was other than Hollywood.

In 1943, Polonsky joined the Office of Strategic Services, or OSS, a most curious precursor to the Central Intelligence Agency. He recalled that he was invited to join not in spite of his political orientation but because of it: leftists were correctly thought to be the most reliable antifascists, and the smartest. He was assigned to work with the British and spent his "active service" in the United Kingdom and in France, where he collaborated with partisans on radio broadcasts to the German Army during the weeks after D-Day. Just before the war ended, he saw a rigid anticommunism overtake decision making; and, in an incident recounted in the final chapter of *The World Above*, the OSS attempted to recruit him to go to China to fight the revolution gathering there. He took his leave as the war ended, continuing to work on a modernist novel, "The Discoverers," accepted for publication by Modern Age Books. The manuscript was withdrawn at the last minute due to an editorial shuffle and probably also to the loose narrative that placed the plot somewhere in the background.

Polonsky's true literary gift had begun to emerge. In a short story, "The Marvelous Boy," published in *American Mercury* in November 1946, he explores a theme that would be considered difficult in any period. A young woman teacher who specializes in the care of mentally handicapped children of the wealthy is given charge of a banker's thirteen-year-old son who may or may not have a gift for sculpture. The boy somehow awakens in her a sexual desire on which she acts, only once and then merely as an exhibitionist; but with such a resulting attack of guilt, she rejoices at the child's death, an apparent suicide. The story is notable for its sympathetic interest in women's sexuality, its concern with issues of repression and guilt in the context of class predation, and, above all, its sophistication in arcane areas of psychology, which would form the theoretical scaffolding of *The World Above*.[14]

He might have continued fiction writing, but Polonsky finally answered Hollywood's call. After a disappointing few months at Paramount, where his intended film about the Gypsy holocaust became a fluffy Marlene Deitrich vehicle, *Golden Earrings*, Polonsky joined the new independent company Enterprise Studios. The budgets were low and the genre limits clear—basic melodrama—but in these environs, the particular postwar social forces of class, gender, race, and culture combined to make extraordinary film work possible. Polonsky seized the opportunity to develop a visual language and a forcefulness of characterization that transcended genre. His first fully realized film, *Body and Soul*, written by Polonsky and directed by a fellow Communist (and former prizefighter), Robert Rossen, was a characteristic mixture of myth and realism, rigid formal plot structure, and flexible psychological interpretation of character. After the death of his black sparring partner, the protagonist (played by John Garfield) makes the fateful decision not to throw the upcoming title fight even after he has secretly bet his own savings on his opponent. He is now fighting not only for himself but for the dead man, for his own proletarian neighborhood, and for everyone else the system has ground down.

While the arc of the story's movement within one of Polonsky's genre myths is meticulously clear, there is another element—the one most remarked on by the film's admirers from the very beginning— that has set his films apart from other American movies: Polonsky's unique use of language. Nowhere is it so completely realized as in his second independent film, *Force of Evil* (1948). Against the simplicity of the story line emerges a Clifford Odets-style "city speech." Here also the sense of political struggle touches everything. The movie's opening shot is of Trinity Church on Wall Street, squeezed into a narrow profile by the slot-canyon walls of the office buildings. The camera pans down to the busy street, and we hear the first line of John Garfield's voiceover narration: "This is Wall Street, and today was important, because tomorrow, July 4, I intended to make my first million dollars. An important day in any man's life." The screen dissolves to an interior shot of one of the office buildings, where we see workers placing small numbers bets at a newsstand. Garfield, as a young, self-seeking lawyer, begins to explain the arcane science of amassing wealth from the collective tiny hopes of suckers who play overwhelming odds. Just because these cheap hoods, including Joe, have law degrees from elite institutions, wear silk hats, smoke pipes, and have offices "in the clouds," doesn't mean they're not cheap hoods.[15]

In one sense or another, everyone in *Force of Evil* is a cheap hood. This is a world unlike virtually anything ever seen in Hollywood, even in other left-wing films noir. There are no colorful, redemptive poor people willing to hold out hope for humanity with swelling speeches, no grandfatherly voices rounded with reassuring clichés. There is only illusion and disillusion, and whoever tries to draw moral distinctions merely plunges deeper into despair.[16]

By a monumental contrast, *I Can Get It for You Wholesale* (1951), for which Polonsky wrote the script but did not work on the production, is remembered today as an early expression of feminist sensibility. Its lead, Susan Hayward, pours her sweat equity into a small clothing manufacturing company, en route making one of the most articulate protests against the coordinated social effort to drive women back into the kitchen. Among his greatest talents, Polonsky was skilled at representing on the screen women capable of boldness and indisputably in charge of their own sexuality, employed and engaged in the changing world rather than mere victims or passive observers. Indeed, it is their conflict with the male characters that provides the narrative engine of the stories, not only of *I Can Get It for You Wholesale*, but also, just below the surface, of *Body and Soul*.[17]

Polonsky had meanwhile set himself on a return to fiction, and as *I*

Can Get It for You Wholesale went into production, he removed to France with his wife and two children to finish *The World Above*. Named before the House Committee on Un-American Activities, as he expected, he had one more major media role a few short years before him.[18] Returning to New York in 1951, joined by two fellow blacklistees and Hollywood pals, Walter Bernstein and Arnold Manoff, Polonsky began writing scripts pseudonymously for television's first acclaimed "quality" show, "You Are There" (1953–55). Produced by Charles W. Russell, with Mike Wallace and other news notables supplying the questions to imagined historical figures from Socrates to Galileo to Ulysses Grant, the series fairly radiated references to freedom of speech and its suppression across the ages.[19]

About writing for television Polonsky would say, like the title character in the teleplay "The Tragedy of John Milton": "my life is my work, and what I write merely the form that my life takes."[20] His preserved notebooks from these years are filled with closely written (or scribbled) pages of ruminations on the essentially literary question of finding a new language for the visual arts, and above all for cinema.[21]

Polonsky finally had the occasion to publish a manifesto about this question, in French, a decade later. This remarkable document, entitled "A Utopian Experiment," looks forward to a time when the apparatus of direction that now frames the dialogue would become something far more lyrical and subjective, substituting metaphorical insights for technical prose and using those flashes of insight as the subjective counterweight to the objective quality of the dialogue. Polonsky concludes the manifesto with the assertion that in such a cinema, "we might have in direct tension with the motion picture a literature of the film. . . . In the end we might escape from the paralysis of naturalism which has for so long distorted the reality of our condition on the screen."[22]

One might easily suggest that Polonsky had made a similar decision about the novel, remaining within the limits that a narrative demands but also visibly straining at those limits. The result is also a long, highly ambitious, and occasionally difficult work, *The World*

Above, that traces the evolving awareness of its German-American, lower-class protagonist through sometimes jarringly episodic stages of life (Polonsky would no doubt add, quite accurately, that they are no more jarring than the effects of real-life shifts of the 1930s and 1940s on millions of Americans). His character evolves from the first pages as an avid scientist in the laboratory to a lover and paramour, a distinguished psychologist, a military officer, and a near-existentialist to a fully realized human, one capable of accepting responsibility for a loving relationship with a woman whose personal history and motivations are as complex as his own.

Not the occasional difficulty of the plot, however, but the intricacy of character development mirroring the historical setting demands the reader's closest attention. Dr. Carl Myers is the same person from beginning to end, but he must realize his own qualities inside the framework of his era. In the first twenty pages of the novel, he is already placed within a decisive triangle, including also his dear friend David Seawithe (who has well-concealed but deep homosexual feelings) and his lover Sandy (also his friend's future wife). By inertia as much as desire, but even more by historical circumstances, Carl remains entrapped within the triangle during most of the novel and can only escape by shattering its boundaries. To suggest an overly easy interpretation, perhaps the triangle symbolizes the forces that come together in the thirties and fall apart in the forties, creating at first a troubled but somehow collective hopefulness and then a stark division of interests.

The boundaries are assuredly ones of class and political circumstance. David, who disappears to the margins of the narrative and then returns again at several critical moments, is not only the scion of a wealthy family but also a vigorous New Dealer. He will become an even more prominent (if less idealistic) liberal diplomat and officer in the European war to come. Without knowing it, he wants the power and celebrity natural to his social class more than he wants social change. That weakness was in the New Deal all along but only becomes clear as the bureaucracy of economic reconstruction is transformed into a bureaucracy for military victory and postwar hegemony over a suffering world. David loves his friend Carl (in more ways than he is conscious) but cannot really help him. Seduced not by the aura but by the research perquisites and public recognition of middle-class professional life, Carl finds his own way only with the greatest difficulty.

The World Above is scarcely less about family, both loyalties and tensions. We learn this gradually, as if discovering with Carl what he has managed to put out of his mind but must relearn at considerable pains. He has no wish to go home again; he also has no choice.

Carl's brother, Bill, is a union organizer for a time in Westchester County, a situation doubtless drawn from real life, as was the scenery, and is close to a few real-life anonymous heroes Polonsky knew and admired. Bill's wife, Juley, a woman whose pregnancy and personal difficulties make her appear both slovenly and contrite, strikes us at first (through Carl's eyes) as physically repellant and later as a blowsy war worker whose looks and behavior epitomize how home-front life has fallen apart. Struggling with an infant and then a growing child, for a long stretch of the novel, Juley is in fact more intelligent and more courageous than Carl can imagine.

If Carl is puzzled by his brother's apparent invitation of beatings and worse, he can feel only a deep sense of fatalism about his own connections with his aging, widowed mother. Faced with the kind of family conflict that reminds us of Odets's theatrical scenarios (Polonsky has, in fact, often been described as the screenwriter who realized Odets's disappointed aspirations), she redresses him as a "self-satisfied selfish middle-class fool" (190). It is, at that point of the novel, a harsh judgment but scarcely a mistaken one. With all their faults, the rest of the family know themselves and their loyalties better than Carl does. The accomplished and promising scientist is the one who most badly needs a real-life education.

Carl gets that education in spades. But before examining the consequent narrative, it is valuable to examine some of the current trends in American psychology that touched ground by mid-century more subtly than the negative fears of women unleashed or minorities revenging themselves on civilization. Polonsky, an extreme admirer of Simone de Beauvoir, was guided into the salvation of his protagonist not by the dour Freud, nor by the alleged "biological determinism" of gender so popular at the time, so much as by the emergence of self-realization theories and even the sexual potentiality of women. The revelations of Alfred Kinsey were still years away and feminism was decades in the future. But the arguments for a distinctly unorthodox and radical approach to individual psychic growth were quietly beginning to be assembled by thinkers as distant as Abraham Maslow, Herbert Marcuse, and the Hollywood psychiatrist Judd Marmor (not so coincidentally the son of a distinguished Yiddish Communist journalist).[23] The escape from the "paralysis of naturalism" led through a different kind of knowledge and insight than Freud or Marx had to offer, albeit one owing considerably to both of them.

Early on, Carl learns that he must give up Sandy in order to receive from his friend David's family what is in essence a bribe: the funds to go abroad and continue his studies. This is not the greatest of sacrifices, because he wants far more to realize scientific discovery than to be a lover. When he returns, to take up residency at a distinguished research facility in Manhattan, Sandy is waiting for him, bored with her new life and ready for an extended affair that Carl is only too eager to be part of. Perhaps her husband, aware of his inadequacies as a lover, knows of her sexual adventures (Carl is not the only one, even if the most desired one) and does not disapprove.

From Carl's limited insight, the disappointments of science for science's sake lie at the center of his growing malaise. The facilities at a state psychiatric hospital in a picturesque village up the Hudson River from New York City are superb. Carl's work is inevitably brilliant. But his chief patient is a stricken little girl, apparently mute and hopeless despite drugs, shock therapy, and above all endless hours of close attention by Carl. The use of insulin sufficient to bring about a coma does prompt a surrealistic explosion of speech, if not communication, "a running flow of words, an effervescence of phrases, of run-on sentences, a million poems in one" (127). The truth about her, which cannot be articulated in this overexpression, is finally sexual, the fate of the passive child who, with puberty, regressed and tormented herself, unable either to return to childhood or to advance to anything like adult normalcy.

It is tempting if extreme to interpret the girl as symbolizing modern society, by the terms Marx uses in *The Eighteenth Brumaire*, trembling in the throes of potential rebirth but unable to complete the transition. This is certainly how Polonsky and a generation of political-minded intellectuals no longer optimistic (or young) were inclined to see the convulsions of the 1930s and 1940s as they looked back on them. Orthodox Communists like orthodox Freudians (and liberals as well as conservatives, for that matter) had their own pat answers. Polonsky had no formulas, only hope for growth of insight and potential, a hope resting too often on the thin reed of contemporary society's capacity to comprehend and act rightly. Or, as he put it in an interview: "I do not write stories which attempt to sell a certain morality to the audience. . . . If we have certain concerns about our nature in [the world], we're going to pay a price for that."[24] Redemption is never painless or free.

No wonder Carl leaps into adultery, significantly after a dismal visit to his family's flat at Second Avenue and Fourth Street, the old Lower East Side, drags him back toward a memory that he would rather repress. He dreams of escape: of the Europe he remembers (now under the cloud of fascism), of making love to women in a picturesque setting. He settles for Sandy.

By this time the gracious hostess to a circle of New Deal think-tankers—still bored, as unwilling as the stricken child to struggle with life—Sandy mirrors no less than her increasingly absent husband the uncertain commitments of the American middle class. Carl, however, is brought suddenly back to reality (perhaps a bit mechanically) by stumbling into the middle of a strike scene, beaten bloody and left for dead in his brother's cabin, mistaken for the class-conscious unionist that the non–upwardly mobile sibling had become more by instinct than choice.

The two worlds, connected through Carl's romance with Sandy but also through his interrupted friendship with her cuckolded husband, connect again still more decisively a few years later. In darkest 1939, American leaders are weighing their European options, and David is the brilliant diplomat facing "his fate, as his destiny, his great opportunity" (195), a moment as exciting to him as the early New

Deal. Two years later, Carl finds himself in London, strafed by V-bombs, a major in an air force hospital, and author of highly esteemed scientific papers. Here, David and Carl meet again, and the gravity of his old friend's (and rival's) feelings toward him become marginally clearer to Carl as events weigh on them.

From this point on, nothing as externally decisive as a world event intrudes on the novel. Like the real-life red novelists, the characters must work out their own fate in the postwar world. The book is strangely optimistic after all this difficulty and misunderstanding. The protagonist begins to straighten things out for himself even if he clearly cannot do so for the world.

It may well be that in Polonsky's mind, the death of Carl's brother during the war seals off those great hopes of the 1930s. He shows it beautifully in a dialogue between Carl and Bill's former union comrade Sam, initiated when Carl learns to his dismay that the man is living in Juley's apartment (and is obviously her current lover). At first outraged, Carl becomes unwillingly sympathetic as Sam describes his disappointment in the postwar world: "Those days are gone. We've flopped . . . and now it's different" (376). That proletarian possibility has vanished. Juley, with all her limitations and with a son to raise, is nonetheless the future. Sam, the lover who is about to be discarded, says to Carl, as if articulating the enduring element of the 1930s for its participants, "You belonged to us" (376).

The reader of *The World Above* will naturally wish to wrestle with the difficult question of what makes it both radical and unique among the other volumes in the series The Radical Novel Reconsidered. Most contemporary reviewers considered *The World Above* a realist epic. A *New York Times* writer compared it to Sinclair Lewis's *Arrowsmith*, in "a doctor's search for a working philosophy that will reconcile his strictly scientific principles with a broadly humanistic faith." Seen from a longer perspective, the characterization of the novel in this way, like the characterization of Polonsky's films via plot analysis, does too little justice to the qualities of his writing. The *Philadelphia Inquirer* review, which praised the book more generally as "fascinatingly rich in psychiatric insights and romantic interest," may actually be closer to the point that many of today's readers will find central to the enduring interest of *The World Above*.[25]

The World Above might best be described philosophically, as a tale written from the inside out, with its storytelling notably removed from the artful play on genre in Polonsky's films (genre being, after all, a tradition of stories created by someone else). As a novel, it is the work of a mind emancipated by its own struggle to create, and its structure is a record of that struggle. What it has in common with Polonsky's films is the marked use of language, which here is liberated from the poetry of film into a different kind of poetry, one that aims at nothing less than the description of the political structure of social reality.

Take this passage from an early scene in which Carl, depressed after a fight with his mother and brother, has just learned that his research funds have been cut off. He is stretched out on his bed and beginning to drift:

He wanted money. He needed money. He had to have money. The whole energy of life, its labor, its worth, lay coagulated in money. It was a money civilization and a money time and even science was helpless without money. Science was dreams without money, and one could not even invent a theory of the universe without money to prove it. It seemed that all history, the death of martyrs and the victories of conquerors, the pain and ecstasy of revolution, the repressions, tortures, pains and joys, were nothing but the slow accumulation of money, the creation of the horde which now like a magnetic mountain raised itself in the world; and each thought of man, each dream of nobility that launched itself upon the seas of life, was slowly and then swiftly attracted to this mountain where the thought was wrecked and the dream drowned while the money was attracted to the mountain and there added its tragedy to the mass. . .

He got off the bed and straightened his clothes, already thinking of who could help him. (64–65)

This is, despite the narrative shifts, still the world of *Body and Soul* and *Force of Evil*, in which anxious young men think about little else but money and worry over whether money has a memory or a moral conscience. It is a world, as Polonsky writes a few pages later, in which there is "enough despair to founder a civilization" (69).

After Carl emerges from the war with a successful record and has an extensive history of practice in a psychiatric hospital, the true novel of ideas begins to emerge. In a remarkable and probably unfilmable scene, he travels from California to New York to deliver his ground-breaking theory of the origins of mental illness, as derived from his study of the broken veterans of World War II, in a paper entitled "A General Theory of Causation." To a lecture hall full of the "pink faces and plump bodies" (350) of established practitioners, Carl begins with a description of his view of normative psychology: "Only when man was looked at not as mind reflecting or inventing the universe, but as an animal in conflict with it, an animal whose consciousness was part of his struggle with society and nature, part of his relation to it, part of his gift to it, in short, only when the mind was not removed from existence but discovered to be its creature, only then was a rational science of psychology actually possible" (353). He presses upon his uncomfortable audience that "no science of psychology can be founded on what man is, but only on what man is becoming, the general rule being that he is never becoming anything but what society itself is becoming" (354). From there it is a logical step or two for him to insist that society is the sick creature and that "mental illness is a form of action, a form of will, a form of struggle, but at the level of accepted social defeat" (358).

Twenty years before R. D. Laing but with none of Laing's cribbing from Eastern religious psychology, Polonsky created social theories, still drawing on the methods of historical materialism, that anticipated in many ways the best thinking of New Left writers. The theory expressed in *The World Above* continues to draw inquiries—Polonsky once told an interviewer that he had heard from medical students at Harvard and elsewhere.[26] The trouble Carl gets into for daring to utter the theory in public has its counterpart, of course, in Polonsky's own life. By the end of the story, Carl is hauled before a congressional committee under a manufactured charge. After a great deal of testimony, he repeats to the committee statements he made in New York:

"You dare to say they are true?" Vaughn [the committee chairman] shouted.

"Listen to yourself and you can be certain they are true," Carl replied.

"You are in contempt," Vaughn yelled, and he shook with fury and banged the rostrum.

"I would indeed be contemptible," Carl told him, "if I did not assert my rights against the gavel and the miseries of the time." (464)

Here, finally, is the radicalism of the novel, one consistent with the efforts of the Hollywood scenarist or unrealized playwright. Carl dares to see. He will pay dearly, but still he sees, and now he can see himself properly in relation to others. This is his small but significant victory in a society gone wrong. Polonsky himself has never been blind (except, of course, in illusions about the Soviet Union), but he too had to learn to see in a new way when the happy years of victory over fascism had fled and the endurance of empire had shown itself, East and West, with all the character deformation inherent.

Polonsky was vindicated when *Tell Them Willie Boy Is Here* hit the screens in 1969 (following numerous disappointments and several lesser films that he successfully scripted).[27] Ill health prohibited him from directing films after 1970, but as an avuncular figure and film teacher he has reached a new generation, influencing a significant group of younger directors, including Stephen Spielberg. He faced other disappointments, perhaps the most significant in 1991 when *Guilty by Suspicion* appeared under the directing and writing credit of Irwin Winkler. This film, which stars Robert DeNiro, is based on an original screenplay by Polonsky and was to have been directed by the French master Bertrand Tavernier. But Winkler took over the project, insisting that the protagonist be "innocent" (of being a Communist, that is), a change that took the sting out of the plot. As far as Polonsky was concerned, that and other changes destroyed the intent of his screenplay, and he was successful in having his name removed from the credits.[28]

The story of Polonsky's life is widely known in film circles. By the 1970s, his early cinematic work was at last being acknowledged by American critics (the British writers at *Sequence* and *Sight and Sound* had already discovered it, followed by the French writers for *Cahiers du Cinema*). This American "rediscovery," attributable almost entirely to the extraordinary critical success of *Willie Boy*, led to a rediscovery of *Force of Evil* by a new generation of critics. Robert Sklar's *City Boys* is now the accepted view of the extraordinary radicalism in both form and content of Polonsky's work: that he has taken noir artistry farther than anyone in film, and that he has stamped his distinct artistic-political perspective on several genres.[29]

Overall critical assessments of Polonsky's work remain too rare. A larger rediscovery still awaits this novelist and contributor to Hollywood's most unusual canon. *The World Above* will be reread both as a distinctive novel in its own regard and as a literary expression of one of the modern era's most restless, most relentless creative intellectual figures. Perhaps Martin Scorsese, speaking as a major figure of the world of film, should have the last word. He notes that *Force of Evil* "appears on the surface to be a tightly structured, 90-minute 'B' film" but "has so much more going for it." Then he adds the pregnant observation, "The moral drama has almost a mythic scale; it displays a corrupted world collapsing from within. In this respect, *Force of Evil* is very different from other films noir. It's not just the individual who is corrupted, but the entire system. It's a political as well as an existential vision."[30] Everything that Scorsese hints about the technique required for the achievement of *Force of Evil* applies fully to *The World Above*. The reader is in for a treat, and a challenge.

NOTES

This introduction is part of an ongoing study leading toward a biography of Abraham Polonsky, based in part on extensive interviews with him and other members of the shrinking blacklist community. Grateful acknowledgment is made to Alan Wald for his encouragement, in many ways, of this project.

1. See, e.g., Wiliam Pechter, "Abraham Polonsky and Force of Evil," *Film Quarterly* 15 (Spring 1962): 47; Jim Cook and Kingsley Canham, "Abraham Polonsky," *Screen* 11 (Summer 1970): 57; Brian Neve, *Film and Politics in America: A Social Tradition* (London: Routledge, 1992), 126–36; and Martin Scorsese, introduction to "Martin Scorsese Presents" video edition of *Force of Evil*, 1996.

2. See Ellen Schrecker, *No Ivory Tower: McCarthyism and the Universities* (New York: Oxford University Press, 1986); and Larry Ceplair and Steven Englund,

The Inquisition in Hollywood: Politics in the Film Community, 1930–1960 (Berkeley: University of California Press, 1983).

3. See Mari Jo Buhle, *Feminism and Its Discontents: A Century of Struggle with Psychoanalysis* (Cambridge, Mass.: Harvard University Press, 1998), 154–56, 178–83.

4. Communist publications often panned films written by individual Communists or near–Communists and occasionally assailed Hollywood writers for political "deviations." See the discussion of the Maltz controversy in note 6.

5. Leonardo Bercovici, interview by Paul Buhle, 2 Feb. 1992, Beverly Hills, Calif., in Patrick McGilligan and Paul Buhle, *Tender Comrades: A Backstory of the Hollywood Blacklist* (New York: St. Martin's Press, 1997), 36.

6. In the famous episode of 1946, when the screenwriter Albert Maltz was severely criticized for an essay in *New Masses* in which he had volunteered that the Communist party view of art as a weapon in the class struggle was a "vulgarization" of Marxism, Polonsky was one of only three in the Hollywood branch who voted against censure of Maltz. The other two were Arnold Manoff, destined to be Polonsky's collaborator in the television series "You Are There," and John Weber, formerly head of the Communist school in Hollywood. This microfaction held its position even when Maltz himself meekly agreed to accept the criticism and retract his stake in artistic independence. Although Manoff and Weber left the area, Polonsky later tried, with some success, to reconstitute a blacklistera Hollywood Left with an independent spirit. Meanwhile, little if any apparent political censorship applied to the Left's own film journal, *Hollywood Quarterly*. From its 1946 inception until 1950, when the political survivors removed themselves from the editorial board, it was conducted in a strictly professional if also generic left-wing manner, treating the technical aspects of films and their popular reception. On the Hollywood meeting about the Maltz affair, see Abraham Polonsky, interview by Paul Buhle and Dave Wagner, 7 Feb. 1996, Beverly Hills, Calif., in McGilligan and Buhle, *Tender Comrades*, 494. This recounting was confirmed in discussions between John Weber and the authors.

7. See Alan Wald, "Introduction," in Phillip Bonosky, *Burning Valley* (rpt., Urbana: University of Illinois Press, 1998), viii–ix.

8. Abraham Polonsky, *Zenia's Way* (New York: Lippencott and Crowell, 1980), 8.

9. Polonsky said of the images in his film *Romance of a Horse Thief* that they "signify something beyond, because they come by way of the tales my grandmother told me. . . . It is her voice I hear all through the movie and it was her voice and her face which toured the locations." Abraham Polonsky, unpublished interview by Paul Buhle and Dave Wagner, 7 Feb. 1996, Beverly Hills, Calif.

10. Ibid. See also Paul Buhle, "The Hollywood Blacklist and the Jew: An Exploration of Popular Culture," *Tikkun* 7 (Sept.–Oct. 1995): 35–40.

11. Emmett Hogarth (a.k.a. Abraham Polonsky and Mitchell Wilson), *The Goose Is Cooked* (New York: Simon and Schuster, 1940). Polonsky wryly commented that neither of the authors took the work seriously and added a note of comedy, for themselves at least, by putting a character named "Polonsky" into the novel. The two wrote alternate chapters. Polonsky, unpublished interview by Buhle and Wagner.

12. Scripts are in the Abraham Polonsky Collection, State Historical Society of Wisconsin, Madison. The Rapp Coudert query, adeptly created by conservative legislators after the Soviet Union signed a nonagression pact with Germany in 1939, permitted a sweeping witch hunt in the municipal colleges, with informers providing "evidence" of subversive intent by any and all Communist party members. The purge ended suddenly with the German invasion of Russia and the shift in U.S. alliances, but it provided a blueprint for so-called hearings to come. See Marv Gettleman, "Rapp-Coudert Inquiry," *Encyclopedia of the American Left* (rpt., Urbana: University of Illinois Press, 1992), 644.

13. Abraham Polonsky, *The Enemy Sea* (Boston: Little, Brown and Co., 1943).

14. Abraham Polonsky, "The Marvelous Boy," *American Mercury*, Nov. 1946, 550–62. Polonsky also published a curious fiction on the dangers of atomic radiation, describing the discovery of imaginary creatures on a Pacific island. See "A Little Fire," *Collier's*, 3 Aug. 1946, 18, 50–51.

15. Larry Ceplair, in an essay on Polonsky, argues with great clarity that *Force of Evil* is "not a film about evil, not a film noir nor a gangster movie, but a movie about the power of love and human attachment" ("Abraham Polonsky," in Gary Crowdus, ed., *A Political Companion to American Film* [Chicago: Lakeview Press, 1994], 334). See also Robert Sklar, *City Boys: Cagney, Bogart, Garfield* (Princeton, N.J.: Princeton University Press, 1992), 183–89.

16. See John Schultheiss, "Critical Commentary: Force of Evil—Existential Marx and Freud," in John Schultheiss, ed., *Force of Evil: The Critical Edition* (Northridge, Calif.: Center for Telecommunication Studies at California State University, 1996), 151–98.

17. On *I Can Get It for You Wholesale*, see Neve, *Film and Politics in America*, 201–4. An examination of the original script in the State Historical Society of Wisconsin archive shows the strongest feminist dialogue toned down but the essence retained.

Polonsky refuses to discuss the films that he "doctored" in the interim, but *Odds against Tomorrow* (1959) is a taut heist film pseudonymously written by him. It features Harry Belafonte, with whom Polonsky was close, as a desperate jazz musician thrown into a bank robbery with a racist, played by Robert Ryan in one of his memorable late performances. *Odds* is remembered largely as one of the last serious films noir to be shot in black and white and one of the best of the minor works of the director Robert Wise. Its ending is still routinely appropriated.

Polonsky actually returned to Hollywood under the sponsorship of the producer Jennings Lang and under his own screenplay credit in *Madigan* (1968), a cop thriller starring Richard Widmark and Henry Fonda. *Madigan* was shot entirely in New York City, adding a special sense of grit to the message, and was popular enough to be made into a television series, also starring Widmark.

18. Document 100-138754-469, Federal Bureau of Investigation Confidential Files on Hollywood, describes FBI agents' suspicions about Polonsky and includes transcripts of two telephone conversations taped in 1948. See Daniel J. Leab, ed., *Communist Activity in the Entertainment Industry* (Bethesda, Md.: University Publications of America, 1992).

19. During 1953–54, Polonsky also contributed scripts to the weekly half-hour dramatic show "Danger." See John Schultheiss and Mark Schaubert, eds., *To Illuminate Our Time: The Blacklisted Teleplays of Abraham Polonsky* (Los Angeles: Sadenlaur Publications, 1993). For recollections of the show and the trio of writers, see Walter Bernstein, *Inside Out: A Memoir of the Blacklist* (New York: Knopf, 1997), 206–24.

20. Schultheiss and Schaubert, *To Illuminate Our Time*, 345.

21. The Abraham Polonsky Collection, State Historical Society of Wisconsin, Madison, also contains scripts of unproduced films and several plays.

22. Quoted in Schultheiss, "Critical Commentary," 187.

23. See Buhle, *Feminism and Its Discontents*, 206–16.

24. Quoted in Schultheiss, "Critical Commentary," 179.

25. Both quotes are from the back cover of Abraham Polonsky's *Season of Fear* (New York: Cameron Associates, 1956).

26. Polonsky, unpublished interview by Buhle and Wagner.

27. Walter Bernstein, interview by Paul Buhle, New York City, 9 May 1994. Polonsky's later film credits are *Romance of a Horse Thief* (1971), *Avalanche Express* (1979), and *Monsignor* (1982). Still later projects, like a script for a television film about the Chilean government assassination in Washington, D.C., called "Assassination on Embassy Row," were not produced. The nonproduction of his screenplay "Mario the Magician," based on a Thomas Mann story, is one of Polonsky's keenest regrets.

28. Polonsky, unpublished interview by Buhle and Wagner; Bernstein, interview by Buhle.

29. Sklar, *City Boys*, 183–87, 206–10. See also Nora Sayre, *Running Time: Films of the Cold War* (New York: Dial Press, 1978), 33; Robert Siegel, ed., *The NPR Interviews* (New York: Houghton Mifflin, 1994), 62–67.

30. Scorsese, introduction to *Force of Evil*. Scorsese specifically mentions his own *Mean Streets* (1973), *Raging Bull* (1980), and *Goodfellas* (1990) as being influenced by Polonsky's first two movies. It is widely believed in Hollywood that some of the key dialogue in Oliver Stone's *Wall Street* (1987) was also inspired by *Force of Evil*.

BIBLIOGRAPHY

Books by Abraham Polonsky

The Goose Is Cooked (with Mitchell Wilson, writing as "Emmett Hogarth"). New York: Simon and Schuster, 1940.

The Enemy Sea. Boston: Little, Brown and Co., 1943.

The World Above. Boston: Little, Brown and Co., 1951.

A Season of Fear. New York: Cameron Associates, 1956.

Zenia's Way. New York: Lippencott and Crowell, 1980.

Reviews of *The World Above*

Cannon, Lee E. "Deep Unfathomed Caves." *Christian Century* 6 (2 May 1951): 561.

F.G.S. "Doctor's Dilemma." *New York Times,* 22 April 1951, sec. 7, p. 20.

Levin, Martin. "The World Above." *Saturday Review of Literature* 34 (28 April 1951): 41.

Morton, Frederic. "Modern Mind." *New York Herald Tribune Book Review,* 3 June 1951, 11.

Other Sources

Buhle, Paul. "Abraham Lincoln Polonsky's America," *American Quarterly* 49:4 (Dec. 1997): 874–81.

Schultheiss, John, ed., *Force of Evil: The Critical Edition.* Northridge, Calif.: Center for Telecommunication Studies at California State University, 1996.

Schultheiss, John, and Mark Schaubert, eds., *To Illuminate Our Time: The Blacklisted Plays of Abraham Polonsky.* Los Angeles: Sadenlaur Publications, 1993.

Talbot, David, and Barbara Zheutlin. *Creative Differences.* Boston: South End Press, 1978. 55–101.

PART ONE

The Crisis

i

IN the experimental laboratories of the River Hospital David Seawithe leaned against the scarred stone table and watched his friend, Dr. Carl Myers, operate upon a white rat. The blood hardly flowed from the tiny skull as Carl scraped the fascia from the bone and with a dental trephine cut a circular hole just posterior to the frontal suture. He used his rubber-gloved hands most delicately, most tenderly as he pierced the meninges with a needle and through the hole inserted a glass cannula, preparing to suck out the tissue of the prefrontal lobes like a man about to drink an ice-cream soda. It was at this point that David turned away, averting his fair frank head and drifting out of range of the brilliant floodlight into the cold shadows of the afternoon. "Disgusting," he said.

"The useful and the real are always disgusting." Carl spoke dryly, never looking up, for the operation was delicate and rats unlike pigeons very easily died of shock. He raised his voice a little higher, intoning in mockery, "Suffering humanity lives off the experimental rat. We should wear rats in our buttonholes, not violets. Congress should open this year, not with a prayer to end the depression, but with a hymn to *Mus norvegicus albinus,* my lovely Norwegian white rats. There should be rat prizes for law and art." The telephone interrupted. "Will you answer that, David, please? There should be rat prizes for politics, horse racing and pure science."

"Especially for you," his friend said and moved slowly toward the roll-top desk where the old battered phone, etched with acids

3

and initialed by bored students, sat upon a pile of French, German and English books.

Once again the bell tinkled and in a corner amid the problem boxes Bozo, the neurotic Dalmatian thoroughbred, whined nervously, shifting position, his black-tipped white hairs bristling because for him bells were mystical symbols of pain, times for emotional storms, signals of strange Pavlovian fate. "Doomed!" David once said. "Irrevocably doomed, now that there are no coaches or fire engines to run after, doomed to science because of a fascinating metabolic rate." "Why," Carl had demanded, "do lawyers sympathize with everything and everyone but their own clients?" But this was not true of David, who was one of the bright young lawyers of the New Deal and a social reformer with courage, beauty and inherited wealth. Behind the open half-glassed doors that led to the animal room the rats mewed softly in their cages or sometimes scratched out needle-sharp squeaks, and over all like a tensed claw was the jungle smell, the zoo smell of urine and formaldehyde.

David picked up the phone. "Hello," he said, "hello." He took the top book from the pile and with it hammered open one of the small glass panes in the leaded window that faced directly on the East River. Gratefully he breathed in the foggy air.

"Dr. Carl Myers?" a girl's voice politely inquired.

"No. What do you want?" The book opened in David's hand and he placed it on the desk and stared at the closely printed pages in which the name of Gibbs occurred and the formula $F = C - P + 2$. This relatively simple if incomprehensible equation was followed by others which soon became as wide as the page:

$$\lim_{N \to \infty} \frac{1}{N+1} \sum_{n=0}^{N} f(T^n x) = \int_0^1 f(\xi)\, d\xi$$

The girl asked, "Is Dr. Carl Myers there?"

And from the operating table Carl demanded, "Is it Sandy?"

"No," David replied. He stared at the mysterious letters and numbers, fascinated by his ignorance of them. "Another girl." He

4

glanced back at Carl. "Are you going to teach these rats how to solve equations?"

The girl asked briskly, "Say, is this the lab?"

"Well, what does she want?" Carl's hard voice recalled the phone. "And who is it? What are you doing there, David, dreaming?"

"Just admiring," David said. He spoke into the mouthpiece. "Who are you?"

"This is the director's office. Who's this?"

"A white rat," David replied, reading at random from the text, "whose brain operates according to the $\int_0^1 f(x)\, dx$ formula."

The girl laughed as did Carl and David looked back to the white-clothed body bent in focus over the work. "It's the director's office, Carl. What do I do?"

For the first time Carl turned his head, a twist of the powerful stocky shoulders, the heavy face, youthful, alert, intent. The gray eyes seemed black above the gauze mask, and the dark sullen head emerged as the single naked thing from the covering blank uniform. There was something obscure, remorseless in Carl, David felt, something painfully attractive, a wonderfully hard ambition which he could not find in himself and yet wanted to possess. And would, he thought, and would. "The director's office," Carl said.

"Yes."

The girl flirted over the telephone. "Is this Georgie?" She was enjoying herself and she playfully encouraged David. "Are you fooling around with me, Georgie?"

As Carl approached David lifted the receiver and mouthpiece for him and imitated the girl's voice. "Are you fooling around with her, Georgie?"

There was a flurry of giggles on the other end of the wire. "Come on, Georgie, tell your little girl friend. Come on, now."

"Shut up," Carl told her. He held his gloved hands soiled with rat tissue behind his back while he bent forward bringing his

5

masked mouth against the telephone. David smelled ether. "This is Dr. Meyers. What do you want?"

"Oh." A shutter closed upon her gaiety. "The director wants to see you right away, Dr. Meyers."

"All right." Carl straightened. "You can hang up, David," and he walked thoughtfully back to the table.

"Who's Georgie?" David asked the girl, but she had pulled the plug and retreated into anonymity. "Who's Georgie?" he asked Carl.

Carl picked up the still limp rat, examining it. "He washes up after the dirty med students," he said, "but he never washes himself and neither does she." He carried the animal back to the cages and there from the obscurity announced, "If the director wants to talk to me, David, it means I've gotten the Founder's Grant to put this experiment on a real long-term basis. It means all the money I need."

David gazed without pleasure at the remains of the operation, the bloody gauze, the forceps, knives, the sharp and pointed tools of torture, pain and science. "For how many years," he asked ironically, "would you like to vivisect these elegant white rats?"

Carl closed the door to the animal room and returned to his table to clean up. He dumped the instruments into the sterilizer and began to scrub the table.

"Tell me," David repeated, "how many years?" And he looked at his wrist watch and saw that it was getting on toward five and that very soon the heavy wooden door would open and Sandy would enter. His skin tightened. Each time he saw her it was like the tiny ring of an experimental bell setting off a whole chain of conditioned reflexes in his heart.

Briskly drying his hands Carl faced his friend. "I'm going to work at this until I can build a mechanical model or mechanical models, electrochemical models of the rat's nervous system, and then—"

"Don't tell me," David said. "I didn't mean to ask. You've got a religious fervor to turn men into machines."

6

"Because men are machines," Carl said. "They are. And when I have models of that kind I can state the mathematical laws that govern their operation and then we will have the beginning of a real science of neurology and ultimately of psychology."

"Good-by," David said. "Good-by, Carl Myers. You're lucky you've just turned twenty-five, because if you were a year older it'd be too late. That's how long it's going to take." He surveyed the laboratory, the cabinets, the files, the neat arrangement of slides, the tools, the weapons, the measuring machines, the bottles, and beyond the leaded windows the night stealing over the smoky shore of Brooklyn. "God help you."

The heavy wooden door to the hall creaked open, and first Sandy's blue training cap appeared and then her blond face, broad and catlike, the eyes squinting with pleasure. "Hello, boys."

David continued more loudly, "You want to prove I'm a machine and you're a machine and Sandy's a machine, all with interchangeable parts."

"I'm no machine," Sandy said. "My parts aren't interchangeable."

"Yes, you are," David insisted. "And when you and Carl get married, if you ever do, if the rats let you, it'll be like connecting up two machines, that's all." He picked up the book again and opened it anywhere, feeling the room tense with emotion for him, averting his gaze from the heavy blond hair of Sandy's head, the frail shoulders in her uniform, the absolute fragrance of her appearance for him. It was for this moment that he absented himself as often as he could from his work downtown, to wait here through the long hours of the afternoon, hoping that she would arrive. And even today, when the three of them had an appointment for the evening, he had come early not to miss a single moment of the pain and pleasure he might experience.

"Are you ready, Carl?" she asked.

"I've got to go over to the director's office." Carl straightened his collar and stooped to see himself in a little mirror set into the wall. He took out a pocket comb and ruffled his close-cropped hair without rearranging it. Then he was finished, ready to visit the

7

director. He stood facing his girl and his friend, his hands in the pockets of the neat blue suit he always wore, neat and tight and shiny with years of cleaning and pressing. "I think I've gotten the grant for continuing the experiments."

Sandy took Carl's arm and gently pushed him toward the door. "Go on," she said, "run. Tell him how happy you are and be back in ten minutes. I don't feel like a machine at all and I'm going to be unhappy."

"I don't know how long I'll be," Carl said, and he was smiling, the shy sudden smile which sometimes appeared magically in his hard face. "If I'm not back soon, you two go ahead. I'll catch up with you. Make her happy," he added to David. Carl moved with a rapid ease and was gone, the door closing, and David was left with Sandy and the experimental rats, the uneasy neurotic dog, Bozo, and his own suddenly agitated heart, all waiting their turn in a hostile world.

ii

ALL the corridors in the laboratory wing of the River Hospital and Medical School were dim and full of quirks, afterthoughts of rooms, stairwells and blunt dead ends. Today they were empty, and the buildings which usually shook with male voices now seemed dreamlike as far off down a corridor two women nurses chatted and smoked a quick forbidden cigarette. White-capped, pale faces above their loose blue capes, they looked medieval and remote, but they both waved vigorously to Carl, who waved back.

He turned a corner past the bulletin boards and went down a steep iron stairway. One naked electric bulb shaped brutal shadows on the steps, which were dotted with cigarette butts, paper candy covers and black buttons of hard chewing gum. At the foot of the stairs was an unlocked iron door used by the nurses when they sneaked out on dates, and through it he entered the courtyard.

The sooty mist floated down into this oblong roofless box, wetting the old brick walls, filling the air (Carl sniffed) with the empyreumatic fragrance of pyridine. This little courtyard, created by accident as the hospital and medical school grew around the first small building, topped sometimes with clouds, sometimes with wind, sometimes with one of those winter skies of pure blue porcelain, was today trembling with the coming on of rain. This prison square had entered Carl's imagination on first sight because it reminded him of the tenement back yards of his youth, and it had become a stony pleasant garden for him the way the laboratory had become his real home.

Slowly he crossed the old slate pavement, avoiding a little pool

9

of water from the morning's rain. He thought with fondness of his two years' work, the neat records, the graphs, the notes, the thousands of quantitated slides; he thought of the colony of rats bred solely for problem-solving skill like a race of mathematicians. He thought now with ambition and passion of the uninterrupted work that lay ahead and the field of honor and discovery that would be open to him. He had no doubts of his ability, of the richness of the material. It was a question of time, of time, of work, of imagination controlled to a specific end. His first paper had received a certain quiet acclaim, mainly because of the technique involved, but for him almost everything up to the present had been essential preparation, the delimiting of the field, and with this work now guaranteed by continuity, by the grant which was to be his, nothing stood in the way but the limits of the subject and his own intelligence.

On the river two boats passed and signaled each other. The phrase, hoarse and melancholy, spilled over into the courtyard and fell delicately on his mind as it so often had in the long morning hours of childhood fever. He listened across the years and heard the boats baying on the rivers and his father's soft step in the bedroom: the sickness of childhood and the terror dreams, the drawn face of his father appearing briefly in the early hours by the yellow light of the hall; the narrow lined face of his father, grimy from twelve hours of taxi driving through the murmuring city; the tender appearance, the concern, the whispered conversation with the mother, "How is the boy? Is he better now?" And then finally the awaited, the cool hand calloused and scratching on the childish skin — his father, dead of tuberculosis and diabetes at forty-one, rushed to dissolution by the Great War, work, poverty, and a hatred of life.

Carl looked up into the sky from which darkness now began to float down. The bitterness of the past, the mere struggle to survive, began to invade his present elation, his growing hope; and he shook his head and hurried across to the administration building where he would find the director and the livelier future. The life he had chosen for himself, the concentration on work and rigorous

10

ideas, the life in which at last he was beginning to achieve a certain success and security, would remove him forever, he hoped, from that fearful world of his youth in which his mother and younger brother and most of the world still dwelt.

iii

"MY only comfort is, on the other hand, that the disaster is general." This was evidently of small comfort to the director, Dr. Ayerdonk, who had the nervous habit of automatic writing, the left hand shielding the right from outside eyes. He crumpled the scrap of paper and flung it impatiently toward the wastepaper basket. It missed and rolled to Carl's feet. "Even a revolution is better than slow rot." The director rose and faced the model skyscraper that was to have been the *New* River Hospital and Medical College, but would not now be built. This delicately wrought miniature of the splendid real estate that he had hoped to administer had for years served as a focus of conversation in the director's office, and he could, with a sharp pencil, poke into windows and terraces explaining each of the various large departments which in sum would constitute "the model medical center." It would never be more than a model now. "That's all it is," he said bitterly, "a slow rot, social gangrene."

Carl used his most carefully controlled tone. "You mean," he asked again, "that my job's finished here, all finished?"

Forced to turn, the director drifted one small sympathetic step toward Carl. "If you weren't a medical man, Carl, I could slip you into some small crevice here or there, some routine little job to survive the storm." His voice died, suffered, revived. "But with a young man of your acknowledged brilliance! How would it look, for *us*?"

This word *brilliance* suddenly permitted the director to make up quite sincerely for the blow he had struck. It was a chance to offer something, a tribute which would in no sense affect the

12

financial problem of the school and hospital. "A brilliant young experimentalist like you, how would it look to be put in some clerical position or other, the young man who won every scholarship offered in college and medical school. Your career," he added most intimately, softly, "is as well known to me as my own." And now the director found an opportunity to hurt himself without actual injury, a great advantage. "My career, however famous, is over, but yours is about to begin, and a slight setback will do no great harm. To be young is money in the bank. It's wealth, good fortune." In this way he made Carl rich. "To be old is a natural poverty, each day an alm, a beggar's life while you wait to die." In this way, although rich, he made himself poor. The director, famous author of the epochal text required in all certified medical schools, *Mass Action of the Central Nervous System,* ached like a successful church for temporal power. He was sixty years old, a wrinkled man, every surface of skin or clothes being netted with patterns of wrinkles and creases: face, hands, shoes, suit, tie, hair. And now when he smiled, embarrassed, all the wrinkles rearranged themselves on his face like metallic filings magnetized.

Carl sat rigid, apparently patient and relaxed. He did not let himself accept these social bribes which would make the brutal conversation easier for the director and himself, this testimonial like the last meal of a condemned man, the warden's handshake, the priest at the grave. He asked precisely, crudely, as if it were his right to know, "Are you cutting the whole staff?"

"To the bone."

"It's hardly credible. What about the public services, the students?"

"My God," the director exclaimed and turned his palms up. He felt that Carl was being ungentlemanly about a difficult affair. "If the country is going bankrupt, the people will have to shift for themselves. Besides, as a private institution," and he emphasized the description, "we don't have to give explanations to anybody." He returned to his desk and looked vaguely at it until his glance was caught by the front cover of a magazine from which beamed the smiling, generous face of Franklin Roosevelt. "Perhaps if things improve, perhaps. As soon as things improve. After all, we have nothing to fear, I quote, except fear itself."

Carl uncrossed his legs and recrossed them the other way, persisting. "You're a famous neurologist, Dr. Ayerdonk, a scientist. You know the possible significance of the work I'm trying to do. You know that a year's interruption — a month's interruption — will destroy the entire experiment, and that two years of work will be lost. Why not sacrifice something else?"

The director did not let himself answer at once. He was too angry and Carl's problem seemed already solved to him. He let himself wander toward the model of the skyscraper again remembering the board meeting and the words that had most affected him. There was no use building the new buildings on charitably given land because the development could not in these bad times increase the real estate values adjoining the project. Simple facts, Merrick had said. Facts. The director ran a regretful finger up the architectural toy. "One of the trustees said, Merrick of the National Bank, pure science is a bribe to get the service of clever men you cannot buy for money. When we don't need clever men, the bribe is withdrawn. It's true. It's true. Pure science goes first. Our trust-fund income has dwindled to nothing during these depression years and we must keep the plant going as a mere institution. That," he said solemnly, "is our public trust. The social organism like the biological one must defend its very existence, even at the expense of one claw or another. We're no better than the lowly lobster." Dr. Ayerdonk was generally an amiable man and now he smiled at his own little simile. Thousands of wrinkles splashed from his mouth and from around his eyes which twitched like fish in a net. "We'll all have to limp along."

Carl arose. "All right," he said. "I'll limp."

Quickly the director was at his side searching for Carl's hand which he found and most generously shook. "You could," he said (he flung out the suggestion like a bonus), "you could try general practice. Thank God! People always get sick."

"But in bad times," Carl said bitterly, twisting away to go out, "they hire death, who works cheaper than doctors."

14

iv

CARL walked down the paneled corridor past the painted white colonial doors with their polished brass plaques, past the early prints of New York Bay, the First River Hospital, the First Cable Car, the First Free Clinic, and the bearded face of the Founder; he walked past the fragrance of old wood on such damp days, old carpets and leather settees; he was at the communicating door opening into the hospital odor of phenol and chlorine washes; he cut to the right down the wooden steps; then to the left through a back corridor behind whose wooden partitions he heard the voices of the cooks and smelled the laundry odor of dinner preparing; and there at last was the outside door.

There it was at last and he pushed it open and found himself again in the open courtyard that was a shortcut between the hospital and medical school. Night had come. Night had come as if the day could not bear this frightful hour. He looked around the courtyard and he looked up at the sky.

A spill of rain shivered on his hot face, a flutter of rain brushed him by as if shaken from a comb, and he heard the drainpipe fed by the roof gutters beginning to tinkle. In a light rain the drainpipe tinkled like the signal bell when *Mus norvegicus albinus* learned a conditioned reflex. It was completely unnecessary to postulate an image in the rat's mind, or consciousness itself, in order to predict its ability to run a maze. Cortical lesions were not fatal to the animal's ability to accomplish appropriate motor activities. On the other hand, when clever men are no longer needed the bribe is withdrawn. Carl's muscles flexed with knotting fury, those wonderful muscles whose physiology strangely enough gave

15

startling clues to the action of the nerves. He felt the flexing wave of it, the shake in the throat, the knees in a slight crouch, the tightness as for a blow to be received or struck. But the blow had already fallen.

With a sudden bound he ran across the courtyard, splashing through the pool of water. He flung open the heavy iron door and let it crash behind him. He took the steps in twos and turned down the corridor to his laboratory and there saw the light shining into the hallway and heard the voices of Sandy and David. He stopped himself suddenly. He stopped and listened to his quick breath and heard the laughter from his laboratory.

He could not bear to see them now and he wavered in the hall, looking down the whole dim length of it to the red exit light at the rear. Why were they waiting when he had told them to leave? A typewriter began to tap, the untrained hands hunting through the keys. There was a side door to the right which opened into the students' main lab and Carl walked in. He did not have the will to see anyone now.

He stood beside one of the slate-topped tables, picked up a Bunsen burner and stared into the darkness which gradually became less dark as he looked and grew accustomed to the soft unfinished shape of things, the sinks, the gas cabinets against one wall, and glass, glass as twisted tubings, flasks, test tubes in rows, the whole paraphernalia of the idiotic experiments made daily in pursuit of the medical degree. This vast room was dark and the large windows composed of dozens of little squares of glass glowed with a mildly phosphorescent mist and rain in which electric signs had bled their colored lights like dyes in water.

The conversation in Carl's office was a duet in which Sandy's off-key, rather hard voice became the banjo and David's clear voice the trumpet. There was nothing musical in the combination and not much variation, but the voices played upon each other, and sometimes together, while Carl listened to hear one word, a sign that they were ready to go. But only the tones carried and not the sense, so that the duet went on all mysteriously, secretly, although overheard like a whispering overheard in a dream in

16

which the dreamer knows the sense of the whisper and hears no single word. He wanted them to leave at once so he could enter his office, his quiet lab with its animals, and be there alone now. He could face no one at the moment, especially not the friendliness he would get from David, the warm outgoing helpfulness, the offer "to do something about it." But worse would be Sandy, worse, much worse. Carl's mind cringed beneath the projection of her sympathy. His hands tightened about the tube of the Bunsen burner as the comfort he imagined did not comfort but shamed him. Her harsh laugh twanged against a solo from David, and in that laugh he heard her desire to please.

Even if he said nothing, Sandy would know. She would sense something at once and try to comfort him. Shame dissolved his pride as death loosens the flesh and runs it into the reservoir of earth.

The typewriter tapped on and they both were laughing now, and then after a long time as he hovered there, confused and trembling, they moved again within the office, and now the outer door opened, and their feet sounded in the hall as the door closed.

Turning slowly Carl looked back to the open door of the lab by which he had entered. A small square of corridor was visible, and there, arm in arm, David and Sandy passed, David in his trench coat, hatless even in winter, Sandy in her blue cape and student's cap, her face peering up, engaged all smiles in David's personality, while she laughed again and again at the joke. They passed, and Carl heard their steps disappear into the general roar of the city, the offstage creaks of the hospital, and a truck going by in the tunnel of the street.

He walked hurriedly into his office and closed the door behind him.

Now he was alone with the fears of night.

This was his own little office in the center of the universe, the filing cabinets and index systems, the typewriter, the desk, and the leather couch on which he had spent so many nights alone, working without reference to the normal day, enjoying it, especially in the early morning hours, three, four, five o'clock. Often at five, Sandy

17

used to come to see him. This was before he had taken the two-room apartment in which to hide their relationship. She would steal across the courtyard, go up the iron stairway past the night watchman's smile. It was comic now to remember and stupid, to think of making love before the day began because it was the most secret hour. Where now in the whole world was there room for love?

The enameled green lamp on the flat desk shone brightly on a sheet of paper obviously placed to be read. Carl walked to his desk, sat down, and picked up the typewritten note.

Dear Carl,
1. *We waited half an hour.*
2. *We will be at your hovel till seven. (Sandy has to dress.)*
3. *Then we'll be eating at Marsala's till eight twenty-seven.*
4. *Then at the theater. Your tickets will be at the box office. (We do not intend to sacrifice our pleasures to your rats.)*
5. *If you don't come, it's because you don't love us and want to count the Founder's Grant.*
6. *I enjoy Sandy's company even if you don't.*
                                     David Seawithe 3rd

This was followed by a postscript in Sandy's elementary school scrawl.

            P.S. He does.
            Sandy (Laura) Carlsen 100th

Here David had crossed out the *100* and replaced it with the sign for infinity: ∞.

Carl's glance roved nervously to read something else, anything, because his flesh, his feelings, his thoughts had begun to seethe. He read the back of a blotter advertising Hilton's laboratory equipment, the titles of a dozen reference books in which editors achieved new editions by changing unimportant footnotes. His glance stuck on a picture postcard, the one Burkhardt had sent

18

from Vienna a year ago. Carl plucked it from its corner beneath the glass and read it again, the quick foolish scrawl of it: *Dear Carl: Food fine, women plentiful and cheap because they are starving; science thorough, and for laughs fairy night clubs and the sex-ridden Freudians. Come to Vienna and study man's nervous system while you titillate your own. Burky.*

Carl dropped the card into the wastepaper basket. He had never answered. What could he say to that fool when he himself dreamed of Vienna and Switzerland and the real work being done there? Burkhardt was the son of a wealthy internist supported by an infinite series of gastric ulcers in the rich, and could afford to titillate in Vienna. Carl thought of the quiet labs, the libraries, the pleasures of learning, of investigating — exciting, and somehow peaceful and deep, as if life were a well-stocked ocean liner adrift eternally on a southern sea.

He found himself slowly being magnetized, slowly being turned around by the weight of the files behind him. It was very clear now.

He arose impatiently and let himself be drawn with that passionate but fatal pessimism that clings to reread death sentences. He opened the heavy wooden drawers and his eyes counted the neat lettering, the references, the summaries, the well-planted facts, indexed and cross-indexed, the whole thing like a giant equation that revealed its motion at any point. Here were numberless hours of used life which if not permitted to fruit would kill. They were now dead. At random he bent and plucked a folder as a farmer squats and tugs from the dry earth a dry stalk of corn with its root like a beggar's hand. Carl recognized the half dozen graphs carefully executed in colored inks: 100 traverses by Rat 804 after extirpation of the left prefrontal lobe. Carl looked up and down the rows of files. Hours, intelligence, stood in line patient as reliefers behind these delicate, these painstaking notations. Nothing would be completed. Everything would be useless. The folder fell from his hand and spilled.

His overwhelmed glance pursued what there was in this room so that each dead thing struck its blow. And beyond through the

19

half-glassed doors where a night light burned was the animal room with its rows of cages and its problem boxes, mazes, hurdles, what David called "a gymnasium to exercise the nervous system of the rat."

Carl surveyed his folders, pulling out one and then another, looking at them with an empty mind, dropping them to the floor. The diagrams crushed beneath his feet, the pages tore, and the folders dropped one by one, now this one and now that as one letter after another reminded him of some bit of work doomed to sterility and waste.

There were the cages, neat, watered, alive with mewing of rats, and here and there an exercise wheel turning, going nowhere, a drain of energy which became an endless line on a drum of paper. Even in this cheap little experiment, the equipment was extravagant, industrial; the dependence on things, money, other people, enormous. An entire civilization had been invented for the experimental rat, machines to serve and measure them, environment and habits to condition them, clocks to time and clocks to shock them, special knives and scissors to cut them, open them, burn them, and finally a generation of trained minds to wait upon them, study them, and learn from them. And in the end what was there to learn bigger than the fact that the knowledge was useless and better not learned?

Furiously Carl grabbed a handful of folders and flung these into the room. The cardboard covers flapped apart and the pages flashed out like frightened birds. Shit. Death. All shit. Never again would he be dependent on things, money, people, anything. He had been bribed not to remember this and now the bribe was withdrawn. Never again. From now on he would have all the power in his own mind and no one would have any use of this experiment, this mistake, this weakness of his to believe that anyone else in the world cared about truth, intellectual honor, science. No one would ever see these records again. No one would ever have the benefit of the work and the technique. No one. He would put it all back into his mind. He grabbed a big iron barrel and

20

dragged it into the center of the room, removed the lid, and started to tip and tear folders into it. The paper cut his hands, balled and fumbled within his hands as if resisting, but he hacked away at it, working at it, working, a work of completion even if it were ruin. He would finish the experiment in the barrel.

He jerked drawers out and dumped them into the barrel. There was too much paper to tear, too stiff, too hard, too much. He started to pour bottles of dyes and stains in, broke bottles into it, smashed boxes of slides, and the barrel swam with color and scent, swam with chaos as the order of the known was reduced to the unknown again. He made such a racket that Bozo began to bark in the next room. Carl ran inside, snapped on the bright overhead lights and the cages came alive with rats.

Carl's shirt was wet with sweat, his hands stained with color, his thumb bleeding. He looked violently at the rat cages, at the generations waiting their turn. God damn them. Their turn was now. With the bribe withdrawn, everything was withdrawn. Nothing was to be left. Nothing.

He slid open a cabinet and took out two pounds of ether. Never again. Everything in the head and nothing that needed people, help, bolts, screws, machines.

Carl set up a row of big bell jars with tight glass tops, and then one by one he opened the cages and dropped the wriggling rats within along with a wad of ether-soaked cotton. The narcotic sweetness filled the air as with skill and swiftness he went about the work. His hands had been trained to handle rats and were sure.

He dumped jar after jar of dead rats into the hall incinerator. This was usual. Everything was usual. The student classes killed their quota of experimental animals and the incinerator absorbed them as cemeteries do the population of towns and cities. This was part of the equation as it moved from beginnings to ends.

And now the cages were empty and a special race of rats had come to an end before their time like a civilization before it could flourish.

21

And now the files were empty and nothing was left but the scientist, Carl Myers, and nothing mattered because the place was dead anyway.

Trembling he put on his coat and darkened the rooms, flooding night in upon the shambles of the laboratory. He left the disorder of his workroom, of his ambition, his hopes, his precise science, Bozo leashed to his hand; and he had no sense of going anywhere because the disorder of the world was unlimited.

Outside, the wind heeled around the river corner, the wind opened like a vast dark sail and flapped. Bozo cringed, trotting dutifully behind, cowering, cold. The mist was everywhere shot with centers and glints of electric light. And subtly, profoundly known from the earliest memory of this city on the sea, the great sea scent emerged from its ocean depths, rose in the air and walked up the bays and channels into the farthest slender river tentacles with which it clung to the land masses of the earth.

v

THIS was one of those marvelous nights in New York, early in spring, with always the threat of that last shock of snow. Between the cold that had been and the cold that was about to strike, already advancing over the northern hamlets, screaming at Boston and looting Buffalo with a half-gale, the city flowered in the wet darkness, in the free false hour, rapt with the smell of pavements and the sea, the old stones dripping their years, the traffic, that unique urban sensation familiar to Paris, London, Berlin and all the monster subplanets of this earth.

This neurotic satisfaction which Sandy felt, this translation of the city's tension, ugliness and pain into a symptom of pleasure, made her feel for a moment that she was a New Yorker. She stood under the dark marquee of the theater looking through the thin rain to the oily glitter of Broadway. Programs were scattered and torn upon the wet sidewalk, the cabs churned up filthy water in the roadway, but electric signs and windows agitated the heavy air, and this color play, this disease, touched her mind with romance. She had been dipped by David in consecutive baths of Italian food, flirting conversation, exotic costumes, the songs of the musical play, and now her senses dripped with fat and pleasure. She wanted to go on with it, to plunge again into this fertile city, but she wasn't free to forget Carl. She said irritably, peering into the eddying crowd, "He did say he was coming, David."

"He said he was coming, but he said he did not want to come."

She glanced shyly at Carl's friend, her friend, at the smiling face, the blond hair tousled with damp. "I don't think," she went on, "that he would waste a ticket. I'm just wondering, that's all."

23

David whistled for a cab. "His telephone in the lab doesn't answer."

"The night operator wouldn't tell you the truth. They all lie and cheat for him. Besides he may be home by now waiting for us."

She sat luxuriously back in the cab while they zigzagged with the traffic lights to the East Side. Flurries of rain washed the window. There was a spray and swish from passing cars. There was the motor rhythm of the taxi and the acid nibble of gasoline. Outside, the city became a harbor in which buildings and street lights rode like anchored ships.

David sat close but carefully so that their bodies did not touch, and carried on with the little joke that had been the victim of their conversation all evening.

"Very well," he said, "I'm willing to take you off Carl's hands, but what will it cost?" He turned his head to smile and they were almost face to face, faces touching, and yet they had not touched all evening except when the convention said touch: the hand on the arm, the hand against the side, the hand against the hand, the bodies meeting in the lobby, the hands about the shoulders as the coat fell, all those impersonal hands through which finally the bodies have been sculptured before touching is a lover's right.

"You're rich," Sandy giggled, "so you'll have to marry me." The taxicab stopped for a signal and the red light bathed their faces, drowned them in blood, a savage violent light. As the signal changed from red to green, ruddy desire seemed to drain from her face which was now cold, greenish, with high cheekbones and skin drawn tight. She died for a moment as the cab rolled on, but came alive in the darkness, murmuring ironically, "And wouldn't that be terrible?" She closed her eyes and thought of nothing, trying not to think of what her life might be.

David listened to her accent, mountain, Western; remembered her appearance, tough, wiry, like a tough mountain hare — flat-thighed, flat-bellied with a small, a beginner's bosom; and she was exotic for him. The one sensual area of her body was her marvelous sunny hair, so fully, generously piled on her head as if for Midas this was too much golden treasure, carelessly touched. He leaned

24

his head against the leather backing of the seat and was sorry that she was Carl's girl. Her uncovered head was a few inches from his face and the uncanny fragrance of her hair, the exquisite richness, tossed bouquets to his imagination as the cab lurched forward.

She came, he knew, from one of those hopeless railroad towns in the Far West, a junction at nowhere, a name and a legend: Elevation 6700 Ft. When transcontinental trains rocked by on the downgrade, passengers saw a handful of yellow-brown buildings (company color), a siding with rusty coal cars, sometimes a freight engine and a few flats of ties and rails, three stores, a main street right-angling the tracks but dissolving into wilderness two hundred feet south, dogs; and then once again, as before for hours and states, death, desolation, the landscape of the moon.

There is a certain wild and fearful poetry about such places, seas of sand and sage, waves of great burnt rock that beat winter and summer upon a few civilized objects and a score of people clinging to the main tracks like swimmers to a lifeline. In Sandy's sky-blue eyes, the desolation, an inward dreaming sense, remote, brought back from time to time the lonely buttes, the endless plateau, space so vast that time decayed within it; the sour smell of the saloon and the drinking; by night the train whistle echoing from divide to divide, sad and thrilling as the songs her grandmother used to sing, and always her father's ingrained silentness.

Arthur Carlsen, a second-generation Swede, had left Kansas during the great strike and taken a company job in the wilderness. He still brooded over it and it troubled him although he had long since adjusted himself to his motives, but he missed the glory which even now in his imagination sometimes brought a glow of triumph as he daydreamed what he then had been afraid to do. He believed that without real money a man couldn't be sure of anything, but by now he had long since given up any hope of amassing a fortune. Instead, he had company security. Sandy was the only child, named Laura after the mother. The older Laura had fused with the great space, the isolation, and lived long with the fear that in one of the drinking bouts at the saloon some passing section

25

hand might remember that day in Kansas when Art Carlsen had walked out under the protection of the Pinkertons. This fear was the real tie between husband and wife, the source of their imagination and whatever intellectual life they led. But it was alive only in their own minds, because the old strikers had long since forgotten the strike, no longer cared about it and would have accepted Judas, or Art Carlsen, as a friend.

Sandy had left home with the same sudden impulse to escape disaster. She endured a short love affair with a brakeman who paid her fare to New York, and she abandoned him on the night they arrived at Grand Central Station. What she wanted most in the world was never to lack for money, but she didn't imagine this would ever be her good fortune. David bewitched her with his good looks and his wealth, but she enjoyed him as Carl's friend, and sometimes in her dreams mixed them up and did not regret it.

So now her pointed chin dipped for warmth into the thrust-up rabbit collar of her coat, she stared ahead through the double window into the street in front of the cab. They passed under the Elevated and slowly wheeled to the curb, stopping under a dripping street light in front of the renovated brownstone. She sat unmoved while David hunted through his pockets for change to pay the fare, and she was afraid she had been too light, too pleasant, too coy with him, and that seduced by Carl's example he hoped merely to become her lover. She wanted him to be more serious, without intending to accept him, for she loved Carl. Sandy had no need of lovers. She was convinced there would never be any lack of them. All her experience had indicated men enough, whether the drunks stumbling from the outhouse to the saloon (one of whom had rather roughly made love to her in the freezing cold), or the doctors and patients in the hospital, or the young medical students. There would be no lack of husbands and lovers, of a sort. The real problem of her life was to rise by one means or another to one of those giant apartment houses, to the safety of the lighted rooms in the towers of the city where the penthouses rode the seas like magic yachts.

26

She had fallen in love with Carl because he had chosen her, and because she was very young it didn't seem possible that she could sit back and make another choice, and now this was her life and that was the end of it, just as her mother had a life in the wilderness, and other women their lives according to the men that had chosen them. She was incapable of meeting a problem but could act to escape, and therefore whatever she made of her life would be an escape into success or tragedy. It would be a flight.

David stood in the light rain, leaning within the open doorway of the cab. "Coming?" he asked. The roof of the cab poured water on his trench coat and beaded his hair with golden drops. He smiled and held out his hands, bending towards her.

She shook herself from her reverie and arose carelessly, striking her head against the cab roof.

"Careful!"

But she cried out in pain, "Damn it," and stumbled forward, her head bent towards him, and her damp hair loosened as the combs fell out, and spilled into his hands, foaming almost, heavy, clinging, winding through his fingers, and then her face, and she was leaning against him, off balance.

For Sandy there was only the sharp pain, but for David it was as if she had taken him in love, embraced and held him overwhelmed in an act of passion. There was the same decay of sense as when matter becomes sheer feeling. He held Sandy in his arms, her loose hair binding her to him. The street light misted by rain spun its diffuse light, gold catching at the gold, and the weight of the hair overcame him.

She rubbed the top of her head and straightened. "Damn it," she said, "damn it." But now threads of hair were caught in the button of his trench coat and as she tugged, she cried out again. He carefully undid them as she leaned toward him, and he looked down upon the heavy golden head, releasing her. Her face came up into the light, the hair falling back, and he kissed her on the cheek. She turned toward the house quickly, not saying a word, not even looking at him.

"Will you close the door, Jack?" the cabby asked, and David

closed the door, heard the cab drive off, and thoughtfully followed Sandy up the short stoop into the hallway.

They took turns ringing the bell, and after some half-dozen tries, Sandy said, "I guess he stayed at the lab, or had something important with the director." Then she stopped and looked vaguely around, not meeting his glance. "I think I'll go up and wait for him or go to sleep; I'm tired."

"I'm sorry," he said a little stiffly, "that Carl missed out on the evening." Impulsively he held out his hand, and she was forced to take it, just briefly touching his hand with her own. "Good night," he said.

"Why good night." But she was confused and she hesitated, and David did not want her to go. He wanted to hold her there, to look at her, to feel the presence of her disarrayed hair, as if she had just risen from sleep or love.

He felt his equivocal state as guilt and he forced himself to assert his friendship for Carl, its priority over this moment. "Did Carl," he asked, "ever tell you how we met?"

"No," she said.

Immersed in the privacy of this little hallway, feeling it as his sensual bond with Sandy, he leaned against the wall, and spoke slowly, each syllable tainted with memory. "It was at Harvard. There was a Professor Chamberlain who used to hold afternoon teas and talk about life in a radical way. And I came late one day. It was in the last week before the exams and the summer vacation. I remember distinctly because it was six o'clock and I had left a book behind and wanted it particularly that night. I came up the steps there out of the heat into the coolness and I saw what I first took to be a waiter going round from teacup to teacup, from plate to plate. But it was the strangest waiter, wearing a brown coat and gray trousers. I hesitated, standing back in the shadow, wondering — a thief, or perhaps a ghost. It was hard to tell what the figure was doing. And I saw he had a pitcher and was emptying the leftover milk and curdled cream into this large pitcher, surreptitiously and quickly. And he was collecting sandwiches unfinished and

28

untouched — there were always so many of them — putting them into a brown paper bag. And then this figure turned to go and softly came out, going quite close by me, and it was Carl."

"He didn't see you?"

"No."

"He would have hated you." Sandy looked past David into the rainy street, and with him felt the sadness and iron of that past, in a way so like her own.

"I found out who he was," David continued, "and we became friends. He used to send all the cash he got from his scholarships home to his family — you know, the cash for living expenses. He was actually starving. And now he still won't try to make a living. He still refuses, and picks out something as useless as experimental work in rats. As if he wanted to show all of us how much he despised the things we believe in, a decent life, some pleasure." He paused. He added softly, "Some love."

"Oh," Sandy said. "I don't think so. Good night." And she hurriedly opened the door with her key and let herself in. "Good night."

He started rapidly to walk away, going down the street at a good pace, feeling the rain on his face and the air growing colder. When he reached Third Avenue he stopped under the awning of a German delicatessen store that was still open. In the glare of the window's light, he carefully examined the button of his coat and untwined from it a single golden hair. He held the glittering thread, this lively filament in his hand. It seemed to him that he too was like a filament through which a current had run and charged him alight, for he was very happy, and everything of the night, the rain and the rising cold, the puddles that splashed to his knees, the shock of the overhead trains, the gutters running and the car wheels fanning great sprays upon the walks, and through it all flashes of garish light or soft and running radiance down lonely streets—all this, perfumed with night and damp, was bound by the single strand of hair which he could not even feel in his hand. He admitted to himself at last that he loved Sandy, and having abandoned his morality, the idea of what he should feel towards his friend's mistress, who would someday be his friend's wife, he felt a powerful access of pleasure like a man giving in to a vice for the last time before the struggle to reform.

vi

IT snowed now and then through the night, through the increasing cold, and it was snowing when the closet door clicked at dawn as Sandy took out her hat and coat, turning tiptoe on the icy linoleum of the top-floor two-room apartment.

Carl wakened in the pale, the wavering light, in the chilled room. He curled closer to himself for warmth, pulling the covers almost entirely over his head to smother himself in his own heated breath, as if to breathe himself back to sleep, yet he was waking all the time. He went through the small automatic motions of putting himself back to sleep, to the sleep from which he had not yet risen, but the more he clung to the soft death of sleep, the more his mind resisted. The senses ran open their channels and let more and more of the room pour in, the sounds of daybreak, the deadened sounds of the cars from the streets coming in to him. He tried like a snail to pull his sensitive probing, reacting mind into the shell of sleep. But he was unsubmerged rolling on the surface of the new day.

He kept his eyes closed and lay still, not wanting to talk with Sandy, waiting for her to leave so that he could fall asleep again. He let himself fall below, let himself go down into the depth of sleep again, unwilling to repeat this morning what he and Sandy had spoken of through the night. She was now on her way to the hospital and he could go to sleep again. The automobiles went by outside with a curious dampened sound. The tip of his face, his brow, his forehead, were chilled by the open window, and he knew it was snowing. He could not hear the snow fall and he did not dare to sit up and see, but he knew it was snowing. He could feel

31

it snow through the chilled air that covered the covers. The motion of the snow falling fell through his mind, and through it the weight of Sandy's body on her toes as she moved to the table and picked up her purse. It was her purse and those were Bozo's nails on the linoleum.

"Sh!" Sandy whispered. "Sh!"

Her voice was pinched small, so small as to be a grain of sound dropped into the silence of the room, but it precipitated more and more consciousness into Carl's mind. Ripples of perception came to him, and grains of reality broke off from the room and settled in his mind.

He waited for Sandy to open the door and leave so that he could be alone, and although he wanted to move, he decided against it because if she came over to look at him he would have to open his eyes, not daring to pretend to sleep if she watched him. He could not talk with her this morning and luxuriate in her sympathy as he had so shamelessly last night. He did not want to remember last night, the shameless rage and craving for relief, for pity. He had so much to think of, so much of his own life to imagine, to count, to number as it were this morning, that he did not want to begin anything with Sandy.

Wherever she was she stood still, and he knew there was no chance now to fall back into sleep since he was thinking of himself, of his problem, and wondering why it was after the monstrous shock of yesterday, that overturn, that he should feel so calm.

His mind was like a city covered with snow. His feelings lay beneath the snow, the smooth, the rounded snow. The sharp edges, the corners, the pits, the heights, the ruin of stones and crazy shapes were all beneath the even quiet snow. It was growing quieter, colder and more numb, and then Sandy moved on tiptoe, and the door was opened, the latch, the knob, everything sounding enormous in the quietness of snow and early morning, in the quietness of his heart.

The door closed, and as she started down the stairs, thumping away, he rolled over on his back and opened his eyes, glad to be awake, relieved to be free of the constraint of her presence, and

32

found himself staring in terror at his laboratory He remembered destroying it, he remembered that he would never visit it again, and now he was there standing by the stone table while a glacial daylight fell from the leaded windows upon the wrecked room. The light had the thickness of standing water and over all was the fragrance of orchids, that is ether, because ether is the unfulfilled fragrance of orchids. He did not dare move because it was absolutely imperative, and the command lay heavily upon him, it was absolutely dangerous to move upon the broken glass which lay splintered on the floor, the torn papers, and the bodies of the dead rats which were strewn everywhere, on shelves, in half-opened drawers, in the pockets of his laboratory gown. If he moved they would hear him outside and find out that he had destroyed the work of his youth. For he knew, with such sadness that he was weeping now suddenly as he knew it, that this was his youth and all its works, this was ambition strewn here everywhere and his youth was dead. The sorrow was unsupportable, impossible, and he turned and faced the three doors that led out at one end of the room. He began to move to the doors, and the naked soles of his feet cringed from the broken glass, but it was safe to be shoeless and not be heard. There was no pain from the glass, only a thin streak of blood that flowed from his feet and ran before him in a thin rivulet, hesitating before the three doors, damming up, and then slowly staining through, flowing in a thin hairlike streak beneath the left-hand door. He waited before the doors and did not know which one to enter. He could not bear to stand there in that terrible icy light which pressed upon him and pained his eyes, and he had to choose and could not choose which of the doors to enter by and he longed to faint. He longed to black out, to die and not be there and not have to choose, and he clung to the thought and clung and clung, until with narcotic sweetness his eyes closed and he started to fall away in the profoundest and most relaxing sleep of all his life, into a darkness soft as hands upon his eyes and mouth and nose. This was the bliss of forgetfulness — and then suddenly the center door flew open with a violent crash.

He opened his eyes as the door banged downstairs in the hallway of the apartment. It was Sandy who had let it crash on her way out into the street, and he half sat up and saw the snow flying above the rooftops outside his window. Chill air attacked his shoulders and he settled back and closed his eyes, wondering about the quick short dream he had had, and the peace at the end of it, and the sorrow of his life which still remained felt in his bones, real as real sorrow, it having invaded the secret tissue of deep feeling, of his unconscious life. The sorrow was dappled with points of pain, and yet somehow the relaxation and the warmth began to drain it off, and far down in his soul he remembered that he had to get up and go down to see his family today and tell them the bad news. But his mother would be singing a song, a waltz, and it was a waltz that was playing in some radio in some apartment in this snow-covered city of Vienna. The vast ballroom was blazing with candles and masked couples floated in vast circles around the polished floor beneath candelabra like stalactites, crystal stalactites that hung and burned from the roofless ceiling. And he was dressed in black and dancing to this waltz, and girl after girl entered his arms and danced a few steps with him only to be cast aside, and he was dancing alone and best by himself, gliding, and the music surged up immensely like a wave carrying him upon its crest and he saw a vast blue ocean and the rhythmic waves rising and falling and sunlight pouring upon his closed lids, sunlight and the liveliest blue, the intensest marvelous blue that poured into his eyes and into his brain and into his limbs while he danced alone across the sea.

vii

CARL always hated going downtown and this afternoon more than ever, for the tone of his second dream had remained, coloring his mind with blue, with delicacy and relief, with the future he wanted which was to go to Europe and continue his studies where psychology had first become a science in the experiments of Wundt and his followers. Going downtown was returning to the past. He disliked the physical sense of the city growing more complex and at the same time more disorganized like an organism infected with disease.

His mother and younger brother lived just above Houston Street between First and Second Avenues. They had a little two-room flat packed away on the third floor with sagging windows overlooking an areaway dotted with masts and strung with wash like a slip with pennant-flying yachts. When Carl slammed the entrance door of the tenement a slop of smell poured over him and a cat flashed its eyes in the dimness, bounding up the stairs as if jerked on a string.

He climbed the stairs and rang the bell which did not ring. He knocked and his mother opened the door.

"Why Carl," she cried out happily, and took him into her plump arms while expertly she closed the door against the cold with a kick of her left foot. His brother Bill, a boy of eighteen, was sitting at the kitchen table eating a sandwich above a cup of coffee.

Bill said, "Hello," and went back to the *Daily News* in whose gossip columns of the sports world he lived most of his mental life.

Carl removed his hat and coat as he breathed in the familiar family odor, cooking smells and soap tinged with the lavender his mother tucked away in drawers, closets and behind pictures. On the cracking walls glossy white paint reflected the light of unprotected bulbs, for his mother refused to shade the lights and waste electricity. Next to the economy of the other world she was mainly concerned with not wasting money in this one. She often quoted the dead father on the subject. "Your father used to say that poor people must never waste money, but they can waste all the time they like. Poor people have lots of time and no money. Rich people have lots of money and no time at all." The mother's belief in the world after death was not fanatic or even firmly based. Rather it was her main intellectual activity, like Bill's in baseball, for she was shrewd and liked to speculate on different subjects although her information was meager and her conclusions wild. She was an orderly, thrifty woman who had once been plump, blond and beautiful the way Alsatian girls can be; and she had loved her American husband with an overwhelming passion although disapproving in general of his radical opinions. Since his death she had forgotten her disagreements and now possessed all his former notions as her own, but distorted, and confused by time.

Carl sat across from his brother while his mother reheated the coffee. "I know you like it very hot," she said, "and you know it's not good to drink very hot things. It burns the stomach and gives you ulcers. But you're a doctor," she added sarcastically, "and know more than I do, don't you?" Saving a fresh match she lit the burner with a burnt match relighted under the evening soup which simmered in a large aluminum pot. "Do you want a sandwich? Bill did the world a favor today and brought home some fresh liverwurst."

Carl looked up with hopeful interest. "Working?"

As always when his emotions were aroused, a stain of pink ran into Bill's eyelids and spread over his face. His voice grew hoarse when he was excited, hoarse and eager, and a great air of sincerity transfigured him so that he appeared to speak out of a mission, out of great passion. Now he said hoarsely, "I quit today.

Maybe you can explain it to Mom. . . . I've tried and I give up."

The mother refused to turn around. Her back was sullen over the stove.

All Carl's feelings withdrew beneath the rock of his face. His bad news was coming at a bad time, but he was resolved to tell them no matter what, and even more firmly determined to say nothing of the two hundred dollars which he had saved. This two hundred dollars was solid time for him, it was time to think and time to plan. Giving it to the family would merely postpone the inevitable descent into the relief rolls. He looked down at the scrubbed white linoleum that covered the kitchen table. They were always having crises in the family because the economic equation never managed to work.

In addition to the thirty-five dollars a month contributed by Carl out of his hundred and ten, Bill had to earn from twenty to thirty dollars more for the family to exist. The jobs he took were incredibly hard to find, incredibly hard to do, filthy, boring, outrageous; and the boy drifted from place to place, never satisfied, yet always driven by necessity and boredom to begin again. The pattern was fixed. Each month the telephone rang at the hospital and the mother wept about the rent to Carl. There were then mutual recriminations with Carl telling the mother that Bill simply had to find work or keep at his job, and the mother upbraiding the older son for not practicing medicine and making a fortune. She considered his laboratory work foolish and uneconomical when so much education had been wasted on him, and never ceased to remind him of the sacrifices she had made to keep him in school. The truth was that she had made none, although she no longer knew this. Carl had supported himself and the mother too on the scholarships he won in the different schools. She had formerly been proud of his cleverness but ever since his graduation from high school, when she was present to see the local honors bestowed upon his dark and sullen head, the course of his career had never been real to her. He was absent from home for long periods and had sent her very little money. While she and Bill struggled to exist, he wasted his time studying at Harvard and Johns Hopkins,

37

and now was in a hospital doing God knows what for practically nothing. Each of these additional requests for money drove Carl frantic with exasperation against his family and he had never found the courage to deny his relatives, to cut himself off once and for all from these millstones around his neck, these petty stupid people who wandered through the world expecting somehow, some way, that they would eat and live and be happy simply by existing. Rather grimly he was glad he was out of work, adrift himself, because now he had a reason to cast off these old barnacles and be finished with them.

He looked up bitterly and Bill retreated behind his paper while the mother set the coffee cup down on the table with a little bang so that it spilled and made a pool in the saucer.

"Well," Carl asked, "what is it?"

Defiantly Bill put the paper down and looked at his mother who dripped gloom to his brother. "Don't you both look at me as if I'm in the wrong. I quit my job on Bleecker Street because I'm sick and tired of carting those rags around. I'm sick and tired of working in cold and dirty lofts surrounded by piles of stinking rags full of all kinds of germs, maybe scarlet fever or something."

"What are you talking about?" his mother demanded furiously. "What's scarlet fever got to do with anything? Besides, you had scarlet fever."

But Bill ignored her, he flamed out hoarsely at Carl. "Maybe you think it's nothing, you and those rats of yours up in that laboratory doing whatever you're doing. But pushing one of those handtrucks around all day and working under one light till ten o'clock just drowned in the filth of those dirty rags is more work than you ever did in your whole life. Just give me a laboratory and I won't complain, or a nice warm library and just a lot of books to read. I don't mind working but I'll be damned if I'll die of some dirty disease in a rag factory. I quit. That's all. I just quit. I'm going to work for the government instead, if you can knock some sense into the old lady's head."

Hysterical sobs caught up the mother, who had been standing there all tense and inward, waiting for the crying to come to her,

38

and now the storm of tears broke and she ran from the room, her big behind shaking, and they could hear her wailing in the next room and a pounding on the walls between.

Helplessly Bill said, "She keeps banging her head against the wall. She's just nuts."

"I don't get it," Carl said. "I haven't heard anything new, except this childish dream of getting a job with the government. You need a high-school diploma just to sweep the floors. What's the drama for? This isn't the first job you've run out on and it won't be the last." He rose belligerently and walked into the next room.

His mother sat on the couch, her back to the wall and rhythmically cried and knocked her head against the wall. Carl noticed quite dispassionately that she wasn't hurting herself but merely making a rhetorical gesture.

The room was clean, neat, and everything was falling to pieces. The one big easy chair sagged. The couch had wild, untied springs. The lamp had a split shade. And against one wall under a picture of the Virgin Mary stood a big brass double bed. It was the bed in which Carl had been conceived and born. It was sturdy, unbreakable and out of place, filling the small room with its presence, and whenever he visited his mother's house and saw it, it troubled him, because he could not imagine that his mother should be loved, and that she should have children and lie in that big bed with its old-fashioned bolsters and goose-down quilts, and make love and later bear in pain and affection the sons that were himself and his brother.

He looked at his mother's fat calves and the twist of rags which she used to hold up her torn stockings. "What's the matter with you?" he asked irritably. "Bill could really get sick on that job. I'm a doctor. I know. He's right to leave it."

She turned a tragic tear-stained face up to him. "I didn't ask him to stay there. And you never practiced medicine and you're no doctor, just a fool who takes care of dirty rats. What do you care? I don't ask him to work. I don't ask you or Bill for anything. I don't need anything."

Carl found himself yelling, just overwhelmed with her senseless stupidity. "Then what are you howling about? He's going to get another job. With the government. Isn't that better?"

From the next room Bill complained. "She won't sign the paper. I'm only eighteen and she has to sign the paper and she won't."

The mother screamed out past Carl, "I'll die first." And then she rose and gripped Carl's arms, begging him. "You don't want to see your only brother killed, do you? You're not cruel enough for that? You're not that bad no matter how bad you are. I know you hate him and you hate us and you wish we were both dead and out of the way of your life, but you're the oldest one, the head of the family, and you don't want to see him killed."

"She's off her nut." Bill came up to the doorway and stood there, his face red, frustrated and guilty. "All I did was make an application for the CCC."

"The army," the mother screamed. "He joined the army to get killed."

Carl turned to Bill. "The what?"

Bill ran an embarrassed hand through his light brown hair. "It's a new racket to help the unemployed. I didn't pay much attention to it or what they said, but you go off and live in the mountains and plant trees or pick daisies or some darn thing, and whatever pay you make they send home. At least a guy can eat and be out in the air and play a little ball on Sundays. It's something like the YMCA, I guess, and anyway you don't have to smell dirty rags all day until you vomit your guts out thinking of the people who died in them or shit or pissed in them, and now you got to sit in a cold loft and count them like they were dollar bills."

Furtively listening, the mother shrewdly asked, "And the name on the application blank was a major or something, wasn't it? An army man, wasn't he? That's the army, isn't it? They'll blow you up with a cannon, that's what they'll do. Whenever there's bad times they make war, don't they? And who do they blow up? You. You, you fool. You."

Bill shouted, "It isn't the army. I told you a million times it isn't the army."

And the mother shouted back, "I suppose you think they're going

40

to pay you money for running around in the woods and playing baseball."

"It's work." The red spots were big around Bill's blue eyes, and his voice grew rasping, agitated, uncontrollable. "It's for six months, not forever. Six months. Six lousy months. And the army is running it. They got nothing else to do so they're running it. I told you a million times when there's no war the army got nothing to do, so the President gave them this job."

"You can fool yourself but you can't fool me!" The mother opposed him, shaking and trembling with self-righteousness. "I wish your father were here to tell you. I know what he would say and I'm saying it to you because your older brother is a fool and knows nothing only how to feed white rats in a hospital for starvation wages. You're the son of a workingman. Why should you join the army? Wasn't it the army and the police who killed my brother René in the big strike in Strasbourg when I was a girl? I remember it. They take children of the fathers they want killed and make them murderers of their brothers. And you want to join it. I'll curse you if you join. I'll curse you so that . . ."

"Oh shut up," Bill yelled. "Shut up, God damn it."

Tense and tearing at each other, the mother and the younger son were ready to go on and on with it, but Carl could see that they were really enjoying themselves in a way, enjoying the fury and the relief of yelling, of letting go, to drain off the worry they both felt, and he thought furiously that he would give them something that would really make them shut up.

"Maybe the army wouldn't be so bad for Bill," he said coldly. "Anyway you both will have to start looking out for each other because I lost my job yesterday and from now on there's no more money from me." He turned viciously on his brother. "Maybe by next week you'll enjoy counting those rags and even eating them too."

But Bill was grinning. "So the depression has hit the white rat business." And he turned and went back into the kitchen, sat down and started to eat his sandwich again.

It was quiet after the noise, and Carl, after a numb glance at his

41

mother's shocked face, followed Bill to the table. His coffee was lukewarm but he drank it anyway, his throat dry from the disgust he felt, the impatience, the need to get away. He heard her shuffling around in the other room and then her slippered feet slapping into the kitchen where now she appeared at the kitchen table and sat heavily down. Her face was still, reflective, and with a knife she raked up the bread crumbs from Bill's sandwich, made a neat pile and then began to pick at them, eating them, thinking.

"Maybe it's not so bad as you think," she said finally. "You've got a medical diploma. Why don't you open an office and be a doctor? People get sick and they need doctors."

Carl wanted to say no at once, to say right out that he refused to, that he would never be a medical doctor in that way. But he didn't know how to explain this complex notion to his mother. "It's not easy," he said instead. "It takes a lot of money to open an office, to wait for patients."

"Things like that can be managed," she said. "If you want to, you can manage it."

"What makes you think," he asked, "that everything you want is easy to do?" Bill was sitting there removed from the conversation, watching curiously.

"Well it's the only thing," the mother said.

"That's what you think."

"What do you think?" Her full round face, so innocent of wisdom, looked up expectantly at him. "You have to eat. Of course, you can live here."

"Don't worry about me." He felt savage toward her, toward Bill who looked patiently on, watching Carl as if from the sidelines of a safe position. "I'll eat. You worry about yourself." And he ripped at his brother: "And you worry about yourself."

"I'm too young to worry," Bill replied.

There were no crumbs left but the mother continued to pick, like an aimless chicken, at the empty cloth. "Of course," she said with a certain comfortable ease, "we can all go on relief now that you have no job. At least that's something. And meanwhile you can look around and see how it is to get started as a doctor. Maybe

42

you'll have a little sense now. Maybe you won't think I've been crazy for advising you to take advantage of your diploma. Why there are a dozen families in this building you could practice with right away without even having an office if you didn't charge too much." It made her hopeful. "You could make two dollars right now by going upstairs where that child is lying with a hundred and two fever and her stupid mother is putting flaxseed packs on her chest as if the germs in the chest cared anything about what went on outside. Right now."

Carl flung out the reply he had promised himself never to make. "I'm a scientist, not a pill pusher."

"A what?" She turned to Bill for an ally, puzzled. "He's not a what?"

Carl rose from the table and got his hat and coat, putting them on with a nervous fury.

"Where are you going now?"

"Away, away!" he yelled, and the buttons were hard to find, but he found them. He stood at the door looking at his mother and his brother, and he did not know what to say to them when after all he did not know how to say it to himself. He stood there confounded by their passivity, by their profound ignorance of his life. He had elected himself to be a scientist, chosen it for himself, chosen himself for that career. He couldn't say I've elected myself to be a scientist. A what, she would ask. She sat there in her plumpness, poverty-stricken and hopeless, the gray apron shielding her old gray dress. Her colorless hair, blond going brown and gray, was looped over her full face, and he felt that she was secretly admiring herself, her judgment that he had been wrong and she had been right.

"Wrong!" he shouted at her. "Wrong! You're wrong!" She did not smile but she was triumphant, he felt. He knew it. She was triumphant with the deadness of the conventional life, of the life that seeks out the youth in children and squanders it. She was the mother, the family, the apartments multiplied a million times in this city, and a billion times throughout the world. She was the enormous trap of the whole society to catch him and form him into

43

one of those numberless martyrs to the already dead; for the world, he believed, was already dead when parents and authority approved of it. It had wasted itself, expended its force and was now a corpse tended by the guardians of the dead. He had no clear ambition, no clear dream in which finally at the end there was a thing, a flag, a mint, a castle to be taken, and then that was a life fulfilled. He had no such idea. He wanted something still unnamed, still unsaid, still mysterious in the universe.

"I will never," he announced quietly, "do anything I do not want to do just to make a living, you understand. And I will not sacrifice myself to get the respect of the respectable, or the fools who run this stupid world. You understand that. I don't care if you starve, if you run barefoot in the street begging for food."

She shook her head looking for sympathy to her younger son. "Ah! You're crazy," she said. "You're just as crazy as your father."

But Bill was not looking at her at all. He was held transfixed by a steady stare at Carl, a gaze incalculable and searching. The light brown hair of his head was uncombed and his light eyes like reflections from the white walls were blank, inward-staring.

They think I'm crazy, Carl thought.

"I'm crazy," he cried. "That's what I am. Crazy. Are you satisfied?"

The mother leaned her head between her hands with infinite hopelessness and very quietly this time began to weep. She murmured brokenly into her hands, "If I have to live like this and have sons like this, why did I have to live all these years after your father died, and suffer all these years?" She looked up at Carl, the tears most shamelessly running down her face and the bitterness thick in them. "There were the two of you so young and you will never know that I was alone here, alone in this terrible city with you two to feed, a cleaner. I went to the houses and cleaned all day and sometimes at night, washing, washing. I think I washed a million floors, a million floors, and I don't know why. I think I'm crazy like everybody else. I think we're all crazy because we don't know how to die when things are hopeless." Out of the depth of

44

her soul she raised a cry. "I hope you will never be happy all your life. Never, never."

And Carl fled, slamming the door behind him, flying down the wooden steps.

The winter struck him on the stoop, stopped him in his tracks, the iron bitterness of the cold shaking him, the stony cold shaking him.

It was snowing again, very lightly, but with the wind blowing the hard crystals like dust about his head. The crystals fell from an ultimate space and had an absolute cold, hard, individual feel like grains of icy sand.

An overwhelming realization of his innocence, his youthfulness, his brazen selfishness flooded him with terror. This was the street of his childhood and it meant nothing to him. It had no memory of happiness. Plum-colored darkness brimmed to the rooftops from the tide of dark that flowed in from the night. In desperation, he plunged from the stoop like a suicide, running up the street as if to escape.

$\overset{\cdots}{viii}$

IT took Sandy one nightful of lies and then another to make up her mind. She twisted and turned in the dark barracks of the training nurses and finally she left the hot rumpled bed and went into the midnight lounge to smoke a cigarette. She sat at an open window and before her was the snowy city, secret and laden, the buildings obscure, with only here and there a window burning unsupported in the muffled vacancy of night. It all seemed simpler now that she was awake, admitting it, and sitting up; but the moment she touched her bed, the moment she stretched her chilled body beneath the warm blanket, the turmoil of half-truths and arguments reappeared as if the horizontal favored the seepage of the unconscious. In the morning, exhausted and irritable, she found herself telephoning David at his office and she became so frightened she forgot what it was she had spent the long night preparing.

"I need your help," she said, "I have to see you." It paralyzed her with shame and self-consciousness to have said the truth, all at once this way, and to recoup she blamed Carl. "It's about Carl." But this was worse since it joined David to her and Carl in some kind of meaning which she refused to recognize. It made her tongue-tied altogether and she could say nothing else except *yes,* that she would meet him at his office and have lunch with him, agreeing to anything to get away from the telephone.

When she walked out of the telephone booth she had decided not to meet David at all, to reassert her independence by breaking the appointment. This made the morning endurable.

At eleven-thirty she started to dress to go out, not thinking of

46

any place in particular to go, only that she had the day free until four o'clock and it would be better to walk around somewhere even in the cold than to stay at the hospital and brood. The right thumb of her one pair of black kid gloves was torn and she carefully sewed it up. And then all at once it was a quarter to one and she was fifteen minutes late. She flew out of the building, forgetting her handkerchief, wondering how she looked, was her lipstick smeared, knowing she was going to be late and afraid she had forgotten the number of the office building.

Sandy was a good half hour late when she entered the lofty humming lobby of the Hudson Trust Building near Pine and Wall Streets. And she was depressed by the banks of elevators, the thrusting crowds pouring out for lunch or returning, the streets filled with dirty snow and wet and the office boys throwing snowballs at each other, a sense of noise, business and holiday. At the fortieth floor the elevator stopped with a downward drag, cushioned and caught her heart with nausea, and there she was in a quiet, carpeted sitting room where twin desks faced her, and mild lamps shone and quietness sat tenderly, delicately menacing her. A woman was reading a newspaper at one of the desks, and she looked up brightly, smiled out of habit, only to frown a little when she saw Sandy. This woman was handsome, seemed clever and was nearly thirty, which defeated the girl with inferiority. Sandy rubbed the scar of sewing on her gloved right thumb, hesitated, looking this way and that as if to escape, but the elevator doors were closed and there was no exit except the closed doors which the receptionist guarded.

"Yes?" the woman asked.

"Mr. Seawithe?" Sandy spoke so low she was afraid she hadn't been heard and she raised her voice, but it came out now too loudly in that quiet gray room. "David Seawithe."

Now the woman smiled again, this time welcoming her. "Ah. Miss Carlsen. He's expecting you. Will you go in?" And she rose to open the oaken double doors, revealing green carpeting, hallways with pictures on them, tables flooding lamplight, and dimly in the distance a library in which an old man in a gray jacket was putting

47

books back into their high shelves. "Down this way and to your left. Mr. Seawithe's name is on the door."

Sandy went swiftly by the receptionist, ducking her head a little as if to escape a blow, swiftly down the corridor on silent rug-softened feet, to the left, and there was the door with a name that dragged her forward to safety, a recognized name against all the silence and power which seemed to squeeze against her from the walls. She didn't even knock but opened the door with a desperate push, surprising David who was standing at the tremendous window of the small room and looking down upon the gray bay, out at the gray sky and the gray water which formed an immenser wall around this so immense city.

"Sandy!"

"I'm sorry I'm late," and she closed the door, breathless and safe. He made her feel safe as he stood there in a blue jacket and gray trousers, his face shining and rosy, smiling, and his blond hair transparent in the light of the window.

"I was just going over in my mind one by one," he said easily, inviting her in, taking her hands, "which of the restaurants should have the honor of celebrating our first luncheon together. Because I want to remember this afternoon, my first alone with you." He took the word *alone* and let his voice linger on it so that suddenly she was intimately there with him. He led her to a chair, sat her down, perched himself on the desk before her looking down on her little black hat from which her hair escaped. Now he opened a cigarette box and held it forward as an offering, "But I hope nothing terrible's happened. You sounded so incoherent and frightened this morning."

"Oh nothing, nothing," she gasped. "Nothing." She took one of the cigarettes and saw the sewed thumb. Immediately she transferred the cigarette to her left hand, and made a fist with her right, her thumb hidden underneath her fingers. "I mean that Carl lost his job." And as David's eyes opened with surprise and then narrowed with thought, she added, "He's finished there and his experiment is ruined."

David lighted her cigarette and listened to her story. His atten-

48

tion was rapt and he never said a word when it was all through, but sat there looking out of the window, his face serious, and, she thought with a catch of tension, very handsome. The silence grew longer and she smoked rapidly instead of talking, until her head began to swim and she felt hot and uncomfortable in her coat. She started to open the collar and this awakened him for he smiled and stood up. "It's no use starving to death," he said. "Why don't we go to lunch and talk about it?"

With David at her side, his arm protective at her elbow, it was easier to retrace her steps and feel her right to walk through the office, to descend in the elevator, to march through the lobby. And walking by his side down the crowded streets she found herself like a tourist with time to look about. David wheeled her around a corner into a narrow street, tiny as a village street but lined not with cottages, only skyscrapers which plunged thick masses of concrete like roots from immense heights, and deafened her mind with their silent weight. Another turn and a doorman was opening dark doors with bright brass handles into a restaurant out of which a tumult of male voices sounded. An attendant took David's coat and he nodded here and there and said hello into the maze of faces and tables, but she could understand nothing, so alien did she feel, as if this were a foreign city and the language a foreign tongue. Now they followed the waiter down a row of tables out of which the male voices continually rose, with only an occasional woman to break the uniform of dark suits and red faces and bald heads and gray heads, as if this restaurant were a tribunal of the old, the rich and the powerful and she were being marched between them to be seen and judged for having dared to call David on the telephone. At one table a bald fat man stopped David and she halted, not knowing whether it was proper for her to wait or go on ahead after the waiter, but David said, "Miss Carlsen, Senator Wilson." The man half rose and nodded to her, and then a bass voice, powerful and rhetorical for all the restaurant to hear, announced, "Why how do you do, Miss Carlsen." And to David, "I haven't seen your father, David, for six months, but when you see him tonight, if you do, tell him from me that I read his dissent in the Crystal case

49

and that his opinion is the opinion of the entire committee. Epochal in these foolish times. By the way, how is he?"

"Fine," David replied casually, to a senator, she thought, a senator of the United States. With David's hand at her elbow guiding her way, they left and David's voice whispered confidentially in her ear, "An old reactionary fool."

She was deposited in a booth and David took her coat, turning away to hang it on a little brass hook on the oaken partition. She took off her gloves and the seam in the thumb opened. Hastily she hid the gloves in her lap and looked up, but David still had his back to her, and now he turned, as the headwaiter and two assistants gathered like a black crowd of fancy beggars behind him, and asked as if nothing else in the world mattered, "Comfortable? Are you warm enough?"

"Yes, yes," she mumbled. "Yes." And she felt her neat brown dress a pitiful thing and was glad for the darkness of the corner and the voices that came to them covering her confusion with even greater disarray.

Neatly and agile David ducked around so that he was sitting beside her on the leather bench with the heavy leather cushions, and they both faced across the open side of the booth, a little raised, looking down on the numerous moons of white cloth and the hurried passage of waiters, a swamp of sound and faces and the warm, feeding smells of lunchtime.

A great stiff white card was handed to her by the thin refined headwaiter and another to David, but he put his down and leaned close to read with her the crowded list of dishes.

He started to explain what was written there, but what he said and what he explained were all lost on Sandy, who was alive only to his presence, the narrow golden head and the clean young smell of face and hair. She sat tightly not hearing and finally uttered a forlorn and helpless, "Anything," which made him laugh. He ordered for both of them, and then half turned, still sitting close to her, presenting a serious countenance, and troubled eyes. It was as if he had two demeanors, she thought, one for the escort and the other for the friend. And perhaps there was a third, a

50

lover; and a fourth, more mysterious than any, the rich young man of the rich family. And even others for fathers, mothers, relatives, a galaxy of characters stretching into his private history and private life which she did not and perhaps would not ever know.

"But why?" David asked. "Did he destroy everything?"

"There was nothing left." This she was sure of.

"But the work, the time, the years he put in on it? Couldn't it all have been continued elsewhere?"

"Where?"

He shook his head. "I don't know, a hundred places, a hundred hospitals."

"There was no time," she explained. "It was something that had to go on continuously."

David frowned. "But at least," he insisted, "at least he should have called me, asked me. I'm his friend."

She was so utterly conscious of this friend of Carl's, his compelling physical nearness and all the troubled uneasiness that she felt near him, that she could only agree. "He should've. But he wouldn't. He couldn't. Not Carl. Oh no." It was a relief to be the expert on Carl's feelings and it made the pleasure of being with David more correct and blameless. She thought *without blame*, and immediately was blaming herself for something still undone, unthought, not even hoped yet. "He's very proud. I mean he won't take any help from anyone. Independent, and he needs help. Can you help him?"

It took David a long time to answer, time enough for the first installment of too much food to arrive and sit there smoking before them, and still David didn't talk, but hesitated, thinking, only at the end to offer her one of his usual engaging smiles and the question, "Can I help you?"

"Me?" she asked. "Me?" And her voice went up in a foolish laugh and fell away musing. "Me? It's Carl who needs help."

David was eating now and urged her on. "Go on and eat. Go ahead." And as she began, he went on, "I don't know if I can help him. I can try and I will try and I want to try. But I want to know, and this is even more important. Just why, I have to find out

51

myself." This was an excusing plea. "But I should like to help you."

"Oh, no one," Sandy said sadly, believing it, "no one can help me. I'm way beyond help. A person has to have a good start to be worth helping. I'm hopeless."

"Hopeless?" He put his fork down and faced around to look right at her, his gray eyes striving it seemed to speak for him, as people will who believe in glances speaking. "Hopeless? Not at all. Just helpless. Not hopeless. Helpless, I'd say, and able to be helped."

This confused her and she bent her head over her food and simply stared at what was there until his voice came through the haze of sound in the restaurant, "Why don't you take your hat off? I should like, if you don't mind, to see your hair."

Without looking up at him, almost mechanically, she raised her hands and removed her hat, putting it beside her, and then brushed back a strand, and began to eat, not daring to look at him, or even out into the restaurant, feeling naked somehow, that she had undressed somehow, been asked to undress, and was now there sitting naked with his eyes on her.

It seemed that many years passed, Sandy felt herself dreaming, many years had passed before his voice spoke quietly to her. "You know the other night, in the cab, you remember?"

This was a lifeline and she looked up swiftly, "Why, yes. That was the night Carl found out. You remember?"

"I can't forget," David said. Light from a lamp above lit one side of his face and the other was in shadow so that he was a picture to Sandy, and an ache pinched her body, a relaxation of tension, a softness flowing from her to him, altogether exquisite and helpless — able to be helped, he had said — for he was beautiful, tender and beautiful, to her. His hands were uncared for, unpolished, almost weather-beaten, but graceful and strong, resting there on the table as he looked at her, and she thought that if such a man should love her he would be a strength to her, to care for her and protect her, and not ask anything but love.

Of love, she had a lover's gift. It was responsibility she hated, and now she felt chained to Carl because he was lost, and unattached, strengthless, and it was hard for her to be the girl she was, the woman she wanted to be, in love with a man who was nothing to the world. She was nothing to the world. Hopeless, that was true, and the man had to be all hope, a man for the world, of it, and strong in it, recognized as such. There would be no opportunities in her life except men. She believed this with all the religious power in her nature, with a mystical faith in her narrow destiny. She could escape, but she could not conquer, and she wanted to love, and could love, and did already love (this shocked her) a man who did not need her. She was, in this sense, a child born for sorrow in the world, a victim of pleasures, starved for tastes. So now she waited, having been asked to remember.

"Your hair," David whispered to her, in her ear, and she felt his breath there faintly against her ear where the tip of it showed through her hair, "your hair is like another man's money, or the talent of a great genius, or the luck that some people have. One single strand was caught in my coat and I took it home with me and I have it there. So you see, I own part of you."

"Oh," she said flushing, "oh, we're talking foolishness."

"Now look at me," he commanded, "and tell me if it's true. One is either foolish or serious and it depends on the way you understand it. The words are the same."

She did not look, but merely repeated. "Foolish. Foolish."

She held one hand in her lap, resting on the stiff linen napkin which covered her gloves, and now he took her hand in his hand, beneath the table, hidden there. "Look," he said most reasonably, "we're both friends of Carl's and we both want to help him. I shall. I'll go to Carl and let him tell me what happened as if you and I hadn't met for lunch," and so committed her to a secret held from Carl. "After that I'll invite him up to my father's house in the country and I'm sure between my father and myself we can help him. In that way we'll both be good friends of his." Again friends, so that he changed her at once from Carl's lover to Carl's friend. She felt the change, welcomed it without believing it was possible or easy, and not even yet feeling the need to change. "I'll take care of that, and don't you worry. It's you I want to help and that's much

53

harder. Much." He paused, waited, tried it out, "Because it's almost like helping myself."

And then as she turned, her face open and shaking, not knowing what else would happen, adrift on the current of the river flowing between them, he changed and became amusing, and started to distract her by telling her stories about everyone there. So the luncheon passed, taking hours, and the afternoon gathered, and streets grew dark, and suddenly she realized it was five o'clock and men started to come into the empty restaurant to have a drink at the bar.

They prepared to leave, and as she rose her legs were stiff with sitting and she was late for the hospital.

"Don't worry," David said. "I hope they fire you and you come to me for help."

As she started to gather her gloves, watching David talking with the waiter, she was ashamed to put them on, to reveal the rip. She could not after this afternoon put on those gloves and seem more a pauper than she was. With an instinctive cunning, like a little blond monkey, she searched the spot, found a space between the leather cushion and the wooden partition and tucked the gloves in. This yielded, like any decision, an access of strength. It was easy then to let David help her with her coat, with her hat, and start out with him.

In the street it was cold, very cold, and David asked, "Where are your gloves?" He took her cold hand. "Did you leave them in the restaurant?"

"No. No." She stammered. "No, no. You've got me all confused."

"Wait here," he told her and ran back to the restaurant, disappearing inside quickly, and there she was alone in the dark street, the wind blowing up from the bay, the streets crowded with men and women, the traffic going by. She was ashamed because David would find the gloves, they would be found strangely hidden, and the tear. She wanted to run away and never see David again. She was discovered. She was in love with David, and she had lost him with her stupidity. She forgot Carl, she forgot even the words spoken, the words lost. Everything loomed up as a disaster and

54

roared down on her, and there was David running back, his face a blur of whiteness, and he was there and caught her arm. "You must have dropped them some place," he said. "In my office?"

"I don't remember," she said.

"Never mind." They turned down Broadway and he guided her down three steps into a warm shop, to a counter, to a pretty girl selling gloves, and there she let herself be fitted with new black gloves, softer than her own hands, and David paid. "It's my fault," he said.

She walked in a daze to the subway, refusing a taxi, and said good-by. They said it several times and she felt the gloves on her skin like David's hands. "Good-by," he said. "We'll meet again. From now on, I'll call you. We've got a lot to talk of yet and a lot to do to straighten out the tangled affairs of Dr. Carl Myers."

She marched down the blasty steps of the subway and stood finally at the edge of the platform waiting for the train to roar out of the black and frightful cold. A train came and she did not enter. And another. She stood there lost in her black gloves, and then, as if this had been her last thought, remembered that she could use an old pair, that she was a poor girl; and with determination she left the station and went back to the restaurant.

Dinner was starting, but the waiter recognized her and she hurried to their corner, their corner, and swiftly found her gloves before anyone could see where, and thus armed left, thanking them.

In the street, she felt triumphant, and let herself go along with the others, passing the subway station, going on in the darkness and the crowd, passing under the electric lights, just floating in black cold, drifting, feeling she had done everything she could do with the problems of her life and from now on all was fate.

My fate, she thought, my fate, and blindly walking welcomed it.

ix

JUDGE Seawithe drove the big touring Packard with a careless speed, guiding the wheels through the loose snow while the chains ground away and one loose link banged like memory against the frame. To Carl, crowded to the door, the wind stinging his face red and numb, this was another kind of father, and just as each child has a father so each child regrets the father he never had. This tall man — so thin, so old he seemed, tanned, wrinkled but erect, his speech smiling and slow, his motions never beyond control — had an immediate unchallenged authority. He wore a floppy felt hat and a leather fur-lined Mackinaw. After a first glance from the clean blue eyes beneath a double patch of gray eyebrow, and after a first friendly greeting from dry assertive lips beneath a tailored gray mustache, he showed no other curiosity about Carl, but drove up the long slippery hill past stores and two churches, a gas station, a grocery, a hardware and drug store, as if he were only the chauffeur.

This final fragment of winter which cluttered up the spring had become the image of the season to Carl. In the city winter was just one of the regular yearly sieges through which he had grown accustomed to live along with poverty and hope, but out here — starting from the Grand Central Station, the tumult of his departure among others, the handtrucks going by with their piled luggage and the vast murmur, hollow as in a hive — out here winter was a wonderful change in the world, and the sense of it deepened as woods took over and a succession of hills, and then south down a twisting narrow road where the snow was deep, trackless on every side except for the parallel ruts ahead and behind.

Carl looked out over the landscape, forgetting Sandy, not wanting to remember her at the station in her shabby coat, hesitant and uneasy, waving good-by with a hand delicate in a new black glove. It seemed crazy to him that she should waste her money on expensive gloves when she needed a coat, for at the moment money to him was more precious than life itself, because he was alive and he had no money.

The judge slowed down for a small wooden bridge under which a black brook, crusted at the edges with ice, flowed bitterly. A wooden fence on the right now opened for a gate and the car turned in and ran up a long incline, and there at last was the farm.

It looked like a small village, a big frame house dirty white against the brilliantly pale snow, smoke from the chimneys, and then large barns, outbuildings and cottages. To one side was a steep hill thickly clustered with a new stand of evergreens, trees fresh as mint, tasty and cool in the dead white of winter; and on the other side a flat meadow beneath which the lines of corn marked their pattern; and beyond a stream, and still further hills rising with their scaffolding of fences.

"You boys go in," the judge said. "I'll get rid of the car."

"Well, let's go in," David said and started for the porch.

There the door was opened and Carl stood aside while David dropped the luggage and affectionately embraced the smiling woman who waited. They kissed warmly on the mouth.

Carl looked at the umbrella elms whose ungathered branches held up the low sky. There were clumps of low shrubs, each bush heaped with snow as a mouth is with kisses, and everywhere the land rose and fell in mild hills, natural without wildness as a woman is made.

"Carl," David called, and Carl turned and held out his hand to the smiling handsome woman who stood shoulder to shoulder with David. A heavy roll of black hair escaped in feathery strands about her neck, which was full, strong, columnar, and she had a kind of thick grace, as sometimes a powerful animal, all muscle compact and close, still in its easy strength, has grace without line. An incredible softness blurred her features running them together in

57

color and smiles as if she were being seen through rain or a rain of tears, and her eyes were small and black set close to the surface of her face. The face was smooth and shining, sensitive and change-ful because it was soft-fleshed, boneless and yielding. It had the beauty of an altering, disturbed surface, and the mouth was the most definite shape in it, round-lipped and heavy.

Carl's hand met hers and the softness was in the hand too, cling-ing warmly, pressing his, and in the same gesture she drew him within the house, almost, he felt, into her arms, and helped him off with his coat.

"We'll be down in a minute," David said, "I want to get Carl set."

Carl started up the steps.

"To the left," David warned him, "or you'll end up in my aunt's room."

Dutifully Carl turned left and went round the balcony that overhung the hall. He stopped before a closed door and David passed him to open it. Looking down Carl saw the hall was empty, but he heard the woman's voice talking to servants in the kitchen somewhere, and she was laughing.

"I know you're going to like it," David announced, and stood aside for Carl to enter. "When the world kicks you in the pants it's good to believe in heaven." He laughed, his face golden red like a child's merry sun.

"I do not," Carl said, "believe in heaven."

"You will," David replied slyly, "when you live in it."

The room was dominated by the idea of comfort and ease. A big double bed stood there with a blue and white tufted bedspread on it, a great butternut chest in a corner, a desk, a wing chair, and colored lithographs of hunting scenes. There was a fireplace and in it wood burned palely with wisps of smoky fragrance. Three windows formed an alcove with a window seat and the radiators were hidden behind metal screens. Another alcove opened beyond a small arch to form a small sitting room where low shelves were crammed with books and flowered easy chairs awaited the reader. Altogether the room with its bath and alcoves was bigger than any

58

apartment in which Carl had ever lived. "I've got a lot of winter things you can use." David dropped the canvas bag on the bed. "We'll be waiting for you downstairs." He began to leave but at the door hung back to ask, "Well, how do you like them?"

The air was so sprayed with softness and love that Carl shook himself like a dog leaving water. "Your father," he said, "is very impressive and your mother quite handsome."

"Oh!" David was at once ill at ease. "You didn't catch it. It's my aunt. Not my mother. It's my mother's sister. My mother's not well."

"I shouldn't have come then. I don't want to be in the way. Why didn't you tell me?"

"Didn't I tell you?" David was troubled. He came closer and looked away from Carl to the fire. "My mother's in a sanatorium. She's been there for years, something wrong with her and completely incurable, a physical wasting away that science can't stop." His face brooded over the thin fire, but as a curtain parts for an entrance or performance, he switched back to a sociable smile. "Don't think about it. We don't any more because it can't be helped." Lithely he was on his way. "Hurry on down. They're making a snack." And he was gone, his smile shining for a moment before the closing door, a clatter of steps down the stairway, a door banging off and then at last stillness.

Carl stood for a long time waiting, listening, but there was nothing to hear except his own anxiety beating in place of his heart.

59

X

AFTER dinner Carl excused himself and went upstairs. From the landing he looked down the carpeted steps and heard the Seawithes moving into the small wood-smelling living room.

Carl stood alone in the upper hall, waiting, listening, overcome with dread. He kept feeling like a man running, out of breath, or a man fighting, out of strength, or a dreamer unable to wake, or a soldier taken from the front lines to a palace hotel to rest. He was restless, at a loss with himself, and everything about him proclaimed the danger he had experienced and soon would be forced to face again.

He moved into his room and saw it again as a stranger. He hurried into the bathroom to wash his hot face in cold water. In the mirror he was the same. The anxiety lived on beneath the flesh which presented its own solid and unconcerned self.

He turned from the mirror, from the alien searching eyes which had become his own, and flung the towel into the bathtub. It was a linen hand towel and there were five others on the rack neatly arranged and waiting. The whole house was arranged, and the land around it, the barns, the garages, the golden pheasant runs, the pine plantation, the fields with their fences, and the fences beside their roads. The place was composed, constructed, ordered with secure wealth, and made up a big expensive universe resting immovable on the real earth. And in it were old things and new things gathered and fitted naturally into the house. Carl could have laughed at a rich man's barbarism, but the house hurt him because it was easy to love. The people were easy to love and the dinner

60

drowned in gaiety and wine, with the smooth flowing face of the aunt on one side and the deliberate judge on the other.

The judge was a man of easy power. His mind was dry, his speech often witty and always careful, his opinions never incomplete. When he spoke he expected to be listened to, but he listened when others spoke although he did not promise to believe. So this father was a real authority, loved, a guardian rather than a ruler. "All my prejudices," he said evenly, "have been carefully arrived at and represent the most accurate thoughts on most subjects."

David felt free to hoot at his father, to argue with him, never to agree, and Carl ate and answered in monosyllables, listening anxiously all the while not to what was said but to his own inner feelings. This inner life of his refused to react to the pleasantness, to candles on the table, to the fire living in its grate, to the casual manservant who talked familiarly with everyone like an old relative and yet kept the dinner going so that in the end the table was empty of food and clean for the fresh fruit dessert. And hours passed with never a silence in the narrow cosy room.

"Well," the judge asked, "shall we adjourn for coffee?" And Carl excused himself and went stolidly out hearing over the murmuring voices the storm in his breast.

Now in his room he opened his shirt and put his hand against his hairy chest, he pressed the muscular flesh and felt nothing except the even tremor of the artery. But the storm was there. A wild feeling was loose in his chest and the body shrunk from it to make a hollow where the feeling roamed. The feeling had no sense or meaning. In a way it had no life to be understood, but it was an object. It was like the Christian's sense of sin, or the savage's sense of fear, or the neurotic's sense of guilt, and it was like the cannon in Hugo's story, battering the ship from within, dangerous, frightening, inanimate and yet a rover running like a living thing intent on destruction. Carl pressed his hand even more firmly in, constricting the space to stop it. But this object was subjective, beyond his ability to control it manually, and it kept rolling in his body, in the cavern of his chest, a feeling, a ghost shape lurching with disasters.

He thought with all his mind to stop it. He called up the rules of his science, his studies, his knowledge. He believed in a mathematical world and complex equations for men too. What was the equivalent for this wild feeling, what value was there for him to manipulate in order to stop this anxiety from so wrecking him inside that he would collapse from without?

He touched himself, both hands to his chest, and fright bloomed with the sweat on his temples because he wanted to cry. This was wilder than anything — to want to cry, to let go, to abandon himself because he had been abandoned. He touched himself and his hand was a parent's hand trying to quiet a child who could not be still, who shrieked with an unknown anguish, whose idea of the world had been shattered by night or pain and could not be restored to order. Order. A child is taken into its lover's arms to gather strength, but no strength flowed from Carl's hands to himself, since he was only himself and not another, and only another could comfort and he was comfortless. No comfort anywhere, not in this white bathroom with its uncreased linen towels, not in the window behind impeccable curtains, not in the night outside, the darkness, the silence of the country.

There was illness, anxiety, suffering in his chest, and without physical cause. Nothing hurt him, no flesh was bruised, no nerve ends torn, no part of the brain had been burned out, sucked out, extirpated. What was the world then, to feel this thing within and not have a cause, a name? The world was impossible, and the impossibility was in him and he wanted to vomit it out.

The bright bathroom light assaulted him with memory, with a remembered summer, and he stood there a hand pressed to his naked chest, his stomach tight and hard with the dinner. Summer breeds in the courtyards and alleys of the city, summer breeds hot light and voices rising, and the violent sensation of the street. In the summer he used to be in the street all the time, by day and by night, and the night which seemed cooler was worse than the day. At night there was violence in play under the street lamps and seriously in the shadows, and everyone was possessed of weari-

62

ness, languor without peace, the children trooping up and down the streets screaming against the shaking night. He had run with the others into the crowd around his father's bakery.

All the lights were on and the faces were crowded together, the electric light from the stores astonishing the startled eyes. He pushed through the brink of the mob whose leaders pressed back not to be precipitated as from an ocean wave into the whirlpool of the bakery. Inside his mother screamed and ran after his father who wielded the big iron bar with which the back door of the bakery was made safe. Outside the mob was grateful for the violence and fearful of it too. Inside the big bar crashed among the showcases, sent the bread and rolls flying, pitted the walls with tremendous crashes, and his mother screamed and could not get close. The bar rose and fell like the strokes of fate, of time, of destiny, upon the store, this hole in the building with its glass shelves and fragile shattering counters, the two white-aproned clerks like hospital attendants cringing and calling. In a few moments, or was it one prolonged moment like the stretched dream of fear, the bakery was a shambles, and the police had arrived and his father sat on the stone step in front of the shop, his head between his hands, and was still. The mother was explaining that she didn't know, a quarrel with a customer, maybe the clerks, she didn't know, but she turned on the father and screamed at him, "You've ruined us." The father did not answer but years later when the incident arose to be discussed, when the father was driving a taxicab because the outside work was better for his lungs than working as a baker, he expressed his version of the affair with simple finality. "I don't mind selling myself, but I'll be damned if I'll sell the work of other people and be called a cheat for it." Round, unsmiling, the mother couldn't understand, and the father remembering a little German from his youth (the family was three generations in New York, all bakers, the mother an Alsatian girl lately arrived to serve a rich German family who owned bakeries) explained it to her. "*Ich bin kein bourgeois.*" And this she understood and accepted, although she thought he was crazy, for she

63

herself had worked in the mills of Strasbourg and her father had died in the Ruhr mines where her brothers still worked. Cut out of an old *Herald* was the photograph of a bearded man which the father pasted on the wall beside the mother's row of saints. "Saint Mark," Carl thought he said. "My saint."

"You will see him in hell," the mother had replied, tearing it down.

Carl ran to the toilet and leaned over it to vomit now.

The nausea was real enough.

He leaned weakly against the wall and wiped the cold sweat from his head. He walked into the bedroom and lay down on the bed.

He didn't care that his shoes were on the spotless tufted bedspread. Rolling over, he observed the ceiling and listened to the quiet of the house.

He thought of his dead father again, of the disconsolate face, of the mouth of his father black with death. That was his weakness, that his father was dead. He was a man alone, and his mind closed like a mouth on his shame and absorbed it. His mind locked itself around his loneliness and loss and absorbed them. His mind emptied itself of these delicacies and softness, because as this house proved, as the time proved, it was a question of money. He wanted money. He needed money. He had to have money. The whole energy of life, its labor, its worth, lay coagulated in money. It was a money civilization and a money time and even science was helpless without money. Science was dreams without money, and one could not even invent a theory of the universe without money to prove it. It seemed that all history, the death of martyrs and the victories of conquerors, the pain and ecstasy of revolution, the repressions, tortures, pains and joys, were nothing but the slow accumulation of money, the creation of the horde which now like a magnetic mountain raised itself in the world; and each thought of man, each dream of nobility that launched itself upon the seas of life, was slowly and then swiftly attracted to this mountain where the thought was wrecked and the dream drowned while the money was attracted to the mountain and there added

64

its tragedy to the mass. Like Sinbad he would have to go back to his city and shrewdly, cleverly, brutally, get this money without which he could not even hope to begin to launch his will upon life. Money was the real thing, and the wild loose feeling in the heart was not real.

He got off the bed and straightened his clothes, already thinking of who could help him.

xi

WHEN Carl entered the living room he understood at once that the Seawithes had been talking favorably of him, for they welcomed him smiling and showed no guilt. David pressed into Carl's hand a glass of cognac which he drank with a hot gulp.

He sat to one side of the fire and the other three persons were grouped around it, the fire completing the circle like a real person. Everything was active in the chimney, the wind, the talking flames, the logs burning, oxidizing and therefore living, moving, restless.

The interrupted conversation began again, comfortable and slow, larded with fat domestic facts, drifting aimlessly toward midnight while Carl tried to make a mental list of possible helpers. But money was a hard thing, a real thing, and did not readily associate itself with the people Carl knew. His mother or brother could be asked, but the poverty-stricken had nothing to give, since for them he was the giver, or had been, he thought cruelly. They could ask from now to Doomsday (and this was Doomsday) and not get a nickel again. He had nothing to give. But they could be asked and the question would not be rejected. They would accept his right to ask them for money. So ended the list of relatives of the blood. There were then the guardians, men and women who had admired him as a pupil and aided him with advice, encouragement and testimonials that gained him his array of scholarships. But if he should go to Miss Graham with her tight red hair and rosy face, with her finger on which there was one connection with life, her sorority ring; if he should go to Durrand, white-haired and Irish with the big drunken nose; or to Dr. Backer, or the three professors who had in turn invited him for summer vacations at

66

Woods Hole; if he should even dare ask them for fifteen hundred dollars, or a thousand, or five hundred, they would feel so great a sense of possible loss as to be suspicious and hostile, since fifteen hundred dollars was for any of them a whole year's work and what man or woman could give away a whole year's work for another's life?

There were then the friends, that is, David.

Carl looked coldly around the circle. A man had to give something to expect money, because money contained lifetimes in it, and Carl had nothing to give but his life which he wanted to keep.

At the moment there were no prospects. He refilled his glass with cognac and drank. But it was still a question of getting money, nothing else. Suppose no money were to be had and instead a new career had to be molded, a living to be got?

Under such circumstances, he thought, was it easy or difficult to die?

His mind continued to harden, and the wild softness which had lived in his chest had now no living space. The hardness went into his chest and became a rock, became anger, while his eyes, now severely surveying the room (for he was now a man calmly thinking of death) observed the objects in it and counted them as commodities that would help him escape. It was daydreaming and he knew it. But it was practice and he did it viciously.

Sitting in this living room Carl had become an enemy guest, a looter, a barbarian waiting to sack any part of civilization for its money value. He was like the German tribes before Rome, or the Christians before Asia Minor, or the merchants before medievalism, or the proletariat before the imperial East and West. He needed the accumulated fortune of the old and dying to live. He wanted not one of the uses that possessions give, only their value in exchange, the stored-up history of effort, so that he could take up his career as a man of honor and science.

He sipped more cognac and noticed its taste for the first time. It seemed bitter but drank easily, quietly, without rawness, and then inside his throat appeared to obey a subtle phase rule and become a scent, a perfume of warmth that blew through his head,

67

his mouth, his hands, his belly. On the bottle was printed: *thirty-two years old*. This, Carl thought, is expensive. Say twenty dollars a bottle. Say the Seawithes have fifty bottles in their cellar. Fifty times twenty was enough to set Carl free. It was a small part to detach from the establishment, from the comfort of their lives. The judge liked to sit for an hour and sip a glassful. Wouldn't the judge be willing to give up this tiny pleasure, this so unrational titillation of his palate, say a moment's worth a day for a year so that a whole life could be organized and thrust into fruitfulness? If the equation were put that way: this infantile, this incredibly primitive and silly pleasure, essentially harmful, against a man's whole life, would the judge hesitate?

Carl didn't waste any time on the answer. There were too many equivalences about.

All afternoon he had walked with David over the old and crusty snow which had partially melted and then frozen again so that the surface was hard and steps skated above the ground, men walking, in truth, on water and only sometimes crashing through. Although the snow lay everywhere in drifts and smooth waves, the land like a beach upon which a season's weather had beaten and flung the jetsam of its tides, the cold unmoving air had softened in spots, decaying with spring. There was an unevenness, a tension to breathing as the unexpected warm draught of a little valley, or a clump of trees, brimmed into the lungs, exotic, alcoholic. The air was an infected membrane now as the year paused between its seasons, and all through the day the sky continued to lower, to grow denser by the hour, and even the smallest wind died down, and stillness fell upon Carl's mind like a stone. He had followed David. The place went on for miles, and now Carl thought, if the judge would break off a bit of field, a handful of rocks, an acre of snow-covered meadow, a hundred feet of roadside for a hot-dog stand near the main highway, something that would never be missed, then Carl would have his life, his freedom. Was it worth a man's whole life not to miss the pleasure of a hundred walking steps on a distant field of this great series of farms that formed the estate? The judge was too old to walk for pleasure. If the land

68

were stolen from him, fenced in and sold, he would never know. Carl felt like a thief in the house, a spy for his own life.

What was his education worth in the open market? His ideas? A man without property was worth nothing in the depression market.

He looked gloomily down at his feet. They had just rested on the tufted bedspread and now they were on the figured carpet which eddied in red and yellow before the fire. He rubbed his feet in the heavy nap. This rug rolled up and taken to any pawnshop would probably buy his freedom.

"In any pawnshop," he said.

"What did you say, Carl?" David asked.

All the faces were sudden moons fixed on the horizon of Carl's glance. They were all looking at him, kindly, attentive, sympathetic to his misfortune, as people read in newspapers that in Shanghai rickshaws must carefully avoid the children dead of hunger in the street, as people read statistical prophecies that because of a crop failure at least two millions will die of hunger in India, as people know the world is crushed with anguish and horror while they open the cardboard boxes of food over their breakfast tables. So here these people so easy to love were friendly and sympathetic to him. He sickened and sweated to realize that he had so far lost his control as to murmur a thought aloud before them. He grumbled now, "Nothing." And when the aunt and the father and the friend exchanged a glance, he added, "Nothing important. Only I was wondering what all my experimental rats might be thinking of the future of experimental animal psychology?"

"What any of the unemployed think about the depression?" David challenged his father with this.

The judge grinned indolently. "The depression is the poor man's penance for the bounties of capitalism. Amen."

"That's the damnedest, rottenest thing I've ever heard." The son arose, wanting to argue and fight, already enjoying it. He flung a bright triumphant glance to Carl, a look like a hand, a hand up, an invitation to attack the ogre in his den.

"Well, isn't it?" the judge asked. "And the New Deal is state

69

capitalism or socialism, which merely means that the bankers will use the state power further to consolidate their hold on the economy of the country. Even a liberal fool should recognize that, when an old reactionary like me who believes in decentralization can see it." The judge smiled unruffled. "The rabble-rousers will rise and the rabble will follow into profounder slavery while the incomes of financiers rise."

"And your income too," David shouted.

"My income too." The judge looked at his cognac, held it to the fire, examining his liquid income. "And yours too." He turned to Carl. "My son's a New Dealer. What are you?"

"A discard," Carl said, "no matter who deals."

After sipping, the judge put his glass down and made a tent of his thin brown fingers. He looked at them, then around, resting for a moment with a secure smile on Aunt Corinne, who smiled back from the controlled depths of her chair. "Why don't you sit down?" the judge said to his son before giving Carl his attention. He was arranging his courtroom. "A scientist, and David tells me you're one, Carl, shouldn't resist the principle of experiment even if for a change he's the fact observed and not the observer."

"What does that prove?" the son demanded. "Tell me what that proves?"

"What history proves." With this a note of judicial finality, the habit of granted authority, entered the judge's voice. He spoke with extreme and patient slowness, his words whispering through his false teeth like wind through dry bones. "Things happen and men happen too. It would be better if they happened to purpose. I suppose in the long run everything is meliorative in some sense, but I accept this on social faith and the religion I no longer believe in. And if things happen to no purpose and men to less, then in fact we have merely happened and sit here now merely happening."

"You're impossible." David wheeled away. The handsome son in his checked hunting shirt was great and strong as nature. He brimmed with health and stood at the cherrywood sideboard on

70

which were ice and drinks. "Do you want any more Scotch, Aunt Corinne?"

"A little," she said in her soft voice. "A little. Carl, what about you, more cognac?"

"Why not?" Carl answered brutally not wanting to be on anyone's side and preferring to have them all against him. "I'll never be able to afford it again."

"That's it." The judge raised a forefinger as if to a recalcitrant witness. "You can't now, but you drink it. History happens." And he laughed out with extreme good nature.

David carried a drink over to his aunt and refilled Carl's glass. "I'll tell you something," he announced strongly. "I'll tell you something about my idea of history. It's rotten and ought to be changed and I'm going to try to change it. I want to change everything. I want to change everyone."

"Change yourself first," his father told him. "You're too noisy for a revolutionist. And too sentimental. If you want to be effective you have to be either a scientist or a force. And you're too eager for a scientist and too intelligent for a force."

"A scientist is an agent."

"For whom?" The father paused and added cynically, "For the Lord? Am I right, Carl?"

Carl wanted to tell them the most horrible thing, but the most horrible thing at the moment was himself which, if extended, might engulf the universe. "I'll tell you what I've learned."

"Of course." Aunt Corinne pushed herself a little forward in her chair to show her interest.

"Well," Carl said, "scientists and coal miners and lawyers are all the same. They each have a profession because they happen to have it, but as men they are not much different from each other. One thing they all have in common. They work for whoever pays them. The coal miner digs coal to run engines to make explosive to kill poor coal miners in other countries or in his own. The lawyer perverts laws so that lawyers become unnecessary and law meaningless. The scientist will make poison gas and invent any

71

monster of equations to kill scientists here and elsewhere. They work for who pays them."

"Why bother then?" David was stunned at this, at Carl's violent cynicism. "Why bother with science?"

The judge still smiled. "Don't try to answer that question, Carl. Generations have without profit or pleasure."

"I'll tell you why," David took the floor, dominated it. "Because you're fundamentally decent, no matter what you or my father say, you belong to those people who resist the general corruption. It's in your natures."

"Thank you," the father said. "People are fundamentally decent or indecent. They are fundamentally part of one section of humanity or another, and what's approved in that section is decent, such as law, science, art and charity. All you're admitting, David, is that you belong to one of those sections of society and you include us, and you like it."

"I don't admit it and I don't like it."

"We'll see."

"I make moral decisions," David said. "I make them in terms of my feelings, my understanding, my will. Carl makes moral decisions."

Carl drank again, swallowed. "My economic situation is such that I'm absolutely incapable of making moral decisions. I get a shock. I react. I live. Shock. React. Bing bang."

They were somehow all looking at Carl as if he were the center of their conspiracy, its object, and he lowered his eyes and rubbed his feet in the rug and stared at the brown liquid in his glass.

"You mean," David asked in a low and unbelieving voice, "that you don't care whether you live or die, succeed or fail, contribute to science or not?"

"Yes," Carl replied most simply. "I want to live, to succeed, to contribute, but no one wants me to except myself."

"There," shouted David triumphantly. "There." He walked victoriously to his aunt, took her hand, lifted her formally from the chair. "Let's have something to eat and celebrate the triumph of spirit over matter." He was laughing as if the argument had meant

72

nothing at all, and Aunt Corinne began to laugh in a furry, strange way, her face quivering with the secret sound that shook her.

"What do you want?" she asked Carl and the judge.

"A million dollars," Carl replied.

And the judge said, "To die." It froze everyone. "That is, nothing." And the room was social again.

As the nephew and the aunt went out through the hall to the kitchen with David playfully shoving his aunt ahead, the judge fumbled in his coat pocket and brought out his wallet. "My son tells me," he said softly, neutrally, "That you would like to go abroad and study in your science. I did so myself when I was a boy, studying in some three or four German universities and even for a year at the Sorbonne. Needless to say, I look back upon that time as the happiest in my life because I was relatively pure in heart and wanted only to learn. I was free then as you are now of that monstrous sense of competition that devours our country after having devoured the rest of the civilized world. My son tells me that a fool ruined a year's work of yours. And my son has told me enough to show that you are friends, something even rarer than a genuine thirst for knowledge. Here."

He put a folded slip of paper in Carl's helpless hand, got up, said, "Good night," and went out of the room, only to reappear suddenly at the door, a look of calm authority smiling and kind on his face. "If you feel able or willing, you may return it. In this sense it would be a loan. But if you feel unable or unwilling, then it is a gift." He watched Carl's stunned face. "In a way I consider that check in your hand an arbitrary act on my part. In all my life preparing to be an old man, the only act that ever seems individual, and therefore moral and worth while, is the power to be arbitrary. You have no reason to feel grateful, for after all doesn't nature owe its creatures their right to live? If there is any natural law, isn't that it? If your experiment could be struck down by arbitrary power, then arbitrary power can refurnish your strength and restore that natural balance old-fashioned reactionaries like myself so admire. In this way we can spit in the face of destiny and a usurious civilization, an old man's pleasure in the very late moments of the night. Good night."

He turned away leaving the entry empty, while his steps hissed up the carpeted stairway, and from the kitchen came David's cheery laughter and Corinne's shushing tones.

Carl opened the check and it was for fifteen hundred dollars. He stood there, expecting it, wanting it, needing it, like Jacob on that magical night when he stole the father's blessing.

PART TWO

The Search

i

HAVING verified the arrival of the *Normandie* a half-dozen times, three calls by his secretary, one by his wife, and finally, to make sure, twice himself, Dr. Wilfred Erdman appeared at the midtown pier promptly at noon, a tweed fall coat with a bright overplaid draped over his thin old shoulders, a snap-brim felt jauntily perched on his long bald head, and a cigar in his mouth. Thus formidably prepared he felt he could find the patience to await the rakish liner being slowly and clumsily herded into its pen. With his sixty-fifth year ending in this fine bright autumn, it was not so much Erdman's energy that had run out, but his patience with affairs, with events, with what he desired. In this his life had rounded out and become young once more, each passion or idea intolerable until it had completed itself, and his desire to see Carl Myers again was an impatience of the highest order. "To the power of infinity," he told his wife, thinking that for him infinity was now hours, weeks, perhaps a year or two, and after all wasn't this the only infinity men ever knew? Infinity was always the itch between desire and its fulfillment and never mere time. And his wife smiled, a light delicate smile coming out of her sensitive body, now twisted, wracked, deformed, contracted in the lumps of rheumatoid arthritis. Mrs. Erdman loved her own son, but she readily granted her husband his right not to be overwhelmed with the child she had brought as a marriage portion, along with her dancing grace, to their common life. When, two years before, Erdman had returned after a year's absence in Vienna, she had first heard of this Carl Myers and soon understood that in her husband's mind this stranger had come to be what her own son had never been able to accomplish, a child by adoption, and therefore intended and so fiercely his own.

Dr. Erdman, gangling, energetic, with a saucy wit and an international reputation as one of the founders of American psychoanalysis, lived in a private house on Riverside Drive. It was one of those minor New York mansions in the style of Florence, a heavy stone base, not many windows, a squarish, solid look as if intended to withstand plebeian mobs. There were iron lion heads mouthing enormous iron rings, and sockets above for imaginary torches. The lower windows were barred and on the roof, after Giotto's tower, was a heap of brick treated like spumoni, its vivid colors long since washed away, and now just standing there, with two midget stories of double windows where the pigeons roosted, while below the wide blue Hudson and not the meager Arno flowed.

Downstairs were the reception rooms for the treatment of patients, the secretary's office, and a large library on whose many-vaulted ceiling the former owner had painted the myth and loves of Venus. "How singularly appropriate for a psychoanalyst," Erdman had told the agent when he purchased the place.

In general the old couple were cheerful, well-to-do, liked jokes and heavy food, and could discuss for hours the early struggles of their radical psychology. Erdman still felt like a wild revolutionist, and while he had received honorary degrees and long complimentary speeches from various respectable universities at home, and only two years before from really famous ones abroad, he believed that society still hated and despised the Freudians, that their truths were bypassed and resented, and that the doctrine of the libido, that magical concept of an amorphous and fluid sensuality, the changeling, Love, still had to be promulgated and its banner set in the very heart of entrenched medical reaction.

Both Erdman and his wife were endlessly interested in proving whether this insight or that had been discovered by this man or that one. The cellars of the building had been fireproofed, organized into steel shelves and filing cabinets, and here Erdman had collected thousands of books and pamphlets on the early days of the movement, and he had letters between himself and Freud,

78

correspondence with Brill, Abrahams, Ferenczi; and here too were the printed polemics against the two great renegades, Jung and Adler, and a particularly vicious exchange with Bleuler when that great and former friend had withdrawn the Burgholzli from the official Freudian line. Unable to destroy the Swiss psychiatrist's scientific work, Erdman had written, "Only the schizophrenia of the director has enabled him to make his profound contribution to that fascinating subject," and so assigned the genius if not to the man, at least to the disease.

But in the main Erdman was not a theoretician and made no pretense of being one. He was a practical scientist, a kind of inventor, the Edison of psychoanalysis, with the happy faculty of having an article or book ready at the opportune moment to develop the latest guess on the part of the master, and a certain American knack for absorbing other fields of science to the general philosophy of Freud. By the autumn of this year and in the autumn of his life, Erdman had ransacked anthropology, history, aesthetics and sociology and left nothing for later Freudians except, as Carl Myers once observed, the problem of turning psychoanalysis into a natural science. "What you want," Erdman retorted (they were sitting in the summer night in a Viennese café), "is to turn psychoanalysis into an unnatural science, into numbers, propositions, and little red and black pictures. They ring a bell. Ding-dong! Dinner's ready! And the saliva flows in the dog's mouth. And he eats. Then afterwards when they ring the bell, the saliva flows, and there is no dinner. You call that science? The problem is what happens to a dog or man when the bells ring and life betrays and frustrates the rational expectation?" Out in the street three young Nazis caught an old Jew and pulled his beard. "You see," Erdman had pointed out, "they ring the bell and expect the gates of Paradise to open, and then low and behold, it is Hell." He touched Carl's shoulder. "Don't stay too long. Come home." And he went home himself finally to work on his great book, a definitive history and critique of psychoanalysis, "Which may never be finished, but usefully occupies old age while it remains a constant threat to the reputations of other old men in the busi-

79

ness." He did not doubt that he had a place in the intellectual history of his times. What he wanted to be sure of was what that place would be, and since no one knew better than himself how much he had done to make the notions of psychoanalysis a commonplace in men's minds, he hoped in his book to establish the more permanent values.

Now stationed in the sunlight at one corner of the vast and buzzing shed, the wind catching the empty sleeves of his coat, Erdman watched the ship drift in, the ship which was to be his ship, for it contained the most precious cargo of all, the guarantee of his place in human history, a disciple.

He had arranged a few days before to be directly admitted to the pier, since one of the steamship company officers was a former patient; he had tipped two porters to hold themselves in readiness to take Carl's baggage; he had, like a dextrous magician, palmed bills liberally among the minor officials, oiled the wheels, greased the treads, all with one aim in mind: to get Carl off the liner, into the car, up to the house, and there to present him with the marvelous offer. This gift which Erdman had in mind was now as heavy there as a child in its mother's womb when the hour of birth is at hand, and he could not bear to watch this great ocean monster, helpless, dangerous, decerebrate, being guided by tugs, pushed, hauled, tugged foot by foot so stupidly into the hole that awaited it. "By God," he cried out in vexation, "expedite, let's expedite. Everything takes too long."

It took so long that the turning earth managed to shift the dark weight of the shed upon his shoulders, and he moved to catch the warmth again while his chauffeur followed a respectful step behind. Despite the roar and bustle of the pier, the rattling hand trucks and rumbling cranes, despite the boats in the river and the urban roar, the whole city lay transfixed in the fine autumn sun, held firmly in place by its immense towers. It was a smokeless day, the wind blowing westward against New Jersey, and everything was clear, luminous as Dr. Erdman's intentions. Nothing melted but things lay neatly within their own shapes, colors within the color, spaces sharply within hard lines. Even the reach of the river did not melt into a haze, but the blue water stretched to its horizon and there at the mark stopped for the sky to begin, and if the roundness of the earth had not dropped away from Erdman's eyes he felt he would be able to see across the seas to Europe and the East.

The old man was too wise to expect from Carl the affection he himself cherished. Each of the thousands of men and women whose lives he had studied and changed, "so that they can stand themselves," he used to say, "even if no one else can bear them," had long since convinced him of the subjectivity of men's loves; but it was enough to receive as he did in Carl's letters the respect, a little admiration, and beyond that sometimes faintly sketched in a flicker of feeling, remote yet touching, which he could fondle for an instant. Self-interest would take care of the rest, for all rational men had self-interest, and the stubborn unconscious was nothing if it were not the vain, egotistic, arbitrary lover of itself. During the yearlong didactic analysis through which Erdman had guided Carl in Vienna, he had come to understand the hard young mind, its rigorous logic, its hot feeling, always hesitating to give itself, fearful of the backlash of a yielded love, "a compulsive type." And he had listened to the strange and ambiguous drama of Sandy and David and old Judge Seawithe and helped Carl search the past, stripping free the mechanism that had tricked him into following his own best interest even when it fruited in despair. Now the old psychoanalyst had no desire to possess the younger man. It was enough to have set free something that was there, to have guided the mind, to have introduced it into the open secret of that theory of existence to which as a prophet Erdman had consecrated his life, to which a disciple could now help erect a permanent monument.

And now Carl was almost home, having written in his last letter, "I suppose it's time to come home, since I've learned here what's possible for me to learn, much or little. Besides, all psychological problems are now political in Europe, the intolerable tensions so prevalent that men have no patience for anything but violent actions and misery. And yet isn't it the task of science to

81

undo the misery of history?" Undo the misery of creation, Erdman thought, and breathed a smile of relief as the *Normandie* began to debouch its load upon the docks.

In such a restless surge of people it was difficult to single out one person, but every lover has a lover's eye, a hunter's sharpness to read inconsequent signs — a shoulder's twist, the poise of a head, a walk — and find there the sought-for creature. So suddenly, among the thronging bodies, Erdman saw the hard stocky figure of Carl in a belted European suit moving steadily and almost indifferently through the crowd, and in a moment they were face to face shaking hands while Erdman cried out with comic bewilderment, "But you? With a mustache? And such clothes? You look like a refugee!"

"I am," Carl said.

"You were," and eagerly Erdman took Carl's arm, shouting for the porters to look lively. "You'll see, you'll see, I've slaughtered a fatted calf for you." And bubbling, cheerful, he eagerly breasted the mob, for he could not wait to confront his protégé with a son's inheritance.

ii

SUNLIGHT moving wheeled the great glowing globe of the afternoon upon the muraled ceiling of the library. The indolent flanks of Venus took fire and Erdman's glance familiarly traced their sweet lines as if his eyes were hands, the flesh real and possessed, and the distant painted sea part of a sensual remembered day. He would long remember this day, so long expected, acted out a thousand times in imagination and variously interpreted, played again and again at night in dreams and never the same although always with the same triumphant end, and now here it was, and time had passed and still the moment had not come to pass. He had waited and waited, nursing the secret against the usual conversations, the talk of Vienna, an anecdote exploding, old friends, Freud's health, and many times repeated Carl's appointment to Castlehill. Erdman had kept the secret intact against luncheon and the tour of the house, the jammed literature of the cellars, holographs of some of the master's finest works, a fascinating letter in which he and not Jung was definitely proved to be the first to advance the notion that it was the mechanism of mind that failed in neurosis and not the content. And all the while, fitful with energy, bustling, he waited for the right moment.

Yet how was he to tell which moment was right and which wrong, for against everything, hints, premonitions, suggestions, the smiling face of Dr. Carl Myers was impervious. Neat and cheerful, he absorbed everything, seemed pleasant, and talked not once of his plans, even when asked. The young man did not appear to have the need to talk about himself, and Erdman held his secret locked away because the occasion would have to come. The thing could not be just blankly thrown out into the open and left there in the presence of this polite and charming young man to be picked up or refused (not that it would be refused or left there as if it could be). There was this at least to be said for the training in Vienna, it had given Carl an easy, flexible presence which did not assert itself, but seemed to rest balanced against any turn of events, a mark of extreme egotism or capability.

When Erdman thought back to that didactic analysis — to the first four passionate months when, frozen and rebelling together, the soul of this protégé had slowly opened under the pressure of disappointment and love — the old man almost regretted the power of a therapy which, by removing psychic pain, often left a neuter and accommodating spirit behind. But this could not be in Carl's case. Erdman knew he was facing a mask. There was power there, but covert, withheld.

"How did you manage," Carl asked easily, "to get me the appointment?" The neat mustache turned above a half-evoked smile, the gray eyes genial, passionless, and this after four long years away from his own country, not a sign of restlessness. It was as if Carl had been here in this library every day.

Gloomily, Erdman replied, "We Freudians stick together like any despised minority sect. I knew a man who knew a man. It was a favor."

"I must thank him. Who was it?"

"Not to you. No one knows you here yet, only myself. It wasn't even a favor to me, but to our secret brotherhood."

The smile increased on Carl's face, crinkling the sunburned flesh around his eyes, and he raised a hand and touched his mustache. "You talk as if the Freudians hadn't succeeded in the world. But they have. They're completely respectable."

"Wait till you get to Castlehill," Erdman told him bitterly. "You'll see how respectable you are in an institution devoted to cold and hot baths, electric shock, basket-weaving, chemicals, strait jackets and all the other medieval paraphernalia of witchcraft they call psychiatry."

84

The afternoon continued to waste, the sun forcing the windows, opening the deep Florentine red of the drapes, gilding the books, bringing life to the murals, and suddenly Carl was saying — Erdman could not believe he was hearing him say — "I suppose I ought to excuse myself now and go. My family will expect a visit from a dutiful son."

"Wait!" The word jumped willfully from Erdman. It burst hard and flat in the soft brightness of the room and took the old man by surprise as he said it. And Carl waited, showing no surprise, merely turning a transparent attention to the desk. A cigarette burned in the ash tray beside his calm hand.

"I said wait," Erdman continued, compelled to go on, "I mean I think you should really think it over before you go up to that modern madhouse and waste your valuable time."

But Carl answered steadily as he had before, "It's just a matter of getting in a good year's clinical work in a first-rate American institution. And even if it's a waste, I'm young."

More sharply than he intended, Erdman took him up, "You're young only if you have an indefinite future, a long time to live. But otherwise even twenty-nine is old. They don't use Freudian techniques there."

The calm soft voice came back again, "I want to see what non-Freudian techniques amount to. I mean, the experience generally."

"They don't use it generally," Erdman insisted. "They use it in bits and pieces, without the theory, like crutches. That's what you'll find. I know. I'm telling you because I know."

As he picked up his cigarette, Carl's head came into the sun and he arose to escape the direct glare. "Well," he asked, "what do you suggest?"

And there it was. Erdman's mind leaped and he rose himself, his bald head glistening in the brightness. At last, a question, an inquiry about Carl's own future. Enthusiastic, eager, Erdman walked round the desk to Carl's side. "Something more practical. A scientist has to be practical. There is very little you can do for suffering humanity in public institutions. That's for two reasons. First, only hopeless cases ever go to state hospitals, cases that relatives can no longer put up with or which the law finds anti-social. These people are in general incurable because psychotics are incurable anyway or because it's too late to arrest the disintegration of the personality. Secondly, the administration of these institutions are in the hands of reactionary fools wedded to Kraepelin and mechanical classification."

"What about the Burgholzli?"

"When I worked there it was in 1907, I think. That's a long time ago, and even Bleuler changed. I tell you it's impossible." Erdman dismissed the whole subject with an abrupt gesture. "I want you to consider something else for a moment. Suppose you could open a practice here in the city with your own patients, and devote yourself to psychoanalysis as we know it should be utilized. And suppose in addition to that, you could spend a great deal of your time on theoretical work in an effort to clear the field, to construct at last a consistent history and theory of psychology?"

"Why," Carl answered frankly, "I do not try to suppose the impossible."

"But it's possible." And Erdman put his hand on Carl's arm, and stood over him, brighter above Carl's head than the sun, pouring the full spate of his eagerness and will upon him. "I can make it possible. You open up a practice right here, with my help. I have more cases than I can handle. And I offer you, I want you, I ask you as a favor to me and yourself to work with me as my collaborator on the book I planned with Freud himself. You see, I speak only of the practical."

It was done, and as Carl turned away thoughtfully, slowly walking down the length of the room to the window facing over the river, Erdman returned to his desk, exulting. He opened the big cigar humidor and selected a cigar, carefully cut it, lighted it, and leaned back, waiting now in peace. His thoughts went on ahead to the days that would follow, the long talks, the companionship, and the book slowly being realized. It would take a long time and if he did not survive, the work would, for Carl would finish it, and could finish it, and at last Erdman's position would be fixed as it should be fixed for the whole profession to see. He basked in

86

the comfort of it, the ease and security of being insured against his own mortality which he so strongly felt. And this privilege he was bestowing upon the young man would in turn create Carl's future, make that certain, for so one generation handed on its inheritance to the next. He blew out blue smoke against the sunlight while Carl turned back to him and came to the desk.

"Thank you," Carl said, softly and affectionately. "I didn't imagine you thought so much of me. And it's because you do that I thank you, most gratefully. And, for the same reason, refuse."

"Refuse? Why?" The overturn wrung the cry from Erdman. The shock bewildered and crushed him. "You refuse? What do you mean?" He searched the healthy face in front of him, this impenetrable mask of good nature, and saw there everything he would wish for but acceptance. There was friendship, gratitude, respect, but he wanted acceptance. "Why?"

For the first time Carl seemed uneasy, hesitating, and he answered reluctantly. "I think it's too soon for me to do such a thing. I feel my period of training is unfinished."

Erdman slapped the desk angrily. "But I don't think so. I know you."

"I know you don't think so or you would never have been so generous. But I think so. I think it's too soon for me to accept the theoretical task."

"I accept it," Erdman said proudly.

"Yes. You accept it and can. But I can't. I feel the need of experience and experiment and still think that psychoanalysis is a long way from being a science. But why? How can I find out without working where the sick are? Not just middle-class neurotics, but the really sick."

"How does it matter whom you cure? Science favors no social classes. They're all human beings."

"You don't understand me," Carl went on more forcibly. "I'm not interested in curing them but studying them. I'm not interested in curing anybody except generally. I want to find out what's to be found out. Why aren't psychiatry and psychology a science? Why? That answer isn't in books or in a half-dozen patients."

87

But Erdman hardly listened to the arguments. He was refused. He saw only that he had been refused, that he was still alone; and bitterness invaded his soul, and his emotions clouded, and he struck out helplessly. "Your trouble is psychological, not rational. That's it. That's it entirely. Just because once before you were helped by an old man, David's father, and given a bribe to leave so that the son could marry a woman you loved, you think every gift is bribe. Why don't you forget that?"

"I've understood it," Carl stood there and looked at the open face beneath him. He moved a step as if to leave, and held his place. "I haven't forgotten it. And I do not regret it. It was a bribe. But I do not expect ever to be bribed again."

"And how am I bribing you? How, tell me. Dammit tell me." Agitated Erdman stood up, towering above the young man. "Tell me out of your infinite wisdom what I have to gain from you?"

The eyes smiled tenderly at Erdman, without anger. "My strength. You need my strength to do what you intend. Because you're old and I'm young. But my strength is for myself, not for anyone, not to be sold for security, for money, for fame, for ease, even for friendship. It's for me and me alone. And I'll learn the way I have to, in my way, helped or not helped. And I still thank you for your offer, for it's something that isn't offered to everyone or anyone." He looked up at the old man's stiff and proud face and then turned away. "Good-by and thank you again." And the neat stocky figure went to the big open double doors beneath the painted ceilings, leaving, going away.

"Wait," Erdman said again. But he spoke out of an immense weariness and defeat. Carl stopped and looked back, and he showed neither triumph nor defeat. He merely waited. "I hope you feel free to use my house and my library and my help in whatever way you do. I wish you could put your unhappy childhood behind you. Because you're lucky. People with unhappy childhoods don't regret growing up."

"It's because I can't forget my childhood," Carl replied, "I do what I have to do." He stopped, listened almost to his own mind. "So you think I'm wrong?"

88

"I don't know," Erdman said. "Perhaps you'll be lucky and one of these days a Newtonian apple will fall upon your stubborn head." Heavily he sat down. "When you have the time, stop by and see me."

"Good-by." Carl released an indefinite wave of his hand.

"The offer is always open."

"I may accept." The figure went away down the wide hall, made a turn and was gone. A little later the front door opened and closed, and Erdman sat exhausted at his desk, looking at his dead cigar, and then being very old he could not find the strength to stop himself, and he wept.

iii

NOT far below Kingston on the state highway there is a sign at a minor crossing which lists some half-dozen towns, among them Castlehill, as if Castlehill were just one of the many river villages on the west bank of the Hudson. But Castlehill is not a town at all. It is an institution, the State Psychiatric Hospital, with a population larger than all the towns put together.

Here on a shelf of land in the Catskill foothills, formerly the manor seat of the great patroon Van Cleemens, with a majestic view south over the lordly Hudson, the state had constructed out of an old Bedlam, sordid, vice-ridden, ancient with cruelty and disease, a new institution for the treatment of the mentally ill. There was a great private park stippled and perfumed with the flowers of the season, patterned with gravel walks, lined with buttonwoods, evergreens, and hard and soft maples. In the spring fruit trees blossomed, in the fall the leaves became exquisite drying flowers, the summers dozed and the winters shook with wind and snow. Slowly working, the flow of weather molded Castlehill into the terrain, covered it with ivy, with serene rains, with the absorbing softness of time, but within there was enough despair to founder a civilization.

There were a dozen two-story buildings for the inmates — complete with balconies, sun porches, workrooms and discreetly wired exercise pens. In the center stood a small skyscraper which on the lower floors housed the administration, the reception and examining rooms, the laboratories and hospital, while the two upper stories contained in padded cork-lined security the violent wards. On the outskirts of the large park but still within the steel fence

90

were pretty cottages, each with a little garden and rose arbor, to house the staff, and in one of them Dr. Carl Myers dwelt with another bachelor doctor in domestic comfort. Castlehill was a modern architect's dream of the functional city in the country, on a small experimental scale, of course. As by-products it grew vegetables and manufactured a small quantity of baskets, wooden furniture and handwoven carpets, but its major industry was the daily intake of hard-to-handle psychotics and their processing into easy-to-handle queer characters and corpses.

Carl soon became part of that process, more expert than most. With that thoroughness and devotion which so characterized his temperament, he absorbed himself entirely in his job in the reception department of the hospital; and months went by, collapsing under the simple physical problem of getting an intellectual grasp on this complex institution, its habits, customs, its theories conscious and unconscious, and its mode of classification. But when his first year was nearly done and summer had settled on Castlehill like a lazy dog, Carl was forced to ask himself whether Erdman had not been right. For what was there to be learned in a place where science lived in the interstices of a hospital routine whose major problem was to get rid of the patients as quickly as possible because outside the gates so many thousands more waited to enter, so many thousand known, and hundreds of thousands unknown?

Walking to his office with his fellow cottager, Dr. Val Curtin, Carl asked himself this question once again. He carried his hands clasped behind his back and a cigarette burned in the corner of his mouth, biting his lips dryly, the smoke ascending to his half-closed left eye. The heat was green and flower-filled and through the narcotic trees the windless sun unshaped his starched white uniform. Curtin was, as usual, speculating and complaining about the sad end of one of his recent cases. "When pneumonia doesn't kill them," he growled, "I do." His bristling voice and a distant train alone disturbed the question in Carl's mind.

Dr. Curtin was a brisk, witch-hazel-scented bachelor in his early forties who made a comfortable partner in the cottage. Immensely interested in the new shock therapy, he had taken to

91

Sakel's classical monograph with a gusty enthusiasm. A passion for experiment, a bottomless curiosity, a humble faith that somewhere there was a drug or a combination of drugs that would be a cure-all for schizophrenia, motivated his life. And as he was a confident man, devoted to his profession, redheaded, pale-eyed, paunchy, with very big strong hands on the backs of which a red fuzz like Cain's profusely grew, no defeat defeated him and no victory amazed. But he had long since forgotten that the patients were the moral vessels and treasured wards of the state. He treated them like guinea pigs or white rats, tried everything and anything, because, "in this big world there is so much we don't know and you have to try everything to find out anything." The staff at Castle-hill claimed that Curtin's work with insulin and metrazol was the only way of solving the overcrowding problem, a nasty reference to a few deaths among his patients (an old man who had died that morning being the last). But Curtin's answer to these cheerless jokes at lunch had been, "Take up religion! You guys are just keepers in a loony house." Curtin himself was a fervent atheist of North Irish ancestry and his hobby was collecting pamphlets against the Roman Catholic Church. He laughed at Carl's psychoanalysis which he called "another cure of laying on the hands, witch doctoring, mumbo-jumbo," but he respected Carl's grasp on materialist biology and his solid training in neuropathology. Carl had aided Curtin in several post-mortems of patients dead of shock therapy, and the old man was scheduled for it that night. "A careful, quiet evening's work," was the way Curtin put it. In his eager way Curtin worshiped Carl's technique, his exhaustive knowledge of the brain both human and animal. "You're a God-damned artist, that's what you are," he used to say over the dining table to the other doctors. "The man's a no-good dreaming artist, a Michelangelo of the scalpel, and when I die I want to be taken apart by him."

"If you stay here long enough," Carl replied dryly, "you will."

Across the river the train hooted and the whistle went across the water like a flat stone, skipping from silence to silence until it struck the hills and was netted in the trees above Carl's head. "I keep wondering each time what you expect to find in those bodies we chop up. After all, Val, it's not the same thing you do in experimental psychology where you destroy part of the nervous system in the living animal and then see what happens in action. How would you know if there was a change in your old man at all?"

"You're a God-damned Freudian, that's what." Curtin was sour, yet teasing. "You're a witch doctor who believes in psychic reality, a medievalist. You think immaterial things can cause actions. Scientists have been burned on crosses to disprove it."

"And burned," Carl said. "Psychic reality, I quote, is as real as physical reality." Remembering his own training analysis with Erdman, Carl knew this was true. He knew it from that difficult, that sometimes painful and always remembering journey through unremembered experience, searching always, sure to find behind this bend of time another stretch, longer, deeper, darker, the river of memory narrowing, tunneling into naked first glimpses of life. And always there were other travelers there wearing the shapes of friends, of enemies, and of that enemy-friend, the lover, and behind each mask was the real face of the mother or the father. Superbly Freud had sketched the geography of the human soul so that men could travel through their hearts without fear, *but not without danger.* For psychic reality was *real* unlike storybook ghosts. These spirits of the past were like the flesh itself, surviving everything but death. But Freud, like many an ancient geographer and voyager, while discovering new continents and opening an era, had like them often given these places magical shapes and presences. First the adventurer, Carl thought, and then the scientist. "In other words, Val," he went on, "you must know not only the neural chain, the glandular sequence, the muscular set and change," and Carl thought of himself wild on that rainy night in Vienna, the black and awful streets of that imperial waste, that shell of Empire; he saw himself sweating, nauseous, bewildered, all physical things, the dampness of the rain and the dampness of his body, because of that cable from Sandy and David, and there was also beyond these mechanisms, these organic although

93

dynamic wheels and pulleys, the heart of the machine, the trans·
posing center of it, "but there is also the content of the impulse
and its history in the psychic pattern."

"Agh." Curtin waved his white-sleeved arm in the sunlight.
"And what's the content? Ectoplasm? It's just words you're using.
Everything that happens must have material effects, and God
damn it, if there are material effects we can see them, or what's
even better, see the machines that measure them. Matter must
move. It must move for things to happen or else there's no science
and no knowledge. There's nothing." He moved abruptly ahead in
front of Carl's enjoying smile. "Let's go in and interview little
Emily's old man. Maybe he'll say yes and we can try the shock
therapy on her. She's young enough for some good to come of it."

Little Emily had appeared a few days before, escorted by representatives of the sheriff's office with a court order remanding her
to the care of Castlehill. She was an undersized girl of sixteen with
straggly blond hair, emaciated, and completely passive. Utterly
without affect, she seemed hopeless from the point of view of
ordinary prognosis. She had to be fed, even soiled herself from
time to time, and if let alone usually sat in sodden apathy.

Her father sat in Carl's office and looked at the papers. "What's
the difference?" he said, and signed his name, deposing that he
would not hold the state liable for anything that happened to his
only daughter. Carl questioned him thoroughly, taking everything
down in a neat self-taught shorthand with which he wrote and
composed as easily as with school script.

Out of a worn wallet the father drew a set of pictures showing
little Emily before things went wrong, a pretty girl with a big
ribbon in her blond hair. "You can't imagine the kind of nice and
obedient child she was before she went and caught this schizophrenia."

Curtin looked indifferently at the photographs, but Carl selected
and kept one with the father's disinterested permission.

"She was late in coming to her womanhood," the father answered
to Carl's question. He lowered his voice at this delicate subject.
"Most girls reach the age about eleven or twelve, I guess, but Emily

was fifteen before she started to . . ." he paused, and his voice nearly disappeared. "Before she started to menstruate. And that's when something happened and she caught the disease in her head because of all the troubles she was having."

Carl asked, "What business are you in?"

"Well, before the depression I was in the hardware business, being always mechanically inclined. I had a store on Eightieth Street near Third Avenue."

"Is that so?" Carl smiled politely. "I used to work at the River Hospital not far from there."

The father brightened. "You did? I had my appendix taken out there in thirty-one, but I don't seem to remember you. I can't say I do, Dr. Myers."

"I was in a different department."

Curtin chuckled. "The white rat division."

In response to Carl's questions, the father revealed the simple facts beneath which bulged tremendous meanings, confusing and contradictory — how everything had been well, and then one day the wife caught little Emily at her purse and slapped her, and how only two weeks later the tragedy had occurred. "A little thing like that," the father complained. And now he was all alone, and they had all been such a happy family. Carl probed and the father answered. Curtin called this the priestly part of the business, the lies of autobiography; and Carl called these lies and half-truths the real windows into the unconscious, into the soul lost and in flight from reality.

But this father's mind was deeply stubborn, and he whined always that he couldn't recall, that he didn't know, he wasn't sure, and after a while he even refused to guess. So Carl let him go, but not before Curtin bluntly said, "I don't know what we can do for your daughter. She's pretty far gone. But we'll do what we can, and learn something too, perhaps, to prevent such tragedies from occurring in other happy families." In the end he couldn't keep the discontent out of his voice, for Curtin was convinced that all families were unhappy families because the family had degenerated into a manufactory of cheap labor.

95

As the father walked out, grateful for the interest they were taking in his daughter, Carl tossed the photograph to his friend. "There's a fifteen-year-old girl dressed like a child of nine. I'll bet that Daddy's impotent, that his wife was cheating, that little Emily knew and was looking in Mama's purse for a letter or something, spying on her. It's too bad we can't analyze the father."

Curtin studied the photograph for some time and then quite seriously looked up and asked, "But do you know that little Emily has a birthmark on the inner side of her left thigh just two centimeters from the *mons Veneris?*"

Carl laughed out. "Do you?"

"Yes, because I looked, Dr. Mesmer. And I also took a quick glance into the child's purse, to use a Freudian symbol, and she's been masturbating a long time, too long in fact, and maybe with a steel file." He shouted with laughter, and went out roaring to take over his new patient.

After examining little Emily, Curtin decided to use insulin for the pharmacological shock. The child was dreadfully underweight, so generally run down and so little amenable to instruction, that some artificial means of stimulating her appetite was necessary. Insulin usually made patients ravenous, and in this way Emily's health would be partially reconstituted and her organism prepared for the terrible strains that shock made on the nervous system. So Curtin left orders and made his usual slapdash preparations, for like most specialists he had eyes only for what concerned him. And then in the evening, Carl surprised him.

Curtin was reading the prophecies of various baseball experts on the chances of the Detroit Tigers and mumbling his discontent. As a young man he had been a rather brilliant second baseman and he still maintained a passion for the sport, never happier than when he was arguing the merits of the different players whose histories he knew far more thoroughly, Carl said, than the records of his patients. "It's a question of sympathy," Curtin admitted half truthfully. "It's because you've never been mad," Carl told him, and Curtin wistfully replied that at least he was a manic-depressive type.

96

Outside, in the delicious windy darkness, there was a soft and constant mewing of the trees, and Carl listened as he observed the bright red head of Curtin. He hesitated still although he had made up his mind, and swam for yet another moment before he plunged into the experiment he had in mind. The open screened windows filtered the air currents, and on each wire mesh blind moths beat and fluttered, and it seemed to him that he too was shaking his life away against an invisible screen, trying always to fly to a light that perhaps did not exist. For how could he be sure, as he was sure, that somehow, somewhere, a route of investigation would open up the pattern of human action and reveal there the basis of a true natural science. It was mere faith based on the supposition that the universe, and therefore man's universe too, was completely knowable. He sighed and decided to go ahead. Perhaps in repeating the experiment himself, an experiment done by others, perhaps with stricter techniques, something could be cleared away, because if not, then only psychoanalysis was left, and his mind could not yet accept a nonbiological basis for human science.

"Val," he said, "if you want me to, I'd be willing to work with you on the case of little Emily."

Turning, Curtin crinkled pale eyes and let out an exulting grunt. "Ho ho said the captain. Welcome to the science of pharmacological shock. It's a deal."

"Now wait." Carl spoke slowly. "I want this to be a real experiment, no matter how foolish it is, really planned, worked out in all its details, to be written up and published later with a history of previous work in the field and an estimate of their results as compared with our own. This means time, and it means you can't go running around with a hypodermic in your hand throwing Emily into a convulsion every time you feel bored."

"Great!" Curtin said. "Fine! Wonderful! Why?"

"Just this. Let's either close this blind alley or find out if it's a door, for ourselves I mean."

"Great!" Curtin said again, and he jumped up and shook Carl's hand. "We'll both be famous and write articles for the *New York American* and get rich." He began to gloat and compose scare headlines, his imagination raging because he was so very happy to have Carl as a collaborator and not merely a friend on the sidelines. In the end he dragged Carl off to town to drink beer and celebrate "the greatest combination of skill and intelligence ever arrayed against the dark powers of the human mind."

It was three in the morning as they started home, going up the long dirt road that led from the river's bank to the heights where Castlehill dominated the countryside. The moon powdered the road with its fragile lights while Curtin sang melancholy songs. Somewhere in the shrubbery a fox barked and Curtin accepted the challenge, raising his great head to bark back. "Can you bark like a dog?" he asked Carl.

"Like a man," Carl replied and barked sharply.

"You would make a good dog," Curtin said. "What more can I say?"

From time to time the river wind stormed at the trees and Carl had the sense as the road bore them aloft, the wind pushing behind them, that they were gliding up into the sky, rising high, held, surging. They passed through deep shadows like gliders going through clouds, emerging again into the moonlight with relief and release.

"How is it, do you think?" Curtin wondered in a chilled voice as they cut across a treeless ridge with grasses clutching at their trouser legs — "How is it to be mad, not a neurotic, but someone all alone and crazy like little Emily? What does it feel like? Does anyone know?"

"We have heard," Carl said, and he thought too of nights in which he had lain awake peopling the dark with terrors, the imagination sculpturing out of the broken fragments of shadows primal shapes and brooding presences. "I think it is to be asleep and dreaming all the time, and afraid to wake up because then you will have a dream of terror that will drive you mad."

Curtin shuddered, his pale eyes lost in the windy moonlight so that they were all white and blank like the eyes of statues, and then he stopped and tried to light a cigarette and his matches kept blowing out in the wind. He turned through the compass and everywhere there was a black mouth that blew against him. Carl opened his coat and made a wall for Curtin, then the cigarette was lighted and they walked on again, going toward the gray city of Castlehill that stood silently before them in the moonlight like a Saracen castle above the city.

"We'll do this experiment correctly," Carl said. "I'll first try to get a transference by psychoanalytic methods, and then we'll use the shock and see if it opens up a richer background to inquiry."

But Curtin was still overcome by the mood of wonder, by the terror of the vast night. "Oh little Emily, little Emily," he cried out. He stopped and bent his back, his face open to the vast plain of heaven. "Which constellation is little Emily? What stars above? How did she one starry night tiptoe into her mother's room and drive a bread knife into her mother's throat?" The archipelagoes of universes poured their soft radiance upon his transfigured head. "You know, Carl, I wanted to study the insane because I felt they were the best people in life, so fine, so sensitive; that life drove them mad, and only the dull, the brutal, the mean could stand to live and be normal."

Carl put his hand on Curtin's shoulder, an act which would have been impossible for him five years before, to let himself put out his hand to comfort. "I once read a mysterious sentence in the Bible which I've never forgotten. The heart of the sons of men is full of evil, and madness is in their heart while they live, and after they go to the dead."

"Agh," Curtin growled. He shook himself vigorously. "I feel ghosts and demons." And then he laughed, booming out against the whole world. "They go to the dead, and we will give little Emily the finest post-mortem in the history of pathology if she cheats us and dies." He strode on waving his hands in the night shouting and laughing, a little drunk with village beer, crying up to the heavens, "Which of you is little Emily? Oh little Emily, which is your star?"

iv

IN the morning Carl announced the project to the director, a nervous executive with an exacerbated interest in sexual perversions. "Excellent," Dr. Sloate said, "excellent! And if she develops anything along my line, call me in. I'll be glad to help." Dr. Sloate had no quarrel with psychoanalysis, shock therapy, or basketweaving, but he felt that all these theories had too high an estimation of human nature which he believed morbid and pernicious when it was normal and wildly pornographic when it was ill. But he was kind enough to put the facilities at Carl's disposal, feeling at last that this brilliant young man, who had come so highly recommended, might have happened on something important which he wanted to test; for Dr. Sloate hoped that some new technique or theory might develop which would be called, for example, the Castlehill Treatment developed under the supervision of its director, Dr. Sloate.

Little Emily was transferred to one of the quieter buildings where tranquil misfits perfectly adapted to institutional life spent their cheerless days. Carl had a few storybook pictures hung on the beige walls, a colorful spread put on the bed, flowers in a vase, and all the little odds and ends that serve as the usual surroundings of the normal life. He set Curtin to work on the entire literature of shock therapy, mechanical, electrical and pharmacological, checking the results constantly, writing letters when possible to other workers in the field, and in general exhausting everything that had been written and done. Even Curtin was astounded by what he found, and he told Carl, "The number of concealed and

100

unconscious theories of illness varies directly with the eminence of the experimenters."

"Your job," Carl warned him ironically, "is to expose everything including your ignorance."

"And yours too," Curtin replied, burying himself in the endless statistics of amateur mathematicians. He used to walk around muttering under his breath, "Magic. Magic."

Little Emily was put through an exhaustive, detailed series of medical tests, charted, described, analyzed until the only mystery left was what kept her alive and why she was ill. But these two questions were, of course, the central point of the experiment, and Carl began to devote four or five hours a day to her, trying to develop some kind of transference, some kind of rudimentary affect, just enough to be marked, just enough to indicate a change. He took her for walks, talked to her all the time of simple things, had lunch with her. She responded to nothing, moving near him or sitting opposite like someone who belonged to the living dead, as if her soul had long since departed this terrible world and what was left was flesh doomed to finish its days, a stranger on earth.

Carl spent many weeks at this dull and melancholy task, coming around each morning at ten, entering cheerfully, with a "Well, good morning, Emily, and how are we today?" Dressed by the nurse, she would be sitting at the window because she had been placed there, staring blankly out on the lawn. A big maple tree branched like a giant umbrella stood in the middle of neat grass which was boxed in by curving paths lined with lilac bushes. He used to put on her cotton jacket and take her for a slow walk around the lawn. Sometimes they sat on the bench and watched the gardener mow the grass or water the peony bushes, and all the while he would be talking with never a reaction from the girl. He developed the feeling that he was trying to communicate with a supernatural world, with a ghost, and that reality stood between like a wall of iron.

Sometimes Carl had lunch with her and sometimes he took her for a drive in Curtin's little Chevrolet. He talked only of what could be seen or heard and was extremely careful not to set up

101

references to her terrible past, yet Emily responded to nothing. But the exercise improved her health and the care in feeding supervised by one of the more conscientious nurses developed her appetite. She began to gather fat and color in her cheeks and her hair, formerly so dead, became springy, began to shine. Carl bought a heavy hairbrush in town and spent a half hour each afternoon brushing Emily's hair. She was not pleased and not displeased. She simply gained weight and her appearance improved.

Curtin, who by now had amassed an enormous filing system, used to call for Carl around four in the afternoon, entering the room with a bounce and captivating smile. "And how is the nursemaid today? And the bewitched princess?" And so Emily appeared, bewitched, with a spell laid on her.

"How long," Curtin asked, "are you going to keep this nonsense up?" He groaned, "I'm reading all that junk for the second time."

But Carl persisted. He believed along with Brill and Bleuler that if enough effort were spent, if enough work were put into the situation (for the psyche operated on economic principles), some affect would be generated. Since Emily was alive it meant that she had, so to speak, a certain amount of energy, of libido with which to meet the problems of her existence, internal and external. At present that libido was devoted entirely to herself. Accepting the distinction between the id and the ego, Carl explained to Curtin, "We might say that the ego was developed through the testing of reality and the discovery of object relationships. In Emily's case she has returned to the point where object relations disappear and the ego regresses to a more primitive, more archaic state, narcissism."

"In other words?" Curtin asked, grinning.

"Emily is an infant again, the child before the discovery of the world."

"That is?"

Carl grinned back. " 'The womb's a fine and private place but none I think do there embrace.' "

"I could use a few embraces," Curtin added ruefully, but they spent the nights on the literature of pharmacological shock, comb-

102

ing it thoroughly for clues, assessing the material, making notes. "By God," Curtin said each night, "I begin to see the difference between baseball and psychiatry. Baseball is a natural science and psychiatry is voodoo."

But if little Emily developed no relationship with Carl, he developed one with her.

He had plenty of energy to let loose on the world and this constant socializing from his side with the girl began to absorb her into his thoughts, his feelings, and even into his dreams. He had many a wish-fulfillment in the hours of the night, and his frustration by day was crowned with success in sleep.

Dreams, like stage directions, exist only in the present tense because the inner life of the mind has no real past. Everything is now, and so Carl's dream had the force, the supreme concern of immediacy. He is walking into little Emily's room, walking with sorrow because Emily is dead, and suddenly she is there, upon him, laughing, her golden hair dancing in the sunlight that comes through the window. The blue dress contains its own light that comes from her body, a dress transparent, the white flesh perfect and moving through the cloth like a body seen in water, her body floating in the blue depths of the blue. Her arms around his neck. She is kissing him and the mouth is cool and moist, staining his cheek with its delicate life. Now he walks with her through the grounds while from the tall administration building the staff waves red banners toward them. Each flag is bright red and distinct, each flag a flutter of red in the blue sky. The music of the waltz is concrete, a current that bears them on its rhythm, making them dance and all around the doctors and patients watch with glad smiles, with hope, with love. The laughter rushes about them as they get into Curtin's little Chevrolet, and the white road winds to the white church where Curtin in a clown's dress officiates at the marriage. The marriage bed is enormous, the room dark and as he kisses her the ribbon unties and like a mask falling reveals the cunning face of Sandy. She wears her wedding dress upon her thin body, the bony body, and the thick lids barely opened, let a smile half grow out of her squarish catlike face. He draws back, and then

103

bliss overwhelms him. Sandy is returned from the dead. Alive, not dead, although she still wears her marriage shroud. The bed is covered with mysterious strands of golden hair, and he is losing himself in them, and is, yes, lost.

Awake the happiness still dreamed within his limbs, but as he opened his eyes he remembered his dream, and remembering Sandy the old anger grew across the physical pleasure of his body, irritating him, driving him out of the bed. He lighted a cigarette and wandered through the dark, familiar cottage, hearing from a distant bedroom the whistle of Curtin's sleep, and the dream persisted within his memory, but like a seed dropped beside another seed. For the fantasy on little Emily only served to stimulate the luxuriant growth of all that rich and troubled content which were his relations to Sandy. It was a vine rooted in his past, and moistened, activated, it suddenly flowered everywhere in his thoughts. It did not matter that he understood why it was that only her marraige to David had suddenly overwhelmed him with useless love of her. He caught himself wandering through Vienna again endlessly spinning stories of how he would undo what was done. He found himself in rainy winter streets, in snowy ones, alone in his pension or dining with other students. And each physical place had attached to it a psychical state, the fact that he loved Sandy. Now that he no longer loved her, and no longer even regretted, and hardly ever remembered, it was particularly vexing to be bothered by a chance dream, to have a secret channel opened into the buried past and to suffer, even for a moment, the anger and frustration he had once endured. It was, of course, his anger and frustration with little Emily that caused it. Not that he wasn't professionally patient with her, but he wanted her to react once so that he could get on with the experiment and finish his work at Castlehill. He decided that there was no use waiting forever, and that the shock treatment should be applied, tested, and finished with. This would only delight Curtin. Carl sighed and went to bed.

In the morning, he proposed to his friend that they go ahead with the second part of the experiment, and Curtin guffawed,

104

made a few ironical remarks about Freud, and hurried off to make preparations. "We'll give her the business tomorrow," he shouted, making a jab into the air with an imaginary hypodermic syringe.

Carl and Emily took a last sociable walk together. The girl walked docilely at his side and he held her arm as they went up the little rise where there was a summerhouse covered with wild roses, tucked away in a copse of paper birches and cool pine. There was no view here, only an open space on which three paths converged, twisting in from the heavily wooded section of the park.

Here the summer was dense and fertile.

Rain had loosened the earth and the sun, hot and constant through the long cloudless morning, had distilled the juices in the vegetation into a perfume whose essence was sappy and green.

Carl sat Emily on a bench in shade that was lanced with light while he slowly paced the path and smoked a cigar. He was imprisoned in a cage of fragrance and the close earthy air untapped his senses. Sensual languor uncoiled within him, an alcohol of sex distilled over these long months. His desire, like one of those wild alley cats in the city, was at present objectless but roving, a kind of neurotic anxiety, but richly pleasant. The royal sun magnetized the trees and the flowers, the grasses surged, and he felt his body opening and swelling with desire, distending and shaking, and languid ease nevertheless touched him as he walked, and he finally stopped in the direct glare, forgetting the cigar, possessed.

On the bench Emily sat remote and cool, a golden butterfly hovering about her passive head. Fragile, docile, childlike, she stared ahead of her, knowing nothing, open in the sun.

The pulse of desire has no morality since it is older than civilization and, like the first nature gods, a brute force; and Emily was suddenly the object upon which Carl's desire dropped. But he thought of it instead of letting his mind go loose and wondered if it were not sexuality which had given birth to consciousness, and looking at her, helpless, naked of power, without claws to scratch and teeth to bite and horns to thrust and matted hair or hide to protect, he wondered if after all the generalized shape of man's body was not based on his generalized sexuality and not on his

105

development as a food gatherer. Consciousness varied directly as the erotic development increased, and would not the mind be then a victim of what had born it? Neurotics and others, psychotics like Emily, were too sensitive, too highly erotogenic in a society so far undeveloped as to maintain sexual conventions and morality which supported other social aims. A purely sexual society would have no lunatics in it. What would it have? He shook his head, amused by the extravagance of his mind. It could have me now, he thought.

"Carl!" Curtin's voice came rudely calling. "Carl."

The white starched coat rounded the path, coming swiftly, calling. When he saw Carl and little Emily, he stopped, and struck an attitude. "Bucolic," he cried. "Bucolic." And then he came close, his red face alight with humor. "You're lucky. That's what, lucky. And you're lucky because you've been good. You weren't a naughty boy last night so Fate sent you a present this morning. In your cabin," and his voice hushed, "in your cabin is a dryad, a nymph such as has not been seen in these walls for many an age, in fact since time immemorial."

"A visitor? Who?"

"A Mrs. David Seawithe," Curtin replied. "Don't you know her?" But he didn't wait for an answer. "Run. Run before she evaporates and I'll tend little Emily. Just one promise, I want a blow by blow description. Is Dr. Myers here, Dr. Carl Myers? Oh Lord! When I think of that waitress, that nurse last night, that raddled flesh. Run! Fly!" And as Carl left the voice pursued him. "You should see her great blue eyes. The hair. The legs. The unmentionables. Oh, such unmentionables!"

V

THERE was a little oblong window at the side of the cottage so overgrown with ivy it could not be opened, and it faced through the arch of the foyer into the deep living room. Carl paused, pushed the vines apart and looked in.

A strange woman stood at the mantelpiece with her back to him, and suddenly the tension dissolved in him for the figure was not Sandy's. This must be a second Mrs. Seawithe then, and he was glad the marriage had gone to pieces for it was what such a marriage, conceived in wickedness, deserved. The second Mrs. Seawithe wore a blue linen suit so deep in color that in the sunlight draining through the big window she seemed to shimmer with violet, and her big straw hat, like a cartwheel, caught the rosiness on its white, matched it with the round bare arms, the tan stockings, and the golden blob of brightness reflected on the photograph of Carl and Curtin which she appeared to be studying.

Carl watched her for a moment or two longer, waiting for his heart to slow down to normal. He had not realized how the expectation of seeing Sandy again after five years could call up such a storm within him. The rather tightly fitting jacket and skirt revealed a mature body, solid and womanly such as Sandy's skinny flesh could never attain, and Carl thought that at least this time David had bought something with his money that was worth the investment.

He turned from the window and went briskly around to the entrance, feeling only a rather sharp curiosity, for after all a second Mrs. Seawithe had even less reason than the first one to visit him.

107

The confidence and innocence with which he approached, the dash with which he flung open the screen door and entered the foyer, the speed with which he gained the threshold of the living room served only at last to paralyze him as the woman turned.

Sandy's face, squarish and catlike beneath her blond hair, looked expectantly at him, and Sandy's face smiled out of its sunburnt smoothness, and Sandy's eyes beneath their thick lids caught at his glance, and Sandy's voice, a little more assured, spoke out of this shape that wasn't hers, out of this sexualized and profoundly beautiful body, out of the smart suit and the shoes that finished as it were with a dance the neat legs on which she stood. "Why, Carl," she said.

He could not assimilate the woman before him, glowing in violet, in rosiness, in sunlit tan, to the undeveloped, the scrawny girl whose flesh and mind he had known so well, better it had once seemed than his own. The double image oscillated before him as it appeared to do for her because she stared at him, then down at the photograph and then back at him again. Finally, as he did not speak, she turned and put the photograph back on its mantelpiece. Her motion freed him for his, and he walked to his desk by the big window and sat down before it so that he had the confidence of a doctor about to receive a patient, except, he noticed, that his heart was throbbing again, and the patient was himself.

The bitterness, the humiliation, the exhaustion of pride all came back now, as real and immediate as if Vienna were again outside the door and this were the pension of Frau Ohlrig. And with a certain hard contempt for her humanity, for the fact that she had for some unknown reason come to visit him, he went directly to the heart of the matter, as if five minutes had elapsed, as if the cable had arrived only five minutes before at Castlehill and not five years ago as he ran in out of the rain into the warm hallway of the old house, standing there laughing and breathless, dripping rain upon the worn rug and Frau Ohlrig calling from her little office, "Herr Myers, there's a cable for you. It's upstairs on your bureau."

He looked brutally at Sandy and asked, "Why?"

108

"I wanted to see you, that's why."

He ignored the present without explanation. "Why," he demanded, holding his voice even and insulting, "why did you and David wait for me to be in Europe before letting me know?"

"Oh, that." She drifted toward him, her face serious but not alarmed at this beginning, for like a skilled chess player unusual openings just gave her a better chance to win. "We let you know when we decided to be married."

"But you knew," he insisted over his folded hands as she came up and stood in front of him, leaning upon the desk, "you knew it was a bribe to get rid of me, lending me that money to go abroad and study. You must have known all the time, from the first. You must have planned it with David."

She looked around the room, the rather pretty furniture, the general cheerfulness and success of it, the books, the pictures, and out of the window to the great trees and the sunlight throbbing on the lawns. She seemed to count these things, to make a sum of them across the years and finally asked, "Was it a bribe?"

He looked up from his hands clasped and steady on the blotter and held them that way. He stared at her with horror, at her duplicity, her meanness, her adventurism to come here after all these years to see him. This new Sandy who did not retreat to confusion and silence when accused had developed a kind of sophisticated viciousness, and this was only proper with the beginning that she had made, the betrayal. "You should know," he said. "Who should know better? Wasn't it planned, my supposed friend and my . . ." He hesitated not knowing which word to use.

In the pause she asked, "Well?" And when he didn't go on, she let herself smile. "It's not easy, is it, to say your old lover. That's what you want to say but you're honest enough not to say it because you didn't love me at all. You remember, I'm sure, that you never even talked with me, never asked me to wait, to come with you, never explained that you were going and why, but just said that you were. And you took it quite for granted that having got the money to go abroad, it was quite natural for me to lose you and for you to leave me since there was nothing to keep us together. And it was true and I accepted it. It couldn't have mattered to you, and in my interest, at least, you should have been glad for me as I was for you when David helped you." It seemed to exhaust her patience to say this much and she moved abruptly from the desk and wandered through the room.

He could not help watching her body so graceful and complete passing in and out of the patches of sunlight, admiring her shape and wondering how it had completed itself out of that poor beginning he had known in his bed. He could not be objective and just admire, because this woman had been his, free to him, available, and even though changed, it was Sandy, a familiar presence. It hurt his imagination at the moment that she had bloomed, triumphed, succeeded in her escapade, formalized it into marriage and then made this marriage the constant ground of her life without regret, without regret, he thought savagely, of him. "You accept," he said harshly, "that he married you to help you?"

"Accept?" She was amused. She moved slowly, swung gracefully about to face him. "Wasn't that the point?"

"He knew you didn't love him and he married you? You didn't lie to him?"

"Oh." She thought for a moment before going on. "You mean, you mean to say to me now that when you left you believed I loved you?"

The attack flung him back in complete disorder. He asked wildly, "What are you doing here now?"

But she ignored the present as he had before, as if he had been the one seeking her out. "You mean you went away without speaking to me of it although you thought I loved you? I never thought that. Never." And she sat down on the flowered cretonne couch. "Why, that's shameful."

He was completely routed and could only answer with half the truth, enough to save himself. "I didn't love you when I went away."

Across a pool of radiance which shimmered on the wooden floor between the strips of straw matting, she sent him a long

110

calculating look like a lasso, a noose that twisted into his mind to catch there whatever truth might exist, to tug it out. "If you were glad to get rid of me," and as he twisted his head to interrupt, she interrupted herself, "to leave me, I mean, because after all you didn't love me and . . ." she stopped again, gave a little tug, "Did you think I loved you?"

"I knew you didn't."

"Very well," she carried on with a flash of real spirit, her cheeks flushing a little, the big brim of the straw hat shaking, "then why didn't you ever write although I wrote three times? What were you angry about?"

"The trick," he blurted out, "the meanness of it."

"What trick? What are you talking about, Carl? What trick?"

"To send me away as if for my sake."

Sandy asked shrewdly, "Wasn't it for *your* sake that you went away?"

He rose bewildered, to be outfought, to be forced to reveal what he had felt during all the years when all he had wanted to do was attack her, humiliate her and in the end revenge himself for the fact that it was only after he had learned of her marriage to David, only after that brutal cablegram, only after the hurt, the pain, the gnawing anger had wasted itself fruitlessly, only after the fury was gone and a space had been opened in his heart that he had discovered what it was that love could be, a constant vacuum in feeling which only one person and no other could fill. Sandy half lay within the corner of the big couch, her arms open, the right one upon the back of the couch, the left one resting on the arm rest, a gloved hand loosely falling, the fingers in their white glove like the long thin petals of an exotic flower. Her legs were crossed, and she was relaxed, watching him. She had the power of the moment and the power now of the past. "I admit," he said trying to regain his ground by at least being honest, "I admit that I went away for my sake."

She countered quickly, she was too shrewd for him, he realized. "Then how does it matter for whose sake you were sent?"

He was drawn to her and approached slowly and stood over her so that she looked up at him from under her heavy lids, from under the brim of her hat, from out of the folds of tawny hair which modeled her face. Her body was curved to him, a bow bent for him, this body so new for his eyes, mysterious for his imagination since this body which still was Sandy's had never been his. "You're shrewd," he told her, "and I apologize." He made up his mind never to tell her that he had loved her, although as he gazed upon her face he wanted above all to find what it was that lived beneath it, to rediscover her, at least, at last, to know what she was. "I'm sorry, and I have no real complaint to make because after all you are a great success."

"And you? Your friend, the redhead, he told me a few things about you. He is one of your great admirers and he tells me, and I believe, you're a great success. And your friend, Dr. Erdman, thinks so too."

"Erdman? You know Erdman? How?"

She emitted briefly a photon of an ironic smile, and this was a new depth in her character that she should possess irony. "I don't know him at all. David does. He's David's psychoanalyst."

And Carl burst into an uproar of laughter, a great rain of it that shook him and carried her off too, until they were both helplessly riding it, dashing wildly down upon the gravitation of the releasing mood, facing each other and laughing; and then still laughing she leaned against him and while they both still laughed they kissed as old friends and linked arms and walked around the room.

Carl asked if she would like to stay and have lunch, "To show you off to the staff. You don't realize how dull their lives actually are and it would be an act of charity to show them an example of life's triumph against misery."

"You think so? I'll be glad to."

"You can see the place, a guided tour if you like. We have time."

"I would. I'd like to see what keeps you here in this country club, because that's how it looks to me."

"Fine," he said. "Of course in some respects it's not exactly like a country club."

112

"May I take off my hat?" She removed the big straw and loosened the folds of her heavy hair.

"And on the other hand, it's a country club but more for the inmates than the staff." He guided her out of the cottage into the sun. "I mean it fulfills the function of the perfect country club." He led her toward the main buildings which lay behind a belt of pine trees on the flat field that used once to be a village playing field, and before that a meadow, and was now colonized by functional architecture inhabited by functionless human beings. "Tell me what made you come up here all of a sudden?"

"I was alone in New York." She had a way of being perfectly frank and easy, an air of confidence when she exposed herself, and this was even a surer sign of strength than her cleverness or new intellect. "David and I came up from Washington to New York on some stupid business of his. I certainly didn't want to come to the city, but he insisted and I did. Then he was called back to Washington and finally left for Europe. And there I was stranded. We have a country place outside of Washington because it's so unbearably hot there, and an apartment in New York where it's equally hot, and I didn't feel like going up to Furnace Dock and staying with his father and aunt, although the old judge likes me, and you too. I think his aunt dislikes me, but she's too civilized to do anything but worry over it."

"Why Europe?"

She said without admiration, just the facts, "He's a great expert on resources, the economics of war, and evidently there's going to be a war in Europe today, tomorrow or next year, and David went off to give his advice or get advice, I don't know. And frankly," she added frankly, "I don't care. He's always preaching about preparing America for war because he claims to have all kinds of secret information. And then when he tells me the secrets — which he always does, I can't stop him — why they turn out to be the same things I've read months ago in the newspapers, especially those long dull Sunday articles. You know," she added, "the parts you skip because they're so long and foolish."

They were passing between two white oblongs with modern

113

windows and a double row of porches with high wire walls. Here a nondescript group of semiviolent cases were taking the air, on one side men and on the other women, all with their arms folded in front of them and held by strait jackets. Sandy looked up from side to side and a wrinkle appeared upon her brow, a wrinkle that was a question mark, a doubt, a feeling that this was a little indecent — to be paraded before visitors. At the far corner of the porch a middle-aged man waited with his face pressed against the wire screen. As Carl and Sandy passed he suddenly called, "Madame. Lady. You!"

"Don't look up," Carl warned her but he was too late, for as Sandy's face came round, the man spit through the wire, and then burst into triumphant laughter, pouring out at the same time a stream of the filthiest abuse. He described with macabre details just how he proposed to enjoy Sandy, naming the parts of her body, describing them and his pleasure to be. And as she hurried away, holding tight to Carl's arm, that loud and energetic voice pursued them, rising in a great chant to the great god Sex, until everything was just one juicy word, his mutilated soul's amen.

"Oh," she said, "oh." She was panting.

"I'm sorry," Carl said. "I should have remembered him and taken you around by the other side. But at least you have to admit it's not exactly like a country club."

She forced a laugh. "He's frank. And once in the country club, don't think you're so different here, I heard a United States senator wrangling with someone and finally he got so mad he spit right in the other man's eye." She looked back over her shoulder, as if still pursued, her eyes wide, still frightened. "Do you always have to keep them tied up that way?"

"No," Carl explained. "Hardly ever, as a matter of fact. But these poor creatures have their seasons and it's to protect them from themselves that we do it."

Sandy clung heavily to Carl's arm and they passed here and there a despondent soul wandering footlessly about, waiting for nothing and going nowhere. "Why do you stay here?" she asked.

114

"To become respectable," he told her. "It's a kind of internship, too, to experience a run of cases."

She studied his face for a long time. "I should think it would make you unhappy to spend all your time with people who are so unhappy."

"Not unhappy. Bored."

Sandy sighed. "Yes, you're right. That's even worse."

They went on and Carl pointed out the various sanitary and splendid installations and meanwhile told her of the case of little Emily. She listened and understood but somehow he got the feeling that she was listening to her own mind at the same time, thinking deeply, remembering, sifting so to speak, a heaped-up collection of memories as if to find one piece she wanted.

At last it was nearly lunchtime and they were standing before the big administration building. "Would you," he asked, "like to see the most miserable, the most abandoned human beings in the whole world?"

She said quickly, "No." And then, "Why not?"

They took the elevator up to the top floor and found themselves in a small white foyer where, at a solitary desk before a paper pad and a telephone, an attendant sat reading a newspaper. He greeted Carl, dutifully inscribed the names, and opened the door with a key.

They stood in a long corridor with doors on either side, regularly spaced, each door with a small pane of glass fixed in it at eye level. Soft clear light took every shadow out of the enclosed space, and the naked corridor just sat there, extending, ending, eternal as three locked propositions in geometry.

"Just walk down," Carl told her, "and take a look. I think one look will be enough."

Slowly she moved forward against the nameless horror which she imagined there, more terrible because of the cleanness, the whiteness, the sanitary hell in which the dread was confined, and Carl watching her fondled in his mind the perfection which she had attained without him.

For a moment she hesitated at the door and then looked.

115

She gasped, and turned a blanched and shaking face towards him, and then drawn by the thing within the room looked again, repelled and avid at the same time for more.

"This," Carl said loudly, his voice echoing within the stone corridor, "is Bluebeard's forbidden room, the Pandora box, the skeleton closet of our times."

The creature in the room was a woman, had been, that is, because what she was now was impossible to say, a category of psychiatry at the best, and at the worst one of civilization's dirty secrets. She was naked because clothes were dangerous for her. The walls and the floor were padded because all hard surfaces were dangerous for her. Her nails were cut because every edged object was dangerous. Her hair was matted and she crouched in a corner, sometimes turning her head, searching, searching everywhere to find one hard or cutting edge on which to fling herself or cut herself to death. She waited for a chance to meet death, to destroy herself on his nails, his claws, his teeth. Her face was frozen, her body emaciated, and she no longer had an age. She sat in her own filth, which was regularly cleaned by three other women who trooped in and while two held her, the third washed her. This was her life, without days and without nights, outside of time, and life would only re-enter with the coming of death. Sandy stared and stared and then, like a sleepwalker, started to go from door to door. "The women," she said in a hushed and beaten voice, "are more frightening than the men."

"You have a better opinion of them, that's all." It was strange, Carl thought, how no one could resist another look, how no one could refrain from seeing what was in each room.

When they left Sandy insisted on walking in the open air for a few minutes before they went in to lunch. She started to ask a few questions and then gave up. "I'll never get over this."

"You will," he said, "because you're normal. The normal person is the one who can adapt to anything." She had, in effect, abandoned herself to him, to his strength there, resting against him, and he took pleasure in feeling her body against him, and in holding her bare arm, the wonderful flesh. "Sometimes I think that the

116

human brain, that is the nervous system which created consciousness because that was its need in the world, has finally loosed a
monster, a kind of life within the flesh which is so complex that it
is relatively free of control. It has its own laws, whatever they are,
and the struggle to bring consciousness into contact with reality
is what we call thought. It's as if man has freed himself in part
from the grave necessities of living in reality and constitutes his
own danger. As Dr. Erdman says, the human brain is the most
dangerous thing in the world and if the world can be destroyed,
then by the laws of this brain, the brain will find a way to destroy
the world."

"Don't tell me horror stories in the sun," she said. "Let's go back
to the cottage."

"But lunch?"

"No, no. No lunch now." Lightly she held his arm as if not to
lose the way while she walked pensively beside him, her air abstract and internal.

Carl's feelings surprised him for he could no longer find a single
trace of hostility toward Sandy, not even the memory of one. A
static charge of resentment had been left over in him through the
years and only her reappearance had been necessary to discharge
it once and for all, to free him forever from the past which now was
the story of two other people. He no longer cared. He did not love
her and he did not hate her. She was simply a beautiful and interesting woman, and as he guided her through the hot sun, his
starched uniform topped by his black head and her dark blue suit
crowned by her blondness, he objectively realized they made a
handsome couple, and so he enjoyed the nods of passing doctors
and nurses on their way to lunch.

He watched her slyly and asked himself if it would not be
pleasant to make love to her, but no desire rose to meet the
thought, although he wondered if it were possible. For after all,
it was not as if she were a stranger entirely, and to begin would
not be to begin at the beginning. He wondered what would happen
if he tried, and he realized that he could not guess although he
knew he would not try. As the screen door banged behind them,

117

ushering them into the coolness within, he understood that this at least was the residue of the past, that he could not casually or curiously approach her as a total stranger. So this was left, that she was not for him. This was the end, and the end was nothing, absolutely and blankly nothing.

Even when she started to put on her hat, saying to him from the mirror where his watching face was reflected, "I think I'll go home now," he didn't protest. She could go home if she wanted to.

"I'm sorry," he said, "that I showed you those poor patients of ours."

"It's not those poor people I'm thinking of." She turned around and looked quite intently at him. "It's you."

Her white gloves were exquisite, he observed, a fragile suede on which blue welts were stitched with the fingers neatly articulated by a thread of blue leather. "And what are you thinking?"

"What are you?"

"Of how nice your gloves are."

She held a hand up. "David sent these from Paris. He always sends me gloves just because the first thing he ever bought for me was gloves. You might even remember the first pair, black ones. I was wearing them the day I said good-by to you when you went up to Furnace Dock."

Carl didn't remember. "What are you thinking of me?" he asked.

"Of something you said. I'm sure that you did love me, if not when you left for abroad, then afterwards."

But he smiled and lied to her. "Never."

"I'm glad," she said.

"And I'm sure," he guessed, "that you and David did plan to send me off to Europe."

"I never saw him alone to plan." She held out the wonderfully gloved hand. "Good-by, Carl. Come and visit me sometimes."

He took her hand, pressed it and let go. "Where do you live in New York?"

"You'll find out if you want to see me." A vague smile took the coyness out of her remark, and he held the door open for her, and then followed her out. Once again the door banged and the sun-

118

light struck them. They walked in casual silence to the parking lot and once again said good-by, and the last he saw was her white glove waving from the car window as he remembered the pair of black gloves in Grand Central Station and recalled with a start that this was before David had even offered the money to him through the father, and that therefore she had lied.

But so had he, and he shrugged his shoulders and slowly strolled to the dining rooms, realizing again that it no longer mattered one way or another, for nothing is so dead as dead love, not even hunger satisfied.

vi

WHEN Carl appeared at the luncheon table, he met an awkward silence, for Curtin and the other two doctors had quite obviously been talking of him and his visitor, and deliberately to enjoy it Carl said nothing but, "Afternoon, gentlemen," and sat down and ordered his food. In the end it was Curtin who could not resist, for he rolled his eyes coquettishly, smirked, rolled himself in it and finally emitted a luxuriant "Ah!"

"What did you say?" Carl asked innocently.

Curtin opened his mouth wide and pointed with his fork inside. "I said ah! That's all. Ah!"

"Something bothering you?"

"Ah!" Curtin said again. "I must have caught a cold or something from that little nurse last night. I've got a queer little tickle in my throat." And then everyone started to laugh and all together asked who Sandy was.

"An old friend."

"Ah," Curtin repeated.

After lunch they adjourned to little Emily's room and discussed her case. Walking slowly up and down within the room Carl summed up the results this far. "The first step, to create some kind of rudimentary affect without shock, is a failure."

"Zero," Curtin agreed. "Although the fact that she looks better can be considered to be something. Usually they look worse."

And she had improved considerably, there was no doubt of it. She sat in unobtrusive quietness, dressed in a neat blue dress, her hair nicely brushed with a blue ribbon in it, and blue sandals on her stockingless feet. The open window with its starched curtains

120

dreamed over the lawn, and from time to time a little languid afternoon breeze opened the wings of the curtains wide and blew across Emily's face, touched the soft ends of her hair, lifting them like tendrils of some exotic aerial plant that seeks the sun. She sat with her back to Carl and Curtin and they looked across her to the outside as they talked over her affairs and how the time had come to start stage two of the experiment.

They were quite used to her being around, motionless, unresponsive, unhearing. And yet she was prettier, almost attractive except for the solemn deadness of her face. Her flesh had filled out and she was clean. She was their pet patient, their pet, their very own and they were fond of her the way people are of miniature fish, pets without responsive personality, but somehow charming even when they have an unanswered name.

"The question is," Carl said as he casually walked the room, "can we consider her general physical improvement as the beginning of an affect, or is it merely the same thing that happens when you water a dried lawn?"

"Well, while you wonder," Curtin replied, busying himself over a sheet of paper with a pencil, "I'll do a little arithmetic with the dosage. We start tomorrow, right?"

"Right." And Carl paced up and down the cool and simple room, the clean and fragrant air sacred about him, while he thought not of Emily but of Sandy.

Why had he for so long maintained within his mind the fiction that he hated her and David, that he still resented the little trick they had played upon him? Could it be that he had maintained this anger in order to pretend that he still loved her? And why did he want to pretend that he still loved her? Because otherwise his life would have been empty of love. He was thirty years old now and without anyone to love.

He heard Curtin mumbling numbers half aloud and he heard his own footsteps but otherwise there was nothing to listen to in the room but his own thoughts. Like anyone alive he wanted to be loved, for the urge to love was the motion that turned the mind outward from its own inner life to the external world. Love was, in fact, the reality principle of life, and while he sought outside himself to be a scientist, transferring to this search the deep needs of his emotions, he would not fool himself into believing that he could live out his days alone this way without that passionate attachment to another creature which alone of all needs could turn the senses into their opposite, an idea fulfilled.

And he started to call up in his mind what kind of woman it would be whom he could love. But here habit like a stupid horse kept turning its head towards the known, to Sandy. He changed the face, but her face was changed; he changed the flesh but the flesh was changed; he changed his mind, but the mind was already changed. That would indeed be odd, he thought, to fall in love again with Sandy as if she were someone else.

"Carl!" Curtin's voice came low and urgent. "Keep walking, and talk to me about anything, but keep talking as we were a moment ago. Keep walking, don't stop," the voice spoke on holding a single quiet level, yet marvel moved within it, "and steal a glance at our patient."

It is not easy to be the same when you know you are already changed, but Carl walked, he talked, his skin grew tight, he felt his breath increase as slowly, very slowly, still talking mechanically, he let his glance stray and catch the window and Emily.

Her head was turned lightly on the stalk of her neck. Her head was turned, and she was watching him. Her face, like matter at the word and beneath the hand of God, had become human. A little smile, a quiver of a smile enchanted her mouth, and her eyes were lively and she was watching him.

As he walked she disappeared from the ambit of his eye, and he continued to talk, and each time he got to the corner of the room where he turned back, there she was, her head turned, her back arched as she watched him. He had the enormous realization of this face and smile, of this moment, and he was deeply moved, his heart touched, his feelings weakened, and he felt that his eyes were beginning to soften, to crush with tears. He talked about love, the reality principle of life, because that was in his mind, when all the time he wanted to run to little Emily and take her in his arms and kiss her as one kisses a happy child who by a simple

122

act unconsciously has crowned a parent's life and care with a common triumph, an act of affection, an act of love. He talked and now his back was to her and he could not see her and this unit of time was immense, this time to walk slowly back to the corner as he was walking, as he had walked, this time until he could reach the corner and in the pattern turn and look at Emily again. He longed to gaze upon her constantly, and yet he did not hurry but walked at the remembered rate and then even more slowly until the corner arrived. There was a chair standing in the corner, and Carl saw the chair which was the mountaintop that he would reach in a moment with one final burst of strength and will, and then he was there, and naturally turned to look back as he walked back, and Emily was watching him and slowly turning back to look out of the window again.

There began then the strangest afternoon in Carl's life, for he walked the room for nearly an hour, until the nurse came in, until he was sure that this glimpse of Emily's spirit was just a peek, a flash of light breaking from the darkness, the inner tension of her soul. He walked and talked and tried to maintain the equilibrium. Such talk he talked, over and over again, not hearing what he said, keeping the emotion out of his voice, but a man divided, for there was a Carl leaning out of his eyes as strangely, mysteriously alive as the Emily that had for the brief minute emerged from the jungle of her inbent gaze. Soberly he paced the room, but passion danced within him. And Curtin's face was enough to make another weep, for Curtin was unashamedly letting tears drain down his ruddy cheeks.

In all the weariness and boredom of life, Carl thought, there are few times like this when a moment fulfills itself and needs no use beyond itself, like this. The recognition of psychoanalysis as a general theory of human action, and of his own actions, had been one such moment almost four years ago, and now here was another. But beyond a triumph of mind this had a sweetness, a gift of magic. The room was magical now, from the jute matting with its red and blue design, and the dark wooden floor shining, and the white walls, and the bed, to the open window and the sun on the lawn with the big maple in full leaf, heavy and green within

123

and yellow with sun and transparent as a pool of water where the light filtered through the broad and lovely leaves. The luncheon bell was sounding its last call, and far off, at upper Caxton Ferry, St. Mary in the Fields was ringing the hours, its fragile ancient bell no more disturbing the tranquil hour than extra grains of pollen floating through the golden light.

After the nurse entered Carl and Curtin left, backing out of the room and saying as always, "See you later, little Emily."

"Will you," the nurse asked Carl, "take our patient for a walk this afternoon?"

"Not today," Carl said. "Not today." And as he closed the door behind him he seized Curtin by the arm. "You see!" A charge of enthusiasm shook his voice, his hand, his body. "You see!"

Arm in arm they went down the long corridor to the head of the stairs which was blazing with sunlight from the opened landing window. A big green beech thrust its leaf-laden branch inside and sweetness floated in and fell upon the cocoa-colored matting.

At the foot of the stairs Carl stopped again. His face was flushed, his eyes shining, his whole personality had taken wing, lifted, soared, carrying him radiantly out of the dark depths of his secret life. He was transfigured. This was the sense of life when it no longer is the object of the mind but the character of living itself. Boyishly he began to shake hands with Curtin.

"It's great," Curtin said again and again and again. "It's great, isn't it?"

"First stage," Carl exclaimed. "Success. Tomorrow the next. Just as if she knew what we wanted, just as if in the poor, disfigured soul of her she's been struggling to help, and what more could we ask? What?" he demanded eloquently. "She has returned from the dead to talk to us with a little smile." He could not in his surprise and pleasure prevent himself from laughing, and they both started across the lawn laughing wildly and triumphantly to the amazement of the staff who, sated and stupidly hot, were coming out of the dining rooms on their way back to normality, routine, and defeat.

124

vii

THE therapy of pharmacological shock is based on the theory that pathological mental states arise from physiological conditions in the nervous system and that massive disturbances of neural patterns will alter these conditions and therefore alter the mental behavior arising from them. "The only trouble," Carl said, "is that this has never been proved, that it rests on a half-dozen assumptions so profound that only the creation of a real psychological science could make proof possible, and that all experimental evidence with animals and in cases of organic trauma indicate that in general the nervous system when destroyed in one part partially assumes the function elsewhere. In short," he added to Curtin, who was preparing the insulin dose for little Emily, "if we shouted boo it might have the same effect."

"Boo," Curtin yelled at little Emily, who was staring wide-eyed at the ceiling, and she didn't even look at him.

"Then let her have it," Carl said.

And so the experiment began.

Deftly Curtin squeezed the pale flesh over her left triceps, inserted the needle and injected twenty-five units of insulin.

It was 6 A.M. in the hospital and the morning sun was just emerging above the hilltops across the river. Emily had been transferred to one of the big rooms in the contagious-disease ward, and there Carl and Curtin had space in a room close by for an office. Three nurses were permanently assigned, and the whole staff was on the side lines wondering what this strange pair were up to. "We don't know ourselves," Curtin announced boldly, "but our mistakes will bring less grief to psychiatry than all your discoveries. *Quod erat demonstrandum.*"

Now Emily lay in her white cotton nightgown under the clean white sheet, and the room was still and the sunlight increased from moment to moment while the insulin ate up the blood sugar in her veins.

Carl went into the little office and slowly and carefully entered the various data they had collected earlier that morning on the charts he had prepared. They had tested everything they could from Emily's temperature to her Babinski. In addition to this Carl had prepared in his neat and almost beautiful way four elaborate charts, following the observations of Ross and Malzberg. These charts traced in outline the progression of symptoms under massive shock and were actually based on the four syndromes, the cerebral, the subcortical, the mid-brain, and the medullary. But there was still a week before they would be used, since the first six days were only steps in which the dosage was slowly increased until the threshold of deep coma appeared.

Curtin poured out fresh coffee from the Thermos into Carl's cup, watched him writing, and offered, "You're so neat. So wonderful and neat. And it's pretty too. Did you ever draw pictures?"

"Yes, in the lab."

"Well, draw me a picture of Mrs. Seawithe's legs. They were beautiful. Does she love you? Is your secret name Seawithe? Tell me something, I'm dying of curiosity."

"Who made this coffee?" Carl asked. "Why don't we get this kind of coffee all the time?"

"Because the nurse who made it for me," Curtin laughed, "only succumbed a few days ago to my advances, and she's just started to work for us."

"The little dark girl in there with Emily?"

Curtin nodded. "Nice, isn't she? But of course, not in that thoroughbred class of Seawithe. Now there's a horse for whom I'd love to percolate a little coffee!"

In a way the physiological observations that Carl made all week on Emily were more like science, more like the science he had

126

known in the past. Precise, mechanical, manual, from day to day, in order, they took on the solid authority of natural phenomena empty of that compelling mystery which analysis always carried with it, that obscure socializing with garrulous psychic ghosts.

One week after Sandy's visit, Curtin administered one hundred and thirty units of insulin and in two and a half hours Emily became comatose. This time she had to be brought out of it by administering the glucose nasally.

They planned to treat her five days a week for a period of about three weeks which ordinarily, in terms of past cases, would bring about some improvement. On the fifth day Curtin administered two hundred and fifty units and Emily had a stupendous convulsive seizure.

She lay bound to the bed, a gag in her mouth, and she seemed to be struggling with an invisible serpent which had wound itself within her body and outside upon her limbs and slowly, inevitably was squeezing the life out of her. And being alive and wanting to live, she fought with this monster.

She sweated and was uneasy in the beginning as hypoglycemia set in. Her cheeks flushed and she tried to get out of bed, to go somewhere, to escape from the room. And before the gag was put in her mouth she began to talk, a running flow of words, an effervescence of phrases, of run-on sentences, a million poems in one.

Carl had heard many a story from the unconscious, but never such a spate of prelogical poetry. Emily had what was rather charmingly called "schizophrenic surrender," or hebephrenia. According to her history in the records she had been a rather passive child during her childhood and then, with the onset of puberty, with the instinctual excitement, a flood of protest, hates, fears, anxieties had erupted into the violence which had brought her to Castlehill. Now, regressed almost to a preuterine level, the effect of the insulin like an earthquake had cracked through the surface of her quiescence and released some of the broken memories. But they flashed out not as continuous stories, logically connected, not as events, but as fragments, phrases, mixtures of sensation and reaction without integration or co-ordination.

127

"Broken stick, break the dog," she cried, a thin flow of saliva drooling from her lips. "Blood, blood on Daddy's finger, blood. The black pocketbook. Open the black mouth. Blood in the black. Run fast, run slow, the clown with a stick. Pink balloons in the sun. The sun is burning me, Daddy. The sun is burning me, Daddy. I love Mommy. I hate Daddy." And so on, the words rolling and running, while Carl listened and heard the terrible clues of her past so jumbled and misbegotten like monsters spawned not in the womb but eggs caught and fertilized out of their normal home, in tubes, on surfaces of membranes, distorted monsters of adaptation.

The shock deepened and she began to grow drowsy and the words slurred into each other and finally disappeared as words altogether, became sounds, breathings, and she began to sink, going away into sleepiness. Now Curtin gently placed the gag in her mouth for this was the quiet before the violent seizure to come.

During the weeks that followed Carl watched this hyperkinetic upheaval with mixed emotions. Attracted by its strangeness, he was upset and fearful of its torment. And he remembered the old magicians of society who thought to release the soul by torture, by the debasement of the flesh. This crude therapy of shock seemed to him to be based on superstition, as if there were a normal mind hidden in the wrappings of disease, as if the disease had to be tormented out of the subject so that at last, free and pure, the mind might emerge. But the mind was not a pure thing hidden in the debased body. The mind was a complex history of adaptation, a wonderful balance of dynamic impulses, experiences, habits, a fragment of social life that was this marvelous person, and to destroy its painfully acquired rationale, to seek to fling the spirit back to its roots by pain and shock, was in fact to contradict the nature of what a normal mind really was.

On the other hand there was the thrill of once again being devoted to a concrete work of exploration, the passion of long devoted hours, of hours in which the routine of night and day was abandoned to the demands of the experiment. He enjoyed the strange hours in which he and Curtin ate, their intimate talks at midnight or in the pale hours of morning, the walks across the wet grass

128

on the way to Emily's room, or a turn through the woods at midnight into the everlasting sanity of the inorganic world, the black
skies, the vast machine of the stars. And sometimes the moon, free
of clouds, opened a path upon the Hudson, and his mind dreamed
along it, as if he were an old traveler searching for a pathway to
some land of incalculable richness and mystery.

He grew to love Curtin, to trust him, for this man was actually
an old-fashioned scientist, a sport in the modern world of prize-
seekers. Curtin was fascinated by the universe, and the universe
he looked at was his own soul. It was for this that he was a psychiatrist, to understand himself and the world.

Both men grew weary and strained and they worked without
pause, trying each day to complete every detail, to note it, to describe it, finding nothing too trivial to be thought about, and slowly
their material amassed, and each day little Emily fought with
death in her brain as the shocks ostensibly ripped the tentacles of
the synapses from each other.

In the morning, at the beginning of the third week, Curtin administered three hundred units of insulin.

Emily's subcortical symptoms were terrible to behold and made
Carl sick at heart. It was Emily's dance the way the shuffling feet
of a hanged man become his dance, his exit from existence. With
her it was a flirtation with death, and her unconscious could not
know that Curtin was ready with a glucose injection to bring her
back to life. If there were any deep instinct to survive, and this
Carl had begun to doubt, then this instinct could only terrorize
the flesh with its pulsations. So, as she passed through the initial
sleepiness after her usual lightheaded oration, the first deep throb
occurred. Saliva poured over the gag and wet her chin. She gurgled, and then the inner beating began. She heaved. Her body
became one enormous muscle which flexed, arched and burst into
a spasm.

Carl and Curtin were standing by the window, smoking, watching, and the nurse waited near Emily, now and then wiping with
a piece of soft paper the spittle from the child's mouth. Suddenly,
somehow, the webbing that held her to the bed unbuckled and in

a moment a teeming mass of arms and legs writhed in fury on the white sheet. Emily's hands tore at her face, her body. The thin nightgown ripped off and the adolescent whiteness danced its death dance. She clawed at her vulva and her gurgles came up from the regions of the damned. Spasms reared her and flung her and the nerves unbound, as it were, the escaping flesh and set her free. Her suffering was immense, unnamable.

"Christ," Carl shouted, and they held her. He put his arms around her, embraced her and she grabbed him around the neck. Her body became his body and he felt through the twitchings, the wild beating of the legs, the convulsing torso, the agony, the supreme, the impossible agony of dying without going to the dead. This was a worse madness than madness itself, and slowly limb by limb they forced her back, bound her back, until she lay against her cage sucking the gag. She had torn her belly in a great scratch and torn the outer lips of her vulva. "Christ," Carl said. "God damn it."

But they waited the required time and then Curtin injected the glucose and almost at once, as if the sun had broken through the most violent storm to calm it, she quieted down and in a very short while lay quietly there, relaxed and exhausted, while the nurse cleaned the scratches and disinfected them.

The two men went back to their cottage without saying anything, and they both dressed to go out and still said nothing, and then Curtin drove Carl down to Nyack where Carl took the ferry across to Tarrytown and there the train for New York City.

He felt himself running, he wanted to see Sandy, to be at least ordinarily happy or unhappy and to forget for a few hours in his own life the wildness which they had unchained at Castlehill.

130

viii

THERE was no Seawithe, David or Laura, in the telephone directory and although Carl continued to read up and down the names as if he had missed the one he sought he was really thinking of how impossible it would be to call Furnace Dock and ask there. This was no time to introduce himself again after all these years to David's aunt or father. He had included them in the general silence maintained towards Sandy and David, and now it was too late to begin again. He let the large volume fall into its slot and slowly walked out of the steaming drugstore where luncheon was being served to a restless mob of querulous and tired people. Hungry himself, he stood irresolutely under the hot red awning feeling the heat draining his will of action until suddenly he recalled that David was a patient of Dr. Erdman's. He re-entered the drugstore and sweated uncomfortably in a booth, waiting for the old man to get on the wire.

"Carl? Carl!"

"Hello, Dr. Erdman."

"It's good hearing from you. I thought perhaps you'd been confined to one of those loony bins along with your cases."

"I have in a way. I'm in New York and I wanted to . . ."

"Of course," the voice interrupted warmly. "The lunch is just about to be dumped on the table. Come over, we'll wait for you." And Erdman rang off before Carl could refuse, leaving him with a general impatience and sense of frustration. He did not know at this moment why it was so important that he get Sandy's number without delay, but he felt the delay as an imposition, and resolved to finish with Erdman as soon as possible pleading an appointment downtown.

131

It was cooler on Riverside Drive because from time to time a slow breeze dragged itself across the limp water and shook its pallid heat into the faces around the dining table. This was not going to be a swift luncheon, and as Carl looked around the table, feeling himself impaled on the torpor he found there, he understood that it would not be a pleasant one either. Erdman's stepson, John, an employee in Washington, was visiting his parents, and he had no pleasure in them and less in Carl. A plump irritable bureaucrat, he had no patience with any subjects but his own, no interests beyond the statistical analysis which was his profession, and no love for his parents or his own family, "a stupid wife," the old man had told Carl, "and two charming children well on their way to hysteria." Above all, John Erdman detested the profession of his father, which he called disgraceful, snooping, and irresponsible. To complete Carl's discomfort, Erdman sported a sandy mustache, rather full and bitten at the ends, and two men with mustaches at the luncheon table appeared ridiculous.

"I have never eaten lunch with a pair of mustaches," Dr. Erdman said gravely. "I have eaten with a beard and a mustache, and once at a great function with seven beards. But two mustaches!" It was his way of changing the subject, of offering up anything to his son's discontent to distract him.

"That's ridiculous," John Erdman said. "My father tells me that you're to succeed him in this occupation of his. You seem young and rather intelligent. How can you take this rubbish about sex seriously? A man is either sexually mature or he isn't."

The old man sighed and handed the salad plate to his wife, who sat silently through most of the lunch, her deep black eyes fixed in adoration upon her son. She was so old and wrinkled as to seem like a restoration and not something genuinely human.

Carl asked as pleasantly as he could, "Is your work in Washington very interesting?"

But John Erdman refused the bait.

"Tell me, Dr. Myers, what obscure mental dirtiness has given rise to psychoanalysis?"

"You think," his father asked, "I have a dirty mind?"

132

Bored, irritated by the endless conversation and the nasty personality of Erdman's son, Carl before he knew it launched an attack, regretting it as he went along because the old man turned toward him a pained and miserable expression, a plea to let this thing alone, to forget it. "Psychoanalysis is a middle-class science," Carl said, "and your father with a kind of provincial loyalty to his own class is trying to help out. Most patients that go to psychoanalysts are hysterical women or intellectuals, businessmen, professionals with profound sexual maladjustments."

"Do you mean to imply," the son flamed out, "that I belong to them?"

"Heaven forbid," his father said.

"Do you, do you?" the son insisted, his anger rising and his hands shaking. "I don't waste my time looking into toilets and the beds of strangers. At least I use my intelligence upon mature subjects. On politics, economics. I want you to know that the epithet middle-class hardly applies to me. I'm a socialist."

"Middle-class?" Carl asked.

Under the bushy mustache the thin lips of John Erdman twisted like slices of lemon peel. "And what are you," he demanded, "a working-class fascist?"

So the long luncheon went on in front of the half-drawn blinds with Carl and the father taking turns at comforting this uneasy and belligerent man, and the hours wasted and still Carl couldn't leave, didn't know how, with the old man sitting there so helpless in front of his wife. But, finally, the mother and the son went upstairs and Carl followed Erdman into the study. The father sat down heavily, wearily, and filled a big pipe from the china bowl in front of him.

"Well," Carl said, "it's a hot day anyway, and I have to go. I've got an appointment downtown." He found it very difficult to ask for David's address when David was Erdman's patient. Now he blamed himself for not having called the farm, for having wasted all this time. He started to rove restlessly about wondering when the exact moment would come like an open door through which he could leave.

133

"When are you coming down?" Erdman asked at last. "When will you be finished there?"

"In about a month. I'll call you. Well, I'd better be going."

"It's about time," the old man said.

Carl noticed how cavernous his cheeks had become, how the veins stood out on his skull and how the hands were slowly turning into X rays of themselves. Yet he could not bear to remain longer and listen to an old man's story or an old man's opinions. His mind was running off, standing in a telephone booth and making up conversation with someone at Furnace Dock.

"And how is your experiment coming?"

"Fine. We'll soon be through."

"Well, hurry. I keep sitting here after my patients leave each day marveling at how bitter and frightful life is, and how in the end all the beautiful struggles are useless, and all the dreams are wish-fulfillments."

Before the conversation could begin again, Carl escaped and hurried down the carpeted steps of the old house, dashing by the office door which was open.

"Dr. Myers," Dr. Erdman's secretary called.

With a groan Carl turned back to make his hellos and there on the desk was the appointment book. He chatted for a moment, turned as if to go and then stopped. "By the way," he said, "do you happen to have Mr. David Seawithe's New York address and phone number?"

She gave it to him and he wrote it down, thanking her effusively, smiling at her, shaking her hand, surrounding her with all the pleased charm he possessed, for now he was free to see Sandy.

At last he was launched on his expectation and joyously he took the bus, riding downtown on the top, the sun beating on his head, the oily fumes dirtying his face, and the hot wind of traffic mussing his hair and collar. But he didn't care and enjoyed the bustle, descending at Eighty-eighth Street, where he walked north one block and then east from Fifth Avenue to Madison. The building was huge and white, aching in the sunlight, and Carl decided to cross the street first and call Sandy from the cigar store.

The phone rang a long time and there was no answer. On the

134

chance that he had dialed the wrong number, he called again. The number rang and rang.

Each separate senseless ring added weight to the stupid rage Carl felt against Sandy for not being home. It was as if she had broken an appointment with him, an appointment he didn't want and one that had taken him out of his way and beyond his interests. He hung up the receiver, retrieved the nickel, and walked disconsolately out into the street, not knowing what to do or where to go, for after all hadn't he come down especially for this?

He walked moodily down Madison Avenue, hugging the buildings to keep out of the sun, watching the streets shake, the cars shimmer, and the people scurrying by in a last exhaustion. And he thought of the greenness of Castlehill, the blinds drawn in the cottage, the coolness of the wooden floors, and the heavy vines which gripped the windows and sprayed fragrance into the rooms. He felt himself sleeping there, asleep on the bed in his bedroom, undisturbed, the whine of summer outside and the purr of sleep within, the softness sinking and lulling him, and how happy it was to live there and work. He longed to return at once, but at Seventy-second Street there was a drugstore, so on the off chance that Sandy had returned he went in to call, to tell her he was in town but had to return at once to the hospital.

There was no answer.

He slouched down at the soda fountain and had an ice-cream soda which was too sweet. He drank two glasses of water and bought a cigar, lighted it, and then automatically returned to the booth and called again.

There was no answer.

It was a few minutes after the hour and therefore an hour and a half to the next train out of Grand Central, two and a half hours for the next train out of Jersey City, so he turned west to the park, and while it was no cooler there it was green, resting his tired eyes. The cigar smoked flat and tasteless but he persisted, strolling along in the hot sun, on the hot walk, or passing into the static shade where the benches stood in the dust, in the airless open, each bearing a full load of sitters like a crowded train.

Each fountain was blocked off by a horde of noisy children, and

135

old men with their coats on their arms moved almost motionless across the yellowing lawns.

He heard the merry-go-round and soon saw the lake, the rowboats stationary within it, the sun bright on the glassy, oily water. At the boathouse he stopped for a drink of cold soda-pop and it was lukewarm. There was a phone there and he called again.

There was no answer.

Nothing remained but to depart because train time was at hand.

More briskly he ascended the steps to Fifty-ninth Street and was about to hail a cab when he remembered that he had not seen his mother for months and that this was as good an opportunity as any. He set out for the East Side and the Third Avenue Elevated. Mothers, he reflected grimly, were always home.

As the train rattled downtown at roof-level, the whole wide city glazed and feverish lay spread before him, a vista of supreme awfulness. There was no poetry in this city, nothing, and he recalled the hot loveliness of Paris, the excitement of its sidewalks, the wonderful narrow coolness of the rue Mazarine and the summer he spent there with a French girl who had come up from Nice to be a nursemaid and ended up as a *femme de chambre* in a small hotel.

Lulled by the repeating clatter of the train, his eyes half closed, the breeze pounding in the open windows, he thought of the girls he had made love to in Europe.

When he awakened the train was groaning into the Battery, and he had to get out and cross over to the other side. There was a telephone booth near the change window, so he stopped to call Sandy again.

There was no answer.

Now he gave up all hope of seeing her, and took a train back to Houston Street where he got off and walked down to Second Avenue and up to Fourth Street.

He noticed how the neighborhood had changed, run down, gone to pieces, and how as usual it seemed even hotter here than elsewhere. Wearily he climbed up the stairs to his mother's apartment, knocked on the door and was admitted.

136

His mother was happy to see him and she poured out a full glass of ice-cold milk that tasted of childhood, and then he had another, and then a sandwich while she talked about herself. She had grown very stout and was content with her life at last. The money he gave her each month permitted her to live with a certain ease and now she had time to lavish on her various illnesses. She told him about certain obscure pains that she had in her left leg, showed him the medicine she was taking, recommended by her friend, the druggist, and a new summer dress she had purchased only the day before. Then suddenly, with a little remembering cry, she brought out a postcard which his brother had sent. Bill was no longer in Detroit and had moved with his wife to Tarrytown where he worked in the auto plant.

"You should visit him," his mother said. "You're right around the corner," by which she meant across the river, "and take a look at his wife, Juley."

"Why should I take a look at his wife?" Carl asked, putting the card in his pocket. It seemed cool in the flat, the windows opening on the narrow areaway, setting up a draught.

"Because she's a dirty pig," his mother said forcibly. "Because Bill has married a pig. And with a big belly, too, and they've only been married two months. You explain that."

Carl laughed sleepily. "You know," he said, "I'm so sleepy. You know I'd like to lie down and rest if you don't mind."

It made his mother happy to hear him ask. "It's your house," she said. "Go ahead." And she hurried into the next room and prepared the bed while Carl took off his coat and shoes and opened his collar.

He lay snugly in the bed in which he had been born, in the voluminous bed of his childhood, and the last thing he thought of was that Sandy might be home by evening.

This was his dream:

Paris, the arches of the rue Rivoli, and he walks alone in the street searching. A woman detaches herself from the shadow and approaches him, beckoning him, and he follows her down the dark streets to an old house whose leaning stones hang in balconies

137

above the sidewalks. He climbs the stairs behind her, and her shoulders, her waist, her legs, her haunches, are familiar. In a small room without light he hears her disrobe and then the bed creaks as she gets into it, drawing a white sheet up above her face. He moves towards her hesitantly on his naked feet and slowly removes the sheet and there is the smiling face of Sandy. He kneels beside the bed and she half leans on her elbow embracing him, whispering into his ear. Her breath touches his ear, the words breathing and he cannot understand what she is saying, but as moonlight opens into the room, she is revealed with her belly bulging, round and white in the moonlight, heavy with child. Now there is another woman in the room, sitting quietly and sadly in the shadows, a dark woman, and he turns to her and she leads him into another room and takes him into her bed and as they embrace he sees over the dark woman's shoulder Sandy standing in the doorway, her hands on her belly, weeping.

He awoke bathed in sweat and overcome with sorrow, a sadness that trembled in his limbs, a feeling of loss, of endless grief.

The apartment was empty and it was nearly six o'clock. In the kitchen as he opened the door he saw that his mother had soup cooking on the stove and he understood that she had probably gone down to buy food for dinner. Hurriedly he dressed, scribbled a note that he had to get back to the hospital, and fled, only feeling safe when he was on Fourth Avenue.

In the warm evening air, he walked aimlessly past the book-stores. He was debating whether to call Sandy again, but he was disgusted with himself and still felt the wrack of the dream within his mind. He would now have to have dinner by himself since it was too late to get back to the hospital before the last serving, and so he decided he would call Sandy again, and if she were home, have dinner with her and leave.

He stopped at a candy store in one of the side streets, bought some cigarettes and called the number. He let it ring a very long time and there was no answer. Then for the first time it occurred to him that she might not be in the city, that she might be at Furnace Dock, that she might be in Washington, that David might have returned. This forlorn conclusion that she was not in New York attached itself to the sadness of his dream, found that dying grief and revived it violently. He stood in the booth hearing the phone ring in the empty apartment, ring in the emptiness of his heart, ring down the past years into the little laboratory at the River Hospital.

He thought miserably now of how happy he had been then, for he had no need to remember the unhappiness of that time, and it did not come to trouble him. He lighted a cigarette and walked out into the street and there stood for a vagrant moment, casting about in his mind as to what he should do. There was a restaurant near the River Hospital and he suddenly felt the need to go there, to eat there, and he started off. He passed a bookstore on his way to the Elevated and the proprietor with an assistant was carrying in the outside stalls. Carl stopped because he needed something to read on the train when he went home, and he asked, "Do you have a copy of *Faust?*" And as the man entered the shop, Carl called after him, "In German." He wanted to read in that language because this would take him away from America and he deliberately sent his mind back into Vienna, to the first years there, and began to remember uneasily his didactic analysis and how he had finally confessed to himself that it was Sandy he loved, that it was Sandy he wanted, and that it was his fault because he had not known it, that he had lost her to David. And they had tricked him. David especially, who undoubtedly had wheedled Sandy into the marriage that had turned out so well for her.

He paid for the book, took the Elevated and had dinner at the little restaurant. He propped the book up in front of him and read as he ate, and he had very little idea of what he was reading until a few phrases reminded him of Freud's quotation from *Faust* in the Autobiography.

Vergebens, dass ihr ringsum wissenschaftlich schweift,
Ein jeder lernt nur, was er lernen kann.

He closed the book, applying it to himself, to his foolish desire to move from the hospital elsewhere, from one branch of psychology to another, as if there were some place where at last, in a particular place, he would discover the secret which would turn a therapy into a general science of human action. That was his weakness. The weakness was in him that he had no gift to discover what was there to be found, and he felt his mind grow cold and doomed, and he felt himself fall into the jumbled ranks of the men who were never to be anything but followers.

He paid his check and went out into the street, thinking of himself as a scientist and what it really meant. But it was the devil talking! The advice was Mephistopheles's!

A drugstore on the corner glittered in the soft warm night, and he went in and called Sandy again. When there was no answer, he looked up the number of the apartment house and spoke with the doorman. He told him that he had been calling and there was no answer, that he was passing through New York and wanted to know if the Seawithes were in town.

"Mrs. Seawithe is in town," the man told him, "but she hasn't returned yet."

A bomb of joy burst in his mind, spattered him with light and gaiety, and since it was still early he decided to wait a few more hours and see her.

Walking down one of the side streets he exulted in his persistence and he began to construct a conversation with Sandy, one in which he reachieved the supremacy he had once had over her. He would convince her this time of her selfishness, of her betrayal, and he felt confidence in his success since he no longer loved her. It was this, he decided, that made him want to see her.

He found himself standing in front of a familiar stoop, a familiar downstairs door, the building where he and Sandy had once had an apartment together. It was amusing to think that the neighborhood had resurrected an old habit which had guided him there, and he looked up to see if the windows were lighted. They were.

As he walked away he seemed to be walking away from his youth, and he said to himself that everything turns out for the best because he would not now change what he was and had become for what he had been.

140

He took a taxi to Eighty-ninth Street and from the cigar store there across the street from the house called Sandy again. There was no answer, but he felt no disappointment since she was in the city and would eventually come home. So he walked down to Central Park and there in the night the coolness had finally begun to move although the air still held its heat where the trees were thick.

Everywhere there were lovers. He saw the light dresses of the girls, the thin dresses, and the white shirts of the boys. On the grass on spread-out newspapers like open bed sheets, they lay in each other's arms and kissed, and the traffic from the streets hissed like gossiping tongues about the enraptured heads and uneasy hands and the bodies that strained upon one another. The lamps made necklaces of lights through the dark lawns and the thickets and the upreared walls of the apartments glowed in the immensely soft, the immensely tender sky. But Carl was glad that he no longer loved Sandy for she was a tainted woman, and yet as he walked, the book held under his arm, as he averted his eyes from the couples and listened to an occasional night bird straining through the underboom of the city, the vast surf of its millions, the stones of night rubbing and sounding through the dark, he longed once again to find someone to love, to find a woman upon whom he could lavish that agony and need which he had felt in Vienna for the absent Sandy. There was no one he knew, but he also knew that if he needed to love someone then she would be anywhere, in this park, in a street, in a friend's house.

Again and again he left the park and strolled past the apartment house, and now midnight divided the night from the next day, and it was too late to get a train.

He felt a cynical satisfaction in this scouting, for Sandy was obviously betraying David with another man, and that lush look of hers, her content, only pointed to a life which David could not enjoy. At least this was to be said for David, that if he had yielded to love and betrayed his friend, he was in other respects a serious man, an idealist, being shamefully betrayed by his wife.

Carl did not see the taxicab pull up in front of the apartment but

141

he heard the door slam and turned. He was about two hundred feet away but he knew Sandy at once. As she paid the fare he hurried up and accosted her.

"Sandy."

The surprise, the naked welcome on her face ravished him with excitement.

"Why Carl, Carl!" she cried. "You. What a wonderful coincidence." She took his hand and laughed with pleasure, with joy.

He found himself saying, "It's no coincidence at all. I've been waiting to see you since noon. I've walked my feet off waiting, and worn out the telephones calling." He found himself shaking, distraught, miserable and happy together, and she became, in her black dress, with a black hat tagged into her heavy blond hair, a miracle of reappearance, a rush of senses, a woman inflaming his heart, tormenting him.

Her face sobered and she hesitated, looking around her, and he sensed that she felt trapped.

So now he was helpless and tried to be offhand. "Well, let's go and have a drink somewhere because I have to be getting back to the hospital."

She stood there vaguely, not even listening to him, listening to herself, he thought. She is waiting for someone else. There is another appointment, another man. He asked, "Is David back?"

She shook her head and still made no answer, and at last overcome with shame he turned away from her and started to hurry down the street. Her high heels tapped and she caught his arm. "What's the matter with you?" And she stood very close to him, staring with wonder into his face, into the darkness of his face, and the heaviness of his eyes and his mouth trembling.

She stepped back and began to breathe with difficulty, as through a hand upon her mouth, and she raised her gloved fingers to her face, pressing her cheek. Although it was she who had stopped him, she continued to stand in the desert he had created about her, listening to that same inner voice, or fragment of feeling loose in her as she had the first day at Castlehill, her head a little turned to one side, her hand to her cheek, her breath short and

142

rapid. And then all at once, a grave smile seemed to release her and she took his arm, turning him toward the fluted canopy that led into the apartment house.

She walked closely at his side, holding him by his arm against her.

"You lied to me," she said without triumph. "You did love me," and she took him upstairs to be her lover again.

ix

IN this one respect at least Sandy loved Carl: there was no one else whom she loved at the moment, not even her husband. Boredom had prepared the ground for her first visit to Carl, as boredom so often was the beginning of some new interest in her life, and during the past few years the gravitational power of tedium more and more weighed down her existence. At the moment, she experienced an extraordinary excitement from Carl's extravagance and passion, and on the strange evening when he stopped her in the street in front of her apartment house, as she stood there assaulted by his desire for her, she had waited listening to her heart, wondering if she wanted to begin this affair at all. And first she had decided against it, knowing him from the past, the imperious demands of his nature, and the strength, the tenacity of his will. It was out of complacence that she had run after him, a sense that after all, this was fate, and since most of her life drifted, she let herself drift into his arms.

Remembering him from the old days, the way he had so casually included her in their love affair, his driving interest in *her* was what now thrilled her most. So each night she waited for him to come down from the country and in the morning saw him return long before dawn so that he could be present for the last week of Emily's treatment. Testing her powers over him she tried once or twice to keep him from going, waking before he did and lying quietly, hardly breathing, hoping he would sleep exhausted into the day. But he carried his own clock in his scientific conscience, and he always awakened, and then no matter how she churned up his passions, no matter how she abandoned herself, she could not

144

hold him, and it was the fact that he left her when his other duty called that made her so anxiously wait for the next night to try again. Above all she wanted to destroy his old idea of her that he preferred another interest in his life to love; and it was still true, she rather mournfully admitted to herself after he was gone each morning, although in every other respect she held him febrile and needy in her arms.

Sometimes by arrangement she drove up to Tarrytown and waited in the late afternoon sun, blinded by the light glaring on the river and the heat reflected in her face. The little ferry would blow its small whistle high and piping as a gull's cry, and then far off, across the broad stretch, with High Tor commanding and the Catskill foothills obediently behind, she would see Carl's blue-suited figure on the prow, small as a doll, and as the boat approached her senses took over, first nibbling, then harsh, driving her, pressing her into a tumult of desire until he became a giant, overwhelming, dark, jumping from the boat to bear her down into the depths of her sensuality where at least there was no boredom with existence, only mindlessness.

She remembered too from the past his sexual modesty and in a fit of curiosity even went beyond her own habits of love, but in this too she found no power, for he thought everything ordinary and nothing was new to him even when he was the occasion and for the first time. "It's because you work with perverted people," she told him. And he replied, smiling at her through his half-closed lids, "Pleasure without pain is never perverted."

She made no effort to conceal Carl's goings and comings from the apartment staff, feeling it was her destiny and whatever happened would happen. It was true as Carl had imagined that she had had other lovers in the years between, and even now one of the young men who worked in the apartment house was a lover, and she worried a little that he would find out about Carl and make a scene, but since Carl came in the front door and the young man through the service entrance, when he was wanted, the one didn't interfere with the other. She had, in fact, more interest in the younger man because he was innocent against her sophistica-

145

tion, but she postponed the development of one affair while she exploited the other knowing that boredom always waited within every situation to destroy it.

Nothing assuaged the restlessness of her moods, neither lovers nor luxuries. With Carl at least there was the slash of his passion, and with Carl at best the unsettling brilliance of the way he talked to her, flattering her mind with the gift of his own.

In trying to understand David she had learned to think with subtlety; in pleasing him she had discovered how to handle the social byplay of a rich woman's life; in running his home in Washington she had become the center of a group of young and ardent New Dealers who constituted themselves her clique, her admirers and sometimes her lovers, the while they educated her to the trends of thought current in their circle.

The intellectual fascination that Carl exerted upon Sandy came from the excessive hardness of his mind which she found more carping than those she had known. The young politicians and bureaucrats were enthusiastic, educated, intelligent even when they were cynical of how they achieved power, but their worldliness, such as it was, had no root in seriousness the way Carl's mind did, and even when they astonished her with their manipulation of society, she felt they fumbled because they had no real goal except to remain where they were or better themselves. In Carl, however, the harshness grew out of his difficulty with mastering reality itself, out of a scientific bias, and she recognized it from the rumors she had heard of such men and such minds out of history.

She was wise, informed, but only from what people had told her. She read nothing but the newspapers, and knew well how to read and disbelieve them. She could talk of economic theories or political trends and since the government of which David was a part experimented with everything, she had a range of the latest ideas on most subjects. At the same time she was really ignorant of what lay behind these theories since she had never believed one or another. So everything was social conversation to her and she made an excellent hostess, gracing the salon that David created to further his career.

A healthy woman sexually, with a pleasure in sensation for itself,

146

she was able to keep hidden from Carl how little he possessed her, so he spoke of love and they made love, and there the affair rested without any end in view.

Watching from the side lines Curtin diagnosed the affair as similar to the common cold, unpreventable, with its own course to run, not dangerous but troublesome, and only fatal when complications set in. He refrained from comment as long as he could, and then one rainy morning as Carl stumbled into the cottage, dog-tired, with a cold and slight cough, he asked facetiously from his bedroom, "Can't you use a pinch hitter once in a while? Maybe she doesn't care but I don't want to lose you."

Carl took a hot shower and an eighth of a grain of codeine sulphate. They ate breakfast and adjourned to Emily's old room where the girl was now recovering from her ordeal.

She had changed enormously both physically and psychologically. The insulin had increased her appetite, made it ravenous, and she was now some thirty pounds heavier, almost fat, which left her infantile expression and childish habits unattractive. She talked more freely and was receptive to primitive suggestions, and Carl spent many hours trying to guide her thoughts into the etiology of her sickness. He knew, of course, schematically, the extent and general causes of her illness, but it was the special reasons, the concrete occasions, that had to be known, the secret materials of her life which had to be raised to consciousness so that she could learn to handle them, and adapt.

His own life oscillated between these two extremes, little Emily who could not adapt herself to the shocks of existence except by refusing to meet them, and Sandy who had in a way adapted only too well and become altogether coextensive with her social world. Neither of them struggled with life in terms of what they wanted. They had both yielded, the one crushed, the other triumphant, and one he desired and the other he pitied. For now little Emily no longer seemed like a strange creature from another planet where, life being different and its needs exotic, different patterns of habit were at a premium, so that young girls murdered their mothers and did not talk and floated blindly and innocently in the dusk of their own inner lives. Emily was a fat little girl, more stupid than usual,

147

almost an idiot, and she gurgled and sometimes talked and often fell into long periods of indifference. But she ate well, loved it, and did what she was told, and the strain disappeared from her features, the thinness from her bones, the fineness went out of her and she exhibited for the present none of the symptoms of her psychosis. The question now was whether Carl could get her to reintegrate her mental life to the point at which she once again became active, spirited and alive to the world as it really was, and for this it was necessary to find out just precisely where in her past and just precisely how she had yielded to the unendurable, and to make her know this through her own efforts. But this effort required a will and, what was more, a certain minimum of active intelligence. At the moment she did not have this will and her general intelligence level was low.

"You work at it," Curtin said, "if you're not too tired."

"I'm too tired," Carl replied, but he worked at it, his attention held to Emily by a great effort of will, listening, probing, suggesting, and all the while his eyes kept closing, and his body kept falling into little local sleeps, as if it were possible to fall asleep only here and there in the flesh and consciousness while in general he remained awake.

The noon lunch bell sounded across the sodden grounds and Carl escaped with relief to his cottage where he could abandon himself to sleep, to fall asleep entirely with every particle of flesh and spirit, to drop off and disappear into warm and comforting sleep.

But as he lay on the bed listening to the indolent rain dripping from the trees upon the house, as his senses lolled coolly on the currents of freshness which blew in through the open window, taking fragrance from the wet vines and the gray Hudson, as he waited for sleep, sleep did not come. He composed himself for sleep, shoeless, tieless, a light blanket over him and his face cold to the air. He prepared himself for sleep, going through all the motions external and internal. He set his mind adrift, let it float out to the wet grass, to the heavy earth, let it wander where the damp wind took it, into the skies, upon the river, to a voice far off that

148

made no sense, to a train at the river edge chugging and whistling, to the pillow, to his warm hands, to his eyelids resting lightly on his eyes, to the breath he breathed, and there was the gray ceiling above his head, and there was the window, and here he was thinking.

In two weeks this part of his career ended. It would be necessary for him to arrange to visit Castlehill several times a week in order to continue the analysis of little Emily, to wind it up one way or another and write with Curtin the article they had planned. Dr. Erdman had set aside two rooms for him on the third floor of the Riverside Drive house, and by the end of the following year the practice would be Carl's with Erdman merely continuing the cases to which he was committed and which in good conscience he could not terminate, for the older man was very tired and no longer interested in the specific. While changing his work Carl also felt the need to come to some decision with regard to Sandy. He wanted to know if he should ask her to leave David, to become his wife, and he often thought of it, going there and returning, and somehow the answer never just suggested itself as it does in love affairs, but appeared as a question. As a psychoanalyst he knew that such questions really mean the answer is *no*. The unconscious does not hold back from its desires; it does not weigh the social objectives of marriage, the good and the bad. It chooses. It flings itself upon its choice, embracing and dissolving within it. And when it does not want something, it does not want it altogether. At such times the ego frames moral questions for it. The ego invents detours, pauses, stalemates, sometimes real ones and more often in the form of judgments postponed, or sensible and rational questionings. Whenever the ego is given a role in love, it is because the id has lost interest. This was what any psychoanalyst knew. And a worldly man knew it too, but in his way. Any time you counted the risks of a love affair, you could be sure you were not in love.

He sat up suddenly in the bed, the blanket falling from him. Sandy had never mentioned, not once, that she wanted to leave David.

He rose from the bed because his thoughts had begun to circle

149

and circle like restless and frightened birds about the one central fact, that Sandy had never asked what he wanted of her beyond this night and the next one, that she never talked about David except in the past, that she did not plan, and this was it, she did not make plans. He put on his slippers and started to walk around the cottage, and spoke aloud with a certain bitter humor, "But man is a plan-making animal, and women even more so." Going from room to room, restless, so tired, the cough beginning to rack his chest, he saw the gloomy rain out of each window, rain on the lawns, rain on the trees, rain on the vast and smoky river. What was this relation he had got himself into? Why had he run so miserably to her? What did he want of himself and her?

He sat down on the couch and then lay back trying to sleep there. The weariness in his bones was sad and droning as the rain, and yet he could not sleep. He could not even hold his eyes closed because his mind, like a nervous gambler, kept shuffling back and forth the same ideas, arranging them this way and that, each time a different combination, when what was needed was a novel notion.

He rose and wandered back into the bedroom, but just as he dropped dog-tired on the bed, just as he felt that he would sleep because he no longer had any strength to stay awake, because he had taken codeine and this was loosening his tension, just then the church at Caxton Ferry sounded the hour, four o'clock, four round bells that rolled through the air like ninepin bowls, one after another through the heavy air, striking with a mournful and desolate air his sleepy brain. It was time for him to go down to Nyack and take the ferry to Tarrytown where Sandy would be waiting with the car, and wearily he started to put on his shoes while outside he heard Curtin's Chevrolet drive up and his friend's boisterous and vulgar voice roaring, "Time's winged chariot is here. All aboard for the tunnel of love."

Carl leaned over his shoes and tied the bows, his hands nerveless, and then, as if this hour came out of a different day, a day of energy, excitement, force, this hour signaled him and his body began to grow dry, his flesh revived, and longing refreshed him, calling him to the golden woman he made love to each day.

150

X

EVERY afternoon a small group of men and women who worked in the automobile plant at Tarrytown waited for the ferry to take them home to Nyack. They formed a provincial minority in the factory who preferred the west side of the river to the east, and they all knew each other and waited for their ride home on the little launch in a compact group unified by horseplay and gossip. What most agitated the employees of the plant nowadays was the intense organizing drive being conducted by the CIO, the resistance of the entrenched AFL and management, the occasional flurries of violence and leaflet distribution; but what most piqued their curiosity, offering itself daily as a romantic bouquet, was the blond woman who arrived to pick up the blue-suited man from Nyack.

This afternoon, as the workers huddled out of the rain under a small open shed at the river's bank, they observed with pleasure that the woman arrived, but were surprised to see her start up the car and drive off just as the ferry put out from Nyack. And so, craning their heads and buzzing with astonishment, they looked across the river stippled with rain and waited to see, as in the next scene, if the man would appear.

And there he was, his raincoat blowing about him, his head bare, and quite attractive, too, the women thought, with his mustache and sullen face. After the ferry arrived, the workers lingered on, wondering to see what he would do, whether the woman would return or not, but the high whistle of the launch blew and they straggled aboard reluctant to leave the drama unfinished. Egged on by her friends one of the more daring young girls finally

151

approached the man breathlessly and blurted out, "Mister, she was here but she left, just as the ferry started from Nyack." And then she ran to the boat, carrying with her the memory of an unformulated smile, an eyebrow of amazement, and a low and rather hard voice which answered, "Thank you." As the river increased between the stern and the shore, as the wind chopped out small whitecaps from the heavy tide, the workers watched the man cross to the shed and stand under it, and all the while everything grew grayer and mistier, and finally the daring young girl alone searched the distant shore for a last glimpse, and at last it was impossible to see anything except the haze and the great factory block, and she sighed profoundly, for she had dipped her senses in romance for a brief second and was already dreaming.

There was no longer any romance in his affair for Carl. A small dry cough repeated itself monotonously in his chest and his wet hair was cold. He stood distrait beneath the drumming roof of the shed, for the rain had begun to take on solidity and a wind came down the river in little bursts, rubbing against the water's grain into whitecaps, and the wind in little waves and shocks blew gusts into the shed, spattering his legs. The soaked earthen floor had taken all the water it could and now began to fill with channels which gathered and increased each other until a broad puddle lay in the center. He restlessly wondered what had become of Sandy, irritated with her because she was keeping him there waiting and wet while she rushed back to town to make a telephone call or something equally futile instead of staying just a little longer for the ferry. And he was further annoyed that their daily meeting had become so obvious to the throng of factory workers. Now time went on and the ferry had disappeared into the rain on the other shore where there was a warm cottage all his own and a warm bed and hot drink and codeine to take to relieve the pressure in his chest. He stared moodily across the fish-gray river, and there the mountains were washing away into the sky, the greenness running like water, diluting and losing its color, oozing, dissolving, disappearing.

Infinitely melancholy the ferry landing, with its little jut of pier, the black slimy stumps standing in the turbid water, signaled Carl's aloneness here where the macadam road frayed desolately out into cracked welts of tar, yellow earthy holes, and wild grass. There was a little dump to one side filled with cans and boxes, rusty iron, old and dissolute objects of the civilization on the shore. And what would they find a thousand years from now, he asked himself grimly, my bones here and the old tomato cans, part of a tin roof, and a coiled and broken spring of barbed wire?

A quarter of an hour had passed and still no sign of Sandy, and meanwhile the rain had thickened, taken on weight, hitting the ground in long stiff shattering rods of chill, with the wind piling up beyond the river turn as if at a threshold, and then when enough force had gathered spilling over in a flood that brought rain into the shed as profusely as it did above it. He looked across the river again but the launch would not be returning for three quarters of an hour and he grimly set himself to wait, lighting a cigarette which tasted harsh in his burning throat. He suddenly realized that he was waiting for the ferry to return, that he did not expect Sandy to come back, and at once, with a brief and startling violence, his desire for her became so intense, so sick and wasting, that he flung his cigarette down into the puddle and he walked out into the rain and up the road as if in this way he could guarantee that she must meet him.

To add to his disgust he remembered that his brother Bill now lived in this forsaken and rainy place, somewhere in the wet hills, in one of those foolish houses.

He hadn't seen Bill for years and thought of him only as a footloose boy wandering from job to job, and yet Bill was married, with a wife, and a child coming. Some people, Carl smiled bitterly, know very well how to fall into each trap that life sets. Here was Bill who could hardly take care of himself, standing in line with all the other fathers in the world, taking his place in the long queue which every day formed before the miseries, the stupidities, the anxieties of the times. Bill was ready to live like the rest. Yet there was a certain power in this easy acceptance, and Carl promised himself to visit Bill among his new immaturities, to surprise him and enjoy him. With the rain beating in his face, he pushed on over the bridge, wondering if he had kept his brother's card and what the address was, and even whether he should visit him now, because anything was better than to march like an idiot in the rain, expecting a woman he did not even love. Here he wandered, a scientist without a science, a man of thirty without attachments, children, or a single comfort of existence.

As Carl walked down the incline of the bridge he came to a crossroad, and there he stopped, for he could not know by which route Sandy would return. He was wet through, so miserable and lost that he just stood in a stupor, looking this way and that, as the cars passed, each whining by in the wet, sowing wide fans of dirty spray, and every car a stranger's. Up the right-hand street there was a coffeepot, with a neon sign that read just blankly: *Coffee* — and he decided to wait there. He crossed the street, but at the corner he discovered that it would be impossible to see the bridge and therefore impossible to know when Sandy returned. In this way he would be sure to miss her. He hugged the side of the building and his mind kept yelling at Sandy as if in the midst of a great argument: where in the devil had she gone and what was taking her so long? It was half an hour now, and that stupid little nosybody of a girl had told him Sandy had left just as the ferry put out from Nyack. It then occurred to him that it might not have been Sandy at all, that she hadn't come at all, that it was some other woman, and it must have been because Sandy would never in all her foolishness have come and left in this way, forsaking him to the rain and the waiting. Their relation was more sober than that, and she would be afraid, too, knowing him.

So she hadn't come at all. That was it. This was the truth. He leaned against the wet wall of the building, and looked at the street, half paved, half bricked over with that yellow Hudson River brick. Ripe, yellow-gray, the swollen sky leaned upon the town, upon the buildings and the street, upon the great box of the factory, upon the signs and chimneys, and the rain filled the space between, and the wind churned it, and yet it was not autumn, not cold, but so chilly, packed on his hot skin, and he shuddered. He

154

was running a little fever from the cold, that was certain. And it was certain that if he stood out here like a fool, he would really get sick, and he could not get sick because back at Castlehill little Emily waited and the experiment had to go on.

The most rational thing was to go to the coffeepot, get some coffee, call New York and find out what had happened to Sandy, and then take the next ferry back to Nyack, a taxi to Castlehill, and into bed. He left the wall and ran up the street into the little restaurant.

It steamed inside, and he drank his boiling black coffee, and the warmth crawled back into his wet clothes. He stood at the window, the hot cup comfortingly within his two hands, and tried to look through the misted glass to see the bridge. By twisting his head, he could just catch a corner of it, but not enough to be sure whether or not a car passed. If she returned he would be sure to miss her, and suddenly he knew he could not miss her, that he would not, that he must see her today, now, at once, and he put the cup down and paid and ran back in the rain to the corner and looked over the deserted bridge.

He should have remained near the ferry because that was where she would go, and at least there was some kind of shelter from this frightful wetness that drowned everything in sadness and gloom. So he started back over the bridge. Rain poured into his shoes and down his collar. His head was wringing wet, and his body ached, and the pulse of the fever beat in his temples.

Why, he asked himself with a frightening ferocity and hate, was he doing this, for whom, for what kind of woman? What did she mean to him that he should trudge through the rain and wait and worry? Why?

And reason, curled like a parasite within his heart and mind, whispered back: because this is love that you should wait this way. But he did not love her. He felt none of the things that he imagined love should be, only worry and vexation, and bitterly and ravishingly present sexual desire. He longed to abandon himself on her burning body, in the softness and fat of her, in the arms and legs and body of her. Was this love? And experience, like a catalogue

155

of disasters within his brain, plucked cards out and showed him that this was love, this was love as he had seen it among the neurotic and the sane, the wild and the foolish, the suffering and the sick. Love was not a thing. It was this man's or woman's energy attached to some object, pleasant or unpleasant, in the world, so bound, so wrapped and delivered to that other creature or image, that the soul could not function without it. And this was why he walked, and this was the reason for his being there, and he loved Sandy. That was all. It wasn't good or bad, or wanted or unwanted. It was the fact of this moment.

He stopped in a daze of anguish upon the bridge, indifferent to the elements, the time, his condition. He stopped and resolved that he would see Sandy tonight no matter what, no matter how, and he would tell her, and demand from her, and force her to leave David, and he would take her to himself, and keep her as his mistress, his wife, his love, and make her into what he wanted, and nothing, nothing would prevent it.

He was so intent on this, so paralyzed by this discovery and desire, that he didn't hear the car come up, but there it was sliding to the curb, and Sandy's face at the opened window, and her voice calling, "Carl."

So, triumphant as if he had willed her appearance and she, like the prisoner of some charm, had been forced to come, he ran to the car, slamming the door which she had opened for him, and slid into the seat. He took out a damp handkerchief and wiped his wet hair and face. And now that she was here, now that they were together, his physical misery reasserted itself and he demanded angrily, "Where the hell have you been all this time?"

She accepted this tone as her punishment, showing her guilt, admitting it. "I'm sorry. But something important delayed me. You're wet, soaked." As he coughed, "You've caught cold. I'm really very sorry." And she took out her handkerchief from her purse and tapped at his cheek.

He shrugged her away, rolled his wet handkerchief into a ball after squeezing it dry and put it in the pocket of his raincoat. "Where were you?"

"I'm awfully sorry," she said again. "But why didn't you wait under the shed?"

Carl didn't answer. He waited for her explanation, his face hard and furious, his clothes clinging to his feverish skin.

Like twin metronomes the windshield wipers wasted the time, the motor purred and the steel roof danced with sound. She reached out her hand and turned off the ignition. "The fact is," she said in a small and very conciliatory tone, "David's back."

"What of it?" he insisted violently. "You were there on time and then you drove off."

"Oh that." She looked at the big electric clock on the dashboard. "I remembered I had to make a call home, and I certainly didn't expect that you'd come marching after me in the rain that way. You see," she went on very rationally, placating him, "my shoebag is in the cellar of the apartment house, and David's aunt came up to help pack, and I wanted it brought up."

Anger flew before his fear. "Pack, what do you mean pack? Why are you packing?"

"I'm trying to tell you." She seemed sad and distraught, and she shifted uneasily in her place behind the wheel. "You see, David flew straight to Washington and called from there and I have to fly down tonight at seven-thirty." She pointed to the clock. "And it's nearly six now."

Because she pointed to the clock, he looked at it, but saw nothing, only the vacuum she was opening before him, her absence, and he could not accept that. "Why don't you wait until he comes back to New York? What's the rush?"

"I'm not making myself clear," she explained patiently. "I know it's really a shock, to hear it this way, and I didn't know myself. But he had to fly to Washington to see his chief. It was important, something to do with his trip abroad. And then he called and asked me to come right down and I said I would. I promised him."

So sharp a misery sprung alive in his heart, so great a loss in his face, that he turned away, and sat tightly, holding himself rigid, fighting to hold back his cry that she should not go, that she could

157

not, that he loved her and she should remain. He waited until he could speak quietly. "Why didn't you tell him that you would wait in New York?"

Indeterminately, she looked out of the window as if the answer lay in the rain, then at the clock again. Under her little black rain hat, her face was richly tanned, squarish, and she straightened the fingers of her red and black gloves. "He made me promise and I did. I had to, after all. He's just returned from abroad."

"What of it? God damn it, what difference does it make whether he's in Washington or on the moon?"

She sighed and put out a hand to his arm which he ignored. "I understand how angry you are, and you've every right to be. Getting wet and making this long trip for nothing. But I called the hospital the moment I heard. I called at once to warn you, to save you the trouble, but you were gone."

"No, no." He made his voice as soft and pleasant as he could, and it was difficult because he was raging within. "I don't mean that. I'm not angry that you kept me waiting, because you're here." He asked for the least, the very least, because tomorrow would take care of itself and it was tonight that he wanted her, to have her, to be with her, to talk with her about all the new things that he knew about them. He could not let her go tonight. "Why do you have to go tonight? That's all, why tonight? It's so late, and you're here anyway."

His reasonableness gave her courage and she smiled affection-ately at him. "It's nice of you, Carl, to feel that way. But he was so excited, just coming back from Europe, and he wanted me there tonight to meet his chief. He promised so I had to promise. And they'll be waiting for me at the airport." She brightened warmly, and took his hand and pressed it. "I tell you what. I'll call you from Washington tomorrow and let you know when I'm coming back." She looked at the clock again. "The ferry will be there soon and you'll miss it if we wait." She turned on the ignition key and started the motor, but he leaned across her and switched it off. "Never mind the ferry," he said.

She suddenly seemed to give up and sat back in the corner

158

against the door and seat, looking vaguely ahead as if she had no way to cope with this thing and it would have to end itself.

The grayness and rain created a false evening that simply extended without growing darker. Carl took out his cigarettes and lighted one without offering any to Sandy. Again the smoke was raw in his throat, so hot, and he felt a kind of tiny heat yawning in his bones. That was fever. But he could not let go, he could not let her go, and he could not understand why she wanted to when he had so great a need. The smoke caught him as he coughed and he choked into a paroxysm, coughing and coughing helplessly as if his entrails were being torn out through his mouth. She patted him helpfully on his back and when he lay back exhausted, she prescribed, "You ought to go home and get into bed. That's what you ought to do." And full of virtuous determination she reached for the ignition key.

But he shouted at her violently, "God damn it! You're lying about something. What's your hurry to get away?"

Sandy shrank back into the corner of the car, making herself small and inconspicuous, not looking at him, and now she was really sorry that she had turned back out of pity for him. For she had fled at first, dreading this scene, and now it was happening anyway, and David was waiting in Washington, and she wasn't lying, only she hadn't told Carl everything, since that would make this dreadful thing even worse. Her raincoat was open and she wore a pale blouse above a sport skirt which had slid above her knees. One gloved hand rested on the wheel, helpless to drive, and a strand of her rich hair curled upon her full cheek. The rain hammered upon the car isolating the two of them against the outside, and Carl felt their togetherness as the prize of his life. All the while he knew she was ready to leave the moment he got out, that she was waiting for him to leave, angry, pleased, satisfied or unsatisfied, but to leave so that she could drive off. She was there but gone from him. His passion was alone within him and she felt nothing. If he could only get her to feel this agony, to share with him his need, to know it as he knew it, then her plans would disappear, he was

159

certain, for the nights that they had spent until this moment burned within his finger tips, and he looked at her hands in her red and black gloves, protected from him. He stared for a long time at her body crouched there in the gloom and then he threw the cigarette out of the inch of open window, and pulled her roughly to him, turning her face up, kissing her again and again while he sought her flesh through her clothes, not even caressing her, not even playing at the usual game of lovemaking, but seizing upon her coarsely, striving with hunger to gulp her down into his passion, to drown her in it, to sink himself and her and choke and drown out time and the world.

Sandy didn't resist, she let herself go to him, her body yielding as he used it, and all the while she kept thinking that it would make her late for David in Washington, and the clock moved unalterably on the dashboard. But she had for so long trained her senses for pleasure, and to be handled this way was so unusual that despite her will she bloomed with desire, and felt the wave, the drag and dreaminess of it, leaning upon Carl, and he exulted. But she still heard far off David's voice, enthusiastic on the phone. "We're going to Europe," he had shouted. "To Europe. I'm going to be there a year. In London. And you come right down and call my aunt and tell her to get our things packed and stored away. Take what you need and fly down. It's big news. Exciting. We leave in three days."

It had thrilled her to hear this, the adventure and the change. It was the excitement and pleasure of going abroad, of the important work of David's which meant new people in different surroundings. A change. Another change. And it was change and change again that fluttered her boredom.

Above Carl's tight arm she saw the clock again, and she pulled away from him strongly, resisting, and he let go. She rested against the cushioned seat, breathing emotionally, desiring him and yet anxious to leave. She wanted to be nice to Carl, she wanted him to remember her with pleasure, with happiness, and she did not want to lose him either, because sometime when she returned it would be nice to have him again as her lover, and he was after

160

all Carl, that Carl out of her oldest past, so dim and almost un-recollected now, but the strongest memory of her life. "Look," she said reasonably, "we're being very foolish. Do you know some place around here where we could go for a little while?" She leaned tenderly upon him, kissing him. "Let's not waste time talking."

Happiness surged into his voice. "No, I don't. Why don't we go to your house?"

"I told you," she said, "David's aunt is there." She straightened herself, buttoning her raincoat over her opened blouse. In a moment she had the car started, turned in the road, and roaring out of Tarrytown.

"Where are you going?" Carl asked.

She smiled to him out of the gloom. "I know a place not far from here where David and I stopped once."

He lighted another cigarette and watched the road and the wetness rolling up into them. "What are your plans?" he demanded brusquely. "Because you must have some plans."

"Like what?"

"About us."

"Oh." She laughed cheerfully. "We've got lots of time for plans. Besides I know you. Any man who can rush out of a woman's bed at four in the morning, because he's got a little scientific experiment somewhere that needs his attention, is no man to make definite plans with."

"You resent that?"

"I admire that." And she touched his face. "And you. Why, I tried to keep you. I made a definite point of keeping you and you wouldn't keep."

I will keep you, he promised himself, and you will stay.

She drove off the road, not even searching, but like someone going home, down a small feed lane, and around a blind turn were four cabins and a beer tavern with a red and green sign winking in the rain. Sandy braked the car and in the same motion was out of it. "I know the man," she said. And ran through the rain into the tavern.

161

Carl sat doggedly and waited, watching the flicker of the sign: *Beer.* It did not seem to be the kind of place where David would take his wife, unless, and pain sprang up in Carl's heart, an attack, unless it had been here that David had taken her before they were married, before Carl had left for Europe.

The door opened and Sandy came running out, waving to Carl to follow, for the rain now was beating down in a fury. She went to the last cottage which was almost hidden beneath a great elm tree, and opened the door, and there she stood beckoning to him. Carl got out and walked slowly over.

The moment he was inside, she closed the door and locked it. The room was damp, cold, the wallpaper yellow and streaked, and the one lamp had a split shade and too bright light which garishly flamed upon the sordidness of the place. She pulled down the shades and ripped off the bedspread, and then with the same continuing gesture took off her coat and clothes, and in a few moments stood there naked, her skin covered with tiny goose-pimples.

"Hurry," she said, "it's cold," but he knew she meant late, while she crawled beneath the sheets.

Her face waited there, her shape beneath the sheets, and on her head was the little rain hat which she had forgotten to take off.

"You've got your hat on," he said, and slowly started to undress.

"My hat?" she felt her head. "Oh!" She took it off and dropped it to the floor.

Gingerly he crawled beneath the damp sheet and lay on his back looking at the dirty ceiling. He was shaking with chill, with fever, but he was happy somehow for he had kept her, and she was his to keep. As she moved towards him he held her off with a question, "When were you and David here?"

"Years ago," she said. "A long time ago."

"And weren't you embarrassed to ask the tavern owner for a cottage, to come here in the daylight and ask?"

"He knows me."

162

But he would not let her escape. She lay tensely beside him, waiting, and this was his will, to spoil her pleasure. "You mean because you were here once before a long time ago?"

"Oh! David and I come back here from time to time, for sentimental reasons. You see, this was the first place."

He could believe it, and it was during the time when she was yet his lover. "And wasn't the tavern keeper surprised to see you with someone else?"

"It was too dark for him to see."

They would never have any comfort out of love, he thought, until all this past had been cleared up, the lies dismembered and destroyed, the past accepted so that the future could be serene. And this was the beginning, tonight, in this damp and filthy room. He turned on his side, facing towards her and put an arm around her shoulder. The bare fullness of it, so flowering in its musculature and softness, possessed often, yet came as a surprise to his eyes, and he pulled the coverlet down although the cold crawled on his feverish body, and looked at her, at the woman she had become. Beside the perfection before him his mind paired the fat and demented body of little Emily, writhing in the torture of insulin shock. And guilt stabbed at him, cut him to the heart, for it was the flesh that was sacred, the temporary, the growing, diseased body. This was the sacredness of life, this the care of life and science, to cherish these bodies, and while in old times they had broken bodies to save the spirit, it was in truth the body itself that was to be saved. His mind tumbled with the past as he knew it, from his studies of his own science, of the way mystics, prophets, heroes of the state had flung upon the junk pile of their pride their delusions, their need for power, the tortured and broken limbs of millions. And this world, so harsh with pain, with fears and frights, violated love at every turn, and violated life, and the victim always was the neat body, the flowering body, the sacred vessel of life. Fever droned and images interlaced while he looked at her through half-closed eyes, and let his hand smoothly touch her. But all at once, as if they had been couched in the jungle of her need, in the darkness secret and breathing of her senses, her two

163

bare hands, like live albino leopards, leaped at him and pulled him down, choking him with sensuality and passion, and he forgot everything and took her as the only woman in the whole world whom he could ever love.

The light was still on when he woke up because someone was shaking him. He swam up out of the deepest, weariest sleep, a sleep that was stuffed with choking heaviness and dry fever. He struggled and came out of it, opening his eyes into the same lighted room. A round-faced man, wearing a big brown hat and a raincoat draped over his shoulders, was standing beside the bed. And Sandy was gone.

The voice was neutral. "It's ten o'clock."

Carl's limbs were helpless in the bed. He didn't want to move. "Ten o'clock?"

"A little after."

Forcing himself, Carl sat up, looked at the dirty room, the gray mussed sheets, the light that cracked the horror of this room out into the open. The man stood there patiently, waiting to be sure that Carl was really getting up. "I'm getting up," Carl told him. "This is no place to spend the night. How much do I owe you?"

"It's paid. Your friend paid."

With another effort Carl jumped out of bed. "Does she pay all the time?" he most casually asked.

"Sometimes. Sometimes the feller pays."

Keeping himself as easy as possible, Carl dressed, put his damp socks on, and feet into the wet shoes. He listened for the rain and heard only a light wind. "The rain stop?"

"Yup."

"Am I far from town?"

"Five minutes' walk."

"By the way, does she use this place a lot?"

"Off and on." The man turned to the door. "Just close the door after you. It's got a spring lock."

"Do you know her name, or her address? I didn't get it."

"She gave me a phony. Just count it as good luck, that's what I say. Juicy bit." And the tavern keeper left.

164

As quickly as he could Carl got out of the room, carefully shutting the door behind him.

The rain had cleared and here and there between moving clouds a few stars blinked, very bright, almost icy. From the heavy woods a wet fragrance rolled upon the road, and Carl walked quickly, weary, disgusted, his feelings disheveled.

It was after ten and the ferry no longer ran. This meant a train ride to New York, the tubes across the river, and another train to Castlehill, a good three hours of traveling. He splashed through dark puddles, and once walked off the road, but at last he saw the distant glare of a crossroads light above the Albany Post Road, and cars passing from time to time with a roar and swish.

Profoundly in his heart he shuddered, despising himself and the passion he still felt, for he felt it still, looking forward to the time when she would call from Washington. He would not let her lie next time. He would drag the wretchedness of what she had become out of her, and all the while he reflected sadly that in the jungle in which she so naturally lived, into which he had so blindly wandered, she was better adapted than he, more fit to survive.

xi

MOONLESS the deep night swallowed up the road in blackness and wet. Sometimes a truck growled by, straining and pounding, dashing the puddles at Carl, or the headlights of a passenger car bore down, searching him out, driving him into the drenched shoulders of the highway against the dripping bushes, nailing him motionless to the side and leaving him again in the indifferent dark. If the drivers saw him, they did not heed him, and after a few futile attempts he gave up trying to get a ride to the village which in the distance below the hill shone like civilization itself, its street lights in a thin pattern like far stars.

A small but persistent wind swirled out of the formless woods to inhabit his damp coat and shoes. He coughed more often, choking deep in his chest, and his throat burned. He did not think he could feel more miserable, and he hurried on, indifferent to the wet patches he stepped in, intent only on getting to town where he could arrange to drink something warm and begin his journey back to Castlehill. He longed for the warm cottage and Curtin's friendly company, something to eat, something to shelter his weariness and ache, and he worried that soon it would be too late, impossible to make a connection with the Jersey train, and that he would be stranded for the night.

The first of the street lights hung over the road now, glaring within the space it had carved out of thick dark. For Carl it proclaimed the end of the bitter day out of which nothing remained but his sense of physical discomfort and emotional wretchedness, and he no longer thought of Sandy or love, but of a hot bath, hot coffee and a warm bed.

But as he entered the town past the first straggling gas stations,

166

all of which were closed, as the houses began to line the streets, their windows dark, retired, he realized that the town was in fact shut up for the night, that there was no warmth here, that he was a stranger, and the street lights asserted no more civilization than do stars. Here and there behind a drawn blind some solitary life dwelt, but so withdrawn as to increase his feelings of not being included, and he remembered this same feeling in Europe, of coming late at night to a small town, dark, contracted, crouched upon itself like a fear-ridden animal, the steeple of the black church peeping aloft like a snail's horn, and the hunt for a small hotel through peopleless streets until the entire affair became distracted as a dream, remote, beyond his will.

While he searched down the forsaken business section, on the lookout for those last two oases of the times, the whorehouse and the saloon, either of which would be open with a telephone available, he projected his private desolation upon the world and heard the insane crying in their wards, the screams of pain and disease in all the corners of the earth, the misery, the discomfort, the madness and fear which everywhere haunted the cities engineered upon the vast globe, and that pessimism which is the exchange value of consciousness loosened the ghosts of his flesh.

He found at last a seedy bar with a half-dozen loafers and a lounging bartender, and when he called the railroad station he learned, as he expected, that the next train would not bring him to the city in time to make the Jersey connection to Castlehill. What was left was his mother's apartment, or a dreary motel. And this was only fitting.

He joined the others at the bar and had a few drinks of whiskey which immediately made him feel much better. The alcohol touched his head with a wandering finger for he hadn't eaten since the morning and now it was nearly midnight, and suddenly the scene reversed itself, and he began to grin. He took his self-pity and dissolved it in the alcohol; and he took his weariness and damp and dissolved it in the alcohol; and he took his own desolation and passed it back to the bartender for a drink.

It was only another day, he thought, and thinking that he remembered that his brother Bill lived somewhere here in Tarry-town, so he opened his wallet and took out the postcard his mother had given him. With the help of the loafers and the bartender he sketched a little map which would, in half an hour's walk, bring him to 57A Locust Street, and then he had another drink for the road, and exchanged cheerful good-bys with the saloon, and went out into the night again.

After an hour's struggle to fit the rough map to the wandering streets, he found himself on Locust Street, which was nothing but a dirt alley running up a little hillside behind a paved road. Three ancient houses, boarded up and rotting, lined the alley, but at the dead end was a new cottage with a light burning in one of the rooms. He made for it anticipating its cosiness and a friendly conversation with his brother, and a change of clothes and some-thing hot to eat and drink, and then a comfortable bed and perhaps another drink. But the cottage door bore in antique iron letterings the number 60, and a strange name. He knocked anyway, but could not get the woman behind the door to open it. She did how-ever tell him cautiously that 57A was a garage apartment behind the second boarded house, and that someone lived there but she didn't know who. He called good-by and thanks to her, and when he looked back over his shoulder as he made his way down the road, he could see a blurred face behind the curtains, looking fear-fully out into the night. Well, it was only natural, he thought, since it was after midnight, and thieves and murderers inhabited the world, while all sorts of strange monsters even more terrible than the real ones inhabited the minds. He cut behind the dark three-story wooden house, through rank wet grass, and felt that nowa-days even more than in ancient times men feared the world they lived in.

In the rear was a dark garage with a flight of open steps going up the wall to an apartment. No light showed, but Carl expected that Bill would be asleep, it was so late now. He lighted a match at the foot of the stairs and saw that number 57A had been sloppily painted on one of the slats, and then he walked gingerly up and knocked on the door. Nothing stirred in the dark so he knocked

168

again and again and then rattled the doorknob, and still there was no response. The little lift given by the alcohol was wearing off and he felt too tired to walk back to town, so he sat down on the steps, first pulling to one side the very wet rubber mat placed there. As he did so he heard a piece of metal ring, and felt around in the dark until he discovered the key, which had been hidden beneath the mat. Elated he rose, opened the door and switched on the wall light.

With disgust he saw what he should have most naturally expected to find, a shabby three-room flat, and on the mantelpiece over a small brick fireplace a winter snapshot of Bill and a dark girl, both bundled in overcoats and mufflers, the film so overexposed that it was impossible to tell whether the girl was pretty, ugly, young or old, and Bill only recognizable because he was a brother. Carl slammed the door and stood there surveying this matrimonial nest.

The living room had brown wallpaper, and the two small windows were supplied with shades. There was an old mahogany table, chipped, soiled, unsteady, on which a cotton tablecloth covered with bread crumbs and stains still rested. A gray daybed stood against one wall and against the other a ramshackle bookcase in which were thirty or forty volumes, stacks of pamphlets and a neat pile of newspapers. The next room was a kitchen, small, painted white, with an iron sink and a black gas stove with two jets. A brand-new percolator stood on the stove, and in the sink was a soup pot rimmed with grease and three dirty dishes and two dirty cups. A broom stood in the corner and beneath it a dustpan, but the dustpan was rusty. Carl walked then into the toilet which contained a sink, a bowl with a cracked seat, a modern tub, streamlined like an airplane, and one nail on which hung a red douche bag covered with dust. Carl had to smile because it simply indicated what his mother had already told him: that the girl was pregnant. He drifted back into the living room and peeped into the bedroom. There filling the space was a big double bed, the pillows out and still crevassed with skull hollows, and a bureau, and a wooden chair.

169

So Bill had finally settled down and got himself a wife. All Carl's finickiness emerged and he kept looking here and there, the contempt rising within him until he almost decided to leave.

But it was too cold outside, too late, and he was too damp and feverish. He returned briskly to the living room and from the wooden box that stood beside the fireplace piled dry slats and broken board ends into the fireplace over a pile of newspapers. He threw a match on the heap and after a moment it burst into violent flame, sending out a cloud of living heat into which Carl dipped like a sybarite. He took off his coat and shoes, and slipped off his trousers, folding the latter neatly in front of the fireplace for the legs to dry. In the bedroom closet he found a woman's bathrobe and a pair of new blue felt slippers with red pompoms on the toes. The slippers were almost his size. Christ, he thought, she has feet like a horse.

From the living room he went back to the kitchen, washed out the coffeepot in cold water, since there was no hot, and put water on to boil. It took him five minutes to find the tin of coffee because someone had left it in the living room. From the kitchen he went back into the bathroom and in the medicine cabinet, which contained toothpaste, cold cream, vanishing cream, toilet water, hairpins, mineral oil, and other ritual medicines of the age, he found also the usual bottle of aspirin. He took twenty grains.

In a little while the coffee was ready and he poured himself a cupful and returned to sit in front of the fire. He sipped his coffee and studied the blaze. It did not seem too bad in the little garage apartment now, but he knew what his mother meant when she had said that Bill had married a "pig of a girl." Carl could not imagine himself dwelling in such disorder.

Having finished his coffee he got up and went back into the kitchen for a second cup, and he found the breadbox with half a loaf of sweet cake crumbling in it. He broke off a piece because he didn't want to wash the greasy bread knife.

He wandered back into the living room, munching the cake, and stopped reflectively in front of the bookcase, crouching at last to read the titles. There were half a dozen cheap reprints of detective

170

stories, some dollar editions of famous novels such as *Madame Bovary, Aphrodite,* a rather torn copy of the first volume of Frank Harris's *My Life and Loves,* various book club selections, *Life on the Mississippi, Moby Dick, McTeague,* a series of works on trade-unionism, *Anti-Duhring* by Engels, a history of the United States, a book on parliamentary procedures, two volumes of *Congressional Reports, Letters of Sacco-Vanzetti,* and a great many CIO pamphlets on different problems in the automobile industry. The stack of newspapers were issues of a local organizing sheet of the CIO and the editor was William Myers, his brother. So there lay Bill's total life, a dirty wife, a dirty job, and a disheveled mind.

Carl took some of the newspapers back to the chair before the fire, kicked up the blaze a bit with the last piece of wood, and then seated himself as comfortably as he could in the dissolute upholstered chair. He sipped his coffee, munched his cake, and read the agitational editorials, the news of successes in other plants, discussions of wages, hours, prices, attacks on the local management for using thugs to intimidate the organizers, snide news stories on the local police and politicians, an open letter to President Roosevelt to return to the economic policies of the New Deal, and various other international, national, and local subjects. It was quite dull to Carl, and he finally let the papers slip to the floor and sat, half dozing, waiting for his brother to return.

The first stages of a high fever are not unpleasant, almost alcoholic in some respects, light and winged, with nervous tension ballooning up and floating loose from its causes, and within the inner ear a giant bumblebee buzzing melodiously as in a honeyed flower. Carl relaxed. There was warmth within him and the floating heat of the fire without. Everyday sensations of space, of time, of care dropped below the new horizon of consciousness and while he did not sleep, he did not feel awake. So he was careless of the car that drove up in the street, of the voices speaking distantly below, and he hardly stirred when heavy steps came up the wooden stairway outside, and moved almost in a dream as he got up to answer the single sharp knock on the door. He was, in fact, smiling, imagining his brother's face as he found the lights on with this comic apparition in a woman's dirty robe and new, bright blue slippers with scarlet pompoms.

Carl opened the door and in the room's light saw a rather burly gray-suited man wearing a gray felt hat standing before him.

"Are you Myers?" the man asked softly.

"Yes," Carl said, preparing to say he was the brother.

But the man was drawing back his right hand as if to take something from the dark, and Carl looked. Suddenly a fist lashed into his face, like a heavy stone thrown up out of the dark. It struck him full and heavy in the mouth and drove him stumbling back and reeling in pain from the door. Carl fell against the back of the chair in which he had been sitting, shaken, dizzy; but pain is more intelligent than consciousness, so the hurt mobilized his strength and brought him standing erect, his hand to his face, while the doorway filled with two other men, one of them in a red pullover sweater, the other in a brown suit.

Between Carl at the chair and the three men in the door was one of the new blue slippers with the scarlet pompom. The door closed but Carl didn't see it. He was watching the man in the gray hat who stood there surveying the room while no one spoke. A pulsation of pain whirlpooled from Carl's jaw into his neck, into his shoulders, and he was beginning to ask himself what this was, to speak out, to grow angry, all the things he had been taught to feel in such affairs, when an earthquake of terror cracked open his heart, for the three men had separated and were now moving closer to him, in unison, with a plan, and one of them, the man with the red sweater, carried in his left hand a little wooden club, thick and ridged, about eight inches long, attached to his wrist by a leather thong. Carl backed around the chair, watching the club. His mouth was so dry he could not breathe, he felt his breath die within him, leaving a vacuum which grew and grew, expanded, yawned, blew up and burst in hysteria, sending him wildly running into the bedroom where he slammed the door closed, and pressed against it while he fumbled for a key or lock. But there was no key. There was no lock. There was just the door.

He was still leaning there, still scrabbling for a lock or key when

172

the weight of the others hit the door from the opposite side and half opened it into the room, jamming him with tense wide legs against the bed. He pushed with all his strength and saw in the band of light from the living room a man's black shoe wedged in the space between. He stamped on the shoe with all his might but his foot was bare, and then the door caved open on him, hitting his face, and sent him back upon the bed, the door swinging wide and cracking against the wall while the opening filled with the bulky bodies of his assailants.

Carl rolled over on the other side of the bed, stood up in the narrow space, tugged the window open, and yelled out of it. "Help!" he cried, just once, and then he was struck from behind on the head with the club. A wedge of iron agony like an immense nail seemed to drive into his skull, flaming into wild currents of pain in his hands and limbs. He shuddered, raising his hands to his head while other hands grabbed his shoulders and pulled him backwards on the bed, and another claw clamped on one of his wrists, twisting his arm back until it almost broke in its elbow socket while he turned with the pressure. Carl screamed out, kicking wildly with his bare feet.

They held him thrashing on the bed, caught in numberless hands, and they beat him across the face and chest with the club, each blow crashing into the pain of the blow before, adding and adding, multiplying and soaring with agony, and he curled up, quivering away from them, from clutching hand to clutching hand, all the time kicking and sometimes feeling their bodies with his helpless feet.

"Get him in the other room!" The voice panted in his ear, as if it were to him it was speaking, to him, to him alone; and caged in pain, in this net of pulling, pushing, beating violence, his mind asked: what is this, what?

They dragged him from the bed, punching him and kicking him, and their heavy shoes abraded his skin, piled turbulent, maniacal agony upon his flesh, and because they were trying to drag him out of the room, he fought to stay in it.

In these first few seconds of roaring terror and pain, his untaught

173

body escaped him, and his mind was loose, chasing fear in and out of the blows, and he kept screaming although he did not know it. He clung to the doorjamb and the man in the red sweater brought the club down upon Carl's fingers and crushed the thumb. This pain was the worst yet, the nail cracking, splintering into his flesh, and the small soft bones of his thumb came through the skin.

He let go, fainting back, blacknesss swirling and holding him, and he felt the softness of unconsciousness lapping him up like a black soft mouth, and he was going under softly and peacefully, dying. The word and idea *dying* hit him, drove harder into his brain than fists and clubs and nails and blows into his soul, and the word *dying* shattered open the deep untapped strength of body, and he sprang alive from the men like a flailing animal from the butcher's knife, and burst from them, free, and ran into the kitchen, banging against the walls, and into the bathroom, whirling the door shut and his hand went below the knob as a drowning man's hand raises above the water to clutch at the air for help, to hold on to the delicate air of life, and there was a lock, which he shut, and the door held as the men hit against it, kicking, heaving with their shoulders, and the same voice of the man in the gray felt hat yelled, "Come out of there, you son of a bitch, or we'll kill you."

He heard their tumultuous breaths, their clumsy, heavy body movements, and the door began to split. There was a small window and Carl wrenched it open and yelled out of it again and again, "Help!" Then he tried to scrabble through, to fling himself out and to the ground below and run away, but the window was too narrow and too high.

Behind him the wooden door cracked and he turned a wild and bloody face to it. The door opened in its center near the floor, opened within like a crown of thrusting spikes, and he saw a big black shoe pushing its way in, kicking in and out furiously, and he looked down at his own feet, at his bare feet pale in the little light that came through the battering, crashing hole in the door, and his feet were bloody, and his hands were bloody and the robe torn. The foot continued to kick, and the door leaned open on the

174

bottom and then was pushed up and pulled from the other side, and the foot kicked and kicked by itself like a battering head of a monstrous machine, a wild and furiously driven thing, and then the door gave all at once, all of it, breaking in, clattering, half in half out.

More than the pain was the fright, the nameless, the overwhelming terror that did not let him stand still, that howled in his ears above the shattering door, and now the small room filled with their shapes. He flung himself upon them punching, hitting back as hard as he could, fighting at last, fighting to hurt, fighting to get free, and they hit him back, all mixed and close in, while slowly they dragged him out into the kitchen, scattering the dirty dishes, tumbling the table, the chairs, the closets opening and falling in a crash of glass and metal, and finally weighed him down to the floor. By now these three men were so enraged that they fell upon him at once, each trying to destroy him, wild and foolish, getting in each other's way, always hitting, always kicking, never pausing for an instant to see what was happening, but furious upon this thing that would not lie still, that kept coming to its knees, its feet, only to be kicked down again, grabbing at his head, his hands, his legs, clasping his body, trying to get him down and quiet to kill him, and at last a heavy heel caught him flat on the floor, drove down like a piston into Carl's chest, and he felt it, he felt it with such awfulness, with horror, with such a warning shriek of agony from his bloody mouth, such a tearing of flesh and nerves as his ribs broke, and blood vomited with vomit of coffee and cake from his entrails, as he rolled over.

He did not faint. He lay in a rhythm of pain and the rhythm was his breath breathing, each breath a stroke and a tear, a monster pressure on his chest, a bellows of agony. He could not move but lay there on his belly, curled, and all their blows were nothing on his back and legs, even the kicks against his head were nothing, for there was this machine within his breast, this invention, this broken machine beating his life out with each breath, and he tried not to breathe but he had to breathe and he choked on his breath and his blood.

175

Somewhere in another world voices talked. "That's enough for him."

There was another kick at him, so useless that he felt it like a shake of the hand saying good-by. He heard them far off in this other world outside the machine, he heard them in this other room somewhere smashing everything, pulling down the lamps, the chairs, overturning the bookcases, the one mirror crashing, while he lay there in this machine which was within him.

Only now, only after this wild flurry in which he had flung himself without thought, did he begin to think. He heard them in the next room and he began to think. And at last he was thinking not with the generation of schooling and work, for that world was long since gone, not with handshakes and kisses and conversation, not with ideas suitable to a world which has no hell, not with the things and images which no longer counted, for he felt himself dying; he was beginning to think with his organic life as he felt it ebb within him under the repeated, the breathing strokes of the infernal machine. He thought with his instinct, his naked, deepest vibration of motion against death, that he was dying, and that he would not die this way. He would not die in here but he would go to those men in the next room. Every bit of strength left in his flesh, every drop of blood that did not drip through his wounds, every twitch of nerve and bone, called him with desire into the next room, with a passion to kill these men, to destroy them, for this was all that was left of the need to live. It welled up in him and like an animal doomed by its instinct to die in the act of procreation, he started to drag himself, to crawl, to edge upon the littered floor into the next room.

The three men saw him coming and stood there. He could not raise his head high enough to see their faces. He saw only their feet, their shoes, their trouser bottoms, and he dragged himself there to their feet. He saw a foot raised to kick and he did not have the strength to avoid it so he met it, taking it on his pulpy face, and grabbing the foot, holding on to it as if this foot wrenching and kicking was his life and he had to hold it to live, and he summoned all his forces, all his years of life, the accumulated power

176

of youth and manhood to hold this foot, and the blows began to fall upon him again, and he twined himself upon this foot, this leg. The other two forces in the room tore at him and beat at him, but he held on, twisting himself like death upon it until the body fell, scratching and beating at him. He rolled over with the leg, now the trunk, now the hands beating up at his face, and a hand wrapped in his bloody and sweaty hair, but he persisted like blind fate until he got his hands upon the face of the man, and he clawed at that face reaching for its life and felt something come soft and pulpy in his hands and tore at it and heard a shriek of agony that did not come from him. He heard this shriek that wasn't his with immense and fateful triumph, and then he let go while they pounded at him and finally clubbed him senseless.

Out and in. A shock, but out and in, a moment, and he still was not dead and he heard a car far off starting and a voice, first or afterwards, he could not know, a voice calling, "Hurry. Hurry. He's dead. You son of a bitch, I told you. He's dead. Dead."

But he wasn't dead. He knew he wasn't dead. He was only dying. He was bleeding within, a well of a hemorrhage. He knew he should not lie helplessly there if he wanted to live. Half alive, he still wanted to live. He would not die. He would not die this way here until those men were dead. That was all he could think. Not to die until those men were dead. He could not wait for help because he was alone in the desert of his pain, the blood gathering loosely within him, pouring out of its broken channels, flooding through the cracked dams of his flesh, and he would drown in his own inner blood if he did not get help to live.

Like a blind beast he crawled upon his belly, each motion an undulation of supreme agony, but he crawled against it over the rubbish and destruction of this room to the open door, remembering as a beacon, as a moth remembers a flame, as the flesh remembers to heal itself, as the lobster's claw remembers its shape to grow into a limb again, remembering a little cottage up the street with a light burning in its window and a woman there, a blurred face in a window. He felt the outside air, saw it vaguely beyond the steps, and face downward hung over the steps that went down into the night. He shifted his weight forward until he lay over the steps, over their hard ridges, and when more than half of him was past the landing, he fell slowly and helplessly down to the ground where he fainted.

His will did not let him lie there. His will unwound him from the softness of the fainting spell and brought him thinking into the world again, and he began his slow, his painful crawl, the inch by inch calvary of wet grass, this road of torment. He was propelled by a will which did not want to die and all the while monster agonies of his body commanded him to stop, lie still, to let himself fall back into the comfort of darkness, of soft and easing death, to go out of this world of horror, this grass, this mud, this slime, this torture without end. Finally it was too much and he yielded, he let himself fall back, but the grass was gone. This was the road, and a blind thing he continued to crawl, for there, he raised his head, he saw it, a light, far off a light, and he propelled himself.

It was no more than fifty yards, a dirt road covered with rain puddles, but between Carl and the house the distance was greater than between earth and the farthest and faintest star, because distance which has real magnitude, the distance of universes, is measured in time, and time for men is sensation and life, and time for Carl was agony, and he crawled for this limitless time of agony upon the dirt road.

He crawled through vast epochs of pain, as slowly, as painfully as the human race has crawled through each of the bloody shambles which men call their history. He gathered and added in his flesh the unique and individual torture which numberless millions have endured in Egypt, Greece, Rome, Europe, China, India, Africa, Inca and Aztec, the fires, the whips, the knives, the wracks, the cells, the camps, the knouts, the tools, inventions, constructions, the apparatus of power and greed, and the unspeakable agony at last of his own time which had flung him bleeding and broken into this road, crawling and desiring to live, to surmount this.

On the steps of the cottage stood the woman of the house who had heard the whole affair and she watched him come to her. He

178

tried to call to her across space, to bridge her terror, but he could not call. At first she did not move, but as this shape crawled up the road she backed into her house and slammed and bolted the door, for she had no telephone and she did not dare enter the night. So he had to go on until he reached the steps, and now it was too much. He had the will, he had the courage, no pain was too great for his spirit but the body would not go. It would not go at his command and he began to revile and curse his body. Go, he shouted without a sound coming from his lips, go. Go, I say. And it did not go.

He called soundlessly to her: Do not be afraid of the night. I come to save you from the fears of the night. I am Carl Myers.

And she did not come.

Where are you? He called again in the silence of his brain. Where are you?

And she did not come.

How can I speak to her against the fears of the night, he asked himself, for only he was alive now, the body was useless to him.

My love, my love, he called to her softly, soundlessly, my love, come to me.

And she did not come.

I will not die, he said as he fell all at once, not even knowing it, to fight again into the unmuscled softness of the dark.

The woman did not come out of her house until her son and his wife returned from White Plains where they had been to see a moving picture. They looked at the limp man upon their steps and believed him to be dead. They were therefore unwilling to touch him and the son drove down to call the police, explaining to the sergeant at the desk that he did not yet have a telephone, and this was the reason that his mother had not called during the fight. Later, the police drove up to the scene of the crime, and when they found Carl alive they called an ambulance.

In the economics of life and death, Carl was almost bankrupt by the time competent medical aid came to undo what had been done to him, but he was strong and he did not die that night.

179

xii

IN the beginning Carl did not know he was going to live, and afterwards when he did know, he did not care.

For weeks he lay helpless in the hands of the medical staff and they could have killed him as easily as they saved him and it would not have mattered to him, for his spirit had been so submerged in pain that it lay torn on every broken corner of his body, so volatile that the smallest pinprick of unpleasantness evaporated consciousness and left him dark.

His friends, of course, were concerned.

His mother, who was possibly his oldest friend, haunted the antiseptic corridors and wept, contributing to his recovery her grief, for what it was worth. Doctors Erdman and Curtin appeared frequently and used their considerable influence to see that Carl got every attention, the older man bringing specialists, the younger man, wiser in hospital routine, concentrating on the best nurses, the constant, devoted attention without which recovery is even more agonizing than the destruction itself.

It was Erdman and Curtin whom Carl saw first, sideways through a bandage, sideways through pain, a shaft of lemon light about their heads which leaned over him. "Why, Carl," Erdman said, "How do you do?" And Curtin grinned, his red hair flaming in an orange halo, his voice booming out, "I had them shave off your mustache so you'll be handsomer." Carl closed his eye again, the one that peeped around the gauze corner. The fine cotton strands, so close up as to be a screen for all the world, made a summer latticework, holding the light back like a soapy bubble in the

180

interstices, often repeating the image of what Carl saw a dozen times as if his one good eye were faceted, gigantic as a fly's. Carl murmured so low that Curtin put his ear against his covered mouth to hear. "Little Emily? Ah, little Emily, yes!" his friend said cheerfully, the remembered tone like old familiar furniture in a beloved room. "Dr. Erdman comes up every day to carry on your psychoanalytic nonsense, and I'm keeping exact notes, better than yours, so forget it. All is well, all is well." The phrase repeated, all is well, all is well, came slow and unfatigued to Carl's memory like the luncheon bell of Castlehill, plump and full and rosy red in the center, delicate pink around the edges, all is well across the honey-dripping maples, all is well across lawns asleep in an afternoon of sun. Carl heard his friends a little way off, talking to the other doctors, and finally it was Erdman who returned within the tiny frames of the gauze latticework, who leaned close, his bald head ripe and mellow as an egg yolk, Erdman whose voice cautioned, "If you're a good patient and do as you're told there'll be no physical incapacities, I guarantee it, and if you're sensible, no mental ones." Carl heard him go away while Curtin rang the Castlehill bell again, a last vibrant note, "Bye!" and Carl saw the Hudson again below the meadow and the merry daisies.

His two most persistent callers, neither of whom were permitted to see him for three weeks, were his brother, Bill, and a local policeman. His brother got to him first with a message through Curtin. "I don't know why," Curtin said in a secret voice, "but he says please not to tell the police anything until he sees you. I told him to go to hell even though he is your brother."

But Bill knows why, and now I will know why, Carl thought. If anything repeated itself monotonously in his mind, anything intellectual at all, it was *why*, why this disaster had happened to him. This *why* was an old word to Carl, so familiar from his working life that he probably was more concerned with it than he really cared to be, but to know that Bill knew why, that Bill would carry the answer in, all round and sufficient, all chiseled and perfect, all white and clean and stainless as the round white electric globe of the ceiling, let Carl sleep at once.

181

When Carl saw the policeman he lay stubborn in his tight bandages and replied vaguely. Finally Bill and his wife, Juley, were admitted and Bill's first question after the nurse left was, "Did you tell anything to the police?"

Carl asked, "Like what?" He actually meant to say, like why, but he felt that this answer was going to take a long time, that it would be very complicated like most whys, and at the moment it took more interest than he could summon up. He spoke with as little energy as possible, living as he did within the sheltered confines of narcotics, those mind-eating flowers that close more softly, more sensually upon the soul than desiring flesh upon flesh, and while he was swallowed his ribs healed, and his broken bones knitted and the torn skin, the welted flesh, worked its way back to the body's overpowering design. At this time drugs saved Carl from himself, redistributing causality, keeping the world distant, nonessential, lackadaisical, holding off the pressure of the why, and always beneath consciousness there kept swirling and fluid heavy sleep, so that with the merest intention he could slip away and float softer and more supple than a cloud's reflection on running water.

Bill acted as if he were commissioned to perform a serious and unpleasant duty, and since he had always had a rather comic way of presenting himself, his first defense to his older and ostensibly more clever brother, a way of shuffling his feet in a little tap dance and making wry asides, little painless jokes, of coloring way up to his eyes while they watered, he used this approach on all occasions, even the most solemn, as this was to him if not to Carl. For Carl had discovered Bill's bald head, the surprising presence of it, not altogether bald, but with the hair line in full retreat from the brow, and he was busy watching it, wondering how *that* had happened. How had Bill who was ten years younger managed to overcome these ten years and even add some ten more so that now as he stood there he appeared older than his older brother? He was pale-cheeked, plumper, sensible in a sensible brown business suit, with a brown felt hat in his left hand on which he wore as a final mark of time's passage a golden wedding band. Carl heard his brother ask, "Did these men say anything to give away what they were after?"

"Tell me something," Carl murmured most softly. "How did you manage to get so much older?" And then an afterthought, "Than I?"

"Than you?" Puzzled, Bill looked around to his wife, and Carl looked that way too, with difficulty but without pain, and saw her at last. So this was Juley, swollen with pregnancy, carrying like a python an undigested child.

"Where," Carl asked, "did you get your wife?"

"Detroit," she said. She said *Detroy-it* in a tough, rich voice whose main tone was spoiled and irritable.

"That explains everything," Carl said and closed his eyes to see the room, the room he would never forget but which was so much more bearable when it was only looked at as belonging to Juley.

She demanded at once, "What do you mean everything?"

"I mean," he told her, "why was the coffee in the living room?"

Uneasily Bill interrupted, giving his wife a warning look, reminding her of his brother's feebleness. "Now wait a minute. Wait a minute." And he came closer to the bed so that Carl, when he opened his eyes again, could not see Juley, and saw instead the emotional and painful face of his brother. "Christ," Bill said with intense feeling, "I can't tell you how I feel to have this thing happen to you. You know that. You see, I know who these guys are, who hired them. But I was wondering if they said anything. You see," and it got more and more complicated to Carl, "I want to know, we simply have to know, if they just wanted to scare hell out of me and chase me out of town, or whether they were looking for anything in particular. They upset the whole house. We simply can't afford to have the police come in on this. Did they ask you for a list?"

Somehow this irritated Carl. Outside it was autumn, so full of rushing clouds that the sun kept spattering in and out of the room, moving across the ceiling in ripples and floods, going in and out dizzily, and this made Bill waver, as if he were standing there, pressing too hard against Carl's body, too hard. The pressure of

183

thinking back was unpleasant. He said abruptly, "Tell me what you want to tell me. I'm too tired to listen much. Too tired, that is. What is it? What list?"

Bill blushed guiltily. "I'm sorry," he choked out hoarsely. "I'm sorry to bother you, forget it."

From behind Bill's brown suit, now in sunlight again, now in shade, the sullen richness of the wife's voice appeared. "It's not your fault. You don't have to apologize. We didn't know he was coming. We didn't know they were coming."

"Oh shut up," Bill said without heat. "I'm talking to my brother. I know your opinions."

But she could not shut up. She said, "You'd think he was the only one that ever got beat up."

And Carl raised his voice. "Dirty bitch. Why didn't you wash the dishes?"

Apologetically the soft voice of his brother, so low and hoarse, always as if with a cold, came to him. "It's the pregnancy. She's not like this at all."

But Carl closed his eyes, abandoning himself to his own feelings, the sense of going to sleep again while Bill talked. "The reason about the police is simple. You see, I'm the spearhead up there at the plant, I'm the guy who's running the movement of the CIO into that plant, and I got the cards of the people who already joined." It was going to be a long complicated story and Carl began to sleep, not very far down in sleep, he was too polite for that, and besides too irritated with the wife. She sometimes spoke even though Bill had told her not to. She was willful and lazy but her voice was attractive when he separated it from the dishes and the bathrobe and the one blue slipper with the red pompom sitting there in the middle of the floor between him and the man in the gray felt hat. He woke up to look. It was his brother Bill, his brother's old and semibald and kind face, his brother standing there, mysteriously his older brother. "Those three are either AFL or management goons come to scare me out of town and get the lists, I think. You see if they can fire the people who've joined, it will scare off the others. And they fire them in spite of

184

the law because the law takes too long, and we'll lose the plant like we did before." What in the world was he so excited about, Carl thought. This had nothing to do with the three men and himself. The meaning of that lay in him, and Bill was like Curtin, just talking. He didn't know a thing, nothing. Carl craned his head to look at the wife. He wanted to hear her voice again, it was somehow very beautiful, not hoarse like his brother's but all rich and rubbed, rubbed like fur rubbed the wrong way, like the whitecaps rubbing against the Hudson tide. He did not want to say anything just like that, so he waited to listen to Bill again, to find something he could pick up, some fragment of words to throw at the wife, and make her speak again.

"The question is this," Bill explained, "if you call in the police and say they were anything but three unknown holdup men, if you help them nail this thing on the labor movement, then the police step in and in a week they'll have everything gummed up. They'll call in our people ostensibly to find out if they know anything, because it's a labor case, a case of violence, and meanwhile they'll go through the suspects, but it'll all be those suspected of belonging to the CIO. Those three bastards are out of town by now."

Carl heard the word bastards and he asked at once, "The old lady says you got married after your friend over there was pregnant. Was that why you married her?" This made a connection in his mind but not in Bill's.

"Aw, come on lay off, Carl," Bill said in embarrassment. "Don't pick on her because she's dumb enough to pick on you."

Carl waited but the wife didn't say anything, just smoked and looked contemptuously at the bed. He tried again, "Why does she wear a dirty bathrobe? It's all her fault. I would have made a better fight with my shoes on. I'll tell the police they were after my money and followed me from the saloon."

Bill's face flamed again, soft and brotherly, and he put out his hand to touch Carl and then drew it back at once, afraid to hurt him. "Christ. Thanks. You got to keep it away from the police if you're in the labor movement. I want to thank you for all of us."

185

Carl gave up hoping to hear her voice again. "Good-by," he said most wearily. He would sleep in a minute, in one small minute.

His brother called, "Good-by," and they were going out.

Carl asked, "Doesn't she even know how to say good-by?"

And suddenly in this room, so white and filled with chasing sun and shadow, a low laugh came, a laugh like a ball of tumbling kittens, soft and furry, and comic, exquisitely rich and somehow languorous and soft to touch, and the laugh went into the words and called, "Good-by."

Falling asleep it was hard to assign this laugh to the house in Tarrytown or the careless, almost unlovely creature who had sat in the hospital room, so Carl kept it apart for its intriguing self, hearing it again and again as a new kind of human sound, fondling it in his mind, assigning to its character a person who decidedly was not Juley. But as the days went on he forgot it, not forgetting that he had heard it, but forgetting its living presence, and therefore trying to recapture it by wanting to see Bill's wife again.

Bill came without his wife the next time, this some two weeks later, and he wore a new overcoat and his face was rosy from the cold that had fallen upon the region, with a sudden winter leap in the midst of warm autumn. There was in Bill a certain forward confidence despite his mannerisms, as if he were a successful businessman, very shrewd about his affairs although naïve generally. He folded the coat carefully, complimented Carl on looking so much better, that is with fewer bandages, and announced that he was leaving for California.

"When?" Carl asked. He was still extended rather awkwardly on the bed, but with much more movement. And so he was able to twist his head rather sharply on this question, and take in his brother's neat haircut like a lawn cropped around a sandy playing field, and beneath the plumpish and pleasant face with its tender watery eyes was a bright green tie.

"By plane tonight. You see," he smiled with embarrassed triumph, "we've had the election and won, and what happened to you helped. At least that much came out of it."

186

"Shit," Carl said. "For my part I'll keep my health and they can lose."

Bill laughed. "Well, anyway, the organizing committee passed a resolution unanimously thanking you for your co-operation and," he laughed again, "your devotion to the labor movement. They wanted to inscribe it on a scroll, but I talked them out of it." And he went on laughing, in a quiet, confidential way that was very charming.

"Well," Carl said dryly, "you can thank them for me too, and tell them I expect them to do the same some day."

Bill took out a new silver cigarette case, snapped it open and offered the contents to Carl, who had to refuse. "Can I smoke?" Bill asked.

"Go ahead."

And then Bill searched and brought out a companion lighter. "From the union members," he said proudly.

"Your own brother's blood you mean."

"You're right," Bill said seriously. "Which would you like to have, the lighter or the case?"

"Ah!" Carl didn't even laugh. "That's more like it. I'll take the lighter."

Bill put it down on the shelf of table across the foot of the bed. "There you are, with the compliments of the membership."

It shone in the cold light that came through the window, a fingernail of brightness, a single blind reflecting eye.

Carl asked, "How did you ever get into a thing like this?"

Bill smiled shyly again. "I'm making a living, that's all. It's a job of work. I got this auto job and then when the union started, I got involved."

"And where's your dear wife?" Carl asked. "Doesn't she want to say good-by?"

"She's not coming along. That baby is pretty close now and I don't know exactly where I'll be yet, so she's staying behind with Mama."

"Poor Mama."

Awkward and a little upset, Bill ambled around the room, try-

187

ing to find a decent way to say it, but couldn't and gave up. He stopped near his brother and just came out with it. "You've got nothing against her, Carl. She's feeling just lousy, having a hard time with the kid, that's all."

Carl dismissed the conversation, and after a few more wearying moments, Bill left promising to write, and Carl remained with himself, feeling generally indifferent to everything, even to the time it would still take before he could get out of bed, and the time it would take to be free of this crippling process of getting wholly well.

There was in his return to health a certain organized process of changing attitude, from the earliest sense of loose and desultory abandonment, to the now growing, the now firming feeling of indifference. His brother, his brother's wife, Sandy when he thought of her (she hadn't called), his mother, Curtin, Erdman, all these people had their place in his consciousness. He knew them all and he knew what he had experienced with them, what they meant to him, in fact. But he did not, he could not care if they came or went, or what they thought about him, because he could not bring himself to think that way any more. He looked forward to being healthy, to finishing the paper on little Emily, to working with patients, and thinking again in his science, but he was profoundly bored with the prospect of human relations. He liked best the empty, relentless days, when he saw no one but the nurses, all the hours of the twenty-four the same except that some were light and some were dark, and in some he slept and in some he did not. Most pleasant were the early hours of morning as he lay awake and waited for the first modulation of the dark to begin like a piece of music with its daylight theme. The hospital was never wholly silent, but these routine noises were no more particularized in his mind than the din of the country on summer nights. He was getting much, much better and no longer had those long sweating moments of anguish, and with a fierce self-imposed discipline he had stopped taking the narcotics long before ordered to. He did not want them any more, and now there was no pain, and yet he was not quite well. He was rather marooned within the pleasant,

188

the peaceful, the empty island of his self, and while deep within him, scratching a little in dreams, he sometimes was face to face again with that awful night, he let it lie there where it was, no longer trying to comprehend its meaning for him. The meaning assigned by Bill had nothing to do with Carl. That was not his meaning for him, and even after the event, he could not elect himself to the role he had been forced anyway to play.

When he was discharged from the hospital and installed at Erdman's, when he began again to see a few patients, and visited little Emily, now completely regressed to her former state, when sometimes of an evening he went down to his mother's house and there had dinner, with Juley in Bill's place across the table from her, he often remembered the long, the placid hours of the coming on of morning at the hospital, that slowly awakening silent light, and how sleep stood aside until full daylight broke and then brought darkness again into the room. From the bed nothing was to be seen but sky, a kind of blank screen with no shapes on it but what morning could accomplish, or stars at night. These mornings were the fullest memories he had of the long stay at the hospital, the happiest, the most essential.

To his surprise he enjoyed the weekly dinners at his mother's little apartment, and she grew fat and kindly on them. Between them they rather ignored Juley, who didn't seem to care, but just slouched through the remaining days, just waiting to have her baby and follow her husband to Los Angeles where he had finally installed himself, but still without an apartment or house. Bill wrote nearly every other day and Juley spent long hours composing interminable letters in a childish scrawl, very large, hardly more than a few sentences to a page.

"They must be in love," his mother told him. "But what anyone can love in her I just can't imagine."

Then dinner would be ready and after she was called half a dozen times Juley would amble in, loose and floating largely in a man's bathrobe, her slippers slapping on the linoleum, her hair disheveled, with a slap of fresh lipstick across her mouth to show she was not going to bed.

189

One night it became too much for Carl, more for his mother's sake, he imagined, his mother who loved order, and he said, "Why don't you get dressed and look decent instead of like one of those sacks of rags that my brother used to push around on Bleecker Street?"

"Now, Carl," his mother said.

But he wasn't angry. He felt cool and unpiqued. It was just that he did not like the way she accepted so naturally that other people would take care of her. But she flamed all red, and pushed her hair back with ink-stained hands, and yelled at him, "If you don't like it, don't come down here."

This was true enough and he admitted it. "You're right," he said.

But his mother tried to make the situation useful. "Carl's right. God knows you're having a hard time, but you can make believe it's not so bad and you'll feel much better."

"I won't make believe," Juley shouted in her rich beautiful voice, like a great tragedienne. "I won't." And she wept.

"You look even worse when you cry," Carl told her.

"And what are you so virtuous about?" The tears dried on her face as she struck out at him. She struck at him as if she had waited a long time for this. "I've heard more than I can stand about you. That great smart brother, that famous scientist. But what do you know? You look awful smug because you just got beat up once. But your brother has been through that a dozen times. Yes," she exclaimed triumphantly at Carl's disbelief, at the mother's gasp of horror. "You don't know what your brother is. You don't care. He thinks you're just marvelous, but I've told him. You're just a smug self-satisfied selfish middle-class fool. That's what you are. That's my opinion. How do you like that?"

And Carl said mildly, "I don't like it at all. But what do you mean about Bill?"

"I mean," she said righteously, "that he takes chances like that on every job he goes on. That's what, and he takes it as a matter of course and doesn't think the whole world has come to an end. It happens all the time, to better men than you."

190

Carl turned to his mother and asked, "Did you know the kind of work Bill was in?"

She nodded, her round full face a little sad. "I didn't think it was that bad, but he's like your father when he was all mixed up in the same kind of thing. And he's like my brothers and my father."

"And now what have you got to say?" Juley asked victoriously.

Carl broke off a piece of bread and began to eat his meat. "I still think," he said, "you should comb your hair, and try to look a little more civilized."

And suddenly once again she laughed that marvelous laugh of hers, and sat down to the table. "I just made up my mind to hell with everything until the baby comes. I give up, that's all, and I hope it's better after the kid is born."

They ate in a kind of formal politeness for a while and her swollen face glanced rather shyly to him and she said with a penetrating huskiness so musical and dominating that he could only smile back at her, "I'm sorry for what I said, honestly. But having a baby, at least for me with all the trouble I have, is like going into a strange room and having three men jump on you and beat your brains out. It's just impossible."

Impossible, unendurable, it was exactly as Juley had put it, and when Carl got back to his two neat luxurious rooms and arranged Erdman's notes in front of him, and Curtin's comments, and the complete filing system on little Emily, impossible and unendurable were the words that echoed before him. This word impossible was louder than the winter wind riding upon the icy Hudson, hurtling between the Palisades in a vast and flowing torrent, shaking the double windows outside like a clumsy thief, prowling and howling in the alley, demanding to be let in to destroy the warm comfort and the discreet lamp which burned above Carl's desk.

It was this impossibility, this inability to absorb the experience, that faced him as childbirth faced Juley. But she at least would have the child and it would be over. But for him, despite the explanation he had received and understood, despite the history, so to speak, of the event, the fact itself was incomprehensible. It was like the night when Curtin had asked, shuddering, What is mad-

191

ness? Or why this person goes down in a fury of disavowal of life and this other person not, a blank incomprehensibility. He sat back in his chair, his face between his hands, and felt fury rising within him: a desire to kill, to step upon and maim, demolish, destroy those three men, all burning and flaming within him, shaking him and crushing him with intolerable tension and desire, overwhelming and wounding his mind, to kill them, to murder and destroy them, to get rid of this impossibility within him. And then it went away in long pulsations, leaving him, departing, and he knew he still lived with this impossibility, absolute as evil.

He went downstairs into the neat kitchen and made himself some coffee and carried it upstairs to drink as he worked. He flung himself into the work, into its impassiveness, into the first stages of writing, the fundamentals, the problems, the scientific criteria, and he began to write out for the first time in sequence the etiology of little Emily's sickness.

The wind was so loud, everything else in the world became quiet. He leaned over the page, writing carefully, neatly, and brought his head sideways into a more comfortable position, only to recreate for a moment in himself the shy look that Juley had given him. Impossible was right, as if the apple which fell on Newton's head had never yielded up its secret, as if Archimedes had drowned in his bath, because he felt that the night he had walked into Bill's house still contained its secret, its secret message for him, and it was impossible because he could not hear it, or read it, or understand it.

Even this experiment, he thought, as he wrote on, had a secret for him which he still did not know, like all his life, like this moment, but he marshaled all his intellect, all his will, to continue his calm, his dispassionate report, and suddenly came in his own text upon her smile, the only one she had ever given him, a smile which had in effect delivered all her life into his hands. The memory of the smile evoked the memory of Juley's laugh, and he stopped writing and rose to walk slowly around the room. He lighted a cigarette with the lighter Bill had given him, and stood for a long time at the closed windows watching the constellation

192

of lights in New Jersey. Then he put everything in order, turned out the lights and went to bed.

He lay sleepless for many hours, thinking it seemed of nearly everything, wondering what had made Bill fall in love with Juley, her voice perhaps, which was as physical an attraction as Sandy's body. He was growing very tired and still did not sleep, so he decided to think in a more logical way.

What, he asked himself, were the preconditions for a natural science of psychology?

In a moment, still smiling, he was asleep.

xiii

ALL through winter and into the windy spring of 1939, while David flew from capital to capital on his more and more mysterious missions, Sandy let herself be marooned in the south of France because nothing satisfied her, nothing excited her, and at last, like a disease long preparing whose first symptoms had yielded to local medicines, to old wives' cures, to changes of climate, of scene, of people, at last her boredom became insupportable and nothing alleviated it, nothing, not sleep, not acceptance, not even sensuality. She was no intellectual and could not make a career out of analyzing her ennui and proclaiming to the world that everything was nothing, that alienation was the condition of man, that disgust was virtue or virtue quiescence, or in effect, that words were everything. She had no way of imposing her state upon the world; she just felt it, day and night, in everything she did and did not do, and finally it began to frighten her. She remembered with horror the scenes in Castlehill which Carl had shown her, the naked women in their cocoons of madness, and in the night with the mistral opening and closing in grand, outrageous gusts upon the villa, the shutters rattling in their frames, the windows tinkling, and outside the palms and pines breathing like breathless runners, she clung to her bed, as to a raft, and stared at the ceiling gilded and sculptured with cupids, and wondered if this was how a person began to go insane.

Yet she did not leave St. Ivrey-sur-Mer, as she might have, and go to one of the monster cities, to Paris, London, Rome, Berlin, Warsaw, or Prague. She did not go home to America. She had been in all those places and not one of them had made any difference

194

to her. In the urban political excitements, the men and women she met, in power in their countries or close to it, all had seemed dull and stupid, no wiser than those who had nothing to say, and even when politicians, diplomats and generals were charming, even when they intrigued, Sandy could not find the brittle adventure in it that her husband did.

David was a man on fire, so excited he could not sleep, so keen, so clever, people said, and so close to the central decisions of the day that even if he had been a thousand times stupider he would have been interesting. Not since the early days of the New Deal had he felt so alive. The peopled life he led had fined him down, worn thin his healthy flesh, his outdoor muscles, but in return revealed a pure and delicate beauty in his features, a fragility there. He was all nervous energy, talkative, witty, entertaining, and he had endless stories, predictions, revelations to make. But all the while he too waited at the edge of that intolerable tension which was the coming on of war and felt it as his fate, as his destiny, his great opportunity. Whatever the certain war brought to Europe, it was going to bring him life and make a history for his country.

By training and talent he was an intellectual, but as some religious men can only express their faith through repudiation of God, he could only express his ideas by rejecting the role of thought. He had come to believe in the inevitability of power shifts in history, in cycles of change against which men could not struggle, and now as in the courts of princes or the shabby ante-rooms of republics he smelt the awful stench of all the human blood that would be spilled; as before his eyes the frightful visions of the near future took their monstrous shapes, a wild elation seized his heart and he had no time to eat, to drink, to love, because destiny was rolling in upon his times and his destiny was to em-brace it. In the beginning he despaired of his country which like a provincial cousin had been named heir to the world's for-tune and did not know how to come into the inheritance, but more and more as he conversed with European statesmen, with leaders in all walks of life, his optimism rose. It was David who

195

had convinced Sandy of the idiocy of the European leadership, no wiser than the leadership at home, but she had forgotten his other remarks because they bored her, and these were that the destiny of America would come out of this war, not because any new ideas were involved, but because in history events moved to give leadership where power, where material energy, accumulated, and the power was at home.

His life with Sandy had been a failure from the moment she showed herself more apt for it than he. She took to the comfort and luxury of the upper bourgeoisie, to their games, their sports, their customs, their habits, even their ideas; and meanwhile he was moving away from it, at present in leaps and bounds, plunging into the chaos ahead to act and act decisively, to embrace the new world of power, to bring it to life and afterwards to administer it. The physical courage to which he had been trained taught him not to fear for his death, for in such gigantic struggles even the luckiest man could die. He gaily accepted the idea of death. It didn't matter. Nothing mattered except devotion to his destiny, and this burned. He didn't put Sandy aside, or leave her. He rather liked to have her around. As her inner discontent matured she seemed to ripen and become more golden, more exquisite, and it was a pleasure to have her with him. She attracted men to herself and therefore to him, for when his affairs were not mere intrigue, they were social. This was the way history was being made at this stage. But at last Sandy refused to leave the Côte d'Azur. Once settled at the Villa de la Tour Sarrasine she found it impossible to move. She waited with the presence within her, as if she were pregnant with it, as if in its growing it would finally fruit, had to, and her only fear was of what it might be.

The villa was named after the ruins of a Moorish tower on the estate. From its crumbling summit Sandy could see beyond the Cap de Croisette the green thumb of Cap d'Antibes. Below to the east was Cannes, to the west the rough Estérel Mountains, and far behind in abrupt barricades of milky stone the Maritime Alps above Grasse, the higher peaks covered with winter snow. A ten-minute walk brought her down to St. Ivrey, in the crowded streets,

196

and in fifteen minutes she could be in Cannes where the hotels were jammed with vacationers from every country in the coming war and the harbor packed with yachts. Although Sandy was alone she was not isolated and was invited everywhere, especially when diplomats hurried down for a week end accompanied by generals who would either soon betray their countries or uselessly slaughter their armies. The weather in Europe was horrible that winter except on the Riviera, the one place where unexpectedly in between immense winds brilliant days would burst, still, warm, sunny, with the waveless Mediterranean surging with blue light like medieval glass. So there were parties and little yachting trips to Menton or Monte Carlo, or even to San Remo, or the other way to St. Tropez, and these European politicians and military people listened respectfully when Sandy spoke, hoping to hear through her what David might have said.

It was the mimosa season and each day the inhabitants of St. Ivrey sought out these flowers of gold with the lust of Forty-niners. On her daily walks to town Sandy used to pass bicyclists with shocks of mimosa riding the seats, or baby carriages piled with the flower-heavy branches while the children toddled on foot in their rabbitskin coats. There was a continuous procession from the little town, almost with a sense of pilgrimage. Old men packed the mimosa on their backs and old women bore it conventionally on their heads, while young couples embraced it more fervently than each other. Just beyond the private road of the estate on the public way there stood one old and very tall tree that some-how managed to become a part of Sandy's life, of the time going by. It had minted its flowers in vast profusion, rich, ripe clusters heavier than grapes, and, standing all alone above the ravine that descended in terraces to the palm-fringed sea, it dominated the windy view. The grownups marched up the road, crossed the stone bridge over the ravine, circled above the town where church bells rang all day, passed between the confining walls of the farms whose stones were pink and cracking, chalky and delicious as the nougat manufactured in Provence, and finally emerged on the level length of road with its great view south and

197

this one big tree undulating in the wind like a sea unfolding golden surf.

Sandy watched the older people break off careful bunches, selecting among the hand-high flowers, and day by day the tree grew greener around its base; but on Thursdays, when there was no school, gangs of boys and girls took the short cut up the ravine, leaping from rock to rock like their own goats, and appeared beneath the laden tree and attacked it. They tore the bunched bouquets, dripping with fuzzy balls of flower, slashed the branches, broke the boughs, and at last the tree stood, torn and disfigured as high as the children could climb and reach, with jagged flowerless leaves, and above, riding out of reach on one long, spearlike branch, a single magnificent cluster, now more valuable than the rest, holding sunlight within its gold against the gray and windy sky. Now each day as the mimosa hunters appeared they walked by this tree, although from time to time a boy would try to reach that last cluster for his girl, only to be defeated by the swaying slenderness of the branch which held it, and this remaining sheaf of blossom became for Sandy like her own life. She seemed to stand all golden to one side while the procession of life went by, and her season would pass, she knew, and time would eat up her youth, and she would die.

She longed to live again and did not know how, and so she could only walk down of an evening and stand before this tree and look at it blankly, hearing the wind in her ears. One morning David arrived and announced they were going home in a few days. He was waiting for some dispatches, he said, and then they would leave, and for Sandy it would be for good. The war was simply a matter of weeks, or days, or hours, or minutes. No one could tell. "It might be going on now, at this second, in motion, and Europe is no place for you."

"And you?" she asked.

"I'm going home for some conferences," he exulted enthusiastically, "and then I'm coming back."

"And me?"

He smiled vaguely, hardly hearing her, and bursting with en-

198

ergy, unable to sit still although the weather had changed and one immaculate day followed another. He helped her raid the shops. "The last chance," he cried, "for such spoils. After this is chaos."

He bought her dozens of pairs of gloves, marvelous as flowers, colored like the tropics, like birds, like clouds, like precious stones, and she followed him docilely and let herself be clothed. When his important papers did not arrive, he telephoned, and frequent telephone calls responded. It would take a few more days and he was bored with buying, so he took the Bugatti and drove her through the ancient cities perched upon the sunburnt rocks. Here was where the floods of history had poured through Provence to leave these stone-gray villages heaped on top of gorges, precipices, and pointed rocks and hills. And he talked endlessly. "Dead. Everything in Europe is dead and even the dead things will have to die some more." He could not contain his impatience for the storm to break.

She was docile, she hardly heard him. She listened only to herself now, to this feeling which day by day crumbled her will to live, to move, to struggle, and she did not know what it was, or what it came from or where it would lead her. She wondered only if David could help her.

They took the car and drove to the seashore behind St. Tropez, and on a hot transparent day changed into their bathing suits and swam in the cold, the sky-blue water. The surf, kicked up by weeks of roaring wind, had dragged tons of seaweed up to the shore which had mixed with the sand to form against the particolored rocks a kind of sandy turf, yellow, dry, spongy. Here they ate lunch out of a wicker basket, drank a bottle of Chambertin 1915, and sunbathed. They lay side by side and Sandy looked at the clean horizon line through sun-drenched lashes, and she put her head on her husband's chest. He began to caress her and she responded, feeling so lost and alone, desiring him. But after a few mechanical gestures, he jumped to his feet, unable to be interested, and began to throw stones into the sea. Then he flung himself in after the stones and swam far out and back again to come up to her dripping. "Let's go," he said. "Perhaps those dispatches have come."

They dried themselves and got into the car and he drove back as fast as he could go. The wind roared upon her, the sun beat, the sickness grew.

At home there were no dispatches and David sat down at the telephone and began to call everyone in Europe, it seemed, while Sandy took a bath.

He burst into the bathroom as she lay almost asleep in the tub. "Tomorrow," he shouted. "They'll be here tomorrow, and we're off." As he started out she stopped him.

"David," she said.

He stood at the open door in his shirtsleeves, so thin, so fine, so wonderful-looking, a kind of dry fever in his eyes, his fair hair thin, cut close, so young-looking.

"What's going to happen to me?" she asked.

He stared at her, at the golden body in the jeweled water, and he did not appear to see her. "You?" His mind danced about his own word for a moment. Then he laughed, a free, a happy laugh. "Why, enjoy yourself." And he bounded out of the room, calling to the servants to be sure everything was packed.

She lay in the tepid water which drained away whatever energy she had left. To enjoy herself? That no longer meant anything and she tried to remember when she had last enjoyed herself. It was like going through a list of securities that no longer had any value because the companies were bankrupt, and she passed through the weeks she had spent with Carl, counting him with the others.

She remembered the afternoon when she had first gone to see David without Carl. That still remained, but as she let her mind loll in it, it too lost value for now David was what he was. And before that was Carl again.

The surface of the bath moved with her breathing, she lay so still. Her body flattened out before her eyes, became almost a single surface. The taps glittered. What would her life have been had she married Carl, she asked herself?

His face began to tremble before her, the night he had stopped her in front of the apartment house, the rainy afternoon in the car in Tarrytown, the walk through Castlehill, and then, dipping, the

200

current of her memories began to run strong and true, began to float up the solid, compact time when she and Carl had been lovers, the River Hospital and the little apartment on the top floor.

She could never have become this if she had not betrayed him for this life which no longer concerned her. He would have saved her for he had a different kind of strength. And his passions, his moodiness, his sullenness, his explosions and softness all returned and filled her with delight and the sense of living. How could a woman find this again, become this again? He probably hated her now because she had left without even saying good-by. But she would confess her guilt. She would go back to him. He was her hope. She longed to cling to him again, to touch him.

She wanted to love him again.

She sat up suddenly and shattered the calm surface of the water. A sickness of desire made her shake as if with chill, and she despaired. She didn't care if he loved her or not, if only he would give her a chance to be with him, to enter his life once more.

It was worth everything to try, everything.

At once the vacuum of her life filled with faith in the miracle her existence demanded, and over her face the subtle contour of hope took shape. She sprang dripping and golden from the water as if into the arms of love, loving the idea of it, a thousand schemes glittering like drops of sundrenched water in her mind, and her time filled up and her imagination flew rapt and transfigured to her first and only love.

She wanted to be alone with this secret to her future, and she dressed hurriedly and went out of the house by the side entrance, hurrying down the road to avoid her husband. She came out by the big iron gate and walked more slowly now in the direction of the great tree, and there she sat down and dreamed over the sea.

Every now and then as if a door had opened somewhere in space a gust of wind came dancing over the sea and hit the shore like the wave of a hand, brushing back the bushes, the grasses, the trees, and the flags in the harbor. The wind blew her hair and whipped her dress against her legs, and then the door was closed and once again the afternoon lay still. She saw the islands like two

201

green water-lily pads in the sea, and against the distant Estérel shore the little white breakers like wash blowing on parallel rows of clothesline. And she sat with her secret.

There was just the question of how. She felt that if she went to Carl and offered him her love he would refuse her. It was not enough with him that he should love her or she him. That was his wonderful strength, she so shrewdly imagined. It would have somehow to go back to their common past, as if they had strayed apart and now slowly retracing their steps could come together and start again. It was David, of course, who had driven them apart, and she heard his voice calling from afar, "Sandy, Sandy."

She stood up and when she did he saw her, loping down the road at a half trot, shouting, "I've been looking everywhere for you. What are you doing down here all by yourself?"

She looked vaguely around for an excuse, and there was the tree with its one big cluster of mimosa out of reach on the soaring branch. "Why," she said most naturally as if it had been true, and in a certain inexplicable sense to her it was true, "I've been watching the people strip this tree every day, and now that we're going, now that there's just that one cluster of mimosa left, why I thought I'd come down and get it."

He laughed at her. "Why, the estate is just lousy with the damned stuff."

And she smiled slyly, her thick lids lowered suggestively, "But it's that one I want." And she looked up. "And I can't get it."

He accepted the challenge at once, freeing her from his questioning, and leaped at the tree like one of the boys from the town. "I'll get it for you."

He scrambled up and soon stood below the one outthrust branch, and it was beyond him. She watched him from below, his white-shirted figure against the sky, and he seemed very high up. "Be careful," she called from below. "It's not worth breaking your neck over it."

He shouted down. "You don't know me."

He took hold of the long thin branch and slowly applied his weight to it, and it bent like a bow, and then holding on only by

202

his hands he very slowly and carefully began to inch out on the limb while it bent lower and lower.

She heard the first cracking of the wood, the first tearing of the bark. "It's breaking," she yelled out fearfully. "David."

His laughing face shone down on her. "Exactly."

He hung there, just shifting his grip a little closer in, so that the branch broke almost in slow motion, letting him down like a parachutist, and when it tore off he was some half-dozen feet from the ground, landing like a cat with his prize in his hand. He broke off the flowers and formally presented them to her. "It's something I remember from my boyhood," he explained. And he stood there flushed and triumphant, his face glittering with pleasure, excited and stimulated by the danger he had overcome.

She pressed the heavy mimosa clusters in her arms as if they were Carl, as if David had given him back to her, and with a bent submissive head followed her husband back to their last home together.

xiv

THREE weeks after the war began Dr. Erdman had a massive cerebral hemorrhage. He had gone down to the cellar library to look up an old paper in one of the early numbers of the *Psycho-analytic Review*. With Carl in the house slowly assimilating the practice to himself, Erdman had time and the inclination to work once again on his book. The volume he sought was on a lower shelf and as he bent down to extract it, he was suddenly struck.

They did not miss him for several hours, but when the secretary insisted vehemently that he had not gone out, a search was made and Carl found him crumpled and unconscious beside the stacks.

Strangely enough, such is the tenacity of a going system, he recovered, although forced to stay in bed with a slight paralysis on the left side. Carl spent much time with Erdman and they talked mainly of the old days of psychoanalysis. Those times were universes away, romantic and exhilarating, the mistakes and brutalities eradicated by time and the death of so many of the participants, and besides, as Carl told his old friend, "The theory won out and is accepted if not altogether correct." He loved to sit and listen to the old controversies, the struggles as between heroes and giants, and like a small boy heard tales of a bygone mythical age.

In the evening after dinner Carl would smoke a cigar with Dr. Erdman and sometimes read him a few pages of the paper on little Emily. The writing was drawing to a close and against his intention Carl found himself indulging in a few last paragraphs of speculation which delighted Erdman. "You see," he complimented Carl. "You can think. You're not just a plumber looking for leaks in the nervous system."

204

Since death lived so strongly in the house they never talked about the war. Toward nine o'clock Mrs. Erdman would come limping in on her rubber-tipped cane and after coffee was served, she and her husband gaily recalled their courtship and life in old Vienna. These memories swung and lilted like old waltz tunes which remained on after she had gone to bed, and the old man smiled queerly up to the frescoed ceiling and said, "You can tell you're really old when you hang on to life just to remember the past and not to imagine the future." He sighed deeply and looked quizzically at Carl. "The future?" he repeated as a question, "You, my boy, take care of the future."

"I'm afraid," Carl told him, "the future will take care of me."

"How right you are!" Erdman grinned broadly, his wasted face almost malicious in the lamplight. "In our times, without facing the fact, young men and women expect to die violently. I think that makes for a very sad future even if a millennium results, which is highly improbable. Not for you, dear Carl, this sad comfort and peace of dying in bits and pieces, by spaced blows, so that in the end you do not care whether you live or die, for living is half death anyway, and death no more than what you have been doing every day for too many years. The true mark of a civilization is its ability to permit its citizens to die of old age in bed, but modern politics is a social invention to make civilization impossible. You will not die in bed."

"Then," Carl replied impassively, "I will die out of it."

Silence came between them and Erdman closed his eyes. Carl thought he was going to sleep and he began to read again the last few pages of what he had written, waiting for the even breathing before he left, but Erdman started to speak again. "Would you like to know what I most regret in life?"

Carl nodded, smiling, because he expected one of Erdman's terrible jokes. But the old man was serious.

"I regret that I married my wife because by the time she wanted to marry me I no longer cared and was ready for new adventures. But I had made such a fuss over her and carried on so much that I had to go through with it. I regret therefore and you will always regret every sacrifice you make for other people because of their weakness, their guilt, or their dependence on you. You will regret the sacrifices you make for truth, for honor, or for love. In fact, you'll regret every sacrifice that isn't to your advantage, because in the unconscious, which is the only mind that counts, everything which isn't a clear personal profit is a total human loss." He chuckled now. "Don't look so reproving. My marriage didn't turn out so badly, but sexuality and love are so fascinating, it's a shame to give them up for nothing. Think of how wonderful life would be if instead of battleships, planes and guns, the only armament industry was contraceptives and beds."

Erdman noticed the wry smile on Carl's mouth. "You think my mind is wandering and you're right. After all, a man so close to death as I am has a right to wander, to hesitate before the final cul-de-sac. But if you think I should be serious and give you some valuable advice . . ."

"I never asked," Carl interrupted.

"You're too polite. Here it is. I've been formulating it for several days now. Listen carefully. A free man always elects himself to the life he is going to lead, and only afterwards does he learn whether or not he has been elected. And this goes further. You must elect yourself to what you will be or else you will be drafted like those miserable wretches all over the world today. And this goes still further, for even if you are drafted you can elect yourself for what you have been drafted and this makes you free again. But if you do not elect yourself before or after, then you are not free, even if you are so isolated from life that nobody bothers to draft you. How's that?"

"I agree, but it's very complicated."

"Naturally. You think I'm the kind of man whose life can be summed up on a tombstone with a '*Here lies a loving husband, May he rest in peace*'?"

At ten o'clock Carl left Erdman who was trying to put this thought into a couplet in German. "What the hell?" the old man said. "Maybe it will keep my name alive, and if not it will put me to sleep."

206

In Erdman's study which now was his, Carl sat under the myths of Venus and worked on the paper. Curtin was leaving Castlehill in a few weeks to take charge of the psychology department in a Western university and Carl wanted the paper on little Emily finished and out of the way. He wondered if he should not eliminate the guesses at the end and let the case stand on its own, but it appeared in that way to contain too little, while with the few general ideas at the end, it seemed to hold too much.

Downstairs the doorbell rang. After a few minutes, there were steps in the hall, and steps went up past the landing behind his closed door, and far off he heard Erdman's door opening and closing. As the maid came downstairs again, Carl opened the door and stopped her. He wanted to know who was disturbing the old man at this hour when the doctor had left specific instructions against it. "That's what I told him," she apologized, "but he said he was leaving the country tonight and I knew Dr. Erdman was up so I called upstairs and he said show him up."

Carl nodded and turned back into the study. The maid went on, "It's a Mr. David Seawithe and he said he would like to see you too."

"Thank you," Carl said. He closed his door again and retreated to his desk. For a brief instant he felt a mild curiosity, but he had trained himself not to think of what was unimportant, and David Seawithe was completely unimportant to him now. He sat down and lighted a cigarette while he slowly reread one of the paragraphs he had written.

He went back to the formulating sentence, reading it again and again to convince himself that he really believed it. *"The biological aspects of psychology are general mechanisms of activity, of growth and decay, and while they condition the possibilities of human action, they do not explain or control it."* Could they, he asked himself? Might they? And he stared at the words until they disappeared, listening within himself for the least sign of hesitation.

He skipped down to the next heresy, for this was what these notions were, heresies. *"We can accept further that the social*

207

history of the human race indicates an unlimited plasticity and adaptability (which means ability to control) and physiological experiments indicate almost as much for the organism itself." This was a still more dangerous idea for it disputed the idea of human nature, of there being any such thing. And he turned back a few pages to a corollary notion. *"Compared with man most animals have only a rudimentary sexual life, and it is this plastic, this infinitely adaptable and controllable sensuality which has given rise to man's complex consciousness. It is sexuality again which drives consciousness into the external world, to reality; and therefore disfigurations in the sexual life, that is, mental disease, are the results of disfigurations of reality, of the social worlds that men inhabit."* He had written another sentence after this which he had crossed out, a question. *"We must ask ourselves whether there can be a science of psychology without a science of history."*

He didn't know whether this question should remain in the text, and he sat back in his leather chair and rested his cheek against his open palm, musing. Would the war, he wondered, stay away from him or absorb him, and if it came to him would he survive to answer any of these questions? The life of Gibbs appeared before him, the vision of this quiet scholar who had unlocked such vast fields of human control over nature without, so to speak, ever leaving his library, and if there was any life that Carl now wanted to lead, it was one such as that. Oddly enough the Gibbsian laws were basic to modern war, and if Carl died it would indirectly be Gibbs in his study who killed him. It would be nice to put on a man's gravestone: Killed by Gibbs's deductions from the second law of thermodynamics. And Carl was smiling when the maid knocked on the door and asked if Mr. Seawithe might come in, and smiling when David entered.

With a trench coat over his left forearm and hat in the hand, David hovered on the brink of the room, taking in the soft lamps shining on the books, the painted ceiling, the heavy red drapes drawn over the window, and on the floor the giant tufted rug with its Chinese designs, and he cried out with his old familiar energy,

"For six years I imagined what you and your life were, but I swear to God I never imagined anything like this." Then he started forward as Carl rose, calling to him across the long length of the room, "And where's your mustache?"

They shook hands and Carl sat down again while David flung his hat and coat on a couch and nervously walked up and down, to pause finally with arms akimbo, his head craned back examining the painted ceiling. He stared with amusement at the myth of Venus and Paris in which the story had been reinterpreted to show a naked goddess giving herself to the young man in exchange for the golden apple. "It's funny," David said, "but every time I look at a naked woman, real or painted, I think of Sandy."

"And how is she?" Carl asked.

"Fine. In Nevada. We're being divorced." And having delivered the news he sat down on the edge of the large desk and looked brightly at Carl, waiting for some appropriate remark.

Carl searched his mind for one and found nothing useful, so he remained silent.

"But no," David insisted, leaning closer to Carl, "you must say something. It must have some significance for you." He picked up from the table a Florentine dagger which Erdman used as a letter opener and played with it, tossing it by the haft from hand to hand, making little cutting thrusts with it. "It does, doesn't it?"

"Why," Carl replied slowly, "it signifies that you two are separating."

David dropped the dagger and stood up again. Little bolts of force flung him from one position to another, as if his organism had no constant flow, only a perpetual agitation. He was always on the edge of another motion, and now he exclaimed, "You must be a better psychologist than that."

"I only psychologize for money. What difference does it make what I think?"

"She thought it would."

"She was wrong."

Having delivered this frontal attack, David now retreated, for he had imagined the conversation would go another way. "I suppose," he said with a charming melancholy which quickly suffused his features, invaded his gestures, and slowed him down, "I suppose you're still angry with me because of the dirty trick I played on you so long ago. I suppose that's your point of view."

"It used to be."

"Isn't it any more?"

"If I thought of it any more, I suppose I would think so."

David approached again. "Look, Carl, Sandy told me you and she had been lovers last summer, and we talked everything over and we both agreed, the both of us, mind you, that we had made a mistake, acted, if you like, selfishly and ignobly, and that since you and Sandy still loved each other it was only right and proper for me to step out of the way. I'm not trying to make anything much out of this for myself. Believe me. I'm here on a diplomatic mission so to speak, that's my business, to tell you that Sandy is free."

Despite his outward calm, and Carl maintained his quietness, resting back in his chair, his cheek in the palm of his hand, a pressure of rebellion and irritation began to shake within his mind. He did not like being routed out of his office this way, out of his mood and life as he had created it, as if these two still had any claims on him. He said flatly, "She may be free, and you may be free, but I'm not."

Worried, David just stood there and stared at this unmoved man whom he had expected to storm into anger, argument, vexation. "You mean you're in love with someone else?"

"Hardly. I want Sandy neither for mistress nor wife."

"But she expects it. I mean she thinks of nothing else, of starting again with you, of being happy with you."

"For Christ's sake," Carl said in exasperation. "She'll just have to find something else to think about. What's this about anyway? What do you want?"

"I?" In all innocence David gestured vaguely above. "Nothing. I came to say good-by to Dr. Erdman. I'm going overseas for the State Department, and I thought since this was my last night in New York and since you were here anyway, to speak for Sandy.

210

We're still friends." And when Carl didn't speak, he darted one roving collecting glance around and said in astonishment, "Here you sit, quiet, retired, like an old man, as if nothing in the world were happening. I thought you were going to be a scientist."

It made Carl smile. "Here is where I practice my profession, or downstairs in a smaller and less flamboyant room with my patients. I've given up the test tubes temporarily."

Without any sense of incongruity, David began to pace the room and speak of the past. "I remember those days at the River Hospital and that strange laboratory of yours, and those rats and surgical operations. You seem like an altogether different man now, quieter, almost old and old-fashioned, and my father was right about you. Why don't you ever go up to see him? He always asks about you and what's happened to your career." But he did not wait for an answer, and finding himself at the desk again, as if surprised to be so close, he bent a troubled face to Carl and asked, "Why don't you forgive me? Why don't you put it down to my ignorant youth and its selfishness? I did want to help you and I did love Sandy, and you seemed not to. Put it down to anything you like, but forgive me." He began to stretch his hand out to Carl, as if he were mesmerized, as if he could not avoid touching the shoulder before him, and finally, almost with a shudder, pulled his hand away and started walking again, distraught, overexcited, torn from one end of the room to the other. "I tell you in all these years I've had no other friend, and I remember our friendship, and I regret everything, everything, you understand?"

Quite simply, and with simple emotion, Carl said, "Of course, if there is anything to forgive, I forgive you." He rose, trying to end this scene which had started so peculiarly one way and now was finishing so unexpectedly in another. And David almost leaped to him, holding out his hand which Carl took, and felt the warm quick pressure, and the eager face spilled its feeling quite nakedly out.

David abruptly turned and got his coat and hat. "I'm going now," he said in a soft and boneless voice, "and I'm glad that you feel as you do about Sandy, because if there had been no Sandy we

211

would have been friends through all these years, and now all that time is gone, and everything that might have been is wasted. It seems a shame."

They shook hands again at the door, and then Carl walked him downstairs and opened the street door for him, and the crisp night blew in upon them. David stood on the steps, his hat jammed down on his head, his trench coat wrapped around him, the collar up, hesitating, leaving and yet unable to leave. "Believe me, Carl, I never imagined that anything I would ever do could hurt you. But Sandy told me what it meant to you."

And Carl sickened, remembering how he had blabbed to Sandy, and poured out the suffering past. His dark face grew pale and ashamed, and he hung back in the darkness, out of reach, withdrawing, going away, afraid to be seen. Past David the black river flowed and beyond the wall of New Jersey, the ascending road going up in its graph of lights, the factory signs blinking, and he breathed the cold air, the neutral air, to revive his indifference. More than ever he hated the idea of personal relations like these, and he kept thinking of the room upstairs, of the silence there, of the unfinished work which was the only life he wanted, the unfinished work that could be finished.

"I wanted to speak to you for a long time," David went on urgently, "but I couldn't. Only now because I'm going away, because in this whole exploding affair, who knows what will happen and how we will end, only now could I face up to this meeting, and I'm glad it happened, in a way glad of the war that makes it possible. I'm sure we'll see each other again." And he ran down the steps as if chased, hurrying away along the drive, the wind catching his trench coat, fleeing.

Carl shut the door and went upstairs again, but as he stood before the rich redness of the library, he could not bring himself to enter. He could feel David's presence still grinding against his will, and he thought it would be better to talk to someone. He went up the next flight and saw the light under Erdman's door, and tapped and heard that rasping voice call out, "Come in."

When he entered, Erdman put down the book he had been

212

reading. "I expected you," he said dryly, "and tell me what your friend wanted?"

Carl sat down in his usual chair. He folded his hands over his crossed knees and said as unemotionally as he could, "David tried to palm off his wife on me. They're being divorced."

"And you said no?"

"Of course. Only I can't imagine why he came, and why after all he was so relieved when I wanted no part of it."

"Excellent," the old man said, like a physician who sees the expected symptom appear at the expected time.

"The whole thing," Carl continued, "had a kind of shameless frankness about it which I didn't like."

"Naturally."

"As if there were something else involved, and whatever it was never appeared."

"Precisely." And Erdman grinned and then began to laugh as he used to years before when he told one of his famous dirty jokes at a psychoanalytic lecture. "The sexuality of man," he intoned, "is a mirror held up before nature. Poor David! We never really got any place with his analysis. He had no time and I had no strength, although I was curious because of you. But he never loved this Sandy, this wife of his, never, never. He couldn't. He is a bitterly repressed homosexual who doesn't know it. And all these years he's been in love and doesn't know it."

"And you do?"

"Of course."

Between his folded fingers Carl felt a film of sudden sweat, and he broke his hands apart, and got up. He went to the door and stood there without looking back to Erdman. In the end he turned and said wryly, "Good night! You dirty old man."

As he closed the door he heard Erdman roaring with glee, shouting through choked syllables, "What a comedy for the textbooks!"

But Carl descended slowly, step by step, his hand sliding along the polished mahogany banister, marveling with sadness and dismay at the awful shapes that civilization stamped upon its people, and how he himself, who wanted only to be a mathematician of life,

213

stood like some innocent Newton beneath the apple tree and did not know until the apple fell how much of the mystery was in himself, how profound the knowledge, how incredible the involvement.

He went back to his desk and directed his attention to the question he had scratched out, and then after much consideration very carefully wrote it in again. In this way he launched his will upon the awful seas of history more terrible now than any before known, upon a struggle in which whole races and civilizations had foundered in failure and a just oblivion because they could not learn and would not change.

PART THREE
The Battle

i

ALL day long and now in the night the pilotless planes, the robombs, *Vergeltungswaffe eins,* V-1, fell one by one and without any rhythm on the filth of London. The dark city, spread over many hundreds of square miles like an enormous colonial animal with thousands of neutral centers, primitive and unintegrated, absorbed these minor deaths and destructions without loss of function, existing through everything, burnings, rapine, demolitions, gutting, for to die it had to die everywhere at once, and as yet the enemy had no such weapon. It lived into the present from its imperial prehistory, calcified in part into monuments, with suckers and feelers going away into the far corners of the earth for nourishment, floating upon a universe which, creating it, had itself been re-created to support the vast needs of this sprawling organism; and it quivered here and there when struck, it died here and there when hit, it erupted here and there when probed with fire, but it lived on darkly in the dusty September night, the blue lamps dull in the streets, curtains drawn, doors closed, throbbing and breathing, the greatest Hydra of them all.

In his two-room lodgings in Mayfair, Carl sat in the light of a single rosy lamp casually leafing through the pages of his book before going to sleep. It was only eleven o'clock but he was tired and his feet hurt from tramping the pavements on a dozen scattered errands.

The housemaid with the dirty and rather pretty face, with black silk stockings on fine legs, with an ugly goiter on her neck, had plumped up the pillows, removed the bedspread, opened the glass door between the bathroom and the alcoved bedroom, seen to the

217

blackout curtains, and then, as she had done so many times this past year, paused behind his chair and thoughtfully run her fingers over his shaven neck, kissed him on the ear and gone off with her two cats. He heard her laughing on the landing below as she joked with the navy petty officer whose room was crammed with all kinds of American supplies, from cigarettes to girdles, and finally her voice sank and became businesslike while she discussed with her partner the various ups and downs in the black market.

Carl could find nothing to read in the book, for his memory was quicker than his eye, finishing a sentence before he could scan it. On his lap the open pages lay unobtrusively while he regarded the dark sitting room with the leaning floor and the frayed rug. One of the strange conditions of this war was to deposit fragments of a man's life in different dwelling places as he moved stage by stage with more and more care to the point most threatening to his existence. This little apartment on Chesterfield Hill Street was a midway point looking south to the beleaguered continent and westward home, more dangerous than New York, more secure than the collapsing front where the armies were pounding to the German frontier. The walls were paneled in dark wood and in odd spots were touches of a shabby elegance. There was an exquisitely light Chippendale table against the wall on which he had piled the packages gathered during the day for his colleagues, and he reminded himself to be here tomorrow noon when the truck from the hospital would come by to fetch the pipes and books, the mufflers and scarves, and the three pairs of nylon stockings which Pamela had extracted from the tycoon below him.

One of his patients had mentioned under narcosynthesis Twain's *Life on the Mississippi* and after much searching Carl had found it and was sending that along too. Tempted to open the wrappings and read that casual, twining work so rich in another era, in dawdling summers and magical youth, he didn't move because in this time of death he could only remember that men had died there too, there in the summer mud and soft sunlight, and it was too much trouble to forget.

Carl looked down at his own book and closed it. The neat wrap-

218

per bore the title: *Scientific Method and Psychotherapy, by Dr. Carl Myers. The Gibbs Lectures: 1941. First English Edition.* It had been Curtin who had gotten the university to invite him, and now Curtin was Colonel Curtin, a very important administrator in Washington, and Carl was Major Myers in an Air Force hospital in England, and here was the book too, very plain in its wartime edition. It was a pleasure to look at it if not to read, and he wondered how much more he knew to say to those earnest and interesting students if the opportunity should arise again.

But at this moment, within the equilibrium of all the heterogeneous noises of London, he heard the distant planted seed of a motor truck roaring into the city from the far suburbs, and while he continued to stare at the end papers of the volume, no longer actually reading, while he forced himself not to stare but to read the scientific blurb, in his mind he had already distinguished between the normal and the abnormal, between the usual and the new, and he understood this was no truck but crude death, and like the memory of a well-known tune, the first notes supplied the whole phrase long before it occurred. If the flying bombs did not reach London with any definite rhythm in time, each bomb contained in its succession of sound and silence an internal order, its own phase rule.

He opened the book again as he listened and read the dedication to Wilfred Erdman, M.D., now four years dead, rotted and dissolved in eternity. To Erdman, Gibbs had merely been a name, but it was Gibbs who had discovered the laws of the equilibrium of heterogeneous substances, and these papers dealt with the most heterogeneous of all substances, the complex behavior of men some of whom across the Channel had sent this flying bomb to Carl, a man they did not even know. As he listened to the noise grinding up greater and greater, filling the sky, absorbing everything, becoming a universal solvent into which all differentiated sound disappeared, he recollected that Gibbs had only been thirty-two when his first papers had attracted Maxwell's attention, and now he himself was thirty-five. The including roar of the bomb dominated the entire city. Nothing else existed. It was like standing

219

at the base of Niagara, at the foot of that vast and overpowering tumult — and suddenly the river froze. It stopped flowing and crystallized into a gigantic pendant icicle and hung there above in absolute silence and cold.

Now, as in some marvelous pause of a Beethoven symphony, after so much preparation, the silence so abruptly formed, flowered, distending, opening a fantastic vacuum, an interval of nothing which the mind tried desperately to fill, to imagine, to complete, and Carl turned to the last page of the last lecture and read the concluding sentences.

> *"It is clear that all psychotherapies whether Freudian or non-Freudian are directed to the same end, which is to re-adapt the patient within himself to the accepted conditions of the social world about him, as if that social world were fixed and eternal, ultimate as the speed of light and therefore hopelessly unchangeable. But the opposite notion is equally possible."*

That was all he had written, the opposite notion. He had never stated what the opposite notion was, confining himself to estimating the degree of scientific method and precision in the descriptive and medical aspects of psychotherapy. But there had been two weeks after the term in which informally with half a dozen doctors various opposite notions had been expressed, and what remained now in memory was the thrill and pleasure of being with such minds, so eager to expose the unknown, so flattering in response, so faithful to truth if it would let itself be known. Carl had suggested a three-pronged approach, the physiological, the subjective, the social. The physiological, as a system of communication and control, would be abstracted to a set of laws, mathematically noted if possible. The subjective system would itself be reduced to its mechanism, conditioned by its social content as realized in the mind, mathematically noted if possible. Finally, the social environment would have to be stated in terms of its historical laws. Then transformation formulas could be constructed which would provide a linking up between all three and in this way a science could be provisionally formulated. There were in existence mathematical theories complex enough to hold all these variables. This synthetic approach had appeared most difficult to the doctors present, for they were trained in their specialties and did not know what really was going on elsewhere in the sciences, even in their own.

The silence still continued, so dense that he could hear nothing else, and he just sat there and listened to it, resting passive and empty, unable to think of anything else any longer.

In combat and in similar situations, such as this one, there were any number of attitudes to be adopted and Carl's temperament had selected a cheerless fatality in consciousness, the most ordinary acceptance he could find. But the unconscious, the soul itself, cared very little for cheerful or cheerless attitudes, useful or useless ones, brave or stupid ones. It retrenched each time at the center of its dark and passionate universe and waited to die.

Stupendous came the orchestral crash and imperceptibly Carl ducked his head.

The curtains facing the street sucked in and a puff of air went by him riffling the pages of the book, subsiding through the open bathroom door where the curtains billowed out into the alley. A few squares off there was a clatter of crumbling brick, of smashing glass. It was over again.

Reasserting itself, the city disclosed its first phrase again. The omnipresent nighttime sounds therefore disappeared.

Carl arose and set the book carefully down on the table beside him. Weren't all things fragile? Even the most massive of concrete and steel showed less power to survive than the soft-bodied men. Audibly he yawned, deciding to go to bed, and put out the light. In the darkness he walked to the windows and pulled back the curtains upon the brightness.

Carl was waiting for his leave orders.

A month in America beckoned pleasantly, if just for the change, and he thanked Curtin who was out there somewhere in the darkness of oceans and continents for writing that letter which would bring him home for an "important" administrative consultation. Curtin's private note had mentioned rather cryptically, "I want to talk to you about an important idea I have for two screwballs like us after the war." Even more pleasant was the fact that his brother's wife was now in New York, having given up her life as a "camp follower." Like so many women she had trotted after her husband with the child, named Carla after himself, trying to be near for the final months, but Bill had merely shifted from one training ground to another in America and when two years had passed, Juley had given up in disgust and returned to New York. Bill was trying by every means possible to get overseas, but he was luckier than most, ending up in the 84th Infantry Division, which seemed to be in preparation for some future war and not this one, as he had complained bitterly to Carl when the two sons, both in uniform, had stood solemnly at their dying mother's bedside and received her blessings. To Juley she had given the furniture and to her children a word of advice, "So you've found yourself a war at last. I can only tell you what my grandfather told my father. If you can stay out of the war, stay out of it. If you can't, try to stay home. If they send you near the battle, stand behind the general." The pain-wracked face had smiled, almost with an un-believer's cheerful irony. But they had buried her with full Catholic ceremonies, and Bill had returned to train endlessly for the battle.

It had turned out to be Carl whom Juley had seen off to the wars, and in the brilliant geometry of the moonlight it was easy to evoke her image and the last rather foolish night in New York. Carl had been sent over to join a unit and so had received his orders along with a certain amount of freedom. He knew when he would leave and had called upon his sister-in-law. They made the rounds of New York, the eating, the dancing, the drinks, and she had expended on him all the emotions she had saved up for her husband. At last, around the corner from the pier where after much secret nonsense thousands of men marched openly into the ship that would bear them off upon the adventure so few desired, she had embraced him, kissing him full on the mouth, and he had felt a desire to remain, holding her close, forgetting she was his brother's wife, feeling through her warm mouth the desire for life which so long had lain dormant in him. They stood like lovers, she in place of someone he might have loved, he in place of the one she did love, and they kissed for all lovers and lost ones. He remembered that now when there was no one else to remember, and he wanted to see her again. It was in these last corroding years, thinking back to his American life, that he had let his attachments fall upon his brother, his brother's wife, and their child named after him. Never close to his family, it was all the family he had, and he adopted them, at least when he felt the need.

On Charles Street the taxis went by and beyond the buildings Carl heard the cheerful voices of the officers who made the Red Cross Club there a hangout. Discharged from the shadows below, three soldiers appeared in the moonlit street, two men and a woman, and they strode by in unison whistling a popular tune. Carl leaned out of the window to watch them, and at last they disappeared in the bottomless darkness, the awful blackness of stellar space which the moon poured down on the burned-out buildings along with its sourceless light, for the brightness where it rested seemed to come not from the moon but to be of it, a phosphorescence, and the night collected in the shadows was hollow and infinite.

The dry warm odor of dust suspended in the air floated to Carl, a cloud composed of an infinite number of heterogeneous particles, the nebular dust of dying civilizations, the powdered fragments of bricks and dirt, the dead, too, of this war and other wars, of all the graveless dead in all the world, the enormous bomb dusts, and even the dry, the choking, dust of the past, of the men gone and dead here, of the savage history of this land, and the dusty exploding dreams, of which America was one, the dust of empire, the dust of India and the hot dust of Africa, the dust of deserts and of Pacific Islands where now too the war was running out. This dust was sterile, not like the dust out of which planets were born. This was historic dust, final dust, dead man's dust, and he let the smell of it crackle in his brain and ascend to lie powdery as moonlight on his brain.

Far off, at last, and he had somehow been waiting for them so he could be released into sleep, he heard the sirens of the rescue squad, and now the people who had that job the way he had his would come to do it, to tend to the living and cart away the dead, put out the fires, shut off the water, gas, electricity, to stop up this new wound in the carcass of London. He straightened back into the room and walked to his bed and got into it.

He rested his head on the down pillows. He lay perfectly relaxed and waited for the process to begin.

Whenever Carl went to sleep, the moment that first disengagement of attention took place, as the outside world was released and permitted to spin away, he found himself listening for the fears of night.

His limbs were snug and stiff beneath the blankets as in childhood. The windows were open, the eyes closed tight, the windows open not to smash from the sound wave, the eyes closed because behind the lids were comfort, withdrawal, forgetfulness of the fearful terrain. All lights out at last, the sun, the lamp, the moon.

The brain withdrew its brilliantly real tentacles of sight, so common-sense and accurate, and let fall dark, hairy spiderlegs of hearing into the tempting dark, a strange world. Unlike the eye, which is like science, the ear is like religion and knows everything by rumor. And now, as every night during these past years, the rumors began upon the edge of sleep, and he heard the cries, the filth of narcosynthesis, the men crying out their hates and fears of the civilization that had borne them, the shit, piss, screw against mother, father, God and country, against the self and all that had created the self. Each night like this, Carl heard them before he went to sleep, a million tongues in every dialect and local accent, in every range of voice, bass, tenor, baritone, and it did not matter, education, creed, race or belief, the clamor of tongues went up, circle on circle into a tower of Babel, it went up screaming against the horror and filth of life, shrieking an anathema against everything known, against the loved and unloved, and in despair against the very soul. He could never escape this moment before sleep, as if his conscience as a scientist needed this rehearsal of agony to

224

remain true to its task, and he feared this moment, and he desired it, for without it he could not sleep.

But a bomb went off and he heard rattling against the windows grains of rubble.

He awoke uneasily to listen and once again his windows rattled, and he got up, very tired, and walked into the violent moonlight and looked down in the street.

A soldier stood there and two women.

"Carl," the soldier cried out. "It's David."

And peering down into the fragmented light that glittered on the silver eagles of David's blouse, upon the gold of his cap, Carl saw his old friend waving a lobster in the air, the face laughing and calling. "Carl. It's David. I've thrown a ton of rocks against your window and two V-1's have blown up your neighbors. Wake up."

"When did you get back?" Carl asked from his window, leaning sociably on it as if this were a scene from one of his dreams.

"Just now. Let me in. London's too dangerous." And he laughed again, for he was just back from the front and could play at fear.

As Carl turned back into the room to go downstairs, he heard David telling his friends, "And that's Carl for you. Fast asleep while everybody else shakes in his shoes."

ii

THIS was not the first time Carl and David had met during the war, but each time was more a first time than the time before, and it was David who made it so. He could not bring himself to let his friendship for Carl grow beyond a beginning, fearing the future of a relationship he did not understand, a sense of attraction and wonder, a desire to explore, and deeply beyond a temptation more frightening than death itself, profound, perilous, cloudy, which threatened to shake him out of control.

Yet each time he was in London David came to visit Carl, and it was always a delight for Carl to see his oldest friend, charged with passion and light, as he was tonight, thin, tanned, looking ten years younger than the forty he had lost. His soldier's career, a combination of politics and combat, a throwback to the warrior priest, had brought him the usual honors, and these ribbons glittered on his tunic above the paratrooper's emblem which had been stitched on in tiny silver beads. David was meticulous in the customs of his branch of service, polished, athletic, smiling, and there had been no danger which he had not invited, no ordeal too violent to survive, wild or foolish, no adventure which he had not undertaken. In a few years the war had shaped him to a kind of ancient perfection which he so well understood, and he himself had helped the times make him over from what he once had been, a man who detested violence, a youth eager to serve the dispossessed, a rebel against received authority.

He never appeared at Carl's apartment without bringing a woman along, and tonight, Carl felt, must even be more special since there were two. These women were the convention upon

226

which David had fixed, a safety valve against himself, and Carl understood it as he understood so many of the conventions which men and women invented to help them through the continuing crisis of their lives.

Remotely in the night behind the blinds that were again drawn, two bombs went off, distant destructions without reference to the four in the room, David in the center, his back to the fireplace, his overseas cap still on his head and the lobster, boiled pink, in his hands. "I have here," he announced, "a *langouste* from France, not fit to eat, but proof that peace is on its way. The war is over, Carl, and those bombs you just heard are merely fun for the civilians, a last warning to look elsewhere for the meaning of life." He threw the lobster into the fireplace and took one of the women into his arms, "And this is Alice Carewe, Mrs. Alice Carewe, of England and Bucks, a dear friend of mine, whom I brought just for you tonight when we go out to celebrate my departure from the ETO."

"For me?" Carl asked. "Is she yours to give away?"

"Oh no," Mrs. Carewe said. "I asked for you."

Carl retied the knot in his bathrobe and made a little bow. "I seem to be the only one dressed for the occasion." And after letting a polite smile go to Mrs. Carewe, he turned back to David who had lighted a cigarette for the ATS lieutenant sitting on the arm of the rickety lounge chair, her tight drab skirt making a little tent over round, attractive knees.

"As for me," the lieutenant observed, "I'm hungry and I want to eat. I've had a terrible day."

"As for me," David added, "I'm hungry and I want to eat. But I've had a fine day. I turned over my little clique of eccentrics to another slave, and after appropriate ceremonies became a free man. Some time here, Carl, on political business, and then the States, and then, don't fall down, China."

"Ah," the lieutenant rose and adjusted her Sam Browne belt. "China. You can have China. I've got a husband somewhere in that God-forsaken yellow hole doing some kind of God-forsaken business for money no one ever gets to see." She turned to Mrs. Carewe. "Isn't your husband somewhere there, too, in a Jap prison camp?"

Mrs. Carewe nodded, a little shake of her fair head, while with her hand she gave a little fillip to her kerchief which fluttered like a dipped flag. "He was."

"What are we waiting for?" David demanded. "Can it be you, Carl?"

Quickly Carl let himself fall into the mood of this little company, although he would have preferred to see David alone, to talk with him about this China affair, and learn on what new misfortune David was thrusting himself. "Where are my pants?" he asked.

"There," said Mrs. Carewe. She turned to David. "But you said he was the wisest man in the world, and he hasn't said anything more profound than where are my pants. And you said he was the kindest, and he hasn't even kissed me hello, and you said he was the bravest, but he's just lazy enough to sleep instead of being frightened. And you said," and she paused, her eyes merry, a very kind smile upon her pale pink face, "I forget what he said, Lieutenant, what else did he say?"

The lieutenant was a slim, broad-shouldered girl, with a good figure and a full bosom that jammed against the too narrow man's shirt she wore. She had a retreating nose, a pile of brown hair which ducked out from under her cap, and she carried her right thumb in the shoulder strap of her belt. She thought for a moment, wrinkling her brows.

"What did he say?" Carl called from the bathroom.

"Do you have any whiskey in the house?" David asked. "And what have you been buying in these empty stores?"

"It's for the fools who have to stay behind at the hospital," Carl answered. "The whiskey's in the cabinet near the bed. I'm waiting for orders to go home."

"Home?" Alarm, like a small bell, rang in David's voice, and as Carl appeared in the bathroom door, buttoning his shirt, he found David there, the whiskey bottle still unopened in his hand, waiting, almost reproachful. "But you didn't say anything."

"You didn't give me a chance." The two women were standing next to each other trying to remember what the other thing was

228

that David had said. Carl called to them. "There are glasses in the bookcase."

"What for?" David asked. He shook the bottle and then held it up to the light. "What for?"

"A leave. And to see Curtin. And then back, that's all, until they let me out of this country."

Mrs. Carewe walked with a rather stately step up to Carl. She had opened her tweed coat and underneath was a gray wool dress, very beautifully cut. On her heavy, smooth white neck she wore a string of pearls, so low in tone, so glowing within, that they had to be real, and a strand of her fair brown hair had fallen loose upon her heavy cheeks, hollowed in the center, a head carved and reposeful, a mouth classic, neither full nor meager, on which no lipstick had been smeared. It made her all the paler, the pinker, with her gray eyes and the beautiful brows, unplucked, a little ragged over the bridge of the nose, but finely arched. She seemed in this way shaped and fine, careless and natural, as was her voice; and her accent was not forced either, it was English but without fantasy as David's was American without any touch of localism. Now she stood up to Carl, his own height, and asked, "What do you mean let you out of this country? Are we going to have one of *those* evenings?"

"In the army," Carl said without letting himself resent her, "every place you are is terrible, goes on too long, and is spoken of as that place you want to leave. England is home to you, but it's just another hospital army camp to me, filled with sick soldiers suffering and bored, just as I am. And I will talk about it as I always talk. If you want to defend England, you don't have to defend it from me. I know nothing about your country, except that my English colleagues are as good as my American ones and a little more polite. Are you satisfied?"

It thrust her back a step, this even-tempered but altogether unexpected answer to what was, after all, just a favorite gambit of hers for baiting Americans. And she looked up to David who was grinning, and then turned to the other girl. "I say, Lieutenant, I remember now. He said the major was the meanest man."

229

"I did not." David laughed. "You invented that."

"I know what it was," the lieutenant joined them now as Carl knotted his tie, and with a strong accustomed hand she helped him on with his tunic. "He said the major was a psychiatrist and we should behave because he understood all our secret sexual wishes. That was it. How could we have forgotten?"

Mrs. Carewe colored a little, a little more pinkly, until in the rosy lamp she almost glowed. "I think the scientific answer is that we're afraid to remember."

"We can get a taxi in front of the Red Cross Club," Carl said. "Where shall I take you for this celebration?"

David offered the bottle to the lieutenant who took a swig, as did Mrs. Carewe, and then Carl and David.

"It's ordered," David said, putting the bottle down on the little table next to Carl's book. He saw the title. "What do we have here? The English edition?" And proudly with a friend's unenvying pride he handed the book to Mrs. Carewe. "Now, look here. I told you."

She picked it up, read the title, and then without raising her head just glanced up, a motion of the eyelids to Carl who waited, expecting anything. "Can I take it along to dinner?" she asked. "I promise to give it back."

"You may have it." He bowed a little.

"And will you write something in it?"

"After I know you a few minutes longer, Mrs. Carewe."

"Oh!" She took his arm as he snapped off the lights. "Call me Alice. I've lived so long in the American wonderland you men brought over from that former colony of ours that I expect every man to call me kiddo, baby, or sis. Alice is quite proper."

"Yes, Alice," Carl said obediently. He closed the door and marched downstairs arm in arm with Alice Carewe. Below David had already opened the front door upon moonlight.

"See how bright the moon is," she said. "Do you admire natural things too?"

"Only natural things," he told her, and entered with her upon the dreaming night, the glitter and softness of it, into the street

230

cut in half by eternal blackness and eternal light like the moon itself. She took his arm again, and he felt through her tweed sleeve the softness of her arm. "I like your unplucked brows and your unrouged mouth."

"That," she said, "is not principle, only laziness and confidence. With so many free men around, one need only have the appropriate organs. The rest is poetry."

As they walked down Charles Street to the Club the rest was invested in poetry, for the moon hung in the blackout windows and transformed the gray streets into a river of brightness, the moon caught upon glass and iron, found jewels everywhere, and the moon was in the trees at Berkeley Square. It was so vast a sky above, cloudless and lighted, and there so close, round and wonderful was the moon, and its greatness was the magic of how it hung in space surrounded with stars, for this was the perpetual enchantment of the firmament.

"How good the moon is to cities," Alice said as they waited for a taxiload of American officers to discharge.

"It's good to all of us," David cried out. "It enchants all of us, and Carl especially, because he's a dark and brooding man and the moonlight shows him up. He's the only shadow here." With an extravagant gesture he waved them into the cab, and his hand flashed in the pale light like a naked swimmer.

They piled in, David the last, sitting on the jump seat while Carl sat between Alice and the lieutenant, and the trim cab darted off to Soho and the Greek restaurant that was a favorite with the Americans.

Just as they turned round the square, the motor noise of the cab suddenly drowned in the frightful tumult of a flying bomb which seemed to be right in the cab with them, and Carl looked anxiously past Alice, out of the open window into the magical sky. There was nothing to be seen there but he leaned, looking, while David continued to joke with the ATS lieutenant, playfully trying to pull her skirt down over her nice knees.

The noise was deafening, immense, and the bomb rode with them. The driver pulled up at the curb, and slid the window

231

back. "I think it's looking for us," he said, "and there's a nice door-way there." He opened his door and ran to the building where an outside stair went down to a grated cellar.

"Come back," David shouted after him. "Come on back. We'll be late for our supper."

The cab began to tremble with the vibration of the bomb, the streets, the houses seemed to rattle, and still Carl could not see anything. He leaned back in his seat. "Where the hell is it?" he asked of anybody.

"I've got a good mind," David said angrily, "to drive the cab myself. What the hell kind of a driver is that?"

Alice pressed tightly against Carl, and as she did so, the tornado of noise stopped dead. It cut off in air and hung the silence upon them, hung silence gross and thick as moonlight upon all things, froze the taxi still, and the street still, and the trees still, and the buildings still and Alice pressed against Carl and cried out in a low voice, "Please. Please."

He put his arm around her, embracing her like a fierce lover, and from her clothed flesh there arose delicately the fragrance of a perfume. "What kind of perfume is that?" he asked.

She tried twice to say it and finally succeeded. "Chanel Number Five."

David put his head out of the window and looked around curiously, his eyes alight, the moonlight blazing upon him, upon the silver eagle on his cap. "Ah," he said triumphantly, "there it goes. Right behind those buildings."

Alice trembled without control and clung to Carl as if he were a wall, as if he could cover and shield her. She tried to press within his body, to disappear, her face against his face, her mouth crushed against his cheek.

The explosion arched sound and wind like an escaping spring into the air, and roared with breaking walls and the wild clatter of glass, and things began to fall everywhere, and the taxi window shattered behind Alice, blowing out, and she screamed against Carl's face, a smothered shriek that penetrated his heart with its agony and dominated his own fright with her terror which, being hers, he did not feel as such but only as a need to protect her, to shield, to comfort her.

"Well," David announced calmly, "it's all over." And he stuck his head out of the window again and started to yell for the driver, who came out of his basement and got into the front seat, started up the motor again, and drove off.

"All present and accounted for," David said, and he put out a gentle hand and pulled the lieutenant's skirt over her knees. "Your laundry is showing."

Slowly Alice disengaged herself from Carl's arms. She leaned her head against the back of the leather seat and turned an exhausted face to the cab roof looking up with an inward glance, the emotion draining from her, leaving her limp. And with that characteristic glance which Carl had noticed before, she looked at him without moving her head, just a sideways glance from the eyes, the lids half closed. "I'm terribly ashamed," she said. "Terribly."

"What for?" David said. "Didn't Carl protect you, and us? He saved our lives."

"And how did I do that?" Carl asked. He took out his cigarettes and handed them round, and each took one while he lighted each in turn, and they smoked while the cab twisted and turned into the depths of Soho.

"Because," David told him, "I do not think it's your time to die, and therefore we're lucky to be with you."

"And what makes you think I have a special time that's different from any man's?"

A secret look passed its hand upon David's handsome face and he seemed to be talking to himself, "It isn't time," he said gravely, "for our friendship to end."

⋯
iii

"WAR is the great provider." David smiled to take the brutality out of his words.

"I suppose you mean," Carl took him up, "that it's provided the atmosphere of this place." And he looked around at the tables crowded with Americans and their girls, in uniform and out of it, at Englishmen and their Americans, in uniform and out of it, at the stuffed birds hanging from the walls and the stuffed fish plastered against plaques, at the mural of the fruits of the sea, pale pink and green, at the round voices, at the whole texture of the Greek restaurant, collegiate, the businessman's five o'clock bar, the newspaperman's late restaurant, and the sodden under-pinning of dear old England in Soho. The bulbs in the chandeliers were tinted with rose and the wall brackets carried electric candles tinted in yellow, the floor was tiled in red and blue and overlaid in spots with thin red carpets. Against one wall stood a great side-board, black with age, heavily grained and polished, and on it the cold fish and colder crustaceans, the cold boiled vegetables and smoked meats, the salt, the peppery, the spiced, waited. The move-ment was constant here upstairs, and downstairs the general public which was mostly the same but more casually present carried on with a great feeding rumble, the building locked away from the world, sociable, noisy, comradely and terribly expensive.

"I mean," David added, this time without a smile, his brown thin face almost black in the strange afterglow of light, "I mean that it makes life serious."

With a little mockery of both of them Alice begged, "Give me, O Lord, the frivolity of peace and crisp bacon with an egg in

234

the morning." She collected a gratuity of smiles from Carl and the lieutenant, but David ignored her, for this was his celebration, and the end of the evening was coming on and there were many things he had to say to Carl.

Beyond the drawn blackout drapes of this narrow, densely thronged room, fragmented and distracting with too many voices, too much alcohol and too much food, out in the midnight streets of London, far off in some treelined suburb where already the leaves were falling, a flying bomb exploded, was heard, and not noticed. The dead were far away like all the others far away, Carl thought, far far away.

"I do not," David explained, "wish to toast war for that would be barbarian. But I toast those events which force whole nations to take their existence seriously."

No one knew what to say to this and the lieutenant, who was the drollest, finally raised her glass and mumbled a cheerful "Amen."

Behind them at a table filled only with men, jammed shoulder to shoulder on narrow chairs, an American journalist was wondering how it would be possible to hold the readers of his magazine during peacetime, because reader interest, overstimulated by the excitement of battles and large events, would be bored by fires, crimes and politics.

"Give me back the days, O Lord," Alice prayed again, "when a good acid-bath murder was the greatest thrill."

But David granted his attention to no one. He spoke always almost directly to Carl, and Carl felt that the women were there so that David could speak of these things, that he had brought them along and arranged everything to provide an opportunity, and everything he spoke of, the way he said it, was to draw Carl to him, to collect him personally and yet in such circumstances that it was social and not personal, to prove he was more than a daring soldier and that his present life was not an accident of the times but the fulfillment of what he always wanted it to be. David spoke again. "It is said that war is merely the continuation of politics. They mean that politics is always a preparation for war.

235

Only in wars, in general cataclysms, do nations move forward or perish."

"Forward?" the lieutenant asked. "And where is that?"

"Into the asylums and graves. And when they perish, likewise," Carl answered.

David folded his hands around his glass and leaned over it, his crisp head pointed to Carl. "Don't they go there in peace and without purpose? What, after all, are we waiting for in peace?"

"At least for an end to the political blunders," Carl replied. "We waited for them to end and they did not end. Now the war that everybody dreaded is forced on us and we proceed to do in the most horrible way what our rulers refused to do in the easiest way. They could've resigned." He drank his Cointreau all at once having no patience for little drops of sugar and alcohol. "Of course, I speak poetically. Rulers never resign. They are kicked out. But now these same idiots are our prophets."

"You think," Alice asked, "that it was a mistake for us English to fight?"

"I have the usual tested opinions," Carl said. "I believe them. Fascism brought war and through war we defend ourselves against their war. There's nothing else to do. But I refuse to be exhilarated even when I do not refuse to serve. Look," he concluded wryly, "at the company I keep."

"Now, wait," David said. "You talk like all the rest, Carl, and you shouldn't. Two bodies cannot occupy the same space at the same time. Kingdoms and states are great organizations of matter and men and there is room in the world for only one at a time. War is inevitable. Ideas do not count, they are only useful. Reforms do not count, they are only useful. The slogans do not count, they are only useful. What counts is which shall win, and that isn't even a tossup, because there is hardly ever any doubt that in the end one will move forward, the one which for the time has the power, the intellectual and material energy. This is the law of history and civilization. A final law like any natural law. Sometimes nations are pleasant places for most of their citizens and sometimes they're not, and for the conscious individual, his problem is not to have

236

a philosophy of history, but a sense of accomplishment at the heart of the whole movement, as deep down as he can get where the thing moves, where in fact a man meets a man, and men meet men as instruments of history. In the end there's a contraction of the civilization in power, it dies. The time to live in a state is when it feels its strength, because then every time you act it's a victory. And I think you and I are lucky because our country, blind, stupid, foolish, blundering, is moving forward. We're forced to. The thing to do is to make the inevitable the faith because then the force, the energy, is in you and a whole life makes sense, through and through. That's it, of course, to make sense through and through."

Carl didn't like the mystical tone of this, but he saw no point to examining it now. He played away from it and answered only because David hung there, tense over his glass, waiting, and the two women who were the defense against personalities sat there waiting too, not quite sure that David meant anything for them. "Well, we're lucky anyway to be on the winning side, if we are on the winning side, and in a position to enjoy it."

"You don't agree with me?" David said. "Perhaps I'm not saying it just right."

"My opinion doesn't count," Carl smiled at him, that same quick smile that David always remembered from their earliest days, so tender in his sullen face, a surprising smile which came very often now in the life he led, a smile that was needed for the work he did and the feelings he possessed in the work. "Besides, I'm a postwar man. I've got the postwar temperament. I don't rise to great occasions like wars. I've got that old postwar feeling already." He nodded his glass at David. "You bring me that future world of yours and I'll tell you how I like it." He knew he wouldn't like it at all, and he felt sorry for David who, not liking it either, had yielded by giving a religious twist to the detestable and thus elevated it into the inevitable.

The journalist behind them was saying to his audience, who listened attentively for the speaker was highly paid, had been to every battlefront and was close to the War Office of the British and the General Staff of the Americans, "To carry on great democratic wars, the mass media are absolutely necessary. Millions of people must be made to understand the issues in simple dramatic terms. Without the press, and its allied fields, modern war would be impossible."

"My God," Alice exclaimed, and turned her head. Carl watched this, watched the life of her body turning and returning, remembering her pressed into his arms, and the fear of death shaking her flesh. "What *is* he talking about?" she demanded of anyone. And she said it loudly so that Carl could see the journalist turn to see who was listening, and saw his face redden in the redness of the stuffy room, saw his head face the other audience again with a determined swing, and heard the voice take up its credo for anybody to listen to now, especially the next table.

Definitely the journalist declared, "It's ideas that win or lose wars. It's the understanding that the masses have of their role in the war that makes it possible to carry on the fight. The press and radio, the films, every means of communication make democracy a living idea so that ordinary men and women are willing to lose everything, even their lives, in order to preserve their way of life against dictatorship."

Alice flung herself gaily into this offstage combat. She had a very clear and even voice, finely modulated, and she raised the level so it could be distinctly heard behind her while Carl saw the malice touch her mouth and glitter in her eyes. "Ordinary people live the same way all the time, under a dictatorship or alongside of it. They work very hard, they do not have much money, and they like to bet on games. They read the newspapers because they have been taught to read."

"Would you," Carl asked, "like to hear something that sounds scientific?"

"Wasn't I?" she asked.

"Listen carefully," Carl enjoined her. "This is my last word on the subject and I just discovered it. The chief tactical and psychological problem in war is to get sufficient numbers of men in such a contradictory position that they think they are or actually are so placed that they cannot escape death or the fears of death without killing their opponents, real or imagined. The press, radio, pulpit and films bend all their efforts to accomplish this psychologically by using whatever ideas, true or false, that come to hand."

David remained crouched in his former position and he looked steadfastly at Carl as if no one else existed in the room. "You let Alice argue with that journalistic hack, Carl, and listen to me."

The journalistic hack heard and he did not like it. He was a very large and powerful man and he twisted in his too small chair and turned his heavy, angry face toward David. "Were you talking about me?" he asked. It was an unfortunate question, a diplomatic blunder.

The lieutenant and Alice exchanged quick delighted looks, and drew their chairs a little to one side, pleased that something more real was going to happen, and somehow, although the journalist had not spoken very loudly, everyone in the room knew at once, and while the war was, of course, the biggest thing in the world, this private altercation was the most interesting.

David did not even look at the man. He held his hands a little more tightly about his glass and paid full attention to Carl. Carl felt no fear of a fight, for all such things were nothing beside the delirium of this time, but he had within him still, hard and indissoluble as a rock, the memory of that fight to which he had been subjected, and he could not bring himself to be near another. He was facing the journalist and so he spoke, "I was not speaking to you, and I don't even know how you managed to hear what I said."

David bent his head a trifle so that with the very corner of his face he was addressing the journalist. "When we want to talk to you, we'll tap you on the shoulder. And when we want you to listen, we'll tap you on the ear. And when we want you to speak, we'll kiss you on the mouth. But since we've done none of these things, I can't understand how you think we know you're here."

Carl felt himself indecently present as this comedy worked out, the journalist egged on by the presence of so many people as well as by his good opinion of himself, and David with the two women and his friend. Carl thrust himself within the stupid argument again. "Perhaps," he said easily so that everyone could forget, "we've all been celebrating too much."

It was a mistake, for the journalist seized this weakness and stood up, and now he was standing all by himself in the crowded room and he was in a fight that he thought he would win. Besides he was a civilian with a soldier's experience, more than most, and he had his pride, and after all, these were merely two officers who by rights should have been in the battle and not in London having a drink and a dinner. It was stupidity mounting on stupidity and he was stuck with it but not too unhappy. He rose to his full six feet, his whole hulking height, and he squared his big shoulders and his great strong face grew tight and muscular. "I," he said as loudly as he could, "haven't had a drink at all. And if you're all drunk that's no excuse."

This was another step in the theory that politics is a preparation for war. For David and Carl there was now the choice of continuing to argue which would end in a fight or leaving the restaurant. But there sat Alice and the lieutenant, sporting and alert, confident that their side would come off best.

Carl didn't know what to do next. He had been insulted and his friends had been joined to him. He did not feel insulted, or angry, or anything but disgusted with the progress of the brawl. As for the white faces of the restaurant where in quietness everyone sat, not eating, but sipping a drink if there was one, or smoking a cigarette if one were lighted, or lighting one if none were, all these faces of both men and women were expectant with the usual attitudes, and since the war had involved them in the customary manly attitudes of combat, they favored his table with their attention and awaited the next step.

As a boy raised on the streets where no honor counted so much as victory, he knew the best thing was to kick the big man in the balls. If not, then the smartest thing was to run. Running was, at the moment, impossible, because here he stood in an army officer's uniform and David was sitting there quietly and David would not run, and the women gave no signs of being afraid of what was to come. The conversation had been too dull and they were too bored to leave the scene when so much excitement was brewing. He looked past the big journalist to the table which was wreathed in superior smiles, a tableful of American officers from the propaganda divisions and a few English civilians. It was intolerable that they should be amused, and yet he cared very little if they were. Had he been alone he would have left, but there was no leaving now, and he wondered if there was something to say that would disarm the big journalist and let the fight peter out in mutual apologies.

But David had been given an expensive middle-class education and trained on the playing fields of private schools and Harvard, and the ritual was more familiar to him. He said to the journalist, "Well, you evidently need a drink. Have one." And he flung the sticky glassful of Cointreau into the man's face.

There was a sigh, a breath of fulfillment in the other diners, for this was so formally the next step, and the atmosphere of the room adjusted up one stage in pressure while a waiter stepped in front of the buffet to protect the hors d'oeuvres.

Now occurred the long count which was only a brief moment, since Carl's table had taken the appropriate move and the next one was up to the journalist who stood there amazed, and yet not astonished, for he had expected something. The alcoholic odor invaded the entire warm room and fat drops of sugary liquid dripped from the heavy face upon his clothes. The two women did not laugh because this was serious. It was the first physical move, the border incident, so to speak, and border incidents were regrettable affairs that ended in mutual bows, or the first stormy signs of war, depending on the intention. The journalist was stuck with the smiles of his table, for the smiles went away, and anger appeared on the faces of his friends and they looked at him stirring with resentment, urging him forward by their attitude and yet at the same time cleverly remaining as watchers.

Carl felt sad and bored with the whole thing as he had with the conversation on war. All the pleasure of seeing David was gone and he was back in the cage with the times, but no longer as a

241

doctor. He would have to take part in this brawl, and it might bring trouble with the authorities, excuses, denials, hearings which would take time and might interfere with his leave. He wondered if he should stand up and bring the first attack on himself, whether it was the right thing to do, or let David go first and see what the circle of friends behind the dripping journalist might do. He remembered the soldiers at the hospital who in their dreams raged against violence and war and lived with fear, and yet when convalescing liked nothing better than to sit around over a beer and remember their brawls in training, or that great night when they broke up a public house in Apsley Guise. There seemed to be no end to the tension generated in their lives. Each layer cleared revealed another layer concealed and more intense, more fiercely knotted, for it was their whole existence that had rotted and not only one little incident that was more than they could bear. They could bear nothing. And yet Carl felt no tension now, even in this fight which was drawing closer and closer, and remembering that David had been through much heroic action and therefore had more of his manliness to defend, he felt it would be better for him to stand up and exchange a few cursory blows which would satisfy the honor of everyone while the waiters and friends rushed in to prevent a real fight.

So he stood up like a man at a tailor's waiting to be fitted to a suit that was not quite his size, and he was shorter than the big journalist who drew back his hand in a fist, and the restaurant grew still and Carl felt a little sick to his stomach remembering his beating in Tarrytown. But he waited patiently so that it would be clear that the journalist struck the first blow and this at a man who had not even thrown a drink in his face. In case there was any trouble, it would be clear who was drunk and who was not. Drunkenness was always the excuse and not the fact that there were so many people around whose expectations had to be satisfied, for this was fame and he recalled, as he watched the fist, how the Mohammedan prince captive in Renaissance Italy had laughed at the knights who risked their limbs in mock battle, saying that such things were fit only for slaves.

242

David who was still seated said dryly, "If you hit my friend, or me, I shall surely kill you."

The journalist's arm was in motion but it arrested and drew back, still holding the stance, the great shoulder muscles knotted in the tight uniform with the white blaze of a noncombatant, and David got up and leaned his knuckles on the table. The left side of his tunic was exposed with all the ribbons and the paratrooper's emblem, and the journalist listened and looked, and everybody knew with a panic sense that David meant it, that he would at least try, and that there was going to be no pleasure in this thing, only something terribly serious. The journalist knew it too, and he waited but could not withdraw.

He had, of course, nothing really tragic to worry about, because his friends understood together with him what might happen now, that this had gone beyond who insulted whom, and that the hard and very thin man leaning on the table did not belong to their civilian code which was the code of the army generally. They felt very strongly that this bemedaled paratrooper had his own ideas of what was necessary to his honor, medieval as that might be, and it frightened them, so that they arose like a flock of croaking crows and surrounded their friend and bore him off, expostulating all the while in a general cackle.

At last they were gone, and there stood Carl, patiently waiting, and David leaning across the table with a serene face, and the two girls alert in their chairs, and the restaurant all white with faces and very still. As the glass doors closed behind the saviors of peace, someone started to talk in a corner table, and voices went up everywhere very loud, and Carl looked over to David who smiled at him affectionately. Carl shrugged his shoulders and sat down and David did the same, while the two women rejoined the table, shuffling their chairs forward. David called the waiter to him and asked kindly to have his glass refilled, and Carl slouched moodily in his seat and felt very tired.

It was difficult to start speaking again and everybody was happy to see another correspondent rush over to the table, this time a man with curly hair and a pleasant round face, plump and peaceful,

243

calling out, "Why, David Seawithe, you old son of a bitch." And he was shaking hands with David who blossomed into geniality and introduced Jack Warren of the NEA, an old friend.

Mr. Warren's arrival, like the first juicy scandal after a serious war, was overwelcomed. He was surrounded with smiles and handshakes and offered a drink, and he sat back in his chair and held a fat pipe to his mouth. "You'll hear from your general about this," he said to David. "That man is a big civilian noise."

David grinned boyishly. "He had better complain before the week is out because by then I'll be a general myself."

It was a relief to laugh again, to laugh at anything that seemed to be funny, but David, who laughed the loudest, stopped first and said, "It's the truth. Next week I'm to be a brigadier and then in a month I'm off to China to take a command." He looked over to Carl as he accepted the general congratulations. "It was what I wanted to talk to you about especially."

"Yes, General," Carl said, and ordered a bottle of champagne.

"But champagne," Alice exclaimed, "is unforgivable. It's even too expensive for Americans. You have to be an Argentinian businessman to afford it."

"In private life," Carl explained gravely — this was what the evening had finally become — "I'm a businessman in Argentina."

"Really," she said, and smiled to him, not for the joke but for his creditable performance during the brawl, and she put out her soft hand and laid it on his and squeezed it a little affectionately, happy to be with men she could respect and still forget this London and the flying bombs she could no longer withstand.

They toasted David with the champagne and the proprietor arrived with a second bottle because he was making a fortune out of the war and was in addition particularly happy that a fight had not occurred. In the end, after a few rounds, David and Warren settled upon each other with great interest talking about China, of whose military and political situation they both seemed well informed, while Alice, her hand still on Carl's, nodded sleepily in her chair. He smoked a cigarette, becalmed in the light fruitiness of the drink, prepared to spend the night this way or any other way,

244

relieved that nothing was happening. After the third bottle was consumed, she inclined her stately neck toward him, her face close, her mouth whispering against his ear, "I'm very tired. Very. And tomorrow at eight I have to report as a secretary to one of your American war agencies and I should go to bed. Would you mind taking me home now?"

Although David was turned away from them and they were together like two people playing at love, he seemed to know at once and sprang to his feet. "It's late," he said. "I want to say a private word to Carl and then he can take you home, Alice. Do you mind?"

"Not at all," she said.

David drew Carl out of the room, behind the glass doors into the cool corridor, and he spoke swiftly, his eyes uneasy and darting everywhere but to Carl's face. "I do have something particularly important to ask you, Carl. We'll get together later, if you don't mind."

"Of course." Carl waited to hear if there was anything else, but this was all, and he realized it was only David's way of showing the two women that it was Carl whom he had particularly wanted to see and that they did not count, but were his private public.

David clung to his arm. "Believe me, it's important."

"Of course."

And smiling affectionately, David steered Carl back into the room and like Alice he whispered in his ear as they marched to the table, "After all, it's always a celebration to meet again, to be alive and meet. You know how important your opinions are to me."

iv

ON the doorstep of Alice's little house in a dead-end mews, attended by an impatient taxicab, its motor running and the blackout lamps drowned in moonlight, Carl said good night.

She unknotted her kerchief and shook her hair loose into the moon which blazed over the low roofs, firing the black slates with a china pearl, powdering her face with a radiant talc, and like a great shining moth clinging to the old black wall of the tall dark church that blocked the end of the way. She extended her hand which he took and pressed. "Good night," he said again.

"Good night," she repeated after him, without dismissal, but as she heard the sound again she looked above his shoulder and he turned to watch over the roofs the fiery tail of a flying bomb as it sailed with dogged swiftness over the distant park and into the piled-up buildings of the city. They waited like experienced travelers and heard first the silence and then the concussion.

"A very busy night." Carl put his cap back on his head.

He was ready to leave and took a backward step when she asked, "And when do you expect to leave England?"

"Sometime this week when the orders come through. Shall I see you again?"

"Please do. I like modest men of energy and talent." She executed a little flurry with her kerchief and added, "It would be nice if this were tomorrow and we were meeting again."

"Thank you."

"Besides, I hate to go to sleep. I suppose I should get sleeping tablets or something. But I've always felt it was even more cowardly than shaking."

246

There was a pause now and the motor ran on at the curb while Carl waited to be discharged.

"Tell me," she asked, "why did you stand up when it was David who after all had invited the fight?"

He contemplated her with pleasure for she was very lovely there in the opened doorway, the darkness of the hall behind her and the moonlight washing across the first few steps. Her coat was open and the pearls glowed, and her eyes caught the shining distant radiance of the skies in them. The moist mouth with a little shadow under the lower lip and a half-moon of shadow underneath the chin was pushed into prominence, made heavier, formed full as the lip of a pitcher. There was no wind in the dry warm night. Behind him he heard the motor cut off.

"We're keeping the driver up all night," he said and he no longer wanted to leave her. "If you're not sleepy, and since I've already shown my good intentions by saying good night, why don't you invite me up?"

She gave a sage little laugh. "I wondered how long you'd wait to accept."

He walked back to the cab and paid the driver who accepted the money and looked past him to the awaiting woman, a cautious glance without malice. After the cab disappeared at the other end of the mews, Carl returned to Alice who still leaned against the doorframe.

She walked in before him saying, "I'll make some tea." He took another look down the street before he followed her in and felt the charge of its appearance sink directly and eternally into his memory, the long double line of low buildings, the round stones of the street, the cascade of light, and there beyond vaulting and serene the awful sky.

From within she called, "I can't turn on the lights till you come in." And he closed the door and stood in the darkness, sensing the house for the first time as a darkness overwhelmed by an ancient woody smell, a little astringent with damp, a tag of wood smoke, and mixed with it faintly her perfume.

The lights went on.

247

She was smiling there at him, one hand still on the switch, and then she wheeled around and started to take off her coat and he helped her. He hung it on the pegs of the wall. "We're shut up downstairs for the duration." She waved at the closed doors in the low-ceilinged hall. She went up the stairs and he followed her, observing her legs for the first time, very full and shaped, ending in low black shoes, the ankles pinched in and delicate. He was enjoying the sight of them when he recalled the stand under the clothes pegs with a man's rolled umbrella and two canes. On the walls along the stairs were posters from Spain, advertisements for bullfights, gaudy and shellacked.

After Alice lighted the lamps upstairs he saw how comfortable and permanent the sitting room was, with fine upholstered chairs, old without being worn, and the walls covered with a rough beige cloth on which were hung many lively colored lithographs and a few drawings.

"Make yourself comfortable," she said, and went up the two steps at one end of the room that led into a small hall. Off he heard her running water into the teapot, and he stood there regarding the room, the Chinese lamp bases, the little faïence pieces set here and there and the fireplace with old wood ashes in it. He tried to imagine what kind of man her husband was but every sign of him, if it had once existed, was gone unless the crayon drawing of a pretty little boy was of her son.

He walked over and stood before it. The child, if it were hers, had no likeness to the mother, and when Alice returned and found him there, she said, "That's my boy. He's in the country with his grandmother."

They sat down on the long soft sofa and he offered her a cigarette and took one himself. "Now tell me," she asked again, "why you stood up first to that man instead of David?"

Her eyes were weary with little patches of darkness under them, and she seemed overtired too, trying to be pleasant. "How will you go to work tomorrow?" he asked.

"I won't. I'll stay home and be ill."

He then answered her question. "I thought since I was so much shorter than he was that he would just tender me a formal blow which I could return. You'd scream. We'd be separated and it would be over, honor satisfied. With David it would've been an ugly thing and even dangerous."

"You think David is dangerous then?" And she was genuinely interested, curious.

"Oh no. Mostly to himself."

"I know. I know," she said impatiently. "You don't understand. I mean he seems to have some kind of theory, you know, as if he were a wild revolutionist."

"A wild revolutionist in favor of things as they are," Carl said ironically. "I suppose that's the most dangerous kind."

"No," she repeated. "I mean you're a psychiatrist and he seems a little bit strange. I've met him any number of times, and he's strange. Very."

"He isn't strange to me."

"That's why I'm asking. What is he?"

"Why do you want to know?"

She scaled at him from underneath her lids without moving her head the sideways glance, so provocative, a calling glance that beckoned him. "You're wrong, if you think it has anything to do with my feelings toward him. I don't have any."

"None?"

"Not one. My deepest emotion is terror of those damned flying bombs. I was here through all the blitzes but this is the worst, this after all those."

"Why not leave London?"

She was actually surprised. "Leave London? I've got a job here."

"Important?"

"No. But it's my job and here I am. I'm not one of those women who can just hide away when all this is going on. It's my duty."

"And if you're killed? What about your son?"

"He'll be proud of me when he gets old enough to understand. Good Lord, we may not be anything much, we English, but at least we're that." She arose. "I think I hear the kettle." And she went out of the room again while he relaxed against the down back of

249

the sofa, tired, in utter comfort, no longer desiring her, for that moment in the street had evaporated and his weariness, pleasant as it was, decayed within him, and he knew he could sleep very nicely now and longed to.

But this night had its own momentum, deep beyond his wishes, and now from the dark continent of France the flying bombs in a last flurry before the not too distant morning came over in a covey of twos and threes.

This bombardment was not immense like sudden death, a drowning in fire and blood, but a slow torture, tortuous as dreams of terror, the fear and paralysis of the body elongated over subjective time, extended and penetrating, slow enough to mount, to draw tighter and tighter with the clattering fury of the motor, each engine of destruction individual and prepared, the cut-out silence and the wait, as if from the universe reversed and hell above, planets swung from their circles and dropped. Carl sat tightly and listened, heard the ones that came near with a kind of cold fatality and the ones that moved far off with relief.

Alice entered with a nervous step and put the laden tray down on the coffee table with a clatter. Each time a bomb came in she stood in whatever position she happened to be fixed to the end, and the room for her was laid out in traps of posture, each more terrible than the next.

At last Carl said, "You must have a cellar here, why don't we go downstairs for a while? This is the last flurry."

"What are you talking about?" she cried. She was blank-faced and although she listened to what was outside the pain was within to hear and her mind alternated, rising to the skies and then dropping into her own heart, like that of so many of the patients he had watched. One bomb exploded not too far off in the park, a large flat malevolence, and as in the taxi, she turned to him and came against him, holding on to him. "I think," she said in the feeblest beaten voice, "I must be going crazy."

Then it stopped and by then the tea was cold but neither of them felt like drinking it.

"I suppose," he said looking at his watch, "it's over for tonight."

250

She was sitting on the couch before the tea tray, mesmerized by its ordinariness, and she looked up with a haggard face, discouraged. "I suppose you want to go now?"

"Would you like me to stay?"

With a desperate call on her strength, she arose and smiled, faced him like a hostess. "You must be dead tired," she said. "I've got a private number to call and they'll send a car."

"Aren't you going to bed?" he asked.

"One always does." She spent a vague look around the room, not recognizing anything, inquiring with her glance, searching, and at last, as if this were dragged out of her by his presence and not by her own need, she asked, "Would you like me to put you up for the night?"

"Do you want me to?"

She looked at the floor at his feet, her head lowered, the handsome neck bent submissively forward, and then as usual raised her lids and looked at him, and nodded.

He turned away from her to relieve her of his gaze and observed the big wide couch. "That," he said cheerfully, "looks like the biggest and the softest couch in the world. I accept it."

In a few minutes she had the couch covered with a sheet, a blanket, a pillow in place, and they shook hands and said good night to each other. She went out through another door into a small foyer and he heard a door close. He undressed quickly, turned off the lights, and then pulled back the heavy brocaded drapes that covered the windows. The two windows of the room looked out on a small walled-in garden, and beyond were dark boxes of apartment flats, and the moonlight still was in the city. A nerveless wind strayed upon him and he took his weariness to the couch and lay down to sleep.

In the quiet he heard the sounds of Alice moving in the bedroom, the doors of closets opening and closing, the drawer stuck in the chest, the familiar economy of the home, and he began to think of her mysterious, imprisoned or dead husband and how this woman like the soldiers that were his patients had also come to the breaking point, and yet with escape at hand, the house in the

251

country, could not bring herself to leave, for was she not the wife of the empire, and her pain the price of the role life had given her which she had accepted without question, the pleasure and the deaths? In love, even when people made mistakes, they always loved what was necessary to them, for what their passions needed. It did not matter that the joined lives were unhappy, and it did not matter that they should stop with one lover and begin again with another. In the end they got the lovers they wanted, the lovers who satisfied the conflicting desires of their lives. He could, he felt, imagine her husband, by understanding Alice.

Now it was silent in the other room and he thought of her, of that big white body going into the bed, and tired as he was, and sympathetic as he was, he felt vaguely disappointed that he was not there with her to make love to her. He stirred restlessly, composing himself against the softness of the couch. He kept thinking of her and loosed another memory of a week he had spent in Cumberland, in the Lake District, and the excitement and loveliness of the weather there being manufactured in the hills, rain in one valley, sunlight in another, the mountains neat with nibbled sheep grass, yet desolate in their crags, in their rocks and mists. The country there was like a patch of wilderness protected in a man's heart or closed in within a cared-for estate. In the reaches of the Pacific, in the American mountains and deserts, in the Canadian backwoods, in Africa, China and rain-soaked forests of South America, civilizations nibbled against the concrete past of the universe, at the mass of convulsed earth, its animal and mineral origins; but in England wilderness was self-contained, almost nourished, so that the weather in Cumberland, the rain in the smooth, high hills, the lakes dappling, and the constant moving sky were like flushes of civilized emotion, storms of feeling, a neurotic's tears, personal, and therefore poetic somehow and lovely. There was this quality in Alice, in the stately body, the placid brow, the very clear and temperate eyes, and inside a stormy childhood, fountains of tears, gray weather, abrupt winds, but managed, kept within its preserve. The English middle-class temperament was on the outside dedicated to the status quo and

252

within to pure Romance, at its best tender and passionate, and at its worst economical and sentimental when it was not downright stupid and brutal.

He thought what it would be to be in love with a woman like Alice, and what was even more mysterious to be loved by her. And once again he turned his face to the back of the couch to sleep, and then as if he had been noticing it all the while, he heard footsteps in the street. They had been there for some time. He heard them now again because he listened, footsteps that walked, and stopped, footsteps that went away and then came back. It could be a policeman on his beat, but the footsteps always managed to sound within the orbit of the house. They were very clear. They stopped. They began again, tentative steps, hesitating steps, but steps dominated somehow by this house, coming to it again and again as a moth outside a window in the darkness comes to the window again and again, against the mysterious wall of the window and the light within.

He got out of bed and slipped his trousers over his bare body. The windows of this room did not face the street, but he could hear the steps, so by the reflected outside moonlight he walked out of the living room, opened the door to the hall and tiptoed down the stairs. He stood at the door listening and he heard the steps outside, and once they came to the very door itself and then they went away. He stood there listening, waiting, and the steps went away.

Alice's voice called to him in a whisper down the stairs. "Carl. What are you doing?"

He walked upstairs to her where she stood at the door of the living room, the pale, almost expired moonlight behind her, a tall, glowing woman in a light silk robe.

He said very quietly to her, "Someone is walking up and down outside this house. Been doing it for some time."

She showed no alarm. "I wasn't sleeping," she said, "and I heard you get up and go out downstairs and I wondered. We can see from the bedroom."

He followed her through the living room into the small foyer and into the dark bedroom. The curtains were pulled back there and he moved to the window and stood to one side and looked out in the street.

There it was as he remembered it, the long double line of houses and the heavy shadow of the street and on the other side, broken by the shape of the rooftops, the moonlight on the cobblestones, for there was no walk. And he saw at last, after seeing nothing for a moment, a man detach himself from the shadow and come on hesitant steps to the house. Carl raised his hand to Alice for silence and she appeared at his side, standing close to him to look.

The man outside was a soldier and he came almost up to the door and in the clear light Carl saw it was David.

David stood there looking up at the dark windows, almost looking at Carl who pulled Alice back with him out of sight, holding her with one arm about her waist and she leaned against him while they watched.

"Why, it's David," she said into his ear.

David stood there and then he walked away ten steps and stopped again, and his face destroyed by the light of the moon had no expression that Carl could read.

"What's he doing here?" she asked.

The realization of what David was doing there came to Carl with an awful sickness. David was secretive about his loves now, now after all that past with Sandy, and Carl had the rotten feeling that it was Alice who was David's lover and not the other girl, and that David had switched with him to hide this, as he hid everything that had to do with his sensual life. When David had said *later,* he had meant *later that night,* and he had undoubtedly gone to Carl's rooms, found him absent and concluded rightly that he was with Alice. But he could not be sure and wanting to be with her he had come and then hesitated and suffered feeling that Carl might be there and with this woman he wanted. So he marched the street, torn by sensuality, or even love, and he marched the street and felt that somehow the affair with Sandy was being matched and returned to him.

Carl pulled Alice close, tight against him, feeling the softness

254

of her body crushing against him and he said in a fierce under-tone into her ear as he watched the lonely David pinned in con-flict out in the street. "Why didn't you tell me he was your lover?"

"What are you talking about?" She thrust her face around to him, so close, almost in an embrace and her voice held low.

It came all clear to Carl now why David had said *later*. It was to be sure that Carl would come home; this woman who un-doubtedly had strange habits might keep him, and only David's insistence on something important, on making an appointment, was the guarantee of keeping her free for himself and at the same time keeping the affair secret from Carl. A violent anger such as he had not felt for years jangled into Carl's flesh and he crushed the luxurious body against himself, holding the face close, for David was still there and he could not raise his voice. "What's he doing here? What are you doing? He knows I must be here and yet he isn't sure and he wants to come up the way he always does. What are you using me for?"

She pulled herself away from him, and darted back out of the light and he couldn't see her face. But at this moment the steps started again and he looked outside and it was David going down the street, walking quickly away.

"I don't understand this any more than you do," her voice came evenly to him. "David isn't my lover. I have no lover. I have no lover now. Call him in. Ask him. What are you accusing me of?"

Carl stood there looking down the empty street, and he believed her. It could only be that David had been looking for him, hoping the lights would go on, a glimpse of them through the drawn drapes. And if this were so, it didn't matter.

Carl turned back to Alice who had stepped up closer to him, into the light again.

"I apologize," he said gently, more for himself than for her. "But David and I a long time ago had a terrible mess with a woman we both loved and who used us both in a way I still don't under-stand. And we were enemies for years and now we're friends again and I thought for a moment . . ." He stopped, smiled. "Forget it, if you can. Excuse me if you can. I'll dress and go home."

But she had come a step closer and stood there, raising her face to him, dazzling there. "Let's assign everything to the bombs. I imagine in these times no one ever thinks of ordinary things as ordinary. But how could you imagine that David and I were lovers?"

It was conversation now again, and he stood with his bare chest and the heavy pink trousers scratching his legs, in this woman's bedroom, and there was the dim bed. He inclined his head in tribute to her star. "Who wouldn't want to be your lover, to be so fortunate?"

She took another step to him, was standing close, a breath between them. "I would not be ashamed," she said in a tender, yielding voice, "if you told David in the morning that you were my lover."

She made love like the weather in the mountains he had remembered, stormy and sunny together, and he was really the only one since her husband had gone away to the everlasting wars.

v

WHEN Carl got back to his rooms at noon, the fine weather was over and a cold rain fell through gloomy clouds. In the haggard, dispirited streets a mist which by night would be fog blew across the squares and seeped into Shepherd Market and down the mews, through the dripping shells of mansions, and waited for Carl at his door. He let himself in quickly, chilled through his tunic, and slammed the heavy door in the musty hallway.

From the basement Pamela called, "Major Myers? Is that you?"

"It is." He walked over to the wooden banisters and looked down into the dimness.

She came out of her cellar apartment where she lived in warmth and dirt next to the hot-water heater and the empty coalbins, and stood there in a rag of a housedress, her hair awry, while beside her like phosphorescent buttons glowed the eyes of the cat. "This," she cried contemptuously, "is a fine time to be getting home."

"It's only noon."

"Did you have a good time?"

"Any messages?"

"Yes. Your commanding officer called. It's very important. He called twice in fact."

All Carl's tiredness left him and he recaptured his energy in handfuls as he hurried to the telephone hidden in a cubicle at the rear of the hall behind a limp green curtain. He put the call through to the country and sat impatiently while Pamela came upstairs and approached, frankly curious.

"So you think your orders've come?"

"I hope so."

"And why do you hope so?" She gauged him, the exhaustion of not enough sleep on his face and somehow an aura of deliciousness, of pleasure which clung to him, and she sensed everything. She went on captiously, "After all, Major, the American women can't be very much when the American men are practically nothing at all. I prefer Italians."

He had nothing to reply and simply looked at the blank receiver.

"What," she asked, "are you going to bring me from America?"

"What would you like?"

She thought for a while and then remembered, "I forgot, but there's a gentleman waiting upstairs for you, and he's been waiting all morning. I've given him coffee, toast, bacon and eggs, and he's very beautiful and kind, a real hero, a colonel. The gentleman who was here last night with those two whores. Which one did you get?"

"Oh shut up."

"Did you get the big white one, the one that was a lady? How was she?"

The connection came through. "Colonel Atkinson?" Carl asked, and in a moment he was listening to the colonel's heavy-handed humor. He endured it because there was always so much of it and then the colonel told him everything was ready, the papers were waiting for him. "But you'll have to hump along," the colonel said, "if you want to get off tonight." Along with a few English expressions the colonel also carried a little English wand which he found useful for poking into corners when he made inspection tours through the kitchens of the hospital.

"Don't worry. I will. And thanks."

"Righto," the colonel said cheerfully with a Midwestern accent. "Righto, old boy, and don't forget to bring back my cigars."

"I won't."

"You've got the brand written down?"

"Yes, sir."

"*Bon voyage.* We expect you back in a month."

"Without fail."

258

"And don't do what I wouldn't do."

"No."

"My regards to Curtin and all that."

"Yes." This was the monosyllabic retreat.

"Cheerio."

"Cheerio," Carl cheered and hung up desperately.

Sitting at the top of the basement steps, smoking an American cigarette, Pamela called after Carl's hurrying back, "That was the stupidest conversation." And she giggled and yelled out sarcastically, "Cheerio."

David was standing morosely at the opened sitting room window, and downstairs the cab released by Carl still waited at the curb, arrested by David's peremptory signal from above. The moment Carl entered, David could not help asking, "What were you doing downstairs so long?"

"Hello," Carl said with a smile, and he flung his cap on the bed. "I had to call the hospital. I'm on my way home tonight."

"I suspected as much when that dirty-faced maid of yours told me they wanted to talk to you. What are you so happy about? You won't like it at home. It's miserable." David was now miserable himself, having spent the entire morning at the window watching the weather grow from bad to worse, wondering whether Carl had actually been at Alice's. And each hour his position became more untenable, the conversation he wanted to have with Carl less possible because it needed ease and time, an atmosphere of friendliness. His temper was frayed and he felt sleepy, and most of all he remembered how he had walked like a fool up and down the cobbled mews when he should have knocked and satisfied himself. But the cab driver would know where Carl had come from. It would be simple. (Will you take me back to the same place my friend just came from, and hurry please?)

Carl, who had been approaching David to shake hands, turned aside to the closet door and brought out his Val-pak. "Who cares what it's like at home. I like the idea of going." He flung the bag on the bed and zipped it open, deciding to take only what was necessary for the boat and buy new things in the States. This was one

259

of the great boons of the army, everything was expendable, not like peacetime when only men were. He returned to the closet for his other uniform and carried it back to the bed, explaining his haste over his shoulder. "I've got to run all over town and get checked and stamped out, all by six tonight." He stopped dead and remembered that the truck from the hospital was to have called by eleven and now it was after twelve. He wheeled and looked at the Chippendale table. It was empty.

"I gave the driver the packages," David said curtly. "Where were you last night?"

About to say thanks, Carl became impassive instead, actually astonished by David's bitter tone, and he went back to the bed and neatly began to hang his uniform within its pouch. "Why?" he asked.

"You said you would be here later and I came by and you weren't."

"I'm sorry, David. I thought you meant today."

"I would have said so."

"What difference does it make?"

Unconsciously David had assumed his habitual attitude of command, remote, fixed within himself, almost at attention, and the gesture of affection which he had especially prepared himself to make, thought out and planned, became stupid under these conditions. "None," he said frigidly.

There was Carl moving swiftly and efficiently between the bureau drawers and the bag, packing rapidly and without thought or delay, and David remembered how Carl had seemed to him in those old days back at the River Hospital, going about the experiments aloof, withdrawn, unapproachable, and somehow he was again that way. Completely frustrated, unable to begin, David gave up. "Well, enjoy yourself at home." And he got his overseas cap from the mantelpiece and put it on and started out.

"I thought you wanted to talk to me about something."

David exploded. "How can I with you bouncing all over the room like any damned soldier with a lucky furlough? I tell you you're wasting your time going home. It's a stinking rotten place

260

full of fat civilians and every woman a whore. That's what it is, and the army there is impossible."

Carl straightened. "I don't know what you're angry about. I've got to get off tonight and I don't have much time, as you understand."

At the door, David hesitated. The conciliatory note pleased him and after all he didn't want to leave this way. He didn't want to offend Carl again as once before he had so seriously, and the loneliness of his intellectual life, the loneliness of his life in general, even in danger, even in death, had begun to be unbearable and frightening. He reacted at once, turning, smiling, conciliatory himself. "I suppose I need some sleep," he said. And he leaned against the door. "What are your plans for the rest of the war?"

"Plans?" Carl smiled grimly and shrugged his shoulders. "I'm not like you, David. I don't make plans with the war. They put me some place and I stay put. I'm a postwar type."

"Would you like to go to China with me?"

David asked this in the simplest and most unaffected way. It was what he had wanted to prepare by much conversation, to explain what it meant to *him* to go to that land where life was still fluid and where his role could be completely individual. There was no time now. He could only ask.

The request was absurd to Carl, and the time operated against him too. He could not talk it out. He found refuge in a joke. "My mother used to say that the best thing in a war was to stay out of the army. If not, then to stay away from the battlefield. And if both were impossible, to stay as close as I could to a general. And you're almost a general." And with these words Carl came up holding out his hand to say good-by, and get David out of the way.

"I can see you're too excited to think clearly, and now I'm glad you're going home. Wait till you see civilian America giving its all for the war. You'll come to hell with me if I can find the way." And David shook hands warmly with Carl. "Have a good trip."

"Thanks," Carl replied. He opened the door for his friend, happy to see him go with his Chinese plans and his strange and still unformulated career, a soldier and not yet one, a politician and not even one, a mystic, but liberal, all mixed up and yet so efficient in his·role.

David was at the stairs when Carl remembered. "Dammit," he said. "Dammit. I've got an appointment with Alice tonight." By now he was completely annoyed with everyone including himself. He wanted to enjoy going home without all this moodiness, and he already felt a loss of freedom. David stood on the step looking back to him, his face indistinguishable in the darkness. "Do you know where she works? I'll send her a wire."

David told him and took another step down, only to stop again before Carl could close the door. "I remember," he said with gentle irony, "when you left Sandy to go to Vienna and forgot to mention that you were leaving her forever."

"I was younger and braver then," Carl said. "Have you heard from her again?"

"Once through my lawyers. She sent a letter, very nicely phrased too, asking if she could continue to have her alimony if she married again, as a favor of course, because we had made a settlement. I said yes for you and me. I decided she might just as well continue to live in the style for which she sacrificed both of us. Good-by." And he whirled down the stairs, going swiftly and easily, running, departing, leaving Carl completely annoyed and unreasonably angry with Alice who had after all done nothing but amuse him with all her loveliness and luxury all the night.

vi

BY four-thirty Carl had unlocked himself from the glorious island and was free till six, too hot in his field coat and too damp and cold without it. He sat in the taxi which he had hired for the afternoon, the Val-pak sitting on the floor like a faithful dog, and tried to think of where he could eat. Floods of rain washed upon the cab and from the shelter of doorways men and women took turns running up to the cab to hail it, retiring in haste and disappointment. There was, of course, tea, the hot rosy water and the doughy sandwiches, and six o'clock was still too far away. Carl searched his mind for any last-minute details that needed care and there was nothing. He was already out of England, disposed of, assigned to the flow that would bring him home.

It was then that he thought of Alice again, and this catch in memory had been as patient for this moment as the truth itself, settled down darkly and only apt when discovered. He was suddenly in her mind and saw the telegram appear at the office after the intimate night, the few typed words of good-by and the vague promise to see her again, and he saw himself as she might see him and flushed with guilt.

He knocked on the dividing glass and gave the driver the Brook Street address, and as the cab wheeled away, Carl thought miserably in his dampness and hunger how easily he had fallen into the pattern of the war, to consider everything expendable, even passion, even pleasure, even himself. A gross impatience, more irritating than a drug, ranged through his nerves, and he could not get to her office too quickly, to present himself, and to destroy the contempt that this woman must already have for him.

263

He did not fear undeserved contempt (and there was Grosvenor Square, and there was Brook Street), but to be judged for what he actually had done was too much even for the next few seconds.

He was out of the cab on the run and into the bare, cold hallway, where at a desk a sergeant sat before a telephone and diary. They exchanged salutes and Carl gave his name and asked for Mrs. Carewe. He signed the book and under business put *Personal*. Then he went up the marble stairway of this old mansion stripped to its bones, cheerless, unhappy and dirty, and on the second floor entered a large office, filled with Wacs and English civilian girls at desks and files, and felt the warmth of an iron stove burning in the fireplace. He asked for Mrs. Carewe again and was directed to a brown wooden door at the side of the room where he knocked and heard her clear, even voice call, "Yes."

She was sitting with her back to the door, and had a letter in the typewriter. The large French window looked down on Brook Street and the rain lurched in gusts outside. She did not turn around but the machine started to go slowly, pecking out the letters. Her purse was on the desk and under it the telegram.

He walked up behind her and when he paused this change in the routine she expected brought her head around, the white face up toward him, curious, and as she saw who it was, as his appearance struck her, flung itself like a dash of rain upon her face, she opened her mouth, and he bent down and kissed her. She put her arms around him and rose with him, holding close to him, kissing him.

The springs of tenderness did not often gush in Carl, but they opened now and he hugged her as if she were his beloved, which she was not.

"You're not going?" she said at last.

He held her hand and she sat down again. "I am," he replied, "in an hour." She looked at her purse and the telegram and back again to him. "The truth is," and he told her the truth, "I saw myself as you must see me, a telegram, just that, and I came running because I don't want you to remember me that way."

This was less than she wanted, which was to have him remain, but more than she expected even if he remained forever, and she turned her head away, and the supple white neck, bent in large and easy grace over her desk, moved uneasily like the free animal it was, stirring and gentle, luxurious and sensual, and as he stood there, that delicious taste of sexuality created between them returned heavily like a door queerly opened on a hot apartment languorous with flowers.

"All I could do was to come to say good-by," he said. And he took the telegram from beneath her purse and tore it up.

Resolutely she rose again and asked, "When do you leave?"

"Six."

"Are you going by train?"

"Yes."

"Liverpool?"

This was secret but it didn't matter. "Yes."

"I'll ride up with you." And her possession of motion, of life's duties and forms, returned to her. "Now let's go join the others outside for tea. Then we'll make the station in time."

He shook himself out of his field coat. "I'm hungry."

"Well, there isn't much, but there's always something. After all, this is an American outfit. And you know what the Americans are like." She was laughing by now, the only sign of her overturn in feeling, and she took his coat and hung it up, came back to him and slipped her arm through his arm, and spoke most solemnly out of her laughter. "You should never have done this."

"Why not?"

"Because you don't love me and this was something for a lover to do, and now I'm just hopeless in your hands," her voice died into moodiness, "imagining what love could be."

With this she opened the door upon teatime and introduced her major.

Carl spent a pleasant if rather wary fifteen minutes there, because everyone accepted as a matter of course that he was Alice's lover, and everybody knew that she had had no other, and the women measured him, estimated him, and made free of his awkwardness. He might have brought the time off more easily because

265

he was used to even more difficult situations, but Alice, charged with delight and expectation, stirred beyond any power over her unconscious, simply radiated with charm and wit, and her upbringing and memory of the life of her parents, the schooling in grace and ease she had, all burgeoned so that she dominated the room like an actress, surprised them, delighted everyone, and each separate delight was redirected each separate time to Carl, who was given the credit for being the cause of it, the luckiest man in the world, the favorite of fortune, the envy of all souls, the happy lover.

Not for nothing did Alice belong to the upper middle class, to the administrators and enjoyers of English power. Generations and centuries had trained her to the sacrifices of station, to the price of power and control, the husbands in foreign lands, imprisoned or dead, the brothers slaughtered, the fathers murdered. And afterwards there would be the sons, for to rule even among the rulers as one of the smallest of them, the price is heavy, and everything is offered up and given away except the rule itself. So she was trained in the art of letting men go, of sending them away without tears or regrets, of sending them away as if they were not going, but had only this simple task to perform which was to go and do what had to be done. And Carl received the benefit of this. She lavished upon him everything that was wonderful in herself, and kept nothing but the sickness, the sense of stupidity, the dullness of this role. It carried him through the huge station teeming with soldiers of both sexes, and the interview with the harried officer in charge of the contingent going home, soldiers being transferred elsewhere, men on leave and furlough, and a troupe of jugglers, piano players, actors and pretty dancers who had been to the many fronts and were now on their way back. To Carl he assigned worriedly the USO troupe, warning him that they were civilians and were to be treated gently. Solemnly Carl agreed, and after an hour in the dampness of too many bodies, of shouts and calls, of baggage being shifted, they entered their carriages and the train, jam-packed with English soldiers and Americans, with people just going to Liverpool, with anybody and everybody,

266

slowly rattled out of the great station into the rainy twilight of factory suburbs and occasional flying bombs, the corridors filled with seated men and women, the compartments tight, everything overwhelmed with the traffic of the war, and riding high above it all a great sense of comradeship and excitement, some songs, while the USO guitar player, far from being a bother, turned into the life of the party and led the groups around him like a scoutmaster on a vacation.

Alice and Carl shared the Val-pak as a seat at the end of the train in front of the toilet. They were disturbed every other minute by polite and slightly embarrassed men and women, and they talked generally and pleasantly *inter feces et urinas.*

Along toward midnight the lights began to go out in the carriage and soon only the blue night lamps burned and everywhere uneasy sleep pervaded the train. People lay or sat in uncomfortable positions, fixed like the enchanted entourage in the castle, and outside the stations rocked by and the whistle shrieked up high like chalk across a blackboard. Alice sat within Carl's arm, leaning against him, her head upon his shoulder, and from time to time they spoke. The track counted beneath them, the doors creaked, and the night covered all who were weary of the harshness of earth.

At Carl's feet, his head on a duffel bag, a soldier slept, his face ghostly pale in the blue overhead light, and there were heads and arms all around. All, all slid down the funnel of history, some lucky to be alive and some not so lucky. Carl made his corner as comfortable as possible. He banged the Val-pak down so that he could stretch his legs and he covered Alice and himself with the heavy warm field coat and she half lay in his embrace, very close, her hand within his open tunic on his breast, her face beneath his face. She had bent one leg between his, as if they were in a bed, and he put his hand upon her hugging thigh, caressing her without passion, but because they were so close together. This constant motion soothed and trembled a little film of desire in her mind, making it so much more intimate, here among these many sleeping strangers, bodies against bodies, and yet each alone except the

267

two of them. She would have liked to make love to him, but she could not bring herself to go that far, so she rested more and more heavily upon him, abandoning her body to the motion of the train which shook them against each other.

He was thinking wryly of the lost ivory tower of science, and whether after all it was true that not enough yet was known to make a science of psychology. Perhaps the trouble with psychologists, and he included himself, was the thought, the doubt, the hope that somewhere still hidden was a totally new principle which when discovered would organize the known and discover the springs of human action. The many schools arose over these new prophecies, and each time, whether fruitful of not, the totally new turned out to be the incompletely understood. At present, the mechanisms of physiology were pretty thoroughly explored. It was the content of action and thought that these mechanisms moved into reality which still seemed to baffle, and yet here was history in full swing, and every man had his history, and the large forces that moved the times were known.

He let his glance pass slowly down the corridor among the twist of shapes and thought again of Gibbs in his cloistered university. Gibbs had with utmost logic and rigor arranged the known into a science of the unknown. He had never lifted a finger to see what was under a rock. It might very well be that a science of psychology was already at hand, its facts partially organized and separated from each other, arranged by prejudices and schools instead of by their own internal order. What might a solid description of the known in psychiatry lead to, a description pared down to the essence of the discovered without reference to any of the theories spun about them? He made a mental note to speak to Curtin of this thought, and having made the note did not forget it, but somehow saw an image of Gibbs driving the buggy around New Haven, doing odds and ends for his sister because her husband who was the librarian was too busy a man with too important a job to be bothered by such trivialities.

The soft flesh of Alice's face moved along his own, and her mouth kissed him and then slid along his cheek to his ear, seek-

268

ing his ear like a little creature, and whispered there, "Do you think this is wrong of me?"

"What?" he asked.

"That I took you to be my lover?"

He smiled against her, but she did not see his smile, her eyes were closed and her mouth was against his ear, her hands on him, and his hand was moving on her body. "Why?" he asked.

"Because I have a husband. And he's dead in a prison camp somewhere under the Japanese. Or perhaps what's worse, alive and suffering horribly, his poor body I mean, and here I am so comfortable and loved."

To make her feel better he joined his guilt to hers. "If it's wrong for you, it's wrong for me," he said.

"Oh, no. With a man it's different. Much different. You're going home to your wife and you'll forget because it won't matter and she won't know, but I'll keep remembering that it was wrong of me."

He said, "I have no wife."

In the opposite direction a violence of sound debouched and a train screamed past, rousing the sleepers to its presence, and afterward the ordinary silence of the single noise taking them off to sleep again.

"And if you had a wife whom you loved," she asked, "because that's important, would you have stayed last night and would you now be holding me this way here among these strangers like this?" And she moved her body beneath his hand, caressing him with the motion of her hip, her hip a hand, his hand the body.

"I believe," he replied, "I've learned from my sad experience as a doctor that anything which helps you through a crisis of life is valuable."

"How comforting that sounds," she said, "how comforting. But would you?"

"I would."

"And if you had a wife whom you loved and she were home now as I'm here with you, only with someone else, another man whom she took for her lover, or like me with you just for one night and

269

a trip like this, taking a strange man into your bed, a strange man into her body which was yours and loved? What would you think then?"

He was silent.

"Ah," she murmured, and stiffened there in his embrace, "there it is."

"I would forgive her," Carl said. "I mean, there's no question of forgiveness since there's nothing to forgive. I wouldn't think anything of it."

A pause again, this time from her, and down at the end of the corridor a match struck and a cigarette was lighted, carving from the night a man's face and the cheek of a sleeping girl. Alice sighed, "How easy for you when you have no one you love."

He was silent.

"Not even me."

He was silent.

"I don't ask you to love me to make this easier, to invent an excuse for you and for me. When you return in a month, will you come to see me again?"

"Of course."

"Unless someone pleases you more."

"Why scratch yourself with such unpleasantness?" he asked. "Why annoy yourself and wound yourself?"

"Because I'm wounded, wounded," she murmured, and her mouth slid away and she rested against him again, her head on his shoulder. "Because you're such a comfort to me." He didn't hear this, it was so low.

The morning hours began to gather and the uneasy sleep in the black train settled heavily like sediment in a shaking vase, and then at three the train creaked into Liverpool, and amidst great tumult the lights went up, and the doors opened, and the cars fragmented into wakefulness. Under the white arcs everyone was a sick ghost, awry, unpleasant, a magic lantern of war, but the jolly, roaring twenty-four-hour day of the station took them over, into its canteens, into its trains going and coming, for nothing ever ceased, neither those arriving nor those going away.

270

Carl took tea with Alice in the canteen, and they sat on a waiting trunk to drink its scalding pleasantness. The trucks were waiting outside to take the returning contingent to the ship and Carl had just a moment before he took charge of his singers, dancers, jugglers and clowns.

"Well, anyway, another night," Alice said cheerfully, her glance drinking in the place, its tremendous energy and the shifting crowds of soldiers and civilians, the voices going away and the train whistles crying aloud in the narrow slots of the tracks. Red lanterns jiggled on red faces, and the rain seeped in and fell from the roofs. The carts groaned and scratched, and people stood in groups, sleepy or lively, talking or shouting. Beyond in the next shed Carl saw the sergeant approaching, looking for him.

Alice saw it too and she put down the heavy tea mug and embraced Carl with a rousing affection.

"Have a good journey."

"I will — " and by the time the sergeant came up to salute, Carl was shaking hands with her and he turned and walked off with his sergeant.

Outside in the cold and settled rain, Carl counted off his wards into the truck and then he remembered he had left a book on the trunk where he had been sitting with Alice. He hurried back into the station to get it. It was an English work on psychoanalysis which he wanted to read on the boat, and there was no way to get the book in America now except through long communications with a publishing firm, for the volume was out of print. He hoped no one had walked off with it, and he came round the pillars and saw the trunk and the book still on it, but as he started to run to it, he saw a woman in a raincoat sitting on a bench nearby. It was Alice. She was sitting with her face in her hands shamelessly weeping while people passed and turned to look and uncomfortably walked by. And Carl couldn't go out into the open to get his book, and he could not go to her, for what comfort was in him? He stood there and felt again that shabby daily death strike him, that death which every day killed off in bits and pieces the happiness of men when it did not kill them all at once, and his heart

271

broke quite openly, driving him away, leaving her there, sitting in the open for all the world to see.

He ran back to the truck. "Shit on war!" he said aloud. He climbed into the truck. "Shit on all of it!"

"What did you say, Major?" the sergeant asked.

"I said shit on war."

The sergeant agreed sagely. "You said it, sir."

vii

BEHIND the ocean where the war was, the cities no longer contended with the blackness of night but welcomed it as their future, and their ancient towers, willful as the unconscious, had been in darkness for centuries anyway, unserved, immobile as rock crystals, milestones in time. This road of hours along which history marched its horrors stretched out even more distantly than the theories which peopled it with progress, and each civilization as it withered on the way left there the towers which it had ambitiously raised. These towers, if not economical, were always necessary for they asserted the existence of power, of the expanding energy which had lifted them, of the church triumphant, of the Saracen war lords, of the spendthrift Renaissance; and when those monuments still were served by men then the civilization was pressing on to its destiny, and when they lay back in time no longer served then destiny had overtaken them and the power was gone and dead.

So as the skyline of the Empire City, New York, came into view through the clear cold darkness, its great towers glittering with light, hard and faceted like those of the instinctual insect, dominating the entrance to home, Carl knew that only here, and not in Europe where the armies were, was the real energy of his time, and that here the pious service was made before the towers, and here these towers marked that concentration of energy, skill and ambition with which men everywhere would have to reckon if not love.

Stepping out of the pier into the night, Val-pak in hand, his field coat flapping open, Carl didn't take a taxi but walked up the busy

273

side street towards the long avenues, Tenth, Ninth, Eighth, and life boiled brighter and brighter, humming with traffic and people, beaded with magazine color, depthless reds, greens, blues, painted by electrical machines. It did not matter that the war was being fought elsewhere, for in mature civilizations only slaves and mercenaries fought in the hinterland. The meaning of the war was here, here where the war existed only as a few trite slogans (our way of life), a certain increase in pleasure (one dollar eighty to see a film), an exaggerated motility in bodies (a manufacturing branch in L.A., that girl in Kansas City, Brooklyn boys in Louisiana swamps, Louisiana farmers on the blank Arizona deserts). Beneath this the actual meaning, the war living as a dense accumulation of capital, of this spiritual money which stood for the gathered labors and sacrifices of hundreds of millions of men and women every-where on the roundness of the earth, knowing or not knowing, willing or not willing, believing or not believing, all chained to the service of the clean, illuminated, living towers.

After two years in England the American energy assaulted Carl's senses like chemical shock. He stood at Broadway and Forty-seventh Street, a tourist, while the victors teemed around him, and then he joined the crowd, drifting down into the rapacious square. He returned slowly to Central Park South. There, after he tried three or four hotels, a manager gave him a tower room for one night only, making it clear that it was done as a patriotic duty to a returning veteran.

In the elevator as he was carried aloft into the tower, he smelled the girls and the sturdy men with fat red necks like rare beefsteaks flavored with face lotion. But Carl was excited and happy, and he ordered Martinis, which he drank in a hot bath. There was a shower, so he took a shower too. Then he changed to clean clothes, a slightly rumpled uniform, and descended through the perfumes and steam heat to the street again and went by cab to Yorkville where Bill's wife lived.

Carl envisaged Juley's surprise, the exploding richness of her welcome, the great warmth of her, running and cascading over her

274

dark and greedy face, for she was one of those magnificent women with such treasures of emotion that even the overflow was enough for a bystander. And Carl was a bystander. She had surprised him after the pregnancy, as probably to the first naturalist the butterfly had appeared as a miracle and come to stand for one. Voracious in appetite, swollen like a badly made sausage, difficult in temper, all that saved her from oblivion had been her voice. Yet one day she had reappeared, coming up with Bill before she went westward with him, and Carl ascending from the cellar library at Erdman's had seen her sitting on the stoop in front of the house, a youngish, dark girl, rather flamboyant in gesture, easy in laughter, with a sturdy, handsome body, and a generous use of it.

Two years later, when she had come to live with his mother while Bill stayed south in the army, he had got to know her better, at least in the few weeks before he went overseas. She was even thinner, exhausted by the boring life of army camps, the small bedraggled southern towns, the hot summers, and the stupid existence. She was thinner and the bones of her face began to show beneath the sunburned flesh, a dark, dark woman, energetic, un-restrained, slapdash and laughing. It was easy to see why Bill loved her. She alternated between extreme laziness, in which she would do nothing, not even care for the child, lying around the house in a robe or a dirty slip, smoking innumerable cigarettes and reading the newspapers, and a whirl of action in which she shopped, cleaned, worked at a job, disciplined and enjoyed her child, entertained her friends of whom she had dozens, men and women, hardly ever slept and never faltered until the household lay exhausted and passive beneath her while she laughed in her marvelous voice and poured her strength boundless around her.

Carl sat restlessly in the cab, looking out of one window and then the other as he reclaimed the streets and neighborhoods of the city, for this was his city and he knew all of it. He was not the kind of man to say that he loved this city better than any other, and truly, he did not love it. He possessed it. Above his head the cab had a glass roof, and from time to time he looked up at electric

275

signs, leaning walls of apartments, or the sky which had no depth but was more like the inner surface of a sphere hazed with colored light.

On Eighty-sixth Street, which was another blazing center of pleasure and commerce, Broadway repeated itself, gaudier, louder, more compact, and then the cab turned north, heading for the Nineties, and then east down a dirty double row of tenements, the ash cans sitting on the sidewalks, and rubbish scattered beneath the street lights. In one of these many houses lived Juley, and Carl felt his pleasure bite off, recognizing a slum when he saw one. It was just like her, he thought as he paid the driver off, to move negligently into the first thing that came along and stay there because it was too much trouble to get out.

He climbed up the unwashed steps, and her apartment was four stinking flights up, and there where a yellow light burned in a wall bracket was the door 5B and a slot for a name into which an uneven piece of cardboard had been forced: W. Myers. He rang the bell.

Inside light steps approached and a girl's voice asked timidly, "Who is it?"

He wanted to save his name for the surprise, but this was a child, his niece, and so he said, "Carl."

There was a pause. "Who?"

"Your uncle."

The door remained closed and the girl's voice said doubtfully, "I think you've got the wrong apartment, mister."

He realized then that this was an older girl and not his niece, and he asked, "Is Mrs. Myers home?"

"No. She's out."

"Well, this is her brother-in-law."

There was silence again, and finally the voice said, "I'm not supposed to open the door to strangers. But if you ring the bell at 5A my mother's there."

He walked down the hall and rang the bell at 5A. Out of family voices within, the door was opened by a young soldier who drew himself up when he saw the officer's uniform and the major's leaf.

276

The hand started to rise to a salute, and then the young man re-membered he was home and just waited. Behind him was the family dining room, and around it the mother, the father, a few relatives. Carl knew the scene at once, the furlough scene, and he knew the people and the flat for he came from such a one himself, the linoleum worn and spotless, the old furniture and the new radio, the shabbiness and family life. He said, "I'm Mrs. Myers's brother-in-law, and I knocked and was told to come here."

The mother came to the door smiling. "That was my daughter. She's minding Carla. Juley's out."

The young soldier stood there, half at attention.

"Do you know when she'll be back?"

"Oh not too late. Do you want to go in and wait?"

"No," Carl said. "No thank you. I'll come back later."

"I'll tell her you were here," the woman said, and then with a certain curiosity and awe, "Excuse me, but aren't you the famous doctor? I mean, she told us you were in England."

Carl smiled. "She exaggerated." But he was happy to hear that Juley spoke of him, and he took pleasurably from this stranger the tone in which Juley must have spoken. "I just got back."

There was a murmur in the room, and now it was the father's turn, a worn, robust man who got up and asked, "Would you like to come in and wait? I can offer you a bottle of beer."

"Thank you very much. But I'll only be in New York tonight and I must see a few other people."

They all hesitated and then Carl said, "Good night."

This time the soldier saluted and Carl returned it, and went off. He heard them talking as he stumbled down the dark stairs, and while he still disliked the slum as a place, he felt better about Juley, for her neighbors liked her and they were his own kind of people.

In the street he debated with himself over what he should do next. He was hungry and now he would have to eat alone. There were any number of doctors he knew in town, but he had no eager-ness to visit them. There was the Erdman Library and Institute, for this was what Erdman had arranged in his will, and Carl was the director *in absentia,* also by terms of the will, with a right to go there and be received. But these were formalities and did not fit into his sense of being back, a little disappointed now, but not dispossessed, for this was New York and all the while its aura settled on his mind turning up softly into pleasure, acquaintance and reacquaintance.

He walked up to Second Avenue and after ten fruitless minutes continued on to Third and there was able to snare a taxi. Once again he floated into the golden belt around the center of the town.

In the next half hour he found out that it was impossible to get a table in any of the restaurants he remembered. They were jammed with people waiting, a tumult of noise and good health, and he wondered, as many another did, what all the soldiers were doing here when the war was everywhere else. The civilians who directed the various business institutions and factories, and their wives or women friends, were out in full force, resting comfortably after a hard day devoted to supplying the needs of the war, and he bore them no ill will, and he did not even feel angry that he who had been away was not better received. He accepted these things as no worse than was to be expected, for if the life here was more raucous than in London and less troubled by bombs, there was always the exhilaration of large profits and the dangerous automobiles in the street. So he found himself an ordinary restaurant which though crowded had room, ordered a steak and a bottle of beer and had his dinner in quiet.

Without bitterness he reflected that this was about all the pleasure he would get out of New York, for apart from his work, his friends were overseas or in Washington. He finished his coffee, paid a surprisingly large bill, and went out into the streets again, having decided to walk back to Juley's. There were strollers on Fifth Avenue looking into the lighted shopwindows filled with the spoils of empire, and he gazed too (was this not his city?) going from one magnificence to another. Finally, he found a cab and returned to Juley's neighborhood.

The door to her apartment was ajar and a dim light burned

within it. Down the hall the neighbor's door was open and he saw the mother sitting at a table reading a newspaper. When she heard his steps she looked up and rose, beckoning him.

"She's not back yet, Major Myers (her son had taught her this because at first she had called him doctor), and my daughter's gone to bed, but I've got an eye on the child."

He answered, "Thanks. I'll go in and wait now."

"Why certainly, Doctor. I mean, Major." She smiled an excuse. "She'll kick herself for being away when she finds out you've been here twice." She trudged before him, a dumpy woman slapping torn slippers on the hall floor, and showed him the way into the apartment as if he were her own guest. She indicated the half-opened door to the dark bedroom. "The child's in there."

"She's named after me," Carl said, almost to prove his own relationship.

"I know," the woman smiled again, "Carla after Carl."

She snapped on a lamp near the chair which Carl recognized, the old sagging chair from his mother's house, and shifted it for his comfort. And there was the damned couch. She went to the bedroom door and looked in and then softly closed it. "Make yourself at home."

"Thank you."

"Not at all." She went to the hall door and was letting herself out when a thought occurred to her of some moment, for she frowned and half re-entered. "Do you think," she asked, "the war will go on much longer?"

Along with her he thought of the young soldier on furlough, and he moved out of his own concern for a moment to see her. She was so much like his own mother, not in face and not in build, but in manner, and the same hands, the pudgy hands boiled red, the hands that were in all their softness more adamant than rock, for the same oceans of water had poured over them and they had not crumbled and broken away. He could not lie to her and so he offered his comfort. "The people who know say that it's on the way out."

She retreated again smiling to him, "Good night." And then as

279

if in excuse to a real soldier, which he was not, "He's only eighteen."

He stood alone in an apartment designed by the same realities as the one in which he had been born and raised. Where it was different it was different through accident. Its skeleton indicated the same species. Juley did not have the patience to clean the way his mother had, but the place was not dirty, only disheveled. He removed his coat and cap and put them on a wicker summer chair (in his mother's house it had been a padded mahogany rocker, the cheapest chair in a secondhand store); there were two scraps of rug (in his mother's house they had been sewn together); there were straight-backed chairs (the same); a table pushed against the wall (different but also a survivor of someone else's more fashionable apartment). Beside this room, there would be a bedroom where the child was, a kitchen, and he walked to a closed door and opened it. He found a piece of string that went up to the ceiling light. A narrow kitchen with wooden cupboards that could not be closed because of years and years of white paint on them. A narrow stove, a washtub, the yellowing sink, but clean. This was different. There were fewer pots, fewer dishes; here, unlike in his mother's house, the culinary life was improvised. He recognized his mother's breadbox with the red handles. There was the oldest, the shortest, noisiest refrigerator. He pulled the light cord and walked back into the main room. He wanted to examine the bedroom, to see if that old brass bed was there, but he was afraid to awaken and frighten the child. Again and again he looked at one thing after another, and he remembered again and again how he had endured all of this and hated all of this and escaped it by luck and never thought to remember that his brother and his brother's family might have to live this way. In Bill's job, moving as he did from city to city, there had been no chance to gather any possessions, and the war striking, the income gone, had made the furnished apartments too expensive, and the empty ones too expensive to fill.

Carl sat down on a straight chair near the wall and he fulfilled his return. How truly he had come home, to the eternal poor man's house of his childhood and youth.

280

An hour passed before he heard a woman's high heels in the hollow hallway outside, and he rose from his reverie and waited, heard the key in the door and saw the handle gently turn. The door was swung carefully open.

The young woman who stood there wore a navy blue fitted coat, unbuttoned. Beneath it was a red wool dress with a square-cut neck, the corners pulled back with clips, and out of it rose the neck and face of Juley. She was breathing hard from the long climb up the stairs, her mouth half open, arrested now in surprise, and the lipstick was smeared the way he remembered it, and beneath her heavy bob of black hair flying every way in loose strands was the passionate, alive face, and the heavy brows, wavy and not arched, the way Boccaccio loved them.

"Carl."

He had thought of that resonant voice a thousand times and believed he knew it, but it came to him with his name more magical than ever. She flung herself boisterously at him, uncontrolled as always, impetuously and awkwardly, her arms out into his arms, embracing him. She kissed him, and it was a savage blow, for from her mouth as from a dirty smoky room, littered with cigarette butts and empty whiskey glasses, shameful with staleness and bodies and drunkenness, there came the breath of decaying alcohol.

She didn't notice how he suddenly revolted from her, she was so overjoyed, and in the tumult of her welcome she awakened the child who called from the next room, "Mama."

Laughing exuberantly, Juley swept into the bedroom, for she was a little drunk and very gay, and called to Carla, "Your old uncle is here all the way from England." The light went on and he heard the child's sleepy protest. Juley's voice died down and started again more patiently, explaining who he was again, while he stood there smelling the frightful odor of her drunkenness, growing angrier and angrier as he thought of the bitch reeling home late at night, forgetful of the child, her husband droning his life away in a lousy army camp, enjoying herself at some damned bar into all hours of the night, whoring around, stinking drunk, part and parcel of that shameless horde of wives whom the war had

281

liberated into the easy traffic of any man's emotion and their own.

Juley reappeared gently pushing before her a very little girl in pale yellow pajamas, a child with a round face flushed with sleep, a child with a cap of bobbed black hair and enormous eyes blinking doubtfully in the light, advancing and yet clinging to the mother.

Carl sat down on the chair behind him and said cheerfully, "Hello, Carla." He had forgotten to bring a present, so he removed his fancy wrist watch with the complicated dial and the stop watch attachment and dangled it out to her. "I've got a wrist watch for you. Look."

With repeated backward glances to her mother, Carla advanced and Carl didn't touch her but held out the watch. When she took it and waited, he pointed to the dial, and slowly she moved within his knees while head to head he explained the mechanism and made the hand start round and made it stop, all the while breathing in the innocence of her flesh.

"That's crazy. What are you doing?" Juley protested.

Carl ignored her. "This is for you," he said to his niece, and she went back to her mother and stood there looking at him and at her present. "Go on," Carl said to Juley, "put her to sleep. It's late." He tried to keep the anger out of his voice and did, but so twisted the tone that it sounded choked and strange. A comical and belligerent smile crooked Juley's mouth, and she stared at him, comprehending the situation at last, and then she laughed, but without pleasure, to reassure herself of her rights, and led the child back into the bedroom. They talked there in the darkness for a while after Juley had snapped off the light, and Carl walked up and down in the main room trying to master his rage.

He could not bear this sight of Juley because his brother was a man of honor, foolish perhaps in his devotion but devoted to an ideal of conduct and hope; and that this woman should betray him like any common wife of the war was insupportable. Carl had joined his life to his brother's (and it descended upon him now like madness) when he had been drafted to be beaten and nearly killed in his stead, and now Carl accepted it and elected himself

282

and stood in Bill's place and for Bill, raging against the injustice of such a marriage, raging with fury against this woman and sick to death as he imagined the life of the child.

When she came back into the room she had removed her coat and straightened her hair, and along with this change adopted a note of bravado and superiority, all welcome gone. She shut the door and stood facing him and she was again in his eyes that dirty bitch of a woman whom his brother had married, months gone in child, shapeless and terrible to behold. "That was stupid," she said, "to give her that expensive watch. It'll be a job getting it back."

"I don't want it back." He held his voice low, but the venom and anger burned in it, and he moved still further from her. All the terrain of this room was dangerous. It was dangerous for him to come close to her, the space electric and violent. He moved still further back. "Where in the hell have you been all night? What are you up to?" Her buoyant health, her youthfulness, made everything worse, for there she was, triumphant over the poverty, careless and slapdash as ever, glittering and colorful. "You're stinking drunk."

Her voice curled to him like a little dark wave. "I'm not. I was at a party and I had a few drinks and a good time, and I resisted the drunken advances of a couple of new draftees who reeled off like returning heroes although they're still wearing their blue serge suits. But what's it to you?" She strolled up to the table and he turned away from her, keeping his distance, violent at the sight of her body in the red dress and her slouching walk and her shame-lessness.

She rummaged in a drawer and took out a crumpled empty cigarette packet. She stood for a moment with her back to him in the neat wool dress, her figure solid and womanly, and yet when she turned again to face him, there was the girl again. "How about a cigarette? When did you get back?"

Only the child in the next room kept him from an outburst. He tried to think of what to say, to calm down, to consider this monstrous thing, and automatically he put his hand in his pocket and took out his cigarettes. She moved up to him, and she came closer

283

and closer, the image of her distending and wavering in his eyes, holding out her hand, a pink, naked hand, palm up to him. He couldn't help himself and dropped the pack and seized her wrist, pulling her toward him with a convulsive strength. "Is Bill dead? Have you left him?"

But the contact, the physical brutality disgusted him and he let go as she jerked her hand away.

So dark a rage suffused her face and she was shaking so with the fury of it that he half expected her to attack him and he withdrew because this was even worse than the state of affairs in the house. She stood there rubbing her wrist, the conflict between them like a torn and jagged object, crusted with resentment and mystery, and she seemed to be crawling over it, trying to fit her body to it, to its frightful shape, to know it. She said rapidly, "I see, I see. Even you." She shrugged away from him, agitated by a point of view he didn't understand, and after a long and difficult moment in which he sought somehow to escape the scene, to find his way out of it, and could not, she cried out angrily, "You've been overseas two years. You know a lot of husbands, don't you? Tell me something. Are they sitting quietly wherever they're supposed to sit at night, or are they out every free minute after any woman that comes to hand?"

"I don't give a damn what they're doing. Or their wives either."

"I'm not your wife, am I?"

There was nothing left for him here and he asked coldly, "Where's Bill?"

She replied in the same tone, "Still policing the state of Louisiana for cigarette butts so far as I know. I haven't had a letter in two weeks."

"When did you see him last?"

The resentment hardened on her face like a cold film, but she forced herself to answer. "I went down to see him four months ago for three days. His health was excellent."

"Is he still with the same outfit?"

"Yes."

He went over to the chair and got his cap and coat.

284

"Give him my regards," she cried out contemptuously.

He ignored her and went to the door, jerked it open, and started out.

Juley didn't follow him, but she said, "You're crazy to act this way, and if you were my husband and not my stupid brother-in-law, you'd know better. And if I didn't know you better I'd let you go and the hell with it. But you're being foolish and what's worse, mean."

He shut the door behind him, easily, not to awaken the child, and halfway down the stairs he regretted leaving and could not bring himself to return.

An hour later he was on the train to Washington, bundled in a corner, the Jersey flats sliding by. He said to himself it was none of his business. It was his brother's wife. He tried not to think of it, to look out of the window, but the train lights made the glass a dark mirror and all he could see was his own face and from time to time lighted factories working through the night.

viii

CARL stayed in Curtin's little rented house which stood on a hillside above the Potomac. There were a few sad trees and one good one, some yellow grass and a patch of green moss; and whenever the wind blew, and it blew frequently, the dampness and chill made free of the house as if there were no French doors and windows. "The trouble with this damned house," Curtin announced, "is that it's built for a climate where there are only summers. But there's more winter in this damned city than summer. I tell you, Carl, Washington is insane. Only second-rate minds could survive the climate, which explains Congress."

Curtin's robustiousness had collected a layer of healthy fat and he stood greater, redder, balder, more agitated than ever, shouting energy and good humor. "Here," he shouted dramatically to Carl, "are the keys to the city." And he showed him a bottle of whiskey and a hundred-dollar bill. His affection was easy, evident and unrestrained. It was with the greatest difficulty that he lived up to the solemnity of his colonelhood, but under his impatient hands the office rattled away and things were always begun if not completed. His general exaggeration of reality stood the army in good stead, for he always ordered more than was needed and so he had enough as the psychiatric casualities started to pour in. "It's nature's way of striking back. Here was the universe quietly and honorably obeying the highest laws of mathematics and along comes this stinking toad, this hairless extravagance called man, and takes these systems, makes a few thaumaturgical passes, and lo and behold! violent bombs assail the earth. What could that old whore of evolution do, dear mother nature? She made an adjustment, and men go mad."

286

Carl added, "And after that they go to the dead."

"Which reminds me," Curtin reminded Carl, "I heard from our dear old alma mater, Castlehill, and little Emily, bless her heart, is dead. She died of senescence at the ripe old age of twenty-one, the age of consent. But she did not consent. Have some more eggs."

Carl refused. Behind Curtin's rosy fringe of hair, the pearly light of another gray winter day in Washington had begun, and across the river everything was washed in sepia and ink, with patches of red earth like open sores upon the muted skin.

"It was pneumonia," Curtin elaborated. "Plain old ordinary pneumonia and the child didn't have the resistance to go on." His mouth was full of food as he talked, and he kept replenishing his plate, stoking himself up, as he said, "for another lousy day on the Home Front." Now he swallowed, loaded his fork and held it suspended before his mouth, complaining, "I've showed you everything and told you everything I know. But you, you haven't said a word about your work." He shoveled the food in and made a gesture with his empty fork for Carl to talk.

"What can I say?" Carl examined the dregs of coffee in his cup, shook them up a little and drank. "We are faced with the mystery of what makes some men more sensitive than others, and by a combination of experience, scientific guesses, kindliness and encouragement, we send some of the patients back into the war to try again, and the others we keep for the ritual of the mental hospitals."

"You sound like a social worker. Can I say less?" Curtin lofted the chromium electric coffeepot and gestured with it before he poured. "What says the scientist?" Carl nodded and the black liquid filled his cup, to the brim, for with Curtin everything went to the brim and overflowed or did not pour at all.

"There's plenty of material, God knows. If we don't find out now, when?"

"Exactly." The big red face with its pale eyes pushed forward and hung in Carl's face like the smiling mask of comedy. "What are you doing?"

287

Carl transferred his coffee to a clean cup and saucer. "Just this," he said.

"What makes you so finicky? Are you an anal erotic?" Curtin roared. "That's it. But listen, dear Carl, old friend and veteran of the mental hospitals. I've got a plan. Simple, fashionable, and practical. Could anything be better?"

"No."

"The war is, as we say in Washington, entering into its resolving stages, and meanwhile in Congress there's a great note of confidence and a desire to do something, God help us, for the boys. Out in sunny California a big hospital for PN's is on the way, a great big wonderful machine, brimming with architecture, swimming pools, knitting rooms, and electrical machines. I can have that hospital for myself, and I thought, now pay attention, I thought, suppose Carl and I took that hospital, and suppose we selected a staff of doctors, hand-picked, and nurses, hand-picked, and orderlies, hand-picked, and suppose we turned ourselves into one of these combat teams and went to work on the thousands of cases that we can have and must take care of, but went to work like scientists. My God, even the riddle of the Sphinx would fall before us. A real co-operative enterprise. No glory boys admitted, no prima donnas, no miracle makers. Just hard-working honest scientists who believe in numbers, experiment, and plain human kindness. What do you think? Could an honest man devote himself to science there?"

"He could," Carl said.

"You call that enthusiasm?"

"It depends on the control we have."

"Control?" Curtin slapped the table. "Absolute control. Those inspections made by the surgeon general's office will be ducksoup for us. Who the hell understands any of this anyway? When we're stuck we'll say something fancy with long words, and when we know something we'll say it very plain and prove it." He waited. "Well?"

"Yes."

"That's all? Just yes?"

288

Carl took the empty coffee cup and threw it at the ceiling where it crashed and fell like hail upon the table, one piece hitting Curtin on the head.

"What's the matter with you?" Curtin yelled. "Don't you have any control?" And he got up laughing. "Now let's go down to head-quarters and I'll show you this and that."

Carl saw everything that was to be seen, mainly rooms in which pieces of paper were processed into other pieces of paper while Curtin explained how these documents actually represented thousands of men and tons of matériel coming together into the unfolding psychiatry of the war. Carl saw all this and he listened, but his mind was adrift within himself, nibbling like an army of ants around the hard corpse of his experience in New York. From time to time he suddenly awoke and saw his old friend, Colonel Curtin, who beneath the bustle and drive sought Carl's approval in every way. And Carl readily gave it, approving easily of so much willingness, of so much kindness. If he hesitated over anything, it was over Curtin's virtue as a scientist, because it was hard to know whether the war had left untouched that old-fashioned morality of Curtin's, his rough and tumbling desire to discover the truth about human life. In large times and in the age of power this virtue was usually among the first victims along with truth and civilian honor. So now and then Carl came out of his inward state, out of handshakes and talks, in corridors, lunchrooms, cars, emerging to look at Curtin again, and he could not know.

Among these administrators of the various phases of the war, the main personal note was the worry of what would happen to them when once the going business was liquidated. No matter what they said, they liked the hierarchy of authority into which they fitted and in which they might advance, and the looming peace welcomed in words was rejected in feeling. They all reflected in one way or another what David had said outright: where in peacetime could a man find so much freedom, so much purpose, and so much money? Almost dreamily Carl saw the sturdy men in and out of uniform, the secretaries in and out of uniform, well fed, well clothed, well housed, floating over the struggle and doing

289

their share, but taking from the evil necessities of the time more than their share of consumption. And like a crown upon the whole kingdom was the paradise for fools. When the whole world was bent like a single muscle to the struggle, all the fat drained away from below and floated up for the bureaucrats, in and out of the services, in and out of business, and there was room enough for the efficient and the inefficient. Any lucky mouth could gorge itself, and few refrained.

Carl permitted himself to be led everywhere, and meanwhile he assessed himself and his role with Juley, and found it disappointing. He had acted badly, angrily, and without control, and while he couldn't approve of her behavior, he could find reasons for it. It was his own theory, after all, that people must do what they could to survive the crises launched against them either from within or without. He had simply thought that Juley was an extraordinary woman whereas she was ordinary like all the rest.

Somehow remembering her, the image he had taken away for the two years overseas had been stronger than she was.

There was a day at his mother's house that had misled him, a day in which groups of people, her friends and Bill's, had come to visit, and Juley laughing and serving everybody, talking and bounding about, had also handled the child, never worrying about her, never scolding, never annoyed at things that broke, at conversations interrupted, never so lost in her own pleasures as to forget the absolutely individual life of her tiny daughter. The child was at her knees, in her arms, making demands, running, crying, a whole lifetime lived in an hour every hour as children live, and Juley had accepted, participated, and still enjoyed her friends. With the day ending, there was the final scene, of an overexcited child being put to bed without impatience or hurry, and this young girl had appeared with great strength and loveliness in his mind, one of the lucky creatures of the world, of his world, for she was his family. It was this same woman he had wanted to see when he returned, to see her in place of the nervous assortment of men and woman with whom he spent his time. And then there she was, crushed like all the rest by the crises, just surviving.

He blamed himself for being stupid and unkind, and while he no longer wanted to see her, he decided to take the pressure off her as best he could, at least with the money. He sent her a check for three thousand dollars, and arranged to have part of his pay turned over to her as an allotment. In this way he washed his hands of what he could not accept, and on the next day asked Curtin, "How about getting me out of here on a nice fast plane to London?"

But Curtin grinned strangely and asked in a singsong voice, "What are you going to do in China, Carl, buy litchi nuts for the psychoneurotics?"

"China?" Carl looked blank. "China?"

"Are you going to open a twenty-four hour service laundry with your friend, General Seawithe?"

"No." Carl's consternation was real. "No."

"Yes, yes," Curtin mocked him. "You're being promoted to lieutenant colonel and going to China. *Aloha*, Colonel Myers, *aloha!*"

"No, no, no." Carl stared for a long incredulous moment at this sign of David's new authority, and he began to laugh. He explained the situation to Curtin. "And you've got to get me out of this. You get me back to the ETO and handle this, Val."

"I'll lose the order," Curtin said. He rattled his fingers on the desk and ended with a thump. "I'll get you right back to the land of Spam. But why don't you stay here? I can handle it from here."

Thinking of David and the mad scheme, Carl said curtly, "I don't like it here. I'll finish the war there."

Curtin sighed and the big red face slowed down into gloom. "Every time anyone decent comes home, the first thing he wants to do is go back."

"You're sure," Carl asked, "you're sure you can handle this preposterous idea of David's?"

"I'm sure," Curtin replied. The heavy head came up, discovering a new thing to smile about. "But at least you should treat yourself to one night out, just for something to tell the boys, and meanwhile I'll figure out a scheme to give China to that crazy friend of yours. Maybe I'll be able to convince you to stay."

"No," Carl said, "no." But all the while he was thinking that to the other cardinal axioms of the psychiatrist's profession should be added the corollaries: whatever stupidity contradictory intention can execute, will be executed; whatever sentimentalities can confuse existence, will be felt; whatever brutality and willfulness, whatever selfishness and silliness, can be imposed on existence, will be imposed. In peace or war it was the same. The contradictions of external reality created the internal conditions of human life, and there was no place to which he could retire and there was no home and would be none. He could not settle down to a life of a particular place, a house, a street. He was homeless. He had no nation, no country, no village, no tradition, no family, no friends, only his scientific morality of whatever value it might be.

In the evening they went to the most popular and expensive night club in Washington, "The large colon of the Home Front," Curtin called it. He was different tonight, more secretive, and instead of his usual fountain of good spirits, there was an inward play, a private little satisfaction which Carl noticed but did not comment on. It was amusing to see his old friend in a new role, as if Santa Claus should play Iago. But the night club when they finally got there appeared to have nothing unusual about it. It was overcrowded, overwarm, overdrunk. The floor show was overlong and overnoisy, the jokes dull when they were not obscene, but the crowd roared, a big, pampered array of men, from young innocent officers who had seen combat to wise old generals who had managed to avoid it, from corpulent businessmen to hard and rosy young ones, and the fatness dripped from them, the richness of health gleamed on their tight skins and beneath their polished clothes, and they laughed and ate and drank and made merry to forget the troubles of the world. Not their troubles, Carl thought, but the world's troubles which might become theirs. The women in general were carefully selected for general consumption, aesthetically and sexually, and along about midnight the place began to romp.

Carl was watching the band and admiring their dispassionate skill when he saw Curtin look past him to the entrance and then

292

rapidly uncover a little triumphant smile. Dutifully Carl looked too and saw four air force officers complete with wings and ribbons enter, and in their midst, shining in gold, Sandy.

"How did you know?" Carl asked.

"She comes pretty often."

"Which one is her husband?"

"Oh," Curtin was a little disappointed. "How did you know?"

"Her ex-husband told me in London."

"I've met her once or twice," Curtin explained, twisted in his seat and watching the group herded to a table in the little raised corner. "I'll never forget that great rainy romance of yours, and the way she descended on us there." He sighed. "A considerable piece of woman."

She still was, although as Carl observed her as best he could in the bad light and constant movement, it seemed to him that Sandy was getting a little overripe. He could not tell from the disposition of her group which was her husband. "And the husband?"

"The captain on her right with all the spinach."

He was very handsome and very young and very dissatisfied, at least six or seven years younger than Sandy. She did not look so much older as more developed, more mature, at a changing point, while he was nothing yet.

"Well," Carl said. "Now that we've seen her I suppose we can leave."

"But I thought," Curtin started, and then subsided, chuckling. "What could have possibly made me think you'd be interested in seeing her again, with all England lying limp and willing on the playing fields of Eton?" He called the waiter and asked for the check, got it, and then the captain saw the better table being vacated and in a moment his party was being steered towards it, and there came Sandy through the mob, laughing and a little drunk, the square face helpless within the many faces, the heavy lids half closed, and her mouth loose and free for any kiss that might happen to fall.

"Pardon me," the captain said, making way for the colonel.

293

"Not at all," the colonel said maliciously, and lithely slipped his bulk to one side so that Sandy and Carl stood face to face.

Carl saw her with complete indifference, but her face lighted with pleasure and then a note of alarm as she glanced at her husband. She said formally, "Why Major Myers," and held out her hand. Carl shook it. She drew her husband forward, "My husband, Captain Meadows." Carl shook hands with him and saw himself examined with hostility. It wasn't easy being Sandy's husband, that was clear, not with Washington raging with eager men and a woman as pliable as she was. The captain finally remembered that he had met Curtin and shook hands with him too, and there they all were arrested between the tables, the place flailing at them, and unable to go one way or another.

"Major Myers is an old friend of mine," Sandy said to her husband, whose face grew even darker at these ominous words.

"Yes," Carl hurriedly added, "she was a nurse at a hospital where I worked a long long time ago." He returned his glance to Sandy. "You're looking very well."

But the captain was not to be put off with this. He cagily asserted himself and asked, "Would you like to have a drink with us?"

"We were just leaving," Carl said. "I'm on my way any day now and I have to do a thousand errands for the men in my outfit."

"ETO?" the captain asked.

"Yes."

"Sit down for a minute," Sandy asked. She could not keep the excitement out of her face although she tried. It was a change again and she wanted to talk and see Carl. It was so obvious.

"Some other time," Carl said.

He shook hands around again, and Sandy squeezed his hand, talking to him through her hand, asking him not to go, to see her again.

They left and in the splendid lobby, where Carl and Curtin waited for their caps and coats, a waiter found Carl and handed him a note. It gave Sandy's telephone number, and begged him to call at eleven any day. Carl dutifully turned the note over to Curtin. "You call her," he said.

294

"I will," Curtin replied, tossing the note away. "I'm sorry for that young boy."

"Well, what did he think he was getting?"

Curtin shook his head. "One always hopes. Don't you ever feel the need of getting married?"

They stood in the cold street waiting for a cab to appear, and the wind blew damply on them.

"I thought," Curtin said a little sadly, "that she might keep you here a few days longer. I sure hate to see you run off like this, Carl."

"I don't like it here now," Carl explained quietly. "After the war we'll work together in that hospital of yours. But now, I think it's better for me to go back, as soon as possible."

"The day after tomorrow. It's arranged."

"And David?"

"Don't worry. You'll never see China." Curtin began to bang his hands together, for warmth. "Tomorrow night at my house," he said, "I'm having a few doctors over for you to meet and talk to. We've got to start picking our men now before they all leave us and go off to hold the hands of neurotic dames for fifty dollars an hour." He jammed his hands into the pockets of his warm coat, and beneath the green and red lights of the overhead sign, emptiness flooded upon him. "Every now and then I think of little Emily, and of that moment in the room there when she turned. You remember, Carl, how she turned and looked at you with that little smile?" He did not smile himself as he looked up into the heavy sky, starless and cloudy. "And I remember the night when we decided to go ahead with the experiment. You remember, Carl?"

"I remember," Carl said.

"And we walked home from the village." He thought for a moment and called softly aloft, "Oh little Emily, where is your star?" He smiled again, standing close to Carl. "I was drunk. I was happy and drunk, and I was afraid too that it would be a flop, which it was."

"Not completely."

"Complete enough. What do you think, Carl? Is there any hope in this business of ours, any at all, to get our hands on the secret of

295

this whole crapped-up existence, this murderous stinking affair?"

The lights of a taxi swept out of a distant circle and headed for the night club where it discharged its passengers. It was a party of Midwestern manufacturers, complete with a procurement officer and three charming whores. They laughed their way into the night club while Carl and Curtin sedately entered the cab.

It was a long ride to Curtin's place and neither of them spoke very much, but in the end, Curtin could not help himself. He put his hand on Carl's knee. "Tell me, Carl. I don't have to say again how much I like you, how much I admire you, how much I think of your ideas of this science of ours. But tell me, what's the use of the whole thing, what's the use of finding a way to help a thousand men, or ten thousand, when in one year ten million of them are ground up into hamburger and mud, on battlefields and in cities, men, women, children, good, bad, indifferent? What's the use of it?"

Curtin did not really expect an answer and Carl didn't offer one. They sat in the humming darkness, each with his own answer, whatever it was, for there was an answer no doubt, but not anywhere where the words they had could find it. It was deeper and less available, nourished in the obscurity of the moody flesh from which life draws so many of its commands and all its persistence.

ix

BY the first weeks of December the historical uses of the war were accomplished. The center of future empires did not belong to Europe. This had already happened. But as deep within the victory of the allies the sickness of the days to come fermented, more battles of this old war appeared on the horizon. It is the great tragedy of history (and perhaps it will be its delight in future times) that long after an historical phase has taken shape, men must swallow the afterbirth. So the dying went on, absolutely meaningless even for politicians, those most voracious and insatiable of man-eaters. The war went on profound and individual for those selected as the last fruitless sacrifices to a civilization so dishonored and stained by suffering and cruelty as to vie with admired Greece and Rome, imperial Spain and England, and the spiritual crusades.

What, Carl asked himself, as he wandered through the bitterly cold and gray city of Paris waiting day after day for a ride to Germany where the 84th Division rested within the Siegfried Line, what rearrangement of events in history could possibly allay the guilt created in the souls of the victors and the vanquished?

He marched through the streets he had known before the war and they were physically the same, radiating spaces whose interstices were stuffed with historic slums. The natives darted for shelter into the cold buildings while the victors rummaged the shops for what the Germans had left behind and hunted down the women whom the Germans had used. To the victor, friend or enemy, belonged the spoils.

He returned to his hotel and sat in the room with the red silk walls and the rigid silk-covered chairs and the big bed from which the down pillows had been stolen and on which some Parisians had welcomed the ferocious Boche into their perfumed crevices while in bloody cellars their neighbors were whipped, beaten, their entrails dragged out, their jaws mashed and lacerated with whirling electric dentist tools, their heads crushed, and finally similar loving genitals ripped apart.

Carl warmed himself with the cognac and longed to get to the armies to see his brother and talk with him. This was the scheme that Colonel Curtin and Carl had worked out. Carl was to go out as a special Washington representative to observe a new division under combat conditions in order to have a realistic view of the way combat traumas were created. Incidentally, it served to delay his transfer to China and gave Curtin time to botch up the wild and foolish scheme of David's. And for Carl, it was an opportunity to see Bill. Now that he believed Bill had lost his wife as a contribution to maintaining the morale on the home front, he saw himself as Bill's only friend, and Bill as his only tie with the more usual mechanisms of living. They were two brothers and they would sit down like brothers and speak of anything, being together, and this at last was what life had left them.

In the evening after dinner at the mess, he went with two chance-met companions to a cabaret and drank champagne while he watched the shivering naked girls go through the acts which a few months before had amused the Germans. In the finale, the big blonde with the narrow breasts, nipples erect with cold, produced, from the kneeling naked handmaidens whose goose-pimpled behinds looked like emery board, the Stars and Stripes instead of the swastika. There was general applause. Later on these girls and others reappeared among the tables and continued with the more profitable business of the evening.

Carl delicately absented himself from the gay celebrants and wandered down the Champs Élysées to the dark gardens of the Louvre. From time to time out of the damp shadows offers came from faint figures ephemeral as leftover courtesans of the great court. The voices cried out in English, "Would you like a little love?" He shuddered as he moved on because like all men he wanted love more than anything else and did not know how to find it.

Along with the wind he circled the dead fountains and passed beneath the statues, wondering when Lieutenant Farrow would depart. He had, through a friend of Curtin's at Versailles, tracked down a vehicle from the 333rd Infantry Service Battalion and arranged to go with the lieutenant and his five men up to Geilenkirchen area. It was possible that Farrow had forgotten or pretended to forget, in this way avoiding a long trip with a strange major. One of the cardinal rules for avoiding trouble was to have as little as possible to do with officers from behind the lines. And this was what Carl was. From Farrow he had learned that the fighting around Prummern and Lindern had been very hard but he could find out nothing about Bill.

He sat down on a backless bench and looked at nothing. The rue de Rivoli was dark, the city was dark, the air was wet, cold, uncomfortable, and the hotel would be no better. After a moment, he rose and started to walk rapidly back towards the Arc de Triomphe, having no patience for anything, even himself.

Thinking of his irrelevance, his obscurity within all the events of the time, it seemed remarkable that David had decided to make so much of an old friend's mere existence. The ambivalence Carl comprehended easily, it was the content of it that escaped him. What did he stand for in David's mind? Why was his life a proof or disproof of some idea or goal of David's? The latent homosexuality was just a current of energy, as heterosexuality might be in another affair. But sexuality never explained the lengths to which lovers went, the sacrifices they made, the brutalities they committed, or the suffering they experienced. Sexuality was, so to speak, the instrument, supple, various, sensitive, whereby the profound social charges expressed themselves.

At the hotel he inquired of the concierge but found there had been no call. He took himself upstairs in the mahogany elevator and stood again in the frigid chamber. It was a mistake to stay here alone and he thought seriously of going down into the streets and

299

finding some girl anywhere and bringing her back with him, when the telephone rang. It was Lieutenant Farrow, very apologetic. "I'm sorry, Major Myers, but I've wasted all day tracking down one of the men and we've just found the drunken bastard. We're a good twelve hours late on starting back and I thought we might as well go now. How is it with you?"

"Fine," Carl said with enthusiasm.

"It'll be an awful cold ride but I'm afraid I'll lose another man if I hang around till morning."

"Where shall I meet you?"

"Oh, we'll pick you up in ten minutes, Major."

"Thanks, Lieutenant."

"It's this gay Paree," the lieutenant said. *"Toute de suite."*

It took Carl three minutes to pack his stuff and he collected the overshoes which the lieutenant had warned him to get. "Just mud, mud, mud," he had complained. "Mud and rain and lots of pill-boxes. I thought this war was over."

Downstairs Carl paid his bill and had the concierge carry out the case of cognac which he was bringing up for Bill. Then he stood at the glass doors and waited.

In ten minutes to the second the blackout lights of the truck appeared and Carl carried out his Val-pak and waited at the curb. The lieutenant jumped down from the cab and helped Carl put the cognac and the Val-pak into the rear. There were three men sitting on the side benches and they greeted him respectfully and gave him a hand up although they were half asleep.

"I'll ride up in front till we get out of the city," Farrow said. "That GI slob is fast asleep on those blankets back there, but he won't know it even if you walk on him." He was a cheerful man, the lieutenant, and not angry at all. "Just make yourself comfortable, Major."

"Thanks."

Carl got in and the soldiers impatiently waited while he found a place on one of the benches, then they pulled the waterproofing tight and went back to sleep as the truck slowly wheeled down the street and started off on its three-hundred-mile journey. The

300

bench was not too wide and had no back, only the stanchions of the frame of the truck. Carl composed himself as well as he could and sat in cold silence while the wind roared against the canvas and flapped overhead in the slack and from somewhere an icy current girdled his ankles and knees.

He did not have the ability to go to sleep anywhere, to pick up sleep when it was available and go without it when he had to. In this way he still was a civilian. But he had learned over many years to sit quietly and not fidget, to turn his mind in and hold it there within himself for whatever thoughts or feelings he wanted to use.

So now with an easy discipline he began to consider Curtin's plan for scientific work in the postwar hospital, whether it was proper to begin again on a purely empirical basis as if nothing important were known.

In the main all therapies followed one of two schools, the historical or the axiomatic. In the latter, the patient's illness was considered as given (like simple space in Euclid) and various methods were used to move him out of it, accepting as irrelevant what had made the particular patient ill. Paranoia was one kind of psychic malformation, manic depression another, and the disease having been diagnosed, general rules of treatment were followed. This school had as a result a tendency to become mechanical and faddist, running after drugs, shocks, disciplines and other gross alterations based on the notion that it was the nervous system itself that had to be readjusted. Its practitioners would not be at all surprised to find a vaccine or serum that could do the trick. Carl rejected this school completely, except for a handful of unimportant diseases. On the other hand, the historical school, while it had discovered various psychic mechanisms that applied in all cases, at the end and most logically got to the point in which every case was special, every treatment personal, and every perfect cure interminable. It was a whole life that had to be understood and as investigation got deeper and deeper into the events of a life, each man became the whole world and each treatment a form of monadology. Carl accepted this school but he rejected the sub-

301

jective swamp in which it inevitably foundered. Only a general theory of causation could save this science from becoming a rather subtle form of artistic expression.

He was running through the various schools of psychiatry, assigning to each the point at which it became wayward, when the truck stopped and two military policemen demanded to see papers.

"Getting any sleep back there?" Farrow asked as they stood in the road on the outskirts of the city stamping their feet in the bitter night.

"It's quiet anyway," Carl told him.

They were waved on by the MP's and Farrow changed to the inside of the truck, sending a sergeant up front to sit with the driver. "And stay awake," he said, "so that we don't end up on the Riviera."

Farrow pulled and tugged among the various duffel bags and finally arranged what he called "Two cozy foxholes," and he and Carl settled in them as the truck began to pound off again into the night.

"How is it?" Farrow asked.

"Fine." Carl felt the knobby musette bag at his side. "I seem to have a bag of potatoes on my right."

"Grenades," Farrow said.

"They short at the front?" Carl could not help smiling.

"I'm supplying this one," Farrow said grimly. "After we get close to Palenberg you can never tell what you run into, and there's nothing like a grenade. You don't have to aim." He lit a cigarette for himself and Carl, and by the light Carl saw the two Browning Automatics stacked in the corner near the sleeping soldier on the floor, and the carbines next to each man.

"Good night," Farrow said, and in five minutes he was snoring and Carl was alone again.

Lolling with the motion of the vehicle, his body relaxed and held in place by the cradle of dusty duffel bags, Carl returned his attention to the scientific problem.

Without some definite and general theory of causation which could apply to every case, there would be no real difference be-

302

tween Curtin's new hospital and any other extant. The Freudian conception, whether refined, masked, or used as originally proposed, attributed all mental illness to constitution and fate, to heredity and environment. This was logical enough, but everything depended on the meaning of the two conceptions. By heredity Freud meant his theory of instincts, and by fate the influence of reality on these instincts, where reality was parental effect operating through malformations of sexuality, and instinct the energy of the unconscious seeking libidinal satisfactions. But no matter how far back into the history of a patient an analysis went, every motion of instinct was itself a product of environmental change. In short the human body produced strong currents of psychic energy, but these could never be isolated as such, and even all inner satisfactions were prepared for by current social habits. For all practical purposes, heredity, except when it was present as a gross organic malformation, could be ignored in a general theory of causation, because this energy was in terms of present knowledge infinitely plastic up to the point of death.

Carl then took up the idea of fate and remembered along with it Napoleon's bitter and penetrating remark: the role of fate in the ancient world is filled in the modern by politics. Like a tolling bell that word politics awakened into his consciousness the notion that he was going to the Front.

The war had rolled up to the borders of Germany and whereveᵣ it had passed, although it left signs and vestiges of its life, these were all in the main directed to that Front. For the rest of France and other countries elsewhere the normal life started again or just went on. The great pressure of social custom was for each activity to approximate the Peace in times of the War, to settle down to the round of events in which men found their usual duties and pleasures. But, of course, during the War this was only possible so long as the Front existed some place else, and Home, therefore, was that place wherever there was no Front. Home had its being only because there was a Front.

So somewhere always there was a place where millions of men fought ultimate struggles in order that elsewhere the ordinary life could continue. From each one behind the Front a little was taken, but at the Front everything was taken. It did not seem at all like a just division of labor. But the more Carl thought of it, the more usual it became. Ever since there had been states, somewhere in the world a war was going on. It was to be presumed therefore that the nature of states was to create wars, and that War was the condition of the existence of the State. Although Carl had been in the War a long time he had never been at the Front unless the blitzes and flying bombs of London were to be considered as flying fragments of the Front which had accidentally happened to him.

He was now on his way to this enormous bleeding wound in the social carcass of the times.

One by one, as the idea of the Front grew clearer within his mind, the particles of his spirit magnetized and pointed east, and he felt the great pattern being stamped on him, and he realized that no one could go to the Front just to go there but had to be embroiled.

Fitfully in the rushing cold he dozed while somewhere in the upper corner of the truck a minor tempest blew and now and then a car passed going the other way. The night was very large and this vehicle caught in a roaring current, almost undirected, so black and empty the night seemed, and the current was bearing it, rocking, shaking, tumultuous to the Front.

He was awakened by the pulsation of a slower convoy going in the same direction. The spaces between the vehicles were breaks in a continuous tumult of noise and wind, assaulting his ears, passed, again, passed, roar after roar, spaced and neat and violent. He waited for the convoy to end so that he could fall asleep again. Beside him the lieutenant was undisturbed. The drunken man slept, the two soldiers slept, and for all he knew the sergeant and the driver up front slept, too, while the truck hurtled forward on its own. He seemed to be the only one awake, and yet they were all going to the Front.

Why should men go or let themselves be sent to the Front? In so immense an affair of the times where so many went to be undone as living organisms, it did not much matter whether they

304

thought they wanted to go or did not want to go and went anyway. It was obvious that they went to the Front because somehow in a specific society the decision had been reached, one way or another, that men should go.

The convoy was gone and now the truck was alone on the road, the vehicle a social invention rolling furiously, rocking with wind and cold along a social road on its socially directed way to the socially necessary Front. They were passing through land where the Front had already gone by, and here as all the way back in the United States people stood so to speak at the roadside and wished them Godspeed on their frightful journey.

It seemed to Carl as the current sucked him forward that a society would have to point to some very remarkable successes at the Home in order to justify the existence of this monstrous condition, that somewhere millions of men slaughtered each other to maintain the place which was not the Front.

For example, he thought, as his mind was wandering with sleep, what great social triumph in the place called Home could justify the necessity of the Front? Would a war of this extent and nature be justified if as a result the men at Home discovered the laws of relativity? Would that be enough? Would great works of art justify a Front? The Divine Comedy of Dante? All of Shakespeare? The impressionist paintings? An Arc de Triomphe? Radio City? What? What sum total of human accomplishment at the place called Home could outweigh the sum total of human possibility annihilated at the Front? A science of psychology? A science of history? What?

As some men count sheep in order to slip out of reality, he began in a foolish, sleep-ridden way to count each man's life at the Front. He started with Bill who was his brother and measured out a space in his dreams where he could pile up what Bill was, but he very soon got in trouble, because the millions of this war mixed with countless hordes from the past, dark men in burnooses, knights of the cross, peasants dragged from their fields; and empires began to sway, and such a procession started towards the kingdom of the dead by War that the Museum of Art, Science, and

305

the Practical Crafts was hidden. The voices ascended out of the release of narcosynthesis, and there was no language in which these men could not scream shit, piss, screw on society, mother, father, God.

He dreamed he was back in London, standing at a Gothic window overlooking a moonlit mews, and at his side was David, the young David of his college days, bright and terrible with a secret destiny, and outside in the moonlight wandered a weeping woman who soon became Juley. He wanted to go down to comfort her, but he was afraid to because out there was the Front. This building in which he stood with David was Castlehill and David wore the uniform of a surgeon, complete with mask and rubber gloves. With an access of strength Carl escaped into the street and stood there with Juley. They stood for a very long time not speaking to each other and then very sadly, and this sadness wept within Carl, they walked hand in hand back into Castlehill, and that was the Front too.

PART FOUR
The Trial

i

THE staff of the Sierra Hospital in Los Angeles County gave a party three years after the end of the war.

As in all such celebrations, there was a certain obscurity in motive: was it a backward glance over triumph or failure? There was a certain confusion of ideas: did they possess a science or merely an occupation? However, there was a great deal of surface emotion, all friendly, even exuberant (in this way they renewed their first enthusiasms), for they seemed to like each other and formed a well-knit social group with common notions, interchangeable friends, and institutional security.

When all the speeches were over, some scientific, some remembering with humor and sentiment, but all laudatory; when the newly completed project film was shown for the first time in a finished state, complete with sound, music and commentary, a film mysteriously real even for the doctors who had acted in it, so great is the magic of mere representation; when all these tributes had been exacted, a plaque was given to the director, Colonel Valentine Curtin, and a gold wrist watch to the Chief of Staff, Dr. Carl Myers.

"Hello!" cried Curtin. "What's this?" He pretended to be surprised although he had chosen his gift himself. "A plaque with letters of gold? In token of . . . Gentlemen, what's this? A premature tombstone? The report of my death is exaggerated." And he burst into peals of laughter in which everyone joined, this enormous man, topping them all with his height and weight.

Curtin bulged out of everything, so lavishly was the hard, sculptural fat laid on him. Seats were too small, rooms too confining, decisions too neat. A great torso on fragile legs, a round red face whose features had generalized into shining rosiness surmounted by a fringe of thin red hair, an overabundance of energy and laughter, a wildness, romantic and comic, so that from the outside as he stood swaying, gesticulating, bending this way and that, he looked like one of those merry giants carried in a fête at Nice. Beside him stood Carl, dark, hard, rustless, a black thin mustache on his sunburnt face, smiling remotely, bearing the aura of an inner stillness, a density of reserve and incredible patience. He held the watch in his muscular hands and turned it over, read the inscription, examined the face and band, all in a way to give pleasure to the givers, and, with a sure knowledge of the ringleader, smiled intimately over to Dr. Grant, who flushed and leaned over to whisper into his wife's ear, "Behold! The ego and the id."

"Which is which?" she asked, alternating between Curtin and Carl, but the director began to talk.

Holding the plaque like a prayer book, Curtin adopted a pious stance and leaned over the invisible lectern to speak to his flock.

"Dear friends in the Unconscious," he droned, and they laughed out of their informal amphitheater of faces, exchanging quick delighted glances in anticipation of one of Curtin's great performances. "So three years have passed in fun and frolic with these, if I may quote my colleague, Dr. Myers, with these terrible children of our times. We are still here. Can I say more? We are not ourselves confined. Can I say less?" Ready to laugh, they laughed again, a single clatter. "We may have discovered nothing in the way of the psychological sciences, but there has not been a single case of divorce or marriage, always a good sign, a little intermittent adultery, a healthy average. Three cases of kissing in the dark, a social disease. Believe me, I'm delighted." Little waves of sniggers went round from each of these extravagances. The voice boomed up into formal loftiness, senatorial and immense. "I am happy to receive this slight token of your disregard. I shall cherish it with my other favorite possessions, a second-class scout pin, three shavings from the pencil of a girl I loved in high school, the skeleton of a frog from Biology I, the manuscript of the paper written by Carl and myself at Castlehill, and the broken coffee cup with which Carl celebrated the notion of Sierra when I recalled him from London to broach the subject during this most recent war." He had not meant to but was becoming more serious. That big red face quieted down and the pale eyes focused beyond the audience, leveling the disparate heads beneath him, beneath a vision. "I know this plaque stands for loyalty to the hospital, to our work here, to the Sierra Method, if I may call it that. I suppose I can. There is a Sierra Method, a group research in science combined with the most flexible methods of cure." His eyes descended again upon the uplifted faces of the staff. "Our motto," and he chuckled, "No Impatience with the Patients. Ha! Our slogan, Down with Basket-weaving and Back to Life."

He let the delighted applause ruffle past him and tossed the round plaque up into the air, catching it professionally like a magician. When the tumult subsided, he continued quietly.

"I think our method works, better than any known before. We don't try to send back one of those useless finished psychological products, a less troublesome *sick* man. We send back a troubled, seeking creature, a man who wants something from life, who will struggle to achieve it, not at the expense of his own personality, but in struggle with the society which has created him and maimed him."

The staff recognized here and there phrases from Carl's lectures, talks and conversations, but these had become part of the general language of the hospital, collective notions by now infused with common ideas, direction, methods and conclusions. These reformulations and alterations of the language of the science were the characteristic mark of a Sierra doctor, appeared in his papers, his work, and, in the end, even in his thinking. The words and phrases no longer revealed their source. They belonged to everybody, and, like a group of actors who form a permanent acting company, when the staff went out in the world other psychiatrists seemed undeveloped and unsophisticated to them, ignorant of the true secrets of the cult.

Curtin talked on, lifting himself into one of his rhetorical flights, and subtly through his voice a low note began to sound, a gathering ground bass that swelled and absorbed the other registers of his voice, a note all emotional affecting him as well as his audience.

"I sometimes see ourselves not as doctors and nurses treating the mentally ill. I see a group of men and women devoted to truth, and as such, blessed, fortunate to have near us these strange, sensitive creatures of our age, people called the mentally ill, but who are in reality the socially ill, unfortunate companions in life upon whom a sudden concentration of negative environmental influences has collapsed. The times and the forces of the times which affect all of us have caught them in a sudden richness of contradiction and violence, neurotic parents, joblessness, unfortunate loves, war, not one by one but all together. Overwhelmed, these men and women lose their power to adapt, to struggle. The will sags. The mind retreats throwing up symptoms as an army in flight destroys resources. But these people are mirrors of the real world and we are blessed to be able to see, to seek, to search."

He paused, held this long chord and then added very, very quietly, "We have set ourselves on a course of action in the continuing crisis of our times, a theory and practice in the psychological sciences with special reference to psychotherapy. We do not try to please any man. We seek the truth. If we do not forget this, we shall never have any cause for regret, because even our failures will in the end create the opportunity for those who follow in our path."

This was the whole point of the party in a certain sense, the repetition of what everyone believed, but said out loud to all at the same time, a ritual blessing, and there was a shattering racket of self-congratulating applause.

Curtin beamed and began to retreat into the golden cloud of approval. He stopped and held out his immense hands in a gesture as close to benediction as his unblessed nature could command. "Another word. In Washington, today, a subcommittee on appropriations for the Veterans Administration is holding hearings.

Under the direction of Representative Vaughan, Republican, Paranoiac, New York, an effort is being made to reduce the funds available for our work. There is, we are dolefully informed, a shortage of funds, since the next war demands the money which might be used to cure the victims of the last one. The dear boys for whom Congress wanted to do so much, so long as the outcome of the war and the next election were in doubt, have now become the old men who are concerned to see that their sons, the dear boys of the next war, have plenty of destructive objects with which to fight. But doctors like us are making a hard fight to prevent this foolishness, and very soon I shall be going to Washington myself to demand more funds, more and more and more." Curtin bowed his head to the loud and vigorous applause. "We know the practical situation. We need more facilities, more staff, more of everything for research, therapy, and prevention. We won't get this money by remaining quiet and acting like good children. We intend to fight. On the other hand, Carl is going to New York where he will speak at the Psychiatric Congress. His paper, which was written, so to speak, with the help of every one of us, represents the collective opinion of the staff at Sierra. It is our paper that is going to be read there, based on our works, on our thoughts. When the old-fashioned basket-weavers and dream astrologers get up and rip him to shreds, it will be all of us that they are destroying. But, thank God, he'll be the one that's there."

Again they laughed, even louder, because it was a joke, and also because they were indeed glad that it would be someone else who would be there.

When Carl followed he merely said, "Thank you," to everyone, adding in an undertone, "I don't have to repeat what Val has said so well for all of us." Then he looked at his new watch. "Besides, it's time for dancing."

The evening dissolved into sheer enjoyment, a mixture of dancing, clinical gossip and macabre horseplay, while the hours piled up against the dam of midnight, leaning heavily and overweighted into the next day, that sad next day in which the war still went on in the minds of the patients, the suffering which had not ceased,

313

the wounds which would not heal, the agony of soul which the external victory had not allayed.

Dr. Grant, his face flushed with a few drinks, a little wreath of perspiration on his brow and a stumble in his step, paused before Carl and said in a husky, wandering voice, "I don't know why it is, Carl, but when you say those things it sounds as if I'm a scientist, and when Val says them. . . ." But Mrs. Grant pulled her husband away. "Oh, come on and dance," she cried.

Grant followed her out on the dance floor and let himself slowly sway and turn, coming out of each gyration to see his beloved chief, a glass in one hand, a cigar in the other, making the rounds of the guests with the same moderate cheerfulness as he made the rounds of the wards.

"Objective," Grant mumbled into his wife's fragile ear. "Sheer objectivity. Is he the ego or the id? The superego or a highly organized system of conditioned reflexes?"

Now, just after midnight, the guests piling pleasure on each other, the long old-fashioned room glowing and darkened, the polished oaken floor smoothed and waxed, the chairs pulled back, the buffet gleaming on its white linen in the dining room, the windows and doors opened but shielded by screens behind which Chinese lanterns, ticking with moths, gleamed above the camellias, the men in dinner jackets, the women in evening gowns; now they danced, now they wandered through the garden paths of the director's house, until a Filipino waiter in a white starched jacket appeared and sounded a mellow gong. The buffet was to be served, and from every corner the guests trooped in, chattering and laughing, while the crisp California night iced the edges of the social warmth and from the orange trees upon the mountainside the wry strong scent eddied down, perfume from the orchards of Paradise.

At this bewitched moment, a young soldier who had already died a thousand times in feeling awakened in the quiet building where those ready to be discharged, those being tested against the temptations of running away, those on the verge of cure, those whose illness was not directed against themselves or the world,

314

lived like ordinary hospital patients, watched, but not guarded, without bars and bolts or extraordinary precautions.

When he awoke he saw the world *through* his mind and not his mind *in* the world. He had no realization of his transcendent state, so magical, so sad, this true idealism, but he came alive suddenly in the darkness of his room and said his name. "Edward Knox." He spoke it several times, tasting it for the strangeness of it, and a desire to see this man whose name he had spoken came strongly to him. It might have been the music that awakened him, for faintly off there sounded a piano, a violin, a horn, a drum, a medley of instruments, a remembered tune, and the young soldier smiled. He knew this Edward Knox quite well, a lively fellow, a born dancer.

The young soldier rose from his bed and crouched to the door.

There he listened for the sound of the attendants and heard the murmur of their late and gossiping voices at the south end of the hall. With great care he opened the door and peeped out, and as the men turned the corridor corner, he darted in the other direction and into the toilet. Like a thief he unlatched a screen and dropped the few feet into the night. He stole into the grounds, the wide lawns with their curved cement walks, into the green and fragrant coolness recovering from the burning day, and, along with the projected ghosts of mind, made his way through the eucalyptus grove which dropped medicinal scent upon his head. He passed the enclosed yard between the locked house and the acute wards and heard within them a man shouting into the night, a voice raised like a cross into the past, a voice calling murder through the nightmare of history. But the young soldier did not pay any attention to this guardian among the damned. He headed for the great wire fence behind which lay the brilliantly lighted house where the music sounded, and behind him in the bolted buildings all through the night the stirrings would go on, the uneasy turning, the voices and gestures escaping and whirling, tense erratic systems, undisciplined, expansive, commanding as are cancerous cells to the flesh.

This passage was not easy for the young soldier. He could smell

315

danger everywhere, and all objects had the ominous shapes of wild animals, thick-necked bushes, open-mouthed trees, branches with hands like leaves.

He would have turned back from this monstrous jungle of wild life, but he had a great need to find Edward Knox. He was not *unaware* that these shapes were trees, bushes, flowers, yet his experience had taught him, especially those long, long weeks so long ago, that these objects were not at all innocent. Some men he knew considered such things to be just what they *appeared* to be, and perhaps for some men they were because these men *did not know*. This young soldier knew that behind the simple façade were forces, wills, motions. It took great courage for him to proceed, but he had proved his courage before and could demonstrate it again.

At last, the most dangerous place of all lay before him, what appeared to be an eight-foot wire fence and behind it, held away from him by this protecting fence, an open space. Fences, he knew, were used to keep dangers away from people and this was why the fence had been erected here. He peered through the repetitive apertures.

There was a wide roll of lawn that rose up to the house, a dark green surface boxed with yellow oblongs of light, an open space, and if jungles were dreadful, open spaces in them were more fearful still. He could feel the force of the earth swelling beneath the lawn. How the grass strained to hold it down and yet bulged with that dangerous unexploded pressure! Who could tell when it would break to engulf a voyager upon it? The young soldier bent over, almost doubled, his breath coming hard and hot, and sought the will to maneuver the lawn.

Behind the screens of the house he saw the shapes of men and women who thought they were safe behind the fence of the screens.

The music was louder.

He shook his head dumbly and was afraid he was dreaming, that this was a fragment of wonderful life he had invented in his dreams, something to talk about to Dr. Grant. He could not get Dr. Grant to pay attention to the things that mattered in his life. No

316

one seemed able any longer to understand him, but it was all so frightfully clear to himself, a suspicion that had become a certainty, that there was no moment at all, awake or asleep, when the lives of men were not in danger. This no one understood and no one believed, and he sadly reflected that it was because he had not as yet died of these dangers that they did not believe him. People could not believe anything unless it was proved, and how was the terror of life to be proved if he did not die of it? Yet he did not want to die of it. He wanted to live and he sought Edward Knox because Knox would believe him. Knox would believe in these unseen terrors, these dangers to all men, and people would believe Knox if Knox could only be told. The young soldier had been working on this plan of action for many weeks, considering what had to be done, examining again and again his knowledge of this danger.

Take the lawn before him.

People saw a lawn there and so did the young soldier. But the others stopped with the lawn. They did not see the space of it, the greenness like water, like the quiet green pool on the island where he had lain for three days, wounded, in the quiet, innocent surface of the water, calling out to the jungle, to his friends behind it, the dangers that lay there concealed within the innocent, iridescent surface. He had tried to warn them, but they had come to save him from what they did not even understand themselves, as now Dr. Grant was trying. They had come crowding in, his loved friends, his comrades, and the trees had suddenly revealed their hidden forces and buckled down, and the pool opened into a thousand nipping mouths, gushing mouths, death raging with thunder and lightning from the center of earth, whips of force that left bloody streaks, the whole thing a turmoil, a horror of screams and shouts, and in the end the quietness returned because all were dead, and still he had lain there. They had not listened then and they would not listen now.

This man whom the young soldier had known in the past, this dancer and lively fellow, Edward Knox, would believe him. Of this, he was certain. For Knox had listened during those three days and was the only one who had not rushed blindly into the open space where the green pool was. Knox had been cunning, even fearful, and hung back, and Knox had survived and would understand and know.

So this innocent lawn, for those who knew, was not as simple as it appeared.

But necessity is a wonderful strength for men, and the young soldier knew that Knox liked dancing and was a lively fellow and was probably safe at that dancing party behind the protecting screens, and so with all his will the young soldier launched himself over the safe fence and in a running flight took the shape of the lawn in quick passage before it could break open, and flung himself against the house, clutched a low window sill and held on to it, safe for a moment, like a swimmer clinging to an overturned boat.

How mysterious, he thought, are the actions of doomed men who do not know their fate!

His face pale and possessed, the forehead pressed against the lower corner of the screen, his body kneeling over the naked soles of his feet, the young soldier marveled at the stupidity of these condemned men and women. How they carried their dinner plates and delicately or roughly munched the white lobster and the red slices of roast beef, the salad, the bread, as if they enjoyed all of it.

All the while his erratic gaze dipped here and there into the corners, searching always for that old friend. He drew back a little when he saw Dr. Grant, the relaxed face smiling absently, the plumpish body weaving through the crowd with a plate and drink for the surrounded wife. The soldier crouched still lower when he saw Colonel Curtin rolling the plaque across the floor like a boy with a hoop, and he withdrew, startled, from the window when he saw Dr. Myers and felt that dark, fatal glance pass unseeing across his own.

Within the room, Carl joined the others laughing at Curtin's antics with the gift. Sometimes it became a halo above the bald, fringed head, and then an Amazon's breastplate, and once a toilet seat, for when Curtin started he could never make himself stop.

318

In the midst of his laughter, without even thinking, Carl looked back to the window to see again a white blur which he had not noticed before and did not expect to be there. He looked around and the object was not there. Still wondering, without examining it, like something that had flown into his eye and out again, leaving half a tear, he turned back to watch Curtin on his hands and knees pushing the plaque across the floor. It had become this kind of uninhibited party.

It occurred to Carl that Curtin perhaps despised this plaque, this tribute from the staff, even though he had picked it, that he perhaps picked it in order to have something easy to despise.

It had been a face. Carl remembered it now. It had been a white face pressed into the lower corner of the screen.

Swiftly, a little worried, he moved away from the shouting crowd who were trying to think up new games with the plaque, and hurried outside. He stood on the great porch and saw nothing but couples strolling, a knot of men, a sense of peace in the darkness and scent of the gardens. Descending, Carl walked around to the window, but there was no one in the hedges, and he kept on walking, moving freely out upon the vast dark lawn through the blocks of light, wondering all the time if he had seen anything at all.

He decided to check with the gate-house guard and put a call through to the different wards, just to be certain.

From behind the white bone trunk of a peeling eucalyptus the soldier watched Carl and feared him. He felt himself hunted, and like a man hunted, since for him to *feel* was to *be,* he melted at once deeper and deeper into the terrible woods, less terrible than being hunted. Where before he had experienced danger, now there was flight, and in the flight a spring of desperation began to wind and turn and tighten, agitating his muscles, pumping his blood, suffusing his mind with thrusting images of night. Where was Edward Knox?

The fragrance here in the concealed thickets was liquid as a swamp of flowers, citrus and honeysuckle, those powers of darkness, roses, those evening goddesses, and for the soldier these were persons because his was a peopled world, even more thronged than

319

the one he had once inhabited, but friendless and barren of understanding.

A glimmer of light arrested his darting head.

He saw the yellow strip of light turning up the iridescent green, the pool; and brilliant illumination, happiness, burst like too old a star in his brain.

He had found his way back. Back.

There it was, the pool, and on shaking, mesmerized feet he made his way through the resisting bushes and kneeled over the edge of the pool and looked down into it, already talking, already explaining, for there was Edward Knox lying face up in the water.

I come to warn you, he thought he shouted, and sought to touch his only friend, to catch him, hold him, convince him, and he plunged into the pool, into the cool lapping waters of death, to die.

ii

"SUCH accidents occur from time to time in all hospitals." But nothing that Carl said was of any comfort to Curtin, who whipped himself from sullen depression to rage and then subsided, losing his force, losing his will, losing the *point* of his anger, only to find in a sudden flurry all his rage again.

It was very late, the night yawning wearily, and already drifting with tiredness into dawn, and too many hours without sleep had taken the edge off the unhappy event, the pale pajamas, the bluing flesh, the transfixed face of Edward Knox. They had fished him from the waters, and his wet hair, drying, had formed small crisp curls, blond and tender, formerly beloved by girls and his mother. The fatless body, already marked by that emaciation which his disturbed state favored, was still neat and youthful, a man's without the too heavy muscles, something light and flying to it, a litheness close to adolescence and not yet corrupted by crushing work. The tensions, of course, were gone from the body, gone from the muscles, gone from the cells, and while life still went on within Knox's flesh, it was not his life, but the life of innumerable creatures and innumerable processes whose fat days had so suddenly begun. The doctors had tried to revive Knox by mechanical and pharmacological means, and when nothing worked, when all hope was gone, the remains had been carted away to that warehouse, the morgue.

And now there was nothing left of this young man, Knox, nothing he could originate except the meanings he might have for those who remained alive, so absolute and terrifying is the disappearance of consciousness, whose slightest irrational flicker, whose smallest

321

irritation of tissue, is profounder than the creation of new suns and more rational than whole solar systems.

Carl tried again with his friend. "When a man really wants to die, Val, the world is just made for it. Everything an instrument. Any time an opportunity."

"Why couldn't the son of a bitch have waited another week? Did he have to hang a crepe on the party?" Curtin brooded within the wreckage of the celebration, the sandwiches mashed like moths within the carpets, a broken glass in the beige chair, the dabs of mustard on the papered walls as if a muddy wave of pleasure foaming into the room had sprayed it from floor to ceiling. Just beginning to evaporate was the dormitory smell of all the people who had laughed and danced and eaten there, a warmth that very slowly was seeping out of the house into the astringent night, and it added to Curtin's irritation, for he saw it all with alien, puritanical eyes now that his enjoyment was over.

Resentfully he stared at the three doctors who were his audience, Myers, Wyler and Sarvis, and then he rumbled up the steps, shouting to the servants, "Get this damned mess cleared up!" They were doing it anyway and Curtin walked among them pointing out one bit of filth after another. From a crease of cushions on the couch he extracted an overturned ash tray. "Pigs," he cried. "Pigs! That's what this damned staff's composed of, pigs!" He tore out the cushions and flung them to the floor.

Carl caught an amused glance between Dr. Wyler and Dr. Sarvis, and while he sympathized with their point of view, he did not approve of it. "Why don't you let me take care of this, Val?" he asked.

But Curtin returned and stood larger than ever, three steps above the big rooms. "Pimps," he said vindictively. "Medical pimps, a sanatorium for malingerers and fools. That's what we have here. The least I expect is loyalty. Why," he demanded, "why don't I get any loyalty from these doctors after all the sacrifices I've made for them? You tell me that."

Sarvis, a Pacific veteran, young and gray-headed, with the bland meanness of a Roman bust, a man so empty of sentiment that Carl

322

often suspected he was too full of feeling, said, and still smiled, "We were as loyal as we could be, Val. You crawled on the floor and we crawled after you."

A swell of fury distended Curtin's heavy face, and the great body arched, growing greater and greater from within, opening the vast and mysterious source of his violence upon this new frustrating object. But before he could speak or do anything the two white-coated attendants appeared, humble and wary, each trying to hang back behind the other, so that as they came in they moved forward without seeming to advance, and only the scenery went by.

Curtin let his breath out slowly. He withdrew his glance from Sarvis with an almost painful recall, unlocking a hold. "Well?" he asked the attendants. "What have you got to say? What?"

Between them they kept saying the same thing over and over again like a pair of cheap comedians.

They had made the rounds at the correct times.

They had noticed nothing unusual.

Knox had been co-operative and quiet all day.

"Perfect," Curtin remarked sarcastically. "The report is perfect and therefore Knox is still alive. Nothing happened." He invited Carl's approval with ponderous mockery. "The whole thing, I presume, is a mistake." When he received no assistance from that impassive face, he turned back upon the attendants. "And the loose screen in the toilet? It's not just supposed to keep the flies out, you know. You know that, don't you?"

They knew it. They had been careful and couldn't account for the condition unless Knox had prepared the window himself, a possibility, because this was the quiet building and the men were not under unusual guard. If Knox had been in one of the dangerous buildings he could never have escaped.

"Well, God damn it, why wasn't he?" Curtin pointed his red face towards Sarvis. "You were the officer of the day. I hold you responsible for any negligence. Walk these men over the building and check everything."

"With pleasure," Sarvis said politely, and he started out followed

323

by the unhappy attendants while Dr. Wyler took his cue and began to tag along.

"Where are you going?" Curtin flung after him.

The plump, middle-aged man stopped. He was insulted and yet he did not feel it proper to defend himself at this hectic moment so instead he looked to Carl for aid.

To the room in general Curtin asked, "And where's that son of a bitch, Grant? What's he doing home now when his patient is stretched out like cold lamb in the morgue? I'll bet he's fast asleep in a drunkard's bed, wrapped in connubial delight. Soft. All soft. Wyler, you get Grant. Bring him over to the administration building. I can't stand the filth here." Wyler backed out, a slight disdain on his usually secretive face, and once again before he disappeared he looked to Carl for some statement but found only a neutral silence.

"Grant," Curtin went on, "I knew it would be Grant. By God, I'm glad it's Grant. I could've predicted it a year ago."

Now that they were alone, Carl asked sharply, "What do you mean?"

But Curtin strode out, dropping behind him an enigmatic, "I'm not blind."

Carl caught up with him and walked down the porch steps with him and out upon the great lawns, all lighted up by the big flood lamps controlled from the guardhouse at the gate. Within the envelope of light, a transformation had taken place. The event of the evening had served to establish in the minds of the healthy what before had only been in the thoughts of the sick. The place was dangerous. These sick green lawns, those burly trees, the path that led to the pond, the wire fence that gleamed like a frontier, these now were fraught with death, with unmentioned fears. It was true for Carl and Curtin at this moment as earlier it had been true for Knox.

At the edge of the pool Curtin stopped and looked unpleasantly at the water, brighter green and brighter yellow from the light hung in the trees. The surface was still. The bottom evident and empty. It was innocent.

324

They felt it deadly.

"Grant did the workup on Knox's case," Curtin said soberly. "Why didn't he realize the boy had suicidal impulses? That's the purpose of the examinations."

"I don't know," Carl replied. "When he comes we'll ask him. I suggest a post-mortem."

"I used to be a great one for post-mortems myself." But Curtin let no humor edge into his voice. "May I quote you? Where will we find a suicidal impulse in a cadaver?"

"We'll find," Carl insisted, "what there is to be found."

They did not speak again on their long walk to the administration building.

When they passed through the gate the guard was standing outside, ready to tell for the third time that he was positive that Knox had not come through the gate, but Curtin walked by and left it for Carl to smile in recognition to the man.

They rounded the wide circle of buildings, dark-windowed, bright-walled with floodlights, and the area was alert with the look of a military encampment ready for an attack.

...
iii

WHEN pale and nauseous Dr. Grant entered Curtin's office he found his two superiors sitting there across the room from each other. They had merely waited without further discussing the incident, for Curtin felt Carl's disapproval and resented it, and Carl refused to speak until all the facts were at hand.

"It's pretty awful about Knox," Grant said as he slipped down into one of the leather chairs, relaxing completely. "I still feel sick. Why doesn't someone say something when I drink too much?" He did not gather much sympathy and he realized it, so he assembled his powers, his throbbing temples, the shaking flutter in his stomach, and asked, "How did it happen?"

Curtin swung back in his chair and folded his hairy hands over his big belly. "That's why we called you. You did the workup on him."

"I know, I know." It was evident that Grant felt no responsibility for the accident and it irritated Curtin all the more. Curtin rested within the cage of his anger, his words like paw strokes waiting to shatter the lock. This hard, unfriendly atmosphere was not lost on Grant, and in all innocence he tried to humanize it by attacking himself. "I'm one of those people who can't drink. And yet every time there's a party, I do." This brought no response. He glanced over to his admired chief for some help in this situation but Carl sat there without much interest in Grant's hangover.

"What would you like to know?" Grant finally asked.

"I'm asking you," Curtin said deliberately and brutally, "I'm asking you about your lapse of duty, your negligence and the death of one of our patients. You did the workup on Knox and

326

reported no suicidal impulses. We have means for protecting such patients from themselves, or aren't you familiar with the resources of the institution?"

Startled, Grant sat up in his chair and stared at Curtin, then he rose hotly to his feet. "It's very late and I've had no sleep. I don't feel very well and perhaps I can't appreciate your humor, but I'll be damned if I know what the hell you're talking about. What do you mean negligence?" He put his hands in his pockets and stood there in all hostility. "I don't know what happened to Knox and at this hour I don't care."

The top ripped off Curtin's rage. "Is that your best scientific opinion?" He was up on his feet, facing Grant. "I know nothing about it. The good Dr. Grant knows nothing about it. The drunken Dr. Grant has no knowledge of his patients. And what the hell have you been doing with him these past three months? Holding his hand, while you daydream about that little private Hollywood practice you've been setting up on the side? What kind of a place do you think we're running here? A saloon? A rest home for medical cranks? A whorehouse to satisfy the casual concupiscence of delinquent psychiatrists? This is a hospital, you understand? A government hospital, supported by the taxpayers. I've pampered the whole lot of you. I've stood aside and let you all play with scientific theories so that in the end you can't tell whether a patient is dangerous to himself or not. I'm not one of these modern experts. Oh, no. I'm nothing. Just a stinking administrator, a publicity expert, an ex-colonel. I'd like you to know, Dr. Grant, if you are a doctor, which I doubt, that in my time I've done more scientific work than you'll ever hope to do. You've got the wrong man in mind, my friend. You made one diagnosis and the patient lived up to another. I'm asking how did it happen, and I want an answer, not a detailed report on your experiences as a drunkard, or your income as social secretary to the neuroses of ten talentless Hollywood stars."

"Well, Dr. Curtin," Grant said ironically, stressing the *doctor,* "I diagnosed Knox and I tell you now that he had no suicidal impulses. Absolutely none. None. You hear that? None."

"I'm glad to hear it," Curtin replied heavily. "Very glad, because he'll be happy to receive the information. You'll find him in the morgue."

"He can be in the director's office for all I care. I don't know how he died. He could have fallen in, banged his head, anything. It's quite possible for a man to wander out of a hospital at night and get hurt. But I know he didn't leave his room to kill himself. I'll stake my reputation on it."

"You're not risking much," Curtin told him. "And it'll be worth less after tonight."

Grant turned to Carl with a certain helpless anger. "Do you believe this nonsense too?"

"Of course not," Carl said. "I think Val is upset, but that's no excuse for the way he's talking." And before Curtin could interrupt he added, "The fact is that I thought I saw someone looking in through one of the windows during the party. It must have been Knox."

"You what?" Curtin was for a moment bewildered.

"You were crawling around with that plaque and I thought I noticed a white face peering into the room."

"And?"

"And what?"

Curtin sat down again. He was upset because he was quarreling with Carl. He said more quietly. "Did you go out to look?"

"Naturally. I couldn't find anyone. I wasn't sure, as a matter of fact, that I had actually seen anyone."

"Why didn't you send out an alarm?"

"I did, but Knox was discovered dead before he was found to be missing." Carl paused for a moment wondering how far he should go with Curtin. He did not like this helpless raging at the staff, suspecting from experience that it masked other causes, but on the other hand, Carl did not expect too much from people, either of control or steadfastness. He said a little roughly, "I am, of course, directly responsible for the medical work here and I believe that Grant's diagnosis was correct. I talked with Knox myself. We have two thousand patients here and despite our care there will be accidents." He turned to Grant. "You go home and go to sleep. We'll go over this affair more carefully in the morning."

"Good night," Grant said and went out, but as he left he smiled to his chief in gratitude for the help, displeasing Carl, who was irritated by this concern with the self and not the dead man.

"Well," Carl said said wearily, "we can't expect everyone to feel the way we do about the patients."

But Curtin was sitting sullenly in his chair and he did not even look up at Carl.

"Would you like to talk about this business now?" Carl asked.

The pale eyes of Curtin, imageless in the amplitude of his red face, raised and fixed without warmth on his friend, and the great bulk settled, withdrawing within its weight, becoming an impassive stone, a mound of unprojecting flesh, inert as a crystal.

The silence of Curtin was not a pause. It was a barrier.

"Would you?" Carl repeated.

"No."

"Good night, then."

Yet Carl waited another moment. The hard seconds heaped still higher between them, a wall of hostility, a hostility which Carl did not feel although he realized it. He sighed and decided to remain. "It seems to me," he said mildly, "that more than Grant is involved in this."

It took a long time for Curtin to answer, for he sat like an angry child with a ball of knotted and twisted string, looking here and there for an end to begin with, never quite knowing how to unravel his feelings, impatient to do so, afraid to begin. He did not know whether to shout, to explain, to protest. He said, "That Grant is the worst of the lot."

"In what way, Val?"

Again Carl waited, and again he felt Curtin's mind going around and around the labyrinth, and now it was another end.

"I don't like my position here."

This, Carl felt, was closer to the tangle. "What's Grant got to do with your position here?"

Unable to sit any longer with the internal knot, Curtin stood up

329

and automatically untied his bow tie and let the ends dangle on his shirt front. He peered from beneath his reddened lids, searching the room, and then asked socially, "Would you like a drink?"

"No," Carl said. "You have one."

"I don't want one." Curtin licked his lips, dry and ribbed, the worn corners of his mouth. He raised his heavy hands and took hold of the ends of his tie and just stood there. He said, "This Knox affair is just another example."

Patiently, Carl asked, "Of what?"

And suddenly Curtin took the whole knotted tangle and held it out without preparation, for Carl to see, beginning with it just as it appeared to him. "A couple of months ago I was walking outside, towards dinnertime, and I wandered over by the pool, behind the hedges there, and I overheard a conversation. Grant was there, and Sarvis and Wyler and a few other doctors of the staff, taking a swim. They couldn't see me and I didn't intend to listen, but I walked in on it and I heard it. They were talking about me." He paused. This was the hardest to say. "And about you." The mere utterance of this overwhelmed Curtin. He found it difficult to go on. "I'm not complaining," he added, "I'm curious."

"So am I," Carl said.

"You must know. I'm sure you know."

"What should I know?" Carl asked.

The room had become too small for Curtin. He stood there sawing on the ends of his bow tie, needing space and ease and could not find it. He forced himself to speak, and forcing himself was belligerent. "That little bastard Grant said I had a fine racket. You were doing all the scientific work here and because I was the director, I was getting all the credit. I mean, this isn't the point. It's what they think of me. Why should the staff here think that my contribution is less valuable than their own?"

"They feel competitive," Carl replied, and he felt the hopelessness of going on with this. "Everybody around competes and they compete too. What's this got to do with me?"

With a quick explosion Curtin cried out, "I'm the businessman here and everybody else is the scientist."

330

"Shall I," Carl asked softly, "tell you how valuable and necessary your work is?"

Out of his great sense of injury Curtin protested, "Why should you? Who would have to, if the opposite wasn't true? I know what I feel."

But Carl could not unlock his reserve. He saw only a difficulty which he could not manage. Yet he wanted to help. He asked, "What would you like me to do?"

"Nothing. Nothing."

"You chose a certain role for yourself when you could have chosen anything. You preferred it. If you no longer prefer it, give it up."

"I don't blame you," Curtin said miserably. "I blame myself."

"And what makes you think that I consider my life a success?"

"They consider it so. They do."

"They have small standards."

"Small or large, they're large enough to run me down." Curtin was already sorry that he had begun to speak. He didn't know where to turn, how to escape from this painful and difficult situation. He felt inferior to Carl, unable to compete with him, because all the words meant one thing, and there within him was the miserable state, the sense of incompleteness, the frustration. "I've devoted my whole life to this science," he said. "All my life. This institution was my idea, the kind of work, the things we're doing. And what does it all amount to?"

Remote, quiet, Carl looked steadily at his friend, and saw there, suddenly drained of force, suddenly old, a fat and defeated man. Against this image, double exposed upon it, was that truly gay and lurching personality that had dared the unknown regions at Castlehill, and between them were too many years of academic success, wartime power, and administrative effort. Against this worldliness the first naïve fascination with experiment had frittered away. In the end what was left of the life?

"There's something wrong with me," Curtin complained bitterly, "When I have to be the one that goes to Washington like a damned fund-raiser for a charity, while you go to New York to present our scientific work here. I don't mean," he added hastily, "that you can't do it better than I can. I merely feel that, I merely say," but in the end he did not say anything. He sat down once again in his chair and stared at the top of his desk, because stronger than his need to understand was his resentment.

Carl wanted to help Curtin, but the fact was he no longer had the patience and curiosity for other lives as such, that roving adventure in personal relations which keeps existence supple and continually new. His life had hardened. He had a cold sharpness in the world of ideas, even a keenness for exploration there, but friends did not collect about him and love did not come to him. So this irritating, painful situation with Curtin had arisen, would continue to exist and could not be solved. It was difficult to remain friends when both were not equals, at least in intention, and Curtin had changed and drifted away, a new force working within him.

Curtin had become a convivial bachelor with all the peculiarities of the state. As he boomed his way towards middle age with a certain renown piling on his great shoulders, everything unexpected became a personal affront, everything uncontrollable seemed dangerous, everything unusual immoral, but deeper than all, no longer being an active scientist himself, he needed renown since he no longer had the work.

In the beginning at the hospital, he had divided the work with Carl and gloried in the administrative power, but finally, as the years went on, he had seen Carl's position increase in influence, in the attitudes of the staff, and felt the corrupting acid of competition. The overexcited incident of this evening proved it, for there was nothing in the facts but an opportunity for Curtin to assert his will.

The slow realization of this unhappy condition had come to Carl over the past months, and as a result he had tried to withdraw. He could not bring himself to compete with his old friend, not that he hoped any longer to safeguard the friendship, for it was in the process of being destroyed. But Carl did not need the hospital, having, so to speak, created its scientific life which could go on without him, and even more smoothly if Curtin felt more secure. But Carl had not yet decided what course he should take. He could fight Curtin and fight to eliminate him from the scene. This did not attract him. He could leave, but he had not yet decided where, under what conditions, and for what goals. So he had slowly retreated, giving up his quarters at the hospital to take a beach house, far away at Malibu.

There, in a four-room, isolated cottage standing on a peninsula that jutted out to sea, he spent all his unofficial time. The living room had a wall of glass where the sea stood by day and night, matchless, muscled with waves, a perpetual uneasiness. One of the bedrooms he had converted into a study where he dreamed over books, over novels he had never read, fictions in which men and women desired and struggled, and out of which like a fragrant aroma reality emerged with all its marvelous gift of surprise and immolation. There was a kitchen in which he sometimes made coffee and a sandwich. From a settlement in a nearby canyon a woman came in to clean. This was all. From time to time, the doctors met at his house to talk with him. Once he gave a party. But everything was becoming less. A round dry hill loomed behind the house. On the other side of the hill was a curving road and behind the road the scorched precipitate mountains began, climbing to the clear hot sky. The beach was white and naked. In the daytime, when he had the time, he walked its length with sandpipers, gulls and an occasional pelican for companions. At night, he very often sat and listened to the ocean. He would soon have to make a choice because, from experience, he knew how futile it was to attempt to convince a man driven by competitive urge that his supposed rival was free of it. It would be like telling a lover in love that there was no such thing as love. It would be like telling the young soldier not to fear life, when it was life that had created the fear.

All Carl could say to Curtin was, "If you feel me as your rival, I do not think I am. You have rival feelings, Val, but I'm not one of them."

He left without another backward glance, going gratefully into the soft and open night. As he walked down the curved paths and cut across the big lawns, he deliberately thought ahead to the psychiatric Congress and wondered if, after it, it might not be well to resign from Sierra and continue his work at the Erdman Institute, where as director he could remove himself from this competitive environment and the presence of leftover personal relations.

At the gate he instructed the guard to turn off the floodlights, heard again the agitated assurance that Knox had not come through the gate. One by one the lights went out over the area, and the sky closed down upon the usual lamps, swarming into the shadows and crevices, while far off in the east, behind the mountains another hot day began to burn.

iv

ALL the windows were open but no air moved within the sweating city of New York.

On such a paralyzed and decaying night, phosphorescent and fatigued, the noisy shouts and quarreling voices from the meeting rooms sounded inhuman to Juley. She sat at her desk in the little outside office, in a litter of union papers and conflicting leaflets, her feet up on a drawn-out drawer, and she dreamed of California, the oranges in their thick dark trees like ice cubes in Coca-Cola. Across the room an electric fan dozed and riffled the thick bulk of syrupy air, the hard lights burned, the ash trays overflowed, and beer and soft drinks had spilled upon the floor. On the walls posters left over from the war still proclaimed in all their advertiser's innocence the great fight and unity, but years had passed and they were tombstones in the graveyard of social hope.

Now, after midnight the meeting still went on.

A gavel smashed mechanically through the jazzed-up tumult, beat and beat until the roar became a murmur, while from the core of the noise Sam Halloran's voice commenced in its fierce oratorical splendor and Juley knew the end was on its way.

She did not even listen.

Her irritable glance moved upon the desk like a housefly, stopping on the open pack of cigarettes (but her mouth was too hot and dry to smoke again), on Carl's telegram, on an untasted sandwich, on her purse. She touched her grimy, greasy face and could not find the energy to rise, to wash it, to put on new makeup. In the telegram Carl had merely announced his arrival, that he could be reached at the Erdman Institute, that he would be speaking at the Psychiatric Congress. There was no word invit-

335

ing her to see him, no indication that he wanted her to. It was a polite piece of information that one sends to a relative. But she was too tired to be annoyed, and he had after all the right to let her know in any way he pleased, since it pleased him to send one hundred dollars a month for little Carla.

Juley sighed. She owed Carla a letter or a visit, and suddenly with pleasure she thought how nice it would be to go with Carl up to the summer camp in the high mountains, into the coolness and fresh green, where that heart-shaped lake lay inserted in the cold leaves and guarded by evergreen hills like a slice of cold cucumber in salad. If she could only cool off and clean up, Juley would have enjoyed something fine and tasty to eat, to chew away the stale cigarettes, the warm drinks, the hot and vapid air, and this long belittling day.

A few floors down in Astor Place, the late busses roared, shattering the emptiness of the great square, running their sputtering motors into the reaches of Lafayette Street.

At last from within, a geyser of boos and cheers erupted, a flurry of applause, and the boos withering to thin last pipings, bird sounds before bedtime, disappeared into a roar of triumphant conversations.

The doors flew open in the wide corridor.

Juley pushed back her damp hair from her hot face, arose, and slowly walked to the entrance door where she stood watching the mob, thrusting and eager to get into the cooler streets, the women unsticking their cotton dresses, the men in their shirts, coats in the crook of an arm or slung by a finger over the shoulder, a host of pale, distracted faces. She saw pass the faces of the defeated, her old friends, friends of Bill, and she saw the victors go by, her old friends and friends of Bill, for this was what the times had become, a pervasive civil war.

Some waved to her and she responded, and some did not wave and she felt the cut of their anger, but she stood there so hot and weary it did not matter, not even when a middle-aged woman in a yellow dress, her hands still burdened with the literature of defeat, stopped in the crush and then as if with a great effort of will came up to her. There was tiredness on this woman's face but it was not emptied of will. It had anger and spirit, and she paused with her bundle and asked in a low tense voice, "And now what about you, Juley?" She had small black eyes, vibrant as two electric poles, a heavy sagging neck, a brisk body, and she almost quivered with the tension and shock of the meeting.

Juley looked beyond her into the thinning crowd, the particolored backs going away in the brown corridor, the mélange of feet on the stone floor, the sign of a sister union across the hall. "What would you suggest?"

"It was a shame, a shame," the woman said passionately. Hers had been one of the active voices in the meeting, and even in this conversation some of the public speaker's fire still burned. "A shameful thing. I never thought I'd live to see the day when Sam would betray his friends. Never. But I've seen them. And I've seen worse," she added contemptuously, looking at Juley. "Much worse."

A tag of anger, strong because guilty, snarled in Juley's mind. "You didn't expect to win, did you?"

The woman shifted the bundle in her aching arms. "I expected certain people to stand up and be counted."

A growling, excited, victorious handful of men came out of the meeting room, the newly elected executive board, with Sam Halloran in the center, his round handsome head excited and flushed. There were good-nights and the men went off laughing while Sam sauntered over to the little office. The woman suddenly tossed the bundle of leaflets to the floor at his feet where they scattered in a flurry of whiteness, turned her back, her eyes filling with tears, and ran off down the corridor. Her low-heeled shoes tapped a finale on the empty floor, took the turn, sounded down the bend, down the steps and faded into the murmur that came constantly from the traffic of the street, the undertone of city noise, the limp blackness of the night.

Sam stood there, grinning and embarrassed, uneasily stepping within the mass of paper, like a man in an unexpected puddle. "Well?" he asked.

337

"Why, congratulations, Judas," Juley said.

He laughed and changed his folded coat from one sturdy arm to the other. "Ah," he cried, "what the hell! I've got you covered like a tent."

She turned away from him with moody discomfort. "I'll send you a thank-you note in the morning."

He shook it off. "In ten years who'll know the difference?"

This was true, because now after ten years, it made no difference to him.

Sam wore a blue shirt sweated under the armpits, a stain running around his neck and down his back, a hard sturdy man with muscles made in the auto pits of Detroit, and a bright savage face, almost wild with the feelings that so easily came to it, one of the great speakers of the union, one of the shrewdest fighters, and one of the bravest. He now made five thousand dollars a year as the union president, with other thousands kicked in for expenses from the International, and he had a big new Buick, a small modern house in the country where he kept his wife and children, and a bank account.

"Ten years from now," Juley said, "I'll come around to see." She picked up her purse and stabbed hopelessly at her hair with a hand. "But meanwhile I'll go home." She took the keys from her purse and began to lock the files.

"Why don't we go out and have a beer and a sandwich?" Sam asked.

"Don't tell me you're feeling good and you want to celebrate?" She snapped the heavy drawers in and turned the key. "This mess we'll leave to the janitor, and I wish they could sweep you away, too."

A low warm laugh, as rich and sensual as a hand touch, came from him across the room and cajoled her. She stood still for an instant, trying to look at him objectively, but she could feel within him the elation, the pleasure of victory, the lift it gave to his spirits and with it a kind of generalized sensuality. It was not easy to escape the habit of her body, but she decided to avoid it.

"Go home to your wife," she said, and went across the room,

338

passing him. "She wanted money in the bank and she has it. She wanted security and a house of her own. She got it. She wanted to bring up her children in a nice respectable neighborhood full of bond clerks, bookkeepers and real estate agents. She got it. But don't go dumping it on my head. You didn't do it for me."

He laughed again and slammed the door closed, hurrying after her to take her arm.

"It's too hot," she said, "unless you're made of ice."

"Three times," he cried out vehemently, "three times, you know it, I've been a damned martyr three times for the union. Once in the hospital, once in the jail, and once at the end of a rope, damn near. You think the dumb bastards appreciate it?"

Juley did not answer this because it was true.

"Now I tail along with the International," he said, "and I'm a hero. You heard the cheers. I dumped a ten-year fight into the gutter and you heard loud cheers."

She refrained from comment and sighed with pleasure as she entered the street.

It was a warm, a humid summer night, but in these early morning hours the heat had somewhat retreated, sagged back a degree or two, and down the cross street from Broadway a thin, an almost moveless current moved and touched her pleasantly. It slid by her bare legs and touched her arms and neck. "That feels good," she said. And she was hungry.

"C'mon," he said, "we'll go down to that place near the park."

She let herself be led.

Here on the outskirts of Greenwich Village the empty streets, cornered and traversed by the old loft buildings with their dangling signs and narrow tall windows, their black, hermetic bulks rising into the tired sky, here it seemed cooler in the dark dusty air, and on Broadway, blacked out except for street lights, a river wind turned, a slow, fatigued draught, yet astonishing and good after the supine day.

"You know yourself," he went on still explaining, "I laid back to see what the membership would do, and they wanted the board

339

to sign those affidavits. So what? The hell with them. I didn't press them."

"You pushed them tonight."

"They were laying down. I just pushed some of the religious boys who can't tell the revival's over. Glory, glory. There's a dead-end sign on the glory road."

This was all true, and yet it was all wrong. In the end there was the moral question.

"They were old friends of yours."

"A hundred years from now who'll know the difference?"

"Oh, don't." Her exasperation was intense. "I know you've got that long-range feeling, especially because it keeps you in where life is easy. If it made any difference, it wouldn't make any difference to you. You're sour way down to the bottom. And I know it."

He laughed uneasily and held his free hand out, two fingers crossed. "Love and hate," he said, "they're like that."

They were at that moment passing a corner and someone reached out and grabbed Sam's hand and jerked him back and around into the narrow side street, still cobbled and dark with a hundred years.

So abrupt, a force seized him, jerking him around and out of sight in a momentous flutter. The outstretched night contracted with fear upon her.

Juley suppressed a scream when she saw the two men, one holding Sam up against the wall, the other with his face in the corner light, a face like a wedge, pale and terrible with anger. She recognized Chamberlain, Ed Chamberlain, an old friend of Bill's. The other man who now stood in front of Sam was immense, with great shoulders, and he wore a blue shirt. It could only be Sanchez.

Without anything being said the situation was clear to the four of them, and Sam crouched tensely against the building wall, afraid but not resigned.

Sanchez had a hoarse, smoker's voice and was bitter. "It wouldn't do any good, but it'd do me good to turn you into scrap."

"What kind of a committee do you call this?" Juley cried out indignantly, trying to get between the two men and Sam.

340

Sanchez held her off easily with an ungentle hand. "Good and welfare," he said, "that's what. How much did you get paid, Sam dear?"

"Well," Sam replied heavily, "you will have a fight here, I'll tell you that. And if you don't kill me, I'll be coming around to finish it, win or lose. That's what."

"Just give me a reason," Sanchez went on ignoring this, "just give me a reason in this dark street with no company fingermen around to take down your song. How come? They beat your brains out like they did mine when we organized this sold-out union. How come?"

"You've been through this," Juley said. "What's the use of going over it again? Again and again."

"You!" Ed Chamberlain nearly spit in her face. "Dirty bitch."

"That's not fair," she protested hotly. "I've used all my influence to make him stick. He just keeps coming unstuck."

"Try getting on top the next time," Sanchez told her, ignoring her, not looking at her, watching Halloran still waiting against the wall. "Bill's wife," he cried out with a sudden, enveloping fury. "What a joke!"

And she cringed away for a moment. "All right, all right. Sam's no good and I'm no good. What's the good of this?"

"No good," Sanchez said. "No good. I just want to know. Sometimes it's good to give a bum a punch in the nose." He could not bring himself to walk away, and yet he was so old a veteran of these affairs he could not force himself to let go and fight, knowing how in the end it would make the opposition only stronger. He knew Sam and he knew he was not to be frightened by force. "What scared you?" he demanded.

But Sam was still careful, knowing this old friend of his (and he did not want to fight if he could avoid it). "I'm right," he said, "and you're wrong. The union comes first and if a few poeple don't see it, they have to be pushed aside."

"I don't like to be pushed," Sanchez said. "Don't push me."

Ed spoke up impatiently. "Give the son of a bitch a punch in the nose or let's go."

341

"Suit yourself," Sam said. He took out a cigarette and a lighter. When he flipped the lighter to make the flame, Sanchez grabbed it.

"Jesus Christ," he cried. "God. Look at this." His body shook with hatred and the lust for violence, the release of it. "Look, Ed. Those lighters the committee got when we won the shop. Remember?!"

And Juley remembered, sick at heart, how Bill had visited Carl in the hospital and given the lighter to him, and the years peeled off like a dead skin, and her heart shook, assaulted by memory and tears.

With enormous force Sanchez dashed the lighter to the stone. "Light your cigarette," he shouted, "on the company's ass."

He turned and walked off with Ed, and they never turned back, nor looked, fearful as Lot, afraid to avenge by a blow what had been stolen from them by betrayal, a quarter of a life's work. They disappeared down the length of the dark and narrow alley where at the end it ran full into another cross street.

His hands on his hips, the unlit cigarette in his mouth, the jacket slung in the crook of his left arm, Sam watched them. "Well," he said quietly, but aching for vengeance, "if that's the best they can do, it's not much."

Juley bent down and picked up the little silver lighter with the inscription on it. Its little lever stood out like a broken semaphore.

"I'll break their backs," Sam said evenly, but he was beginning to pant, the suppressed rage boiling within him. He took the lighter roughly from her and looked at it. "I paid for this like Bill paid for his, like they did, and it's mine! I'll break their backs for it."

But Juley no longer had any heart for the middle ground. That concealed anguish with which she had lived for so many years had broken through, and she could not live with it, and stand here, and go on this way, ignoring what so humiliated her memory of life. "Good night," she said. "I'm going home."

Sam caught her arm. "Oh, the hell with them. I've got some personal things to talk about."

"Not with me," she replied. It was so easy to decide at last. "Not with me."

"With you, with you. C'mon."

"No." She wrenched away. "No."

His voice suddenly escaped, got free like an uncaged hawk, flew up in a rage. He had not lost his strength, only the point of it. "I'm tired of going back to the losing side. Tired. Fed up. I don't believe any good can come out of it and I'm tired of only thinking of a decent life. I want it now, and everything that goes with it, and everything I've got. What do you want? Christ, I'm getting rid of the whole shebang, the wife, the kids, everything. No more of this crap. Out with it."

She giggled, almost with hysteria, it was so funny. "Respectability. For me too. The big gift. Because *you* love it, I get it. No." And she just turned as if she had not been this man's lover for over two years and went away from him, leaving him there by himself. He was so astounded, not believing this, and she trudged down the street the way she had come, down the dusty dead New York night, back to the office to get her things and quit at that moment.

She could not explain to herself why she had gone on so long, fighting all the way against what Sam was becoming, and yet giving in each day, because each day was so little, so that the mole had become the usual sore, and the sore a constant itch, and the itch a pain and the pain the cancer itself eating her heart and spirit out. For this man had been her violent love and sensual forgetfulness.

She entered the confined heat of the office building, gloomily ascended the stone steps, went down the hall and stepped through the scattered leaflets. She opened the door and clicked the switch.

The overhead light disclosed the disordered filth again, and that was all Sam's victory amounted to.

Juley went to the desk and unlocked it, rummaging in the drawers for her few belongings, things she could have left behind, cleaning tissue, vanishing cream, a box of emery boards, two old

343

letters, the mate of a torn stocking which no longer could be matched, but she did not leave them, feeling the impossibility of leaving anything of herself within this surrendered citadel of her old life. She made a packet of these things in an old newspaper and was turning to go when she saw Carl's telegram beneath a beer bottle. She took the telegram and reread it, and this time she was glad that he was coming because she wanted to talk with him. More than anything, she needed someone to talk with, for now the war's fatal gift to her, that poisoned vacancy, had come to life again, and with a moody, desperate gaze she looked up at the wall where the big wooden plaque with its gold-painted names was, and there Bill's name led all the rest. Died for His Country, it read, William Myers. The only one, the only only one, of all the hundreds whose names followed, the men who had returned, some wounded, some crazy, some untouched, but all returned, only Bill had not come back.

Now it was after all these years that she wept, only now.

She did not yet know what it meant for Bill to be dead, but she knew he was gone, having left her and been away, and somehow she had heard that he had been killed in action, having died heroically for his country. Only Carl had written from Prummern that Bill had been uselessly killed like an unwanted dog on a foolish scouting party just before the Bulge.

But these words heroic or foolishly dead did not mean much for her. She had grieved and not having seen him for a long time, she continued to live not seeing him, sometimes almost expecting he would return.

He did not, of course, return, since he was dead.

And she had tried, being a woman of common sense, to love someone else, in this case Sam Halloran, who was at least a friend of Bill's, a man like him in some respects in the life he led. But it was not the same, and yet she had persisted, and she persisted in her weeping, the long waves of it beginning to sound and sound upon the empty beaches of her life.

She was a woman with a passion for relationship, to be involved in the lives of those she loved, of those she liked, of those she

344

admired, and she had drowned herself in work like Bill's, in friends of Bill's, so that she could have her dead husband without possessing him. Now she knew it had not been love for anyone. It had been flight, and in flight, to escape, one abandons all the possessions, and so she had dropped them one by one until tonight she had awakened to discover that she had dropped the very loyalties of her existence, the very core of her husband's life, his honor, all that was left of him.

She felt extremely sorry for herself, and she longed to cry in the presence of Carl, to go to him for comfort, for he was more than anyone else like Bill, an iron man, she felt, for so she saw him, and saw him now on the hospital bed after the beating he had accidentally taken in Bill's place. She was afraid of Carl, of his mind which seemed far beyond her ability to comprehend, and she had incorporated into her idea of him all Bill's admiration. So she continued to weep, and started blindly for the door.

She stopped suddenly and looked again at her husband's name on the memorial board. With a grim hard fury, she went back to the desk, put down her purse and bundle, and took up a letter opener.

She then very rudely and vigorously scratched out his name.

Now she was ready to leave, and her hands still shook from the violence of her feelings, but she was leaving nothing here in this office where in all shame the men and women who had benefited by her dead husband's sacrifices were now betraying other friends, other comrades of the long fight in which this union had been created.

She flung it all from her, all, everything, and now she knew, she knew it in the profoundest corners of her soul where dreams continue to resurrect the dead, that Bill was dead, her husband was dead, and there no longer was any escape from that fact.

She had lost him forever, absolutely, completely, but even in this frightful moment she was honest enough to think that it was worse for him to be dead than for her to remember him alive.

345

V

AFTER the heat in New York there are summer rains, sweet and lavender as lilacs.

During such a long and fragrant day, Juley waited for the night, and by evening the rain had stopped and in the drying streets she walked two blocks from the bus stop down Riverside Drive to the Erdman Institute where Carl would be giving his talk. There was a weightless charm in the air, a definiteness to the Jersey shore, a radiance on the river, and here along the fringe of park the trees stood like censers breathing violet perfume. She had called several times that day but Carl hadn't been at his hotel and she had not been able to find the courage to leave her name. Some unconscious need beneath the formal requirement that she call him was gratified by his absence. She wanted to see him without being the object of his attention. She did not want to be anything definite to him until she could see what he was to be for her. There he would stand on the platform, if there were a platform, and she would be in the audience and she could look at him and see what this meant. She could listen like the others in the audience and feel what she should be. She could be lost among all the others before presenting herself to him, for this was how she had first seen her husband and his brother, so long ago in Buffalo. She did not urge herself to comprehend all that she was feeling, so remote and devious were her desires. Instead, there was the pattern. She had seen Bill at the auto convention, watched this stranger from the gallery, a tentative but obstinate young man rising to argue from the floor, rising amid boos and catcalls and even threats, yet nevertheless rising, and finally dominating through his shyness and persistence, through

346

his sincerity and good sense, the impatient delegates. Juley didn't expect this to be repeated, but ever since the break with Sam Halloran she had been thinking of her dead husband, and guiding her thoughts along the way of his life which had once so deeply been hers.

Yet there were differences between this evening (the summer about her having suddenly dried and opened up a fragrance, mild and penetrating as an envelope of sachet) and that afternoon way back in the late thirties, a million years away, for so rapidly had the history of feeling and of the times progressed. In Buffalo she had come to watch her father and found a friend of her father's, a young disciple in some way, naïve and earnest. There was this enormous difference. Now, she was going to watch her dead husband's brother, no disciple and not even a friend of hers, something more profound and less favorably related. But these were confusions of emotion, stray feelings, obscure thoughts. She tossed them off in her impetuous way and went ahead.

Like someone going out for a job, or like a lover to an assignation, she had dressed herself for all the beauty that was in her, and the new coolness of the weather favored her black cotton suit with its bolero, and the best sheer stockings in black shoes, and the white gloves and white purse, almost a sketch in black and white (she wanted somehow to be striking even though at first unnoticed). Her heavy black hair was cut thick and loose, and tiredness and excitement made her eyes luminous.

This was the first time since the war that she had dressed with such care. She remembered with mockery the night Carl had paid that flying impassioned visit to the house and caught her out and raged so foolishly when she had wanted to hold and kiss him with all the affection in her, so glad that he was alive and back even temporarily from the wars. Without feeling guilt (that only arrived after she learned of Bill's death), she had stopped thinking of herself as a woman and become some forlorn waiting creature of the war, released finally by Bill's death for what now seemed even worse. But it had been Carl's fault. She forgave him. It had always been this way between them, opposed, and drawn to each

347

other, with Bill as a moderator trying to compose the hostility of a beloved wife and an admired brother.

In the street as she approached the Institute on slow womanly steps she remembered with a dragging desire how marvelous it had been, how comforting and nourishing to be beloved as Bill had loved her. There was, she remembered also, a secret quality which Bill did not have, a kind of bitterness and stubborn, raging seeking in passion which he didn't possess, which she had experienced without love in Sam Halloran. She stopped beneath one of the heavy maples, in the damp circle beneath its weighted leaves whose undersides were still wet with rain. She felt a recollecting shudder of sensuality which belonged to her and her most recent lover. The atmosphere of the tree like the earth's envelope sustained the mood, fed it with wetness and languor. She withdrew from it slowly, starting to walk again, coming up like a netted mermaid, losing the animal tail in the serenity of the daylight world, for that everyday world had been her husband, Bill.

The strange fortresslike Institute with its queer tower on top came familiarly back. She had gone there with Bill just after Carla was born to say good-by to her brother-in-law, and she had been sitting on the stoop, she recalled, when he appeared at the open door, three dusty books in his hands, a smear of dust on his cheek, still pale and thin from the affair at Tarrytown. It had been autumn then, late afternoon in autumn, not too cold, the river shining pale lemon in the evening sun, and a great still sky upon which frayed clouds were smeared. It had not been much of a good-by between Carl and her. Mostly it was between the brothers, with Carl distant and making abstract bad jokes and Bill so earnest and still feeling guilty because of what had happened. From time to time Carl had darted glances at her and she had remained seated on the stone stoop, swinging her legs and feeling quite fine because the baby was born and she was free of the awful sickness of pregnancy. She smiled to herself even now as Carl's delayed, intentionally delayed and yet still startled, words came to her. "But you're quite nice to look at. I never imagined."

348

She was nicer to look at now, one of those lucky women for whom real maturity is a fountain of youth, a new beginning in the flesh, and when she felt good, as she did tonight, her slapdash personality began to shine in her skin and her bones, a personality and a shape always on the verge of excitement and immolation.

Middle-aged men arrived in taxis and most of them knew each other and stopped to chat in little groups on the sidewalk and steps. They looked curiously at her as she went up the steps, and smiled and she averted her head, wondering, until she realized that she herself was smiling out of the memory: "I never imagined."

Within the doorway at a small table a middle-aged woman sat with a little metal box of filing cards and a checklist of names. "Dr. Andrews. Dr. Wokals. Dr. Blumstein," the names intoned before Juley, and she hoped she would be able to enter without having Carl know she was there.

When her turn came she presented the telegram that Carl had sent from California and the woman looked up and smiled. "You may find it quite dull," she said. "Perhaps you'd like to wait in the library or return in several hours?"

"Why no," Juley replied gravely, for gravity was the note she found there and she took the protective coloration. "I think I'd prefer to wait in the audience."

"As you please," the woman said, "it's going to be terribly technical."

Juley thanked her with a smile and followed the others up the carpeted stairway through the magnificent hallway. The building was something like a museum with its pictures and little busts, among them a death mask of Freud. This, too, was unlike the first meeting with Bill, but everything was going to be different tonight, Juley felt, and yet everything though different was somehow the same, for it is the sense of beginnings that create similarities.

The great library with its painted and mosaicked ceilings had been converted into a small lecture hall, with neat copies of Renaissance chairs facing a small dark platform on which stood

349

a lectern and two small chairs, a pitcher of water and a glass. In this way, she thought, all meetings are the same.

The room was nearly full and she found a seat in the next to the last row.

A mingled low-voiced hum rose on all sides, subdued and casual, while expectancy hung in the air without vigor as at a theater before the curtain goes up. Juley sat within herself, neatly, her legs drawn up primly, her purse in her lap, and tried not to be too different from the others. She was alone, however, the way the others were not, and she kept looking out of her tower at the pink faces and plump bodies until looking up she saw the painted ceiling, and found something startling to stare at.

Soon the lights were partially dimmed so that the platform stood out more clearly, and a gray-haired man in a dinner jacket entered followed closely by another man in a similar uniform.

Juley's clothes were suddenly too tight. She felt breathless, and she tried to breathe slowly so as not to breathe loudly and attract the attention of her neighbors, an elderly woman with a slight German accent and a sturdy, ruddy-faced man in his early fifties who seemed to know everybody and whose left leg was shorter than his right.

Juley followed the neat figure of Carl with a rapt glance. She saw him with so great a pleasure, so great an interest as to surprise herself, and she was anxious with the same dedicated anxiety she had so often felt when her husband had stood up to address a meeting, wanting him to be a great success, so submerged and identified with the speaker as to lose her relation with the audience, hostile to the audience even on the chance that they might not respond. She felt this way again now and remembered how Bill had called her "a back-seat speaker."

Juley had spoken at many meetings, large and small, in her time and each time the moment approached all her strength disappeared, all her ideas became foolish, and all her flesh alien to her. She used to stand at last in front of the faces, friendly or hostile, her mind thoughtless, and speak and speak, never remembering what she wanted to say, and yet somehow always succeeding. This premature death of the will she imagined was common to all speakers, and she now imputed it to Carl.

There was polite applause and no need to call the audience to attention. They gave their attention at once. Carl sat down in one of the chairs and the gray-haired man stood at the little carved desk and smiled out into the quietness.

"Good evening, ladies and gentlemen," he said. His voice was dry, without much feeling, almost self-critical, so that he appeared to be discounting the meaning or importance of his words before the audience could estimate them. "I will not waste your valuable time with any unnecessary words. We've spent all day on the business of this Congress, and tonight is the time for pleasure. You all know Dr. Carl Myers. Need I mention our respect and admiration for his work? He has been so kind as to come all the way from California to read this paper in person. The very title is fascinating: *A General Theory of Causation.*"

There was a murmur from the audience, a kind of smacking of the lips, for nothing engaged the appetites of psychiatrists more than disputes on theory. The title for Juley was without significance, and she heard the feeble voice go on to speak of the work at the Sierra Hospital and other things, but this all was noise to her, a kind of monotone of a machine while she fixed her attention on Carl.

Carl had none of the nervous habits of Bill. He did not shuffle his feet. He did not uselessly consult his sheaf of manuscript. He did not touch his face, his mustache, his hair as if to console himself that they were still there. He did not change his position one way or another. He did not even cross his legs. He merely sat very quietly, looking easily from side to side, listening to the introduction as if he were not the object of it.

A vast glow of admiration suffused Juley's heart. Her palms were wet with anxiety for him and affection flooded her feelings. She kept looking from side to side to see the other people, to see if they were respectful enough, admiring enough, polite enough, but they were all so old and undistinguished, with so little force, that she shook her head with contempt for them. She had a fierce

351

sense of possessiveness towards her brother-in-law. He was her family, her very own, and in spirit she sat on the platform with him and defied the whole mob.

Carl looked thinner to her, his face very sunburned, almost mahogany-colored, and his black suit reduced his stockiness. He seemed so young, younger than herself, younger than her memory of Bill. She remembered how Carl himself had said that in the hospital ten years ago, how in a way the older had become the younger brother.

The monotonous vacuum-cleaner noise of the introduction was over and a riffle of applause blew through the audience. Carl rose and stood at the lectern, opening his sheaf of manuscript, already speaking, saying, "Good evening." He went on to add how gratified he was to be present, how honored he was to address this audience, and how overemphasized had been the previous speaker's description of his work in psychiatry.

As he spoke his glance surveyed the audience and again and again fell upon Juley who imagined each time he had seen her until she realized in truth he saw no one, only the undifferentiated mass of faces in the semidarkness. She sat up straighter in her seat.

He stopped, and in the slow pause lowered his eyes to the manuscript and started to read. As he read with a certain lack of emphasis, letting the words do all the work, he looked up from time to time, perfectly easy with his material, altogether familiar with it, and the audience seemed to settle down, listening, waiting through the preliminary remarks, a résumé of the field which they also knew.

Carl's control of the audience, the respectful quietness, had their effect on Juley, and she relaxed and began to listen too, but she could not be really interested in what he was saying. Technical words occurred that lost the sense for her, and after a few minutes her own thoughts revived and played beneath the speaker's in a personal counterpoint.

"To sum up this little review of previous general theories of causation, I would like to indicate," Carl said, and he smiled at the audience, "that only after psychological processes were con-

352

sidered to be not thoroughly rational did a science of psychology begin to develop. Only when man was looked at not as mind reflecting or inventing the universe, but as an animal in conflict with it, an animal whose consciousness was part of his struggle with society and nature, part of his relation to it, part of his gift to it, in short, only when the mind was not removed from existence but discovered to be its creature, only then was a rational science of psychology actually possible."

Here there was a murmur, and in this murmur Juley returned from her own reverie to the meeting. She sat up again into a pause, and then a single hard sentence.

"The truth is that we haven't gone far enough."

From the audience Juley caught the anticipation of a mystery about to be unfolded, a series of half-formulated guesses, a certain leaning forward into the speaker's next remarks, and she enjoyed the way Carl now paused to drink a glass of water while everyone watched, counting time, waiting for him to begin again. That was good, she thought. Good for him. She knew the trick and had seen Bill use it, and Sam Halloran too, and she never imagined that Carl might be just thirsty.

There was the small click of the glass as Carl put it down, and he did not read the next sentence from the text. He leaned over the lectern and projected himself into the midst of the listeners. "What I have to say about the work at Sierra is not special, and although all the cases are casualties of the recent war, they are not limited in their significance to the fact that they occurred during and after the war, for God knows," and he stopped here, he paused, he said slowly, "the war today is the peace around us."

She responded to the shock of this statement, the dagger it thrust into the audience, and at the same time with a little lift of intellectual pleasure she understood what he was saying, she heard it as a meaningful important thing which she, too, believed, said in a polite way, but the kind of thing that might be said anywhere, even at a union meeting. She was listening now like the rest. She was forced to. It meant something for her.

Carl started to speak again but more rapidly, as if what he were

353

saying was ordinary, known, and merely still a résumé. "In striving to organize a system of cure, we were forced by our investigations and experience to discover an obvious secret. We found out that in investigating the many mental ills we were in fact observing what constitutes social reality. If biology is the science of man as a going physical system in relation to himself and the world about him, psychology is the science of man as a going system in terms of the mechanism and content of his social inheritance. When psychology is less than this it is biology, and when it is more it is history. Since the social inheritance is not the past but what the present is becoming because of that past, we found ourselves attempting to assign the causes of psychic malformation to the specific society from which our patients came. Such an attempt would be, of course, no surprise to an ordinary man, but to psychiatrists it was a novelty, and still is. We were forced to assert the hypothesis that no science of psychology can be founded on what man is, but only on what man is becoming, the general rule being that he is never becoming anything but what society itself is becoming."

At first Juley thought the audience hissed, and she looked around startled, to discover that what had really happened was a general intake of breath, almost all at once, and then a stir, heads turning, face to face, neighbor to neighbor, each one in turn looking to see if the others had heard the same thing. But the speaker pulled them back again.

"Now I do not want you to think this point of view is unusual and that there is little or merely problematical evidence to support it. There is an enormous mass of experiment and observation in the social sciences which support this notion. The scientific journals are filled with such proof. Somehow, this great range of material is never utilized, never thoroughly organized, and this is because it appears without its fundamental premise, its fundamental concept. The evidence is without force because it is constantly presented without a general approach. As for ourselves at Sierra, we were led to a few obvious conclusions. If mental illness is the result, the direct result of the influence of society on the individual, if we accepted this, then we were faced with a dilemma. We could strive to readapt our patient to the society that had made him ill, and this is certainly possible, if not quite a cure; or we could accept the notion that society would have to be altered if we wanted to cure the patient, and that the patient himself would have to participate in the understanding and alteration of those societal influences which had damaged him. The first method, the method of accepting the society as a constant, is the general practice in psychiatry, no matter what the school, and, irrespective of vocabulary, inevitably leads to a rejection of social influences as the main causes of mental illness. The alternative notion is objectionable, difficult, and raises serious practical difficulties. Yet if one is to believe that life in society causes mental illness, one is forced to say that no cure is possible in any case so long as the patient is being readapted into the source of his disaster."

This time there was a real sound from the audience, a general, communal hostile note, almost a growl, if so violent and crude a noise were possible among these domesticated creatures. It had no beginning and it had no end. It was a stirring undertone, the kind that is heard among captive animals or in the uneasy streets when some social danger threatens. And Juley felt a cringe of fear, for herself, for Carl, a fear that he was losing this audience, that from now on they would listen but only with hostility. The sound continued as Carl read on, as he broadened and particularized his first points, and Juley couldn't understand exactly what he meant, what he said, only that the space between the platform and the seats was widening with opposition, with rebellion, with discomfort, and even with anger.

She found herself mastering an urge to get up and go to Carl's side, he was so alone up there, so far away from any friend. She knew these dangers of bringing the bitter truth to people, how necessary it was not to be alone, to have the sense of allies about. And Carl had none. The hostility had stabilized at a certain accepting level as his voice went on, and she had time to look around her. It was difficult to see everything in the audience because of the dim lighting, but the woman at her side was saying to herself,

"But no. No." The healthy man to Juley's right was leaning forward, his face stern and threatening, and he tapped the shoulder of a bald-headed man in front of him who snapped his face back, his rimless glasses flashing and opened a plump little mouth which said nothing but breathed discomfort.

The whole audience was moving. It remained in its seat yet it had come alive in a way that was more than intellectual. Its muscles were in motion, its glands were secreting. It had begun to feel, to resist actively.

A panic alarm seized Juley's mind. What if they got up and walked out? What if they got up and booed, or yelled? Rapidly she surveyed the faces again and she could not believe that these people would react this way. They were too polite. But the poison that dripped from the platform, the burning painfulness of those abstract and technical expressions that Carl used, weapons she could not feel because they were beyond her sensitivity, were real enough for these highly developed creatures. She was alone with them as Carl was alone in front of them. She longed to help Carl and did not know how, and she anxiously leaned forward, gazing at him with all her heart and mind to help him, to understand him, wondering if he understood the effect he was having.

He had turned a page and suddenly looked up with the same mild smile. "Be patient," he said, "I have still more painful things to say."

A man tittered in a high voice, unable to restrain himself.

"I hear a Freudian laugh," Carl replied to it. "Let the Freudian remember that his master was called a sensual old goat because he ventured to say that sexuality played a part in the emotional conduct, in the spiritual systems of human beings." And he laughed himself, a rather winning laugh, filled with strength and relaxed. It set the audience back and Juley's mind took an extravagant and desiring leap, her soul flooded with applause for Carl, and a wild pride of identification replaced her former fear.

She settled back in her seat, she withdrew within the security of her anonymity and watched the combat between Carl and the audience, for she could no longer pay attention to what was being

356

said. She felt the feeling, and her brother-in-law, so neat, so dark, so calm before all of them, had become her hero. She had gone through this state a hundred times before in a hundred meetings during Bill's career. It was the fatal role of the minority leader, and even more dangerous when he seemed to stand as a minority of one. How rapidly all the rules of conduct disappeared. She remembered a black night in Cleveland when Bill had actually been driven from the platform under a hail of shouts and boos. It seemed impossible that here in this hall, this room like a museum with the naked women and strange animals on the ceilings, in this audience of dinner jackets and sleek necks, that the same thing could occur. But the feeling was the same, the danger as clear, the hostility as real.

She tried to imagine what Carl must be feeling now. He did not have her training and Bill's in such affairs. She felt that his career had been nothing but one long success, of admiration on every side, of the usual honors in the profession. A wave of melting sympathy ran through her, affection for him, a desire to protect him from the hard reality of this struggle, which as he continued to speak, continued to mount.

She watched his hands, sunburned and hard, but they did not shake with excitement. She watched his feet and they did not shuffle. She watched his eyes and they did not dart in search of aid. He appeared stolid, although not indifferent, and she detected a lurking smile, a lurking playfulness in his face which delighted her.

The ruddy man beside her was talking to the bald-headed man in front of him. They no longer were listening and she whispered, "Sh."

The two faces, one plump and pale, the other haughty and strong, faced her like two lamps, shone a terrible disapproval, and then darkened into quietness, and a little thrill of triumph elated her. She had helped Carl in this little way. She had made her presence felt and told them he was not alone. The ruddy man withdrew to the furthest corner of his seat away from her.

"The fact that most people are not mentally ill," Carl was saying,

357

"does not mean that society is not the cause of mental illness, just as the fact that most people are not unemployed doesn't mean that social conditions do not cause unemployment. When the negative conditions are not generally distributed, when the contradictions and strains occur all together as so often happens, then the organism falters, begins throwing up defenses, finds refuge in symptoms, and becomes mentally ill. Mental illness is a form of action, a form of will, a form of struggle, but at the level of accepted social defeat. In every case of mental illness you will find not a single cause, but a whole history of individual defeats that begin in the earliest stages of childhood and continue up to the point of breakdown in the present. In general, the most advanced of psychiatrists accept this history as the condition of the illness but prefer to examine these accumulations of events as being first causes instead of results of the world around the patient, a world which is not extraordinary but general for all of us, the healthy as well as the unhealthy. I would attribute this reluctance in assigning the cause specifically to society to a general reluctance to criticize the environment which guarantees the psychiatrist a living, to social prejudices, and to a hostility towards social change. Psychiatrists are also citizens of a certain income and habitual cultural loyalty."

A man got up in the third row and started to walk out as Carl continued to read his paper. The whole audience watched this man depart, the heads turning, a rustle growing among them, conversations rising, chairs shifting, and suddenly the meeting was a shambles, and still Carl read on. But as the man reached the rear where the double doors were, Carl stopped. All the heads turned to look at him and a pressing silence intervened.

Carl raised his voice. "In discussing scientific questions it is sometimes necessary to doubt old axioms, to abandon them for their opposites. Naturally, we find this painful, and even vulgar."

The man stopped at the door. He was very dignified in his dinner jacket, with close-cropped gray hair and horn-rimmed eyeglasses. He said with an icy penetration as he faced the platform, "I came to hear a scientific discussion of certain psychiatric problems, not a lecture in radical politics."

358

Like watchers at a tennis game, all the heads turned to Carl, while a thrashing of applause swept the audience.

Carl leaned his elbows on the lectern and looked calmly out upon his adversary, waiting for the response to cease. He said, "There are over six hundred thousand patients in public mental hospitals today, and at least one half that number in private ones. Each year we have one hundred and fifty thousand new admissions. One person out of twenty in the United States will receive psychiatric treatment during his life. Government agencies estimate that eight and one half million citizens of this country need psychiatric care. The rate of institutionalization has increased one third since 1925. These figures omit the millions of unfortunate people who run to quacks, astrologers, faith healers, and other unlicensed parasites who earn a living from the existence of widespread mental illness. I would venture to say that the number of cases will increase in the near future rather than decrease. Do you think it improper to examine the environment in which this disaster occurs?"

Three or four people applauded this vigorously and Juley joined them. The dissenter left.

"I shall now," Carl went on calmly, "take up a number of classical cases, the evidence of some of our own work at Sierra, and interpret these in the light of individual histories and the social conditions in which these private lives occurred in order to indicate the usefulness of this approach." The audience fragmented, altered sides, responded impatiently as he went on, and meanwhile Juley sat in triumphant loyalty, her heart swelling with love and partisanship.

Within the agitated motions of her mind a memory asserted itself, brooding and fragrant, momentous and compelling, the night on which he had gone overseas, the night in which they had wandered within the ambiguity of a relation that went beyond being a brother to Bill and a wife to him. The streets of the city, the places where they had danced, the music and fears, projected themselves and filled this fanciful hall, displaced it and obscured it, and she found herself returning in imagination to the loneliness of the night and tears she had wept, the beating of her heart, the irrevocable tenderness and loss of his departure, and she found

359

herself clinging to the figure of Carl, to his hands and mouth, to the paralyzing and unalterable conviction that she loved him. She had loved him all along. She knew it now. She had loved him without admitting it. She had not for a moment been able to do so with Bill alive, and with Bill dead she had not been able to recall it, but now suddenly it was present and she sat within the tumult and conflict of this lecture, her whole life at stake again, for in love, everything is thrown into the sweep of passion, even regret, old loves, old habits, even enmity, sorrow, and defeat.

Carl was approaching the end of his formal talk and his audience was at the same time coming to the end of its formal patience, unable to remain still, wanting to talk, to argue, to attack. As if sensing it, realizing it in all its complex hostility, Carl began to speak not from the written paper but from what he felt was necessary at this moment. The audience responded with a new quivering of attention.

"I have, like the rest of you," he said, "listened to the thousand babbling tongues of our patients, and I have not been able to separate myself from their torments. Even the most unusual of their experiences were not hostile to my most ordinary ones, springing from the same terrible conflicts of the world about me. We have been fortunate, and it is mainly luck, that the strains of life have come one by one, giving us a chance to survive each defeat and reorganize our forces into new strength. Others have been less fortunate. People do what they can to survive in terms of what they understand and know, in terms of what they need, in terms of what they hope. When nothing else is possible, they become ill. But whether it is the sexuality of man that takes monstrous shapes, or his dreams, or his acts of social drive within the community, in every case, at every point, the malformations are symptoms, no matter how deeply they exist, even to the earliest days within the parents' house. Parents are, after all, vehicles for the thrust of society into the learning of the child. There is no wickedness in all history that did not come from the social environment, and there is not an act of heroism or goodness that did not issue from the social cause. We must move back from symptoms to real

360

causes. Of course, even without this radical step, we have had cures. We have taken patients who could not act at all and sent them out as active persons who would not be arrested for murder, vagrancy or voyeurism. We have sent out patients who have been retrained not to insult the mores of their social betters. But these are not cures in any scientific sense. They are substitutes for thoroughgoing changes, and we are forced to provide substitutes so long as we do not recognize man's real role in society, and our own role, too. The task of science is to help undo the misery of history. Science is one of the social forces that must liberate the human spirit from its social prisons. But the spirit is a spirit of the flesh, the flesh of the society, and so in the end we are forced to act actively within that society as part of our system of cure. Every honest psychiatrist should long for the day when his branch of medicine, like epidemiology, is a minor field within the area of human knowledge, an old memory of horror and pity such as we sometimes feel when we look back on the miseries of the past. I do not believe in original sin, and therefore I believe psychiatry must some day disappear into a general science of human life and become one of the minor branches of biology and history."

There was a scattering of applause and then a violent roar of questions, half the audience rising and clamoring for attention. These soft shapes could howl like lions, and they did. They rose in full anger and bitterness, defenders of the faith, soldiers of the *status quo* in science. They were willing to die for their position and to kill for it, although for the moment the choice was not presented. Aphrodite, with her adventures and loves, floated remotely upon the ceiling, an old goddess no longer worshiped by man. She was a myth. Her followers did not object to it, since they were dead, but the younger myth-makers and worshipers below resisted with all the passion at their command the expulsion of their gods, for as the gods depart so do the priests and all their splendid privileges.

Juley drifted on the sea of conflict and battle, besieged by her own past and seeing everywhere within it the dear body of her beloved. He stood before her in the smoke of argument, sometimes

361

obscured by a dozen speakers shouting at once, but always surviving, and as the time went on he grew sharper, more cutting, and the howls became more intense. It seemed to Juley that her whole life was a preparation for this occasion, for this moment of insight, her love of Bill a test, a training in readiness to recognize what now dominated her whole life. She could remember every moment of seeing Carl, from the very first in the hospital to the very last when he had returned from overseas and with a curt and melancholy bitterness narrated the death of his brother.

A stumbling guilt touched her, like a reef in the seas of her immolation. What if Bill were alive now? What would she be? What would she feel? And she realized that it was his death, his disappearance from her life which was one of the causes of her love. Without this absolute fact, she could not love Carl and would not have loved him, for Bill would have still taken from her all the tenderness she had, all her affection, all her loyalty, and without these freed, she could not love, just as her moody affair with Sam Halloran would never have had occurred if she had not been left abandoned by her husband's death. It was as Carl himself had been saying. It was everything coming together, piling up, overwhelming the mind, that made a man ill, that made a woman love, that made a life take a certain shape. She was like everyone else a creature of the life she had lived, and in such times she could only love certain kinds of men, and in her life Carl was that man as in another life some other man might have become her lover and she herself a woman of another world.

Given the opportunity, Juley thought, holding with triumph the secret happiness of her life now, she would not have exchanged anything in her past and present for any other past or present. And she remembered the words that Bill so often had quoted, the words he had called "the morality of every revolutionist's life," words that had gone beyond words, become a faith in action, so superb is the power of illuminating love: *This is what I say: I would not wish to a dog or to a snake, to the most low or misfortunate creature of the earth — I would not wish to any of them what I have had to suffer for things that I am not guilty of. But my conviction*

362

*is that I have suffered for things that I am guilty of. I am suffering
because I am a radical and indeed I am a radical; I have suffered
because I was an Italian, and indeed I am an Italian; I have
suffered more for my family and my beloved than for myself; but
I am so convinced to be right that if you could execute me two
times, and if I could be reborn two other times, I would live again
to do what I have done already. I have finished. Thank you.*

The mood of these remembered words continued to sound
within Juley's mind, continuing on with an almost pure emotion,
as in remembered music, and she had no sense of the room and no
sense of time, only this feeling connected with her own need to
love, thankful for her whole life which had flowered into happiness at this moment.

Suddenly the meeting was over.

The chairman had been reading a long list of subjects and
speakers, announcing the panels and the lectures, dry, round, inorganic words that fell through Juley's reverie without touching
her, and she was sitting there lost within herself, utterly isolated
from the people and his voice, when the audience arose, a vast
brush of clothes, a surprising burst of voices, a shock of motion,
and she was within the meeting again.

The moment had arrived.

She was startled and overwhelmed with shyness. Her flying
glance twisted through the crowd to the platform. She saw Carl
rising, and then he was hidden in a press of forms, in confused
movement, and she sat astonished that the time had arrived. She
sat amazed, unprepared.

Almost frightened, as if not yet ready, she fled.

She was the first one out of the doors into the hall, the first one
at the stairs, and behind her she heard the rising tide of voices.
The audience was leaving. Carl would be coming out. Her right
hand slid down the banister, her toes slipped on the carpeted
stairs, and she felt the descent, the going down, the escape, in
little shocks of motion. She hurried by the death mask of Freud
whose closed lids and weary face revealed little hope for his
disciples and humanity. She passed the woman at the door, who

363

stood now with throwaways which contained the schedule of the Congress.

"Well, at least it wasn't dull," the woman said.

"No, no," Juley replied. There was the door. There was the street.

"Did you speak with Dr. Myers?"

Juley shook her head. "I'll be waiting outside."

And she was outside. She ran down the stone steps to the sidewalk. She hesitated, looked back at the doorway, and saw the feet beginning to fill up the stairway. Then she darted through the traffic, feeling the hot exhaust of a bus go by, to the other side of the Drive into the shadow of the trees and stood hidden in the darkness above the great emptiness of the river.

She put a hand on the rough parapet and looked across to the Jersey shore, feeling the mild chill of so much space upon her, on her flushed face — her cheeks were burning — on her bare forearms, so terribly empty, on her throat, speechless, on her hands, empty and unfulfilled. The stone beneath her hand was gritty, hard, implacable, a solid anchor for her feelings, and she passed her hand over the surface again and again, irritating the palm of her hand on it, bruising her fingers, holding on.

She felt completely exposed, afraid to be and yet shamelessly ready for it, and very slowly she turned and looked back between the two maples which concealed the street lights and saw the first dark-suited figures appearing within the doorway of the Institute, each with a leaflet like a small white flag.

A silt, slow-pouring and resistant, the audience began to flow down upon the sidewalk and jam up against the dam of the street, spreading out on either side, breaking off here and there at its edges into couples who drifted away, yet holding the great mass of itself before the building, reluctant to leave. Above the impatient irregular passage of the traffic, the buzz of voices sometimes broke, for if the meeting was over, the meaning was not.

Juley lighted a cigarette and watched the doorway for Carl. She saw the other men without seeing them, faces, shapes, meaningless objects. Her intent selective glance, sharp with anxiety, let the whole world pass. It had a single bias, a single strength, a

364

single meaning, and behind it was her whole life waiting to fulfill itself.

A new, highly polished sedan broke from the traffic and came to a halt before the Institute, blocking off the sidewalk crowd, and she leaned back so that she could just see over it the upper half of the doorway.

There was a stir there and she saw three men appear, and pause, and beckon, and now they started down and Carl was there in the doorway, smiling, shaking hands with someone within.

Juley became transparent, became merely a vehicle, merely a hand which she unconsciously raised to call him.

Then it happened, the impossible thing that she had not imagined. For Carl disappeared down the steps. The traffic built up in front of the car, opened a moment, and she saw him sitting inside, near the sidewalk window, and the sedan pulled away from the curb, going, gone into the traffic, its red taillights joining the others.

He was gone.

She stood there, watching, shaken with cold, a castaway, her arm still out.

It was almost terror she felt now. It was real pain, emptiness, unfulfillment.

She hesitated, and she knew as she hesitated, on the verge of running after him, confused, turning to look at the building across the street, and turning back again to search the anonymous motion of the traffic, she knew with a sudden and absolute sorrow that she would have to wait.

There was this whole night to wait, a night as long as the inward road of memory, a night infinitely dismembered by time, a time to worry, a time to need, a time to desire.

There was this immense night.

Her happiness in discovering her love for Carl began to melt beneath the awful fear, the terrible uncertainty, before the abyss of a possible unhappiness as she realized that all she felt was all in her and before her lay the mystery of what her beloved might be, might want, might feel, and the possible truth that he had no need of her.

vi

CARL arrived at the Institute at ten-thirty in the morning to chair a panel discussion on Pharmacological Shock and Therapeutic Surgery, old fields of his. When he entered the building he found the middle-aged secretary standing guard and directing the visitors to the proper rooms. "Dr. Myers," she said with a flutter, "I'm afraid there was a mix-up last night. I'm so sorry."

Carl agreed, smiling. "There was, indeed."

She twittered with misplaced amorousness. "I mean, Dr. Myers, that is, I don't mean your talk last night which I assure you I found most interesting. But your sister-in-law was here and she sat through the whole lecture and then you went off before you could meet her."

"That's too bad," Carl said. "I'll get in touch with her." And he thanked the secretary and hurried in to his meeting.

The room was already full, buzzing with talk. Carl took his place at the head of the long table, greeted the visitors pleasantly and opened the discussion. After a brief talk he turned the meeting over to the main reporter, a juicy man with a gustatory way of talking about brain incisions, and let his own thoughts idly drift back into the history of himself and his sister-in-law. There were his mother's first remarks, contemptuous and belittling, and that last somber, almost speechless talk, a dead afternoon when he had come to report Bill's death, and hardly speaking of Bill had murmured fragments of horror about the war. Juley had always been a puzzling creature to Carl, attractive in so many ways, her voice compelling and artistic as a bird's, great beyond the powers of a fine actress, yet artless and incomplete; her abrupt, all-absorbing clutch at life, experience, and affection; and beneath it all that continuous experience with some of the harshest realities of the world, the struggles of men and women against the bitter economy. So he admired her. And still he disliked her, found so many things, so many actions and qualities that repelled him. He began, with an almost cheerful slyness, to compile the list of her disadvantages, commencing with her hostility toward himself, but he got no further. An objection was being raised, and he was forced to turn his attention back to the subject at hand.

After the panel was over, it was five-thirty, and Carl refused an invitation to have dinner with several of the doctors, although promising to return for the evening's main talk. He got away as easily and smoothly as he could and took a taxicab up to Juley's apartment house.

This time he did not make the error of forgetting to bring a present for his niece, and he stopped off at a toy store at Madison Avenue. Waiting his turn before the glittering shelves and neon lights, he found himself somewhat depressed when he saw the objects being sold there, the whole miniature apparatus of war, constructed out of the latest and most fashionable materials. It was difficult for Carl to imagine the callousness of parents who in this way prepared their children for the miseries which every day he was forced to face within the wards of Sierra. In the end he selected a doll, which at least was human, and a set of building blocks, since these were rational, but his last view of the place as he walked out with his pink-wrapped packages was of an elderly woman with a kind and gentle manner buying a complete outfit of toy tanks, planes, guns, and soldiers, and he wondered how many wars such a woman had to survive, and how many of the dead she had to count before she realized her own role in such disasters. The salesman was passionately recommending the educational value of a new gadget called the atomic gun.

Carl crossed the hot sidewalk to the waiting taxi and wondered what the great Oppenheimer might think of this, and all the other atomic experimenters, and where they believed their roles ended and the task of the millions who disliked premature radiation began.

Carl was quite tired from these busy days and he planned to keep his visit with Juley down to a minimum. He lay back on the leather cushions and watched the hot dusty city shake by, feeling like every expatriate New Yorker a sentimental attachment for this impossible, uncomfortable place. No region and city were too miserable to become man's home, just as no life was too miserable, too narrow, or too painful to seem normal when it was the only life completely known. And this was the dividing point between Carl's notions and most current psychiatric opinions. He could not accept the general conditions of social life as normal, healthy, ordinary, but it was hard to disturb the minds of scientists about such things because it messed up the fields within which they worked. He was still not sure that he had not gone too far, gone too hard at the audience, but it had appeared to be the only way. After all, there was only this one life to live, and a man could not wait forever because he might seem impolite.

Carl had no confidence that the doctors at Sierra really felt and understood the approach. He did not doubt their honesty, or even intellectual ability. What was at stake, what made the difference, was their lack of need to have an organized general approach. Everybody, more or less, believed in a social approach to everything, an orientation that *took into consideration* social factors. But they simply would not face the logical consequence that it was not a question of another contributing cause, but of a new system of causes, the dynamics of social history itself, which in turn altered the relevance of purely psychological and biological factors, reframing and changing them in an absolutely novel way. He smiled as he thought of Giordano Bruno. How perceptive that old Inquisition had been to realize that there was no harm to Copernicus as long as he paid lip service to the old cosmogony. In truth, they had burned the real enemy, the man who questioned the basis of that old society, even as a dreamer. Thinkers who limited their thoughts just to the naked facts never threatened anything, only the fact seeker who had worked before. What was needed, Carl thought, was a general attack on the problem right down the line, everywhere at once, at the heart of the matter, at the fundamental

368

premises. Only out of this would come a real science of the mind that would not stand aside and brood over the mysteries of the spirit while history rattled ahead making each mystery just an old and gladly forgotten confusion, while disasters collected in the guise of fate.

He was smiling a little grimly, remembering the initial chaos of the lecture, when the taxicab stopped in front of Juley's tenement.

The dreary slum street with its crumbling houses and tiny stores looked more decayed than ever, and Carl went up the stoop into the musty, cool hall and began the long climb up to the top floor. How long ago was his own life in such places, his youth and Bill's! And in this way a man recognized that he had passed the center of his time, when places and persons, emotions and ideas, altered from novel experiences to remembered ones, no longer appearances, but reappearances, no longer charged, but accepted.

He arrived at the final landing and went to the door and rang the bell. It did not ring, so he knocked. Filtering through came the fragrant odor of freshly made coffee, relaxing, domestic.

There were heavy steps and the door swung open on a man's voice saying, "It's about time."

Dark, heavy-set, with rolled up shirt sleeves, the stranger showed his surprise, and Carl was annoyed because Juley hadn't bothered to write him of her new address.

Carl said, "I'm sorry."

The man inclined his head. "It's all right. Who you looking for?"

"Someone I knew used to live here," Carl said, and started to turn away. He paused and looked back. "Perhaps you know where she might have moved? She used to live in this apartment. Mrs. Myers?"

The stranger observed Carl with a certain steady insolence and then flung the door open. "She still lives here."

But Carl didn't enter. He waited there on the threshold and saw beyond the man the same living room, newly painted, with some new chairs in it, but still Juley's place. He felt an actual physical shock as if someone had struck him on the chest. "Is she home?" Carl asked.

"No."

"Is my niece?"

"Your niece?"

"Yes," Carl observed in a dry and rather neutral way. "I'm Mrs. Myers's brother-in-law."

"Then come in," the stranger said. "My name's Sam Halloran. You can help me wait."

Carl rejected the whole idea of seeing Juley. "Is Carla here?"

"No. She's away at camp."

Carl balanced the two packages in his hands, then he extended them. "These are some toys for Carla. Will you give them to Mrs. Myers and see that she sends them to my niece?"

But Halloran made no effort to take them. He stood away from the open door and said, "Why don't you come in and wait? I don't think Juley is going to be long. I've been waiting half the day for her myself."

Irresolute, wanting to leave, nevertheless Carl found himself entering, and the door swung closed behind him and the strong voice of Halloran was saying, "I just made some fresh coffee. How about some?"

Carl placed the two packages on a small end table near a newly upholstered chair. "All right. Thanks."

Halloran went by him, leaving a quick, energetic look, a gathering look, an itemization, and then his broad back in its white shirt was in the kitchen, and the voice came out, "The house is upset. I don't think Juley put her hand to it this morning."

Carl stood there. He was more upset than he imagined he would be, ill at ease, and he saw through the open bedroom door the bed, its covers tumbled above the footboard, the white sheets wrinkled and awry, a pillow in the center with a pajama top flung upon it. The ash trays were full, and a few newspapers, opened, read, lay scattered at the foot of the couch. The place reeked of domesticity, and not of a woman alone.

"Milk and sugar?" Bright-faced and cheerful, Halloran was in the doorway.

"Plain," Carl replied. "Just black."

Carl looked around to find what was there to find, but all he found were his own feelings, so abruptly disarrayed, so unsettled, and a gnawing discomfort, because this Halloran could only be Juley's lover. Carl knew this. He let himself down, not wanting to. He let himself remain, not wanting to, and he took from the man's hand the cup and saucer and let himself say, "Thank you."

"Well," Sam began, sitting himself affably on the broad arm of the old couch, "this is kind of funny, you coming here. You don't know me but I know about you."

Carl sipped the hot black coffee and waited. He had an increasing sense of his own stupidity for remaining, a sense of peering into the window of a sordid house scene, and yet this man was admirable, admirable to look at, strong, with a fine masculine face, strong brows and an easy powerful voice, a man who was familiar with his own life, living it, knowing it, resolute in it. This was not something vicious. It did not seem so. It was simply that Carl had not imagined this affair for Juley. He had kept seeing her alone here in this apartment, her life just as it had been during the war, a waiting life for Bill to come home. Carl knew that Bill was not going to come home. He had just not thought to imagine that Juley might have begun to live with the knowledge that Bill was gone from her life forever.

"I've heard about you from Juley," Sam said. He put the cup down on a folded newspaper on the table and took a packet of cigarettes from his trouser pocket. He did not offer one to Carl. "I heard about you from your brother."

This was another shock, not that Halloran knew anything of him through Bill, but that Bill was alive yet in this room just as he remained alive in Carl's mind, his brother, not present, but living on as Carl had known him.

"Did you?" Carl asked.

"Sure," Halloran explained with an easy conversational air. "I was with him when we organized up in Tarrytown. I'll never forget the meeting when we voted you the official thanks for taking that

371

beating." He laughed. "We certainly were dewy-eyed then, real dewy-eyed, voting you thanks for getting your block knocked off like we were doing you a favor."

The one big window in the room looked out on an areaway. Summer light fell from the skies, reflected against the whitewashed walls, and spread a rosy radiance, tinged with gray, within the dusty atmosphere of the living room. Carl looked at the wall and did not speak, but the past reflected back within his eyes, shone there, and he felt somberly that long hidden night, suppressed, bewildering and not yet assimilated.

"Bill and I went through a hell of a lot together." Halloran stopped himself as if he had been prepared to say more. He did not say it. He put his coffee cup down and got up, moving slowly around the room, smoking with long deep draws, and he was ill at ease. Something had occurred to him, and he stopped far off from Carl and watched. Finally, he asked, "You sore finding me here?"

The terrible directness of this found Carl unprepared. He asked the least thing. "What do you mean?" But he knew what Halloran meant and would not face it.

A plain malevolence, daring itself, showed within Halloran's words and voice. "I'm not the Fuller Brush man, you know. I live here."

It was the note, the single note Carl needed to find his control, for he had faced even more difficult situations with his patients. He very calmly put down his cup and saucer and rose. "I'm Bill's brother, not Juley's husband," he said. "Tell her I was here."

"What's your hurry?"

"I'm not in a hurry," Carl said. He, too, was smiling now, feeling his strength come back within this situation, feeling his mastery of it again, knowing it didn't matter to him. "I came to see Juley."

"I didn't mean to upset you, talking about Bill. I just wanted you to see that I wasn't a stranger."

Carl looked around, not seeing anything. It was the gesture he meant. He said, "I can see that."

372

A warm, an almost cunning, intimate laugh came from Sam. "Hell, life goes on."

"Are you married to Juley?" Carl asked. "I'm asking because she never wrote about you."

"No. I'm married myself. We've got problems." He said this with a kind of innocent candor, as if to see for himself how innocent it might be. It was, after all, not so innocent.

"Is she working? Is that where she is?"

Sam hesitated. "Well, she was working in the union office but she quit the other day. I'm the local president. Where can she reach you? Does she know?"

"I'm at the Sherry-Netherland on Fifth Avenue." Then he asked bitterly, "Is my niece in the way of this great romance?"

"Don't be sore." Sam approached Carl and he seemed genuinely disturbed. "Sit down a minute. This isn't an easy thing for me. I want you to know that Bill and I were real friends. But everything's tougher now, all mixed up. She picked a fight with me the other day and I'm beginning to think it was because she might have known you were coming to town. You being Bill's brother, I mean. You see, it's important, the way she thinks of you. Hell, I'm nothing to be ashamed of. I can stand on my own feet. But I've known Juley almost as long as Bill. I don't say we were rivals or anything. This all started after the war. But we were all friends."

Carl was rejecting the whole thing, not wanting any part of it, not wanting to see Juley either. "My only interest is my niece," he said. "I wouldn't want her to be hurt by this. That's all. I'm prepared to do anything for her. To take her off Juley's hands, if that's important. Anything. For the rest I don't care. It's Juley's business and yours."

Sam drifted back to his cup and stared down at it meditatively. "I've known Juley so long but I still don't get her." He turned around. "Do you?"

"It's your problem," Carl said brutally. "I don't care what she does."

But Halloran did not react with anger. He waited patiently, waiting almost as if Carl had to be appeased. "I guess my problem is stepping into another man's shoes and having a woman look at you as if you were someone else. I get the idea I'm still competing with Bill. That's why I'm talking to you."

Despite his resentment, Carl felt an urge of sympathy. "They were very close and Bill wasn't an ordinary man. He takes a great deal of forgetting." He paused and struck. "More than you'll be able to forget, or my sister-in-law either."

At this Halloran flared, for the first time, oddly, suddenly. "What do you think I am?" he cried. "You think I'm nothing? I've been out in front all the way down the line from the first days in Detroit. I broke Bill into the business. He followed me, you understand? You medical Charleys live off somewhere in the stratosphere and that's why you never heard of me. But I signed the original agreement with General Motors. My name's on that original committee."

"What's the trouble then?" Carl asked. He still waited at the closed door, leaving but not ready to leave.

"Trouble." Halloran took his cigarette, looked at the burning end and then dipped it with an expiring hiss into the coffee. "The trouble is everywhere. Everybody lives back in the dear old past. I do myself. They were great days but we were all young, almost kids, and when you're young and you think you're going to live forever, then you don't count the cost of what you do. But I'm like you, now. I'm no kid any more, and there's no fun in it. Nothing. It's a job. A job has to have some sense to it. It's got to be regular and not one crisis after another." He started nervously to walk, crossing and recrossing the window, blocking out the dying light, while grayness like disease crept within the room. "I talk to you because you're Bill's brother. He never was tired of talking about you. He said you were smart, smarter than any man he knew. He said you were the kind of guy who started out on something and never would quit. Don't you know that? He said you were the one who influenced his whole life. Don't you know that?"

Evil and anguish suddenly flooded within the room, coming on more darkly than the evening. Masses of memory, jagged, hurting, undigested, floated upon the poisoned tide, began to strike upon Carl, began to pile upon him and choke him. This man, this

374

stranger, this alien presence in Bill's house, stood great and triumphant within it all, letting the flood of it in, and Carl's heart darkened. He found it difficult to breathe, and all the while the tenderness was being pressed to death within him, his love for Bill, the envy for his life, the life that envied, had refused to die.

Carl stood hard as a stone, his face masked, his arms still. He listened. He stood there as if refusing to listen, and yet he was listening, trapped at last. I will not listen, he thought. But he listened.

"I remember one night," Sam said, and not for nothing had he learned to speak before great meetings of men and women, to stir them, and lead them, to make them feel their destiny as acts of their unique will. "Christ, it was long ago." And *long ago* entered on shaking steps with the coming on of night, the shadows that began to breathe where the dying light no longer reached. "We were distributing leaflets in front of a parts plant in Detroit and we got pinched. They threw us into the city tank along with the drunks and pimps and crooks, and we sat there in a little circle, a dozen of us talking, laughing at first, mostly at Bill. He was high as a kite. This was his first time. And it was a ball to him, a ball. Then we got to wondering what the hell we were doing there and what for. Men talk. They get to talking. And each one of us had a story. I mean, why go on? What makes a man go on? You're on a job and they're sweating your ass off and so you fight. That's one thing. But there's always something personal that's there too, and it gets all mixed up with everything else. There's always reasons, personal reasons, each man to his own. And Bill told a story about you."

"Me?" Carl's mouth was dry with sorrow, and he felt the pain of remembering his brother and that stone cellar in Prummern came up, the long stalks of rain, and everywhere the soft and shattered ground, and how he stood there looking at the sterilized emptiness of that cellar where Bill had died. Now, the front having sputtered out there, was suddenly pressing him here, here in this shabby apartment, in the apartment of Bill's wife, in the face of Bill's rival, the wife's lover. And here he stood, oppressed, shaken to his most ancient memories. "About me?"

"Sure, you. We bought a bottle from the guard and passed it around. It was cold there and Bill told us how one day, it must have been when you were both kids, I think you lost your job at the hospital. Yes, that was it, and you came down to write off the family because you were graduating to the bread line. Christ, those days, you start to think back and those days come back."

The days fell in a dark rain upon Carl, the violent laboratory, the director, a city doomed to snow. The days fell with their different weathers, warm days and cold, spring days and winter nights, that infinity of times, yet measurable time of one man's life, the various but meaningful life of one man's time.

Halloran shook his heavy shoulders, standing too within the wash of time. "He said you had to pick between going out and making a living and being a real doctor, a scientist, and you picked the real thing, so that when he had to make the same choice, it was easy. His father had done it. His brother had done it. So he did it. That's all."

"He said that?" Carl said.

"He said it," Halloran went on. "It came up again after you walked into that beating, and we were scared stiff you'd go running to the cops with the story, and open up that can of peas in Tarrytown. He never worried. I remember how he got up in the committee and said, don't worry, that's my brother, and while we're taking it down here in the shops, he's taking it somewhere else. You belonged, he said, I remember how funny it sounded then. You belonged to us. Well, he was right, and that's why I'm talking to you. Those days are gone. We've flopped. All those days all pissed away, and now it's different."

His voice stopped and the room stopped dead too. It had congealed with grayness, stopped up in its corners, choked in its center, and only against the whitewashed alley wall did the pale evening light still shine, delicately immersed in the end of day.

Halloran sighed wearily. "It's all different now. I'm not ready to start all over again as if I were turning twenty-one. I'm not ready to make believe any more that we're just around the corner from a great circus. And that's how Bill is gumming it all up between Juley and me. She wants a man to be living way back in the past, and it's all gone. Bill's gone. The thing is out of hand now and it's a fresh start again, and the people in the shops don't have the feel for it any more. It's different and harder and, I'm sure, a bust. Every man for himself now, with the thing out of hand and running wild. I'm tired of it all, and she doesn't understand. She still thinks like it was the old days sometimes, not all the time, and I guess it's Bill who's got her still confused. That brother of yours keeps walking around wherever I want to walk. I'm too old to go on fighting with ghosts. Why don't you talk to her? You're a doctor, a big man, she tells me. You know people can't go on living like this. It's not worth it. A man has to settle down with his personal life at last. I've seen these broken-down hacks still fighting like they were twenty, broke, living off a little union charity, bumming a drink and meal. The teeth knocked out somewhere in the South, the stomach ruined somewhere in the West, the wind gone somewhere in the East, the whole stinking geography of the country killing them. It's like being a fighter and not quitting when your strength goes." He was pleading with Carl, and it was all so unexpected, so terrible to face.

Carl could no longer bear his brother's dead body being dragged through this festival of betrayal, the wife, the man, the whole life so fully given and now so fully lost. Without saying another word, he turned and opened the door and went out into the hall. Walking slowly down the stairs, controlled in his body, he felt himself running again in memory down the steps of his mother's house, and outside now, as then, was the undiscovered world which in the end had turned out to be even more frightful than any youthful despair of it.

vii

ALONG about midnight when Carl came out of the lecture hall at the Institute, damp with sitting and too much talk, weary, his mouth wry with smoke, dull-headed and burdened, there was a cool, a naked sea wind blowing up the river, and the trees along the high riverbank were moving their overweighted branches. The leaves were turning upon each other and people had come out of the hot stone houses and were wandering in the youthfulness of this fine and vagrant air. Carl stood on the sidewalk with a handful of new friends, and no one spoke, but they turned their sweaty faces towards the river and let the strength flow upon them.

"I can drop you off on Central Park West," one of the doctors said to Carl, "and you can catch a bus or a taxi across."

There was a vague conversation within the car. It didn't amount to much. Someone remembered one of the speaker's remarks. Another thought he might have objected more strongly from the floor. This all meant little, and meanwhile the smooth run of the car with its windows open funneled the fine air, distilled from the coolness of a distant ocean storm, upon the passengers, and they began to live again.

At Seventy-ninth Street the driver changed his mind and insisted on taking Carl home, but Carl politely got out and said good-by. After the car had gone he stood on the edge of the park, waiting for a taxicab, and then he decided to walk to his hotel. He had not walked through Central Park for a very long time, not since that dim evening, so far away was it, when he wandered, waiting for Sandy.

Even at midnight there were many strollers abroad, couples and old men with dogs, groups of young men and women, amorphous and changing hands, and now and then a solitary, greedy for pleasure, lurking behind bushes, shy, sexual. Carl walked slowly beneath the park lights glowing like sea lamps in the dark and overpowering shrubbery. The wind had no real force here, but lapped heavily in, long tired gusts that made the lamps wink, and sometimes blew unfolded newspapers like huge awkward moths along the gritty walks.

But the night was not without beauty.

He walked without seeing anything, just heading generally in the direction of the East Side and south, taking whatever path seemed to lead that way. He could not see anything for his mind was unfree. All during the evening, even when he was on his feet talking, he had been thinking of his brother who had sprung alive, more real now than in the days when he walked this mournful earth. In only one sense was Bill actually dead. He could no longer create an action for himself, but as a force, as an influence, he had his vivid shape, shuffling his feet in the hospital room, odd and businesslike in his new brown suit, or as the rival to Juley's lover, or in that old apartment downtown, staring over the kitchen table as Carl shouted the foolishness at his mother. So in this fashion Freud was right. Man is a reservoir of old ghosts, night shapes and presences, haunting colloquies, adventurous in dreams.

The auto road stopped Carl with its belt line of cars. Stiff and formidable, the lights swept up the paving, a continuous flashing that beat upon him and resurrected again the disaster in Tarrytown when he stood in the after wetness of the rain and tried to get a ride. At his side, a little above his head, the signal changed, arresting the panting flow with invisible force, nevertheless real, like a psychic force, unseen, internal, but nevertheless real, a signal for him. He hurried across the formidable array. As he reached the opposite side, the belt line began again, but behind, and he was in another area of the park.

Here, although the paths were still marked by lamps which dropped patterned shadows more than real light upon the pavement, there were thickets, clumps of trees, and sometimes empty

379

lawns, and Carl made his way, still keeping to the same course.

The afternoon at Juley's apartment, the afternoon with Halloran, had set loose more memories, more of his life than he wanted to consider, but he was in fact considering it. He could not help himself. In the end, how did it all add up? What a man wanted from the world was an easy question to answer. What he wanted from himself, more difficult, but ˙easy or difficult, he had come at last to a questioning point, and this conversation with Halloran, that long and strange confession, the blaming on Bill — so strange that was with Bill dead so long. What was this point?

The path Carl walked on ran alongside an outcropping of bare rock, and on a sudden impulse, he clambered up and stood on a mound, below him the trees and the immense rectangle of the park, and all around, so very high, glittering with innumerable lighted windows, the great stone city, while behind the façade, two-dimensional, rose all the mythological and frightful towers.

The utter weariness of the summer wind, almost cool, strayed among the lower trees, and he heard above the continuous rain sound of the cars, the mesh of the leaves, the washing of the leaves upon each other like plaintive hands. Against this, geometrical, thin and transparent, yet real in the night, stood the walls of the city, and he was there at the center watching it and himself.

He realized the extent of his disturbance, the shocking truth that Juley was no longer Bill's wife. She was a woman available to men, therefore free, free for anyone she chose, and free to be chosen as Sam Halloran had chosen her. In all his life Carl had never imagined that Juley could some day be such a woman. She was somewhere within this city, wandering, and Sam did not know where she was, nor did he know himself. This had become a burden to him. Carl felt the awful weight of knowing this, that Juley was free to wander and free to choose and free to be chosen. Nevertheless, she was Bill's wife.

Carl looked up. The stars did not show very clearly within the night, despite its clearness, for above was that dome of reflected light, light caught in smoke, in dust, in straying mist, the great and impalpable dome beneath which this city lived.

380

Again the wind moved. It spilled in a shudder within the thick trees and the leaves moved and disclosed lamps and covered them. On such a night, but stormier, Carl and Curtin had climbed their way back to Castlehill, and on such a night Curtin had called out to the clearer stars, "Little Emily, which is your star?"

But little Emily was dead, dead before her time, as so many of the young were dead, Emily, and Bill, and only lately, face-up in a green and yellow pool, Edward Knox. It was impossible to think of the millions dead before their time, dying not in the comfort of old age and the domestic bed, but dead because of this city and cities like it everywhere. The civilizations of the earth hardened into cities, lived in cities and died and left the hollowed stones behind like shells of soft-fleshed sea animals on the beaches of history.

Carl did not want to think. He did not have the energy or will to organize, but he let his thoughts, which were feelings, run loose. He let them play and felt himself played upon, a soft and lonely animal in this great nighttime.

He did not *think* to choose. He *felt* it.

There was such a weariness at last in many decisions, in a life held to a conscious purpose and lived through it, and there was relief, even if much pain, when a current like an utter wind broke through and set up the playing and changing upon the memories, thick as summer leaves.

He was no longer young. Yet he was not old. He was a man of science and yet his science was not pure. Passion and sympathy had brought him into the arena to contend with those who loved power, who loved possessions, who loved their grasp upon life, and therefore upon lives. He remembered how as a young man he had dreamed of a remote and careful life, restricted to a few searches, to knowledge and discovery in which the search, impassioned and pure, was its own justification. But he had not been able to bear the thought of so many dead and so many upon the brink of death, the young dreaming and hoping, desiring and yet crushed to death before their time. He had not been able to separate himself from his work with the litter of the war, a handful

381

only, for who could hope to gather even in a thousand institutions that great wealth of the times, the sick, the halt, the lame, the blind. In a dozen factories of death the recent enemy had sought to exterminate whole nations and did not have the time. The cure did not have the time.

Slowly Carl turned and looked around him with wonder. The city was indeed wonderful.

It was a maze, glittering here, softened at its roofs, flowing with abstract shapes and designs, gaudy with color, traversed by winds, by wails, by calls and cries. It stamped upon its creatures the sign of the maze, so that fixed in their brains, they were able to traverse it and somehow not know that man was not born to live within a maze. He was born for anything and everything, capable and plastic, infinitely various, infinitely promising. Why should he therefore see his life only by the sign of this maze?

Yet to shatter the maze was to elect to live within it.

Not to shatter the maze was to remove the self from it. To think it, know it, find out its laws but not to undertake those laws.

He felt a little cold. The wind was colder. The leaves still made their washing sound, their beach sound of the sea receding and dribbling through a million crevices of sand. He was drawn. He was tired. Very, very tired. Very, very upset. He did not want to feel these thoughts any longer. It was obvious enough, obvious enough, he thought. Everybody lived the history of the times, but some sought out that history as their search, as their need, as their work and love in life. An animal falling within a maze was lost there. An animal born to the maze was therefore born to traverse it. Stamped with the pattern, it had the way to surmount it. In the end there was an act of will even if the will itself were a product of its conditions.

He took a last, full look around and felt again the temptation of the mind, which is to retreat to its own particular virtue and let history fulfill its own struggles, for a man did not have to strain always to be at the neat point where the times, contending, first change. He could drift upon the swelling currents, take peace

382

within the backwaters, or even die within the flood, no better or worse than the man beside him. This was to feel history as inevitable. To seek it out was not to alter the inevitability but to make it inevitably his own.

He scrabbled down the stone to the path and with a sharp and impatient energy started for Fifth Avenue and his hotel. As he walked along, as his blood warmed, his body took on the rhythm of his walk, and he shook these dreams, these frustrate half-disclosed images from his mind. It was too easy to think in visions, an old self-indulgence.

Leaving the park past the darkened zoo, he came upon the crowded walks of Fifth Avenue. In all the prodigious buildings the inhabitants had sensed the coolness coming on and taken to the streets, and where they could, the strollers gravitated to the parks, especially to this one in the heart of New York. Carl hurried the last few blocks to the brilliantly lighted hotel.

The lobby was quiet, and he went up to the desk and asked for his key. The clerk returned with it and a note. There had been a long-distance call from Curtin. "And sir," the clerk said, "a Mrs. Myers has been waiting to see you."

Although Carl was reading the operator's call number, although he was looking at it, it suddenly disappeared from his sight.

The clerk continued, "I think she's in the bar, Dr. Myers. She's been waiting since seven o'clock."

And now it was midnight. Now, it was after midnight. Carl looked to his right where the big clock was and it was half past twelve. He looked back at the clerk who averted his eyes, embarrassed for Carl. "That is, she's been in and out."

"Thank you," Carl said.

He did not ask himself why Juley was there. He knew, and as he opened the glass doors and felt the arctic cold of the bar, he knew that he did not want to talk with Juley about it.

She was sitting at the far end of the counter, a young attractive woman in a silk print dress, talking with the bartender.

"Hello, Juley," Carl said.

383

She had seen him in the mirror and slowly turned her head without moving her body, and smiled. "This," she said, "is a very expensive place to wait."

Carl sat down on the stool beside her and ordered whiskey with soda and ice.

Juley pushed back her heavy hair from her cheek, using her hand with a loose expansiveness, and her expression was wayward and defiant. "I've been waiting too long," she explained. "I think I'm a little high."

"I didn't know you were waiting."

"I know you didn't know, but still it was too long. Every once in a while I started back for home." She lifted her heavy brows, the wavy brows which were so odd, and her voice slightly unbalanced from the alcohol seemed to wave also, to curl and uncurl in its resonance, "Home. Then I came back and continued to wait."

"Well," he said, "I'm glad you did."

"Curious, you mean." As the bartender put down Carl's drink she ordered another for herself. "I'm curious too, curious to know what you're thinking about that dear friend you found in my house."

Carl drank his drink down as if it were a cold glass of water. "I'll have another," he said to the bartender.

Juley laughed. It was more a giggle than a laugh, but with her rich voice, with those penetrating cadences, it became a laugh anyway. "You'll have to work harder to catch up."

"I don't intend to," Carl replied. He placed the note from the hotel on the bar. "I've got to make a long-distance call."

"Go ahead," Juley said. "What's another hour in my life?"

"Why don't we go upstairs?" Carl asked. "It'll be more convenient."

"Why not?" she replied. "What's another place?"

They sat quietly and finished their drinks and Carl paid. She jumped down from the stool and swayed a little, holding onto the bar, but he made no effort to assist her. She picked up her purse and walked out in front of him, going steadily and yet on delicate steps, intending each one of them.

In the lobby as they waited for the elevator, she said, "It's awful hot out here, but I guess it's because it's so awful cold in there."

They rode up in another silence to the midpoint of the tower where Carl had a suite facing the park. The blinds were pulled up, the curtains drawn back and before them in three large windows the skyline glittered and, below, the park.

"How pretty," Juley said, going to the windows. She stood there looking out as Carl closed the door. He immediately got the operator and put the call through to Curtin. As Juley heard the phone click back into its cradle, she turned around and sat down on the window sill. "It's a little cooler here. Anyway, I think it is because we're up so high."

Carl sat there waiting for her to begin. He had decided to make no effort to aid her.

She was looking at him without smiling and then she was smiling. She slid off the window sill and walked over to a chair across from him and fell back in it, stretching out her legs and kicking off her shoes. "Whenever Bill and I talked about you," she said, "I used to say you were a cold fish. I didn't really think so, but now I say, you look like a cold fish."

"And what did Bill say?"

"Bill used to say, when a man catches a fish and looks at it, he says there is a cold fish. And when the fish looks at the man, the fish says, there's a poor fish. So I'm a poor fish and you're a cold fish." She laughed merrily. "Oh, I'm pretty high, you know. That's your fault for keeping me waiting so long. But I'm nice and relaxed. That's the fault of the alcohol. And I'm pretty mad, too, but that's Sam Halloran's fault. He told me a long story."

"I'm very glad to see you," Carl said, "but I don't give a damn about your friend."

"My boy friend. Well, lover, better. I guess, my old lover. He's a fish too."

"How's Carla?"

"Fine. I've got pictures of her in my purse. But my purse is on the table next to the door and I just don't have the energy to get up."

385

Carl rose and went over to the table and got Juley's purse and brought it back to her.

"Take them out yourself," she said. "They're in an envelope which I put in there especially for you to see. She looks like me and you."

He opened the purse and took out the envelope and went back to his seat on the couch. The pictures of his niece were casual snapshots, some of them from the camp, and Carla looked happy and healthy, the way a child should be, and remarkably like her mother. He said, "She looks like you."

"But, thank God!" Juley said explosively, "she doesn't feel like me."

"How do you feel?" Carl asked.

Juley had subsided, her eyes half closed. After a moment she opened her eyes and said, "I'm analyzing myself."

He found himself beginning to laugh. "I don't think you're in the right condition for that."

"No?" She contemplated herself again. "Maybe you're right. But I'm in a condition to talk."

"That's true."

"Only I don't know where to begin."

"You don't have to begin."

She sat up angrily. "Why not? You think you can run into that bastard Halloran and prevent me from talking? I'll talk if I want to."

"Go ahead."

"Ah," she said, and slumped back against the seat again, "you feel superior. That's a great feeling for a doctor. Being superior."

The phone rang and Carl picked it up. "I have your party," the operator announced, and in a moment Curtin's robust voice was booming away on the other end.

"Carl? Hello, Carl? How's the female situation in New York?"

"Hello, Val," Carl said.

"How did the talk go?"

"The way we thought. Lots of heat, some light, plenty of resistance."

"Why didn't you call up?"

"I don't know. I didn't think of it."

"And we're waiting here like a bunch of Penelopes. You call that loyalty? Anyway, Carl, I'm coming East tomorrow. For the hearings."

"Yes."

Carl saw Juley getting up from the chair, drifting out of sight. Her print dress came back into view and Carl looked up and saw her face. She was quite pale and disturbed. "The trouble with you is," she said, "that you never liked me."

"I've always liked you," Carl replied.

"Thank you," Curtin said. "And who is the dame in your hotel room?"

"My sister-in-law."

There was an obscene, gargling laugh. "I never heard that one." Curtin spoke with someone else at the other end of the wire. "I'm leaving tonight and I'll be in Washington tomorrow. I've got reservations for both of us. It's a question of an hour or two of jawing. It won't be a complete waste."

"All right," Carl said.

"Au revoir," Curtin boomed and then he whispered, "Why do you lie to me, gallant Carlie, who's the dame? Does she have a friend?"

Carl hung up. When he looked around Juley was nowhere in the living room although her purse was still on the arm of the chair.

Carl was profoundly annoyed with the notion of going down to Washington to proselytize among the staff of the Administration. So much energy went into useless work, when he wanted to devote all his time to his project, and he wondered if, in the end it was worth it. And now also there was the problem of getting Juley to go home and leave him in peace. Any explanation she felt she had to make to him of her life seemed utterly futile. He had no reason to be her confidante, or judge, or her advisor.

He started to walk up and down within the sitting room, catching glimpses of the great city beyond the windows, and he became increasingly impatient with himself for waiting. He stopped and looked into the bedroom.

Juley was lying face down on one of the twin beds.

She raised her face to him and it was shattered with tears.

Something about hotel rooms made all emotions dissolute, and Carl felt it. He said, "Now, what is it, Juley? What is it?"

She lowered her head within her arms, hiding her face again upon the bedcovers, and he stood over her, looking down upon the sprawled body, somehow remembering an incident of the war, when he was awakened one night to hear a woman screaming, "I want my baby. My baby is dead. Dead dead dead." There was a fearful racket in the next room, the sound of feet and bodies, and this woman's voice hysterically weeping and screaming. Carl got up and went into the hallway and knocked on the door. An air force captain opened it and behind him Carl could see a nude woman rocking herself on the floor and crying. "It's none of my business," Carl said, "but I'm a doctor and I thought perhaps you needed help."

"Come in, Doc," the young man said. "I don't know what's wrong with her. She's all likkered up, hot as a mink, and then all of a sudden this. I think she lost a kid in the air raids."

Suddenly the woman was at the window, shrieking for her child and trying to get out. They pulled her back and Carl persuaded her to take another drink in which he dissolved a sedative. In the morning, when he left the hotel, he met the young captain. "Thanks, Doc," the young man said. "She got up in the morning and it wasn't a total waste."

But the reason Carl remembered this was because of the hotel room, which, like this one, was tastefully furnished, and yet contained the passage of too many bodies, a sense of paid feeling, paid comfort, not a place to live or die. It ran down everything, tenderness becoming drunken sentiment, desire a vice, anger a mockery. It annoyed him to see Juley exposing herself this way, in these hired walls with strangers on every side. But she made no sound.

She merely lay there. In that other room the shade had been flapping, he recalled.

388

Carl sat down on the bed beside her crumpled body. "What is it?" he asked. "What are you slobbering about, and why are you slobbering here?"

She made no answer and she didn't move. He sat there in the half-darkness, light coming from the open door to the living room, and he had no way to end this scene. He thought it might help to offend her. "Shall I call your lover to come down here and take you home?"

She was not offended, and he felt stupid, he felt the contempt he had for her turning on himself, the inward anger. He put out his hand to touch her shoulder. He touched her shoulder, and the shoulder cringed away from his hand.

Slowly her head turned up to him, the face obscured by the tumbled mat of hair, coming out of the darkness of the hair, here in this dark room, the soft shining whiteness of the face coming out of the strands and thickness of the hair. He could not really see her eyes and mouth and yet they were there alive in her face, and he withdrew his hand.

She continued to stare at him and he looked away, for his hand was shaking, pulsing, and a long wave of desire ran from his hand which had touched her, ran along his arm, into his shoulder, into his heart, into his body. He was suddenly wild with alarm. This is my brother's wife, he thought. My brother's wife. He held his head stiffly forward, awkwardly, in a vise away from her, staring at the floor in front of the open door to the living room, at the sandy light there on the beige carpet, and like a man whirled aloft into a thin and dangerous altitude he felt the pressure of his living blood swelling against the thin drums of his ears, and the pulse there like a quick hand drumming, the fingers drumming.

In the ambit of his eye he saw Juley's foot. It was there down in the corner of his field of vision, simply a foot, a stockinged foot, the toe pointing sideways down, and it seemed to him he felt the full unfolding growth of it, this mute, this twisted foot, this foot growing into a calf, the calf slowing down into the crevice behind the knee, and there her dress, and there her other leg, and there the body swelling and growing beneath his gaze, the marvelously

389

full and growing body, the body composing and filling all his eyes, growing into his desire as it grew into its shape, the shape commanding and distending the thin air, the terribly fragile air of this room, so hard to breathe, so hard to live in, and again her face.

Without knowing, he put out his hand and brushed the hair out of her face.

With a sudden twist she was in his arms, holding tightly to him and he was holding her, her face against his chest. She did not speak. She did not weep.

As he held her, one arm across her back, the other hand upon her thigh, because this was the way she embraced him, his body alive with old habits knew at once that this woman, even if she were Bill's wife, was seeking him. A guilt, more terrible than fear, a murderer's terror, assailed him along with a passion for Juley, and he began to caress her and she raised her face, kissing him, and it was like dying of agony to be so possessed with passion and guilt.

He dropped her from his arms and sprang to his feet, panting and overwrought. An inner tumult hammered at his flesh, and he cried out, "What are you doing here?"

She simply lay as she had fallen, looking up at him, and he smelled the odor of the whiskey as on the night when he had returned during the war. She spoke in a monotone, "I didn't want you to know about that . . ." She could not say Halloran's name. "It was nothing, only loneliness. That's all."

"Why do you talk to me this way? I've got nothing to forgive."

She sat up on the bed, swaying a little, all disheveled. "What do you want me to do?" she asked. "What? You tell me. I don't know what to say or how to act. Shall I call on you? Should we take walks together and go dancing, and talk about nothing, and slowly pretending, pretending and pretending, start to fall in love like people do when they're children and just beginning? I don't know how to do that now. I don't want to. I can only tell you. What else can I do?"

She rose from the bed and stood before him, her white and bewitched face open and pleading. "Say no, and I'll go away."

"No," he said without thinking. "No."

390

They were only a foot apart, her face from his, and she was shorter than he was without her shoes, shorter, younger, more helpless.

She was untouchable, an untouchable for him, and she seemed to feel it at last, for she averted her glance and with her head sideways and lowered went by him into the living room, where she bent down and put on her shoes. She opened her purse and took out a small mirror, a compact, a lipstick, and she remade her street face to go down into the street. He stood silently watching her, saw her going, saw her disappearing, and yet desiring her and despising her as untouchable, he let her go.

She did not even look back as she went through the door.

He heard it slam shut, and he continued to stand there.

He did not doubt that she loved him. He did not doubt that his brother was dead, but to love Juley was to finish what the murdering war had only begun, and he shuddered.

He decided to leave for Washington that night, to move, to keep moving, to fly, to escape, but there were more terrors loose in this night than a man could run from.

viii

IN one of the basements of the Capitol (*the Republican Party's catacombs for fifteen years, was the way Rep. Jos. X. Vaughan, R., N.Y. put it*) distributed between massive supporting walls, narrow monastic corridors, and the bases of great pillars which held aloft a dome surmounted by a statue of Freedom, the lunchroom of the Lower House survived thinly, like a parasite in the skeleton of a Leviathan. There was always a pullulation and tumult of diners, Honorables of the House, messengers, visitors, while white-coated Negro waiters softly slid in and out bearing their oily silvered trays, the tarnished silver service and Southern-style cooking. There was always a Midwestern congressman, expansive as a cornfield, with a party of high-school boys and girls, always the remnants of a press conference fragrant with alcohol and old tweed jackets, always constituents ("just passing through, Congressman"), supporters ("a little matter if you can put in a word to the Postmaster General"), small financial contributors (a smirk, a laugh self-conscious, "I just wanted to see what I got for my two bits"), with a sprinkling of inventors ("it came to me in a flash"), grandmothers ("they haven't mowed the grass on my son's grave"), all boring their duly elected representatives to death.

Outside in the last supine heat of summer (lynch weather in the poolrooms and bars) the strange unfinished city burned, the classical city plan which had never quite come off, the history which had never flowered, the Age of Reason which had never come of age. In air-cooled hotels and in this dark conspiratorial basement the real business of government which was business whispered ahead, and no matter who was elected and when, the

392

perpetual president was Six Percent and the vice-president, Jim Crow.

"The American Century," Rep. Jos. X. Vaughan (R) N.Y. said at a Communion breakfast, "is everywhere a thing of majesty and beauty, whether in China or on some remote and tropic isle, but in Washington it looks like a secondhand clothes dealer in a Greek temple. At home we are a nation of peddlers while abroad we bear the Pax Romana." He remembered how the bishop smiled; meanwhile he averted his gaze from the insisting face of Dr. Bowman, psychiatric advisor to the Veterans Administration.

Dr. Bowman stared at the unfinished pecan pie before him. His meal had been a succession of unfinished dishes, the shrimp cocktail overspiced, the turkey drowned in white sauce, the salad garnished with grains of sand, the coffee bitter and the pie too sweet. Most keenly he felt that his conversation with the chairman of the Subcommittee for Appropriations was unfinished too, and unfinishable. Nevertheless.

Dr. Bowman assumed a cheerful look which went well with his salmon-pink complexion, his bald salmon head with ears rosy and tender as breathing gills, and behind his rimless glasses his sharp eyes twinkled, cheerful, cheerful. It never paid to lose one's temper with politicians since they were elected *just because* they shared the vices and weakness of the electorate, and all his life Dr. Bowman had labored to advance the backward state of this same universal creature, this crime-ridden, loose-moraled, ignorant collective. He had taught them that the mentally ill were not madmen, not beasts, not to be treated as such. He had striven with all his strength to inform, and there was much strength in his plump pink body and clever mind. He had fought to make the hospitals humanitarian, to collect funds, to raise the standards of nurses and attendants, to carry on the great work of Pinel, Tuke and Hill. Nevertheless.

He said with cheerful earnestness and his habitual qualification, "I tell you, gentlemen, that is, I suggest, if I may, I merely wish to indicate, that steps have to be taken, or at least a warning given, one way or another, before this thing grows popular with the

393

personnel of our mental hospitals and leads to all sorts of unfortunate trouble and neglect of our real moral duties, since in the end it is a moral duty which we have to our unfortunate charges."

The chairman, Rep. Jos. X. Vaughan (R) N.Y., exchanged a secret glance with his colleague Rep. Tom Larrabee (D) Tex. "My moral duty," he said, "is to the taxpayers' almighty dollar."

Neither of the congressmen had much sympathy for Dr. Bowman. Like all the rest he was always demanding more money for his pet projects, more buildings, better quarters, radios, more staff, facilities for play and education. "The son of a bitch," Vaughan had more than once commented, "acts like he was in the construction business." By now fifty per cent of the patients were psychoneurotics, the bill was fantastic, the future inordinate, the problem insoluble. But Bowman was an important man, a professor in a leading medical school, a member of international organizations, an advisor to the United Nations, an editor of a conservative psychiatric journal, and from a family with an independent income. He could not be just ignored or refused. He had to be handled.

With his usual freedom Larrabee laughed out. "Now, come now, Dr. Bowman." He drawled like a cowpuncher although he was a businessman with sulphur mines in Galveston. "You're not really serious. You couldn't be serious. I think all psychiatrists are crazy, or else why would they be interested in crazy people? Temperance people always have a God-awful desire to get drunk. A man has to have the need before he looks for the cure. Who listens to a madhouse doctor? Not even the patients, I'll bet." He liked the joke, he liked it fine, and he roared out like a rodeo, and then he leaned backwards, stretching his long turkey's neck around, and said the joke again to a colleague just behind a post. "I say, Judge," he said.

"What's that, Tom?" the judge asked. He was a Mississippi man, formerly a justice of the peace, and he retained the title by feudal prerogative.

The posts and walls were everywhere, a narrow labyrinth, and loud voices rose all over, voices loud with that careless ease which comes with power in the social situation. These voices belonged and knew they did, and they sounded up like the Minotaur's roar, and only whispered when they planned. There was the odor of food and cologne, lavender and spice on the ruddy necks, the heavy faces, hot breads in the mouths, and now beginning at the meal's end the dark sensuality of the cigar.

Bowman did not permit himself to grow angry. He was a careful, honest, completed man who knew that all good things are done through personal influence, because one man knows another man even in a case with fools like these before him. So he laughed too, showing his even white teeth, all his own, his pink healthy gums, and with this laughter asserted his common sense, that he was not a crackpot psychiatrist who had no sense of the stern realities of political life.

Joe Vaughan complained a little petulantly, "My subcommittee's been in session a whole week, Dr. Bowman. We've listened eight hours a day while one doctor after another comes to the stand, takes his place and reads a statement one hour long. They write in a language that no human being can understand. They say things no human being cares about. They ask for money no government ever had to spend. Now you and I know these men got together beforehand to bring this pressure on the committee. Well, we're doing them the courtesy of listening, but I'll be damned if I'm going to ask a single one of them a single question. We'll never come to the end." His voice had risen so that he was almost shouting and he saw Bowman's eyes flicker nervously with embarrassment. Vaughan decided to go on, to let himself go, to be appeased. "Do you know what'll happen if I ask one single tiny question about one single tiny idea? Do you think we can stop these men talking? I used to be on the Education and Labor Committee, God forgive me, and I assure you out of my own experience that teachers, doctors, women and union leaders just don't know when to stop talking. They're not practical. I don't understand them. I don't care to. All I want to know is how much does a thing cost, and I can tell you right now, that everything costs too much."

"You'll excuse me," Larrabee said, standing up. "I've got to say a few words to a friend of mine before he leaves." Vaguely he looked about him as if to prove this, although in fact no one had risen to depart except himself. Happy to escape from a bore, he learned over the pinkly glowing head of Bowman, he arched his shoulders with confidence and secrecy and whispered in that voice of perpetual promise which is the true mark of statesmanship, "I want you to know, Dr. Bowman, how grateful we are and how much we appreciate your coming up here to talk to us and to give us the benefit of your good advice. You just tell Joe what you want and I assure you we'll do what we can, if we can. We aim to please." He clapped Bowman on the shoulders, almost patted with love the tempting roundness of the head, bare as a buttock, and in a moment was around the wall and gone. Then suddenly he reappeared and warned, "Don't forget, Joe, we're on again at two."

Joe Vaughan consulted his watch. "That's right. The hearing resumes at two."

Bowman was furious with these cheap tricks. Nevertheless. Carefully he pushed his plate away and made room for his elbows. Carefully he leaned forward, keeping his voice moderate and cheerful. "We have a few minutes yet, if I may, that is, if it's not too much trouble."

"Not at all, certainly, Dr. Bowman. I wasn't trying to hurry you."

"Believe me, Congressman, I wouldn't trouble you, it would never occur to me to annoy, but the situation is fraught with difficulties. I could call these men from Sierra in to my office. I could talk to them personally, as I have in the past with others. These are duties. One doesn't shirk. I might or I might not influence them. But in the end we would be face to face with a whole scientific discussion which is exactly what they want. I mean, Congressman, that bringing this discussion into the Administration this way, opening up the whole field is exactly the kind of cheap advertisement they want for their crackpot theories. I want to avoid this." Bowman saw nothing but inattention on Vaughan's face. The face of a clock and the minute hand was moving across it. "You should know that this mass descent on your committee was planned by Dr. Curtin of Sierra. I had nothing to do with it. I was not consulted. You have to admit, Congressman, that while I've not been backward in my demands for funds, I've never tried to bring public pressure on you, to inconvenience or embarrass the committee. You must admit that."

"That's true," Vaughan said.

Seeing a breach, Bowman shot home a bolt directly. "It's one thing to demand more money to make the miserable lives of these poor wretches under our care more comfortable. It's another thing to spend government money on experiments and foolish theories."

"Well, naturally, I agree, I agree." Vaughan at last could not conceal his impatience. "But, Doctor, how can you tell whether a theory of what makes men crazy is crazy or not? I know when a government bureau is spending too much money, but if they're spending their money on lunatics . . ."

Bowman observed his own pink, neat hands, small and succulent as baby crabs, and there opposed were the meaty paws of this Irish upstart, harsh as his voice, obscene as his mind. Bowman withdrew his hands and elbows, already sorry that he had brought up the whole subject. "I'm suggesting," he finally said, but less cheerfully, "that you avoid the whole affair, that you put an end to a certain movement among our doctors which ultimately can only embarrass the Administration. You can effect this by merely raising the question and then saying government funds are not to be used for experimental projects without the direct approval of the department itself. I know these scientists. They'll back down at once because they'll be afraid to lose the opportunity to study large groups of patients. It'll stop the whole thing dead."

Vaughan shook his head slowly, already preparing to rise. The muscles of his body made tentative moves, little assaults on posture, and he had to will not to rise, to finish here. "You're wrong, Dr. Bowman. I can't just afford the time to let these men start talking."

"I believe," Bowman said, "that a man has the right to hold whatever scientific theories he pleases, but he has no right to put these notions into practice in our public hospitals and to turn our patients into guinea pigs."

397

Suddenly Rep. Jos. X. Vaughan (R) N.Y., already rising, already on the verge of departure, going, gone, felt a little itch of interest. Not much, a mild and distant sensation, a little heat in the suburbs of his mind. The House of Representatives contains 433 men and women, an unusually competitive body of individuals even for a competitive economy, and after years of practice and exposure its members learn to be exceedingly sharp for issues which can become personal, proprietary and public. From his father, who had been a building contractor with good business connections in the Catholic Church, Joe Vaughan had learned the fateful role of money and influence in American society, and so when he made his first blundering steps within the political arena he had specialized in appropriations, budgets, and the saving of public monies. At first, this had opened up chances for rapid advancement and preserved him intact through the spendthrift days of the New Deal, but in the end, as he somewhat sadly realized, people do not get terribly excited about saving money, low taxes for corporations and honest business administration. War, labor, and political differences excite the mob. Now he was chairman of this dull subcommittee and there simply was no future in it.

He sat down again, he settled himself and looked across the dirtied table at the pink candy face of Dr. Bowman. It was an innocent countenance, and Vaughan wondered if it concealed a trap. He couldn't imagine the purpose of a trap.

He was in the habit of complaining to intimate cronies that he was fast reaching the "bonus age," that time when a grateful political machine bestows on its respected servants the final respectable honors: important judgeships (the theory being that old dogs do not question the collar and chain); chairmanships in large corporations (since the labor unions and public cannot question the public interest of men without large inherited fortunes); presidencies of universities (because teachers are not to be trusted with the social role of education); or the directorships of eleemosynary corporations (since ex-members of the legislatures know the ropes and can prevent radical tax policies against large real estate holdings). But these fruits were reserved for men

398

with a record of the larger successes, that is, the scandals of American politics, and Joe Vaughan's life had not worked out that way. Capable of large affairs, he had lived his life within small ones.

Vaughan, in turn, leaned forward upon the table. He asked softly, "What do you mean, guinea pigs, Dr. Bowman?"

"I was concerned," Dr. Bowman said as softly, "profoundly concerned. It was my duty to be concerned after that talk delivered in New York. You know new things don't alarm me, and yet, I felt that my responsibility was such . . ." He paused, took a breath, lowering modestly his tender red lips, clasping with pleasure his soft and juicy hands. "I decided to call the area medical director in San Francisco and asked how things were at Sierra. Fine, he said, fine, although he mentioned that just recently a patient had committed suicide. There was, he felt, a question of diagnosis. I don't mean to imply," he hastened to add, implying all the while what he meant to imply and noting the rapt look that slowly spread like benediction over the congressman's face, "that this theory was the cause."

An adumbration of the startling, the horrible, the strange, eddied within Vaughan's imagination. Soldiers. Mental hospitals. Insanity. The wild insane. An old memory fluttered behind his concealed gaze and he stirred uneasily in his chair. He had a sister who was a nun and early in her vocation she had been assigned as a nurse to a lunatic asylum for crazy nuns. Crazy. Crazy. The word kept repeating in his mind, a screaming word. Crazy people. Insane. Mental. Soldiers. Once as a boy he had visited his older sister and heard behind the elegant lawns, the dark brick walls covered with ivy, screams. There had even been rows of red tulips. Yes, it was spring. Red and bloody tulips in the spring afternoon, bleeding there above the Hudson with a cold wind coming from the Jersey shore. Insanity, screams.

Vaughan had only one nervous habit, a constant itch around his testicles which the doctors called psychosomatic. He applied a cream which contained an anesthetic and he had trained himself not to scratch, but he forgot himself now and began to scratch again. He felt first relief, and then pleasure, and then a little pain, so sensitive is the skin there, so sensitive the region, so concerned with all life that dark region of the seeking flesh. He smiled, yielding suddenly in all softness of will, rubbing, rubbing. "Guinea pigs," he murmured; and then a question, a gentle question, really letting himself listen for the first time, "What theory, Dr. Bowman?"

ix

THERE were about thirty people in the committee room that hot afternoon when Curtin finished reading his typed statement and looked up to smile. With his appearance the hearing was at an end, and from the respectful attitudes on the raised bench, some good would come of it. His notion of a real concentrated descent on Washington by leading men from the different hospitals had been a good idea, and in taking leadership Curtin had satisfied that lean and biting envy of which he now was ashamed. He turned his head slowly to look at Carl, who was sitting in the third row at the end beneath the windows, and felt again with a melting sympathy the concern, the affection, he had for him. He still did not know why Carl seemed so unhappy, irritable, bored with everything, especially after that wonderful battle in New York. In all the preparatory conferences with the doctors for this hearing, again and again they had referred to Carl's lecture, and it was Curtin who had expanded on it during the evening hours while Carl wandered about the city, coming in so late, exhausted and indifferent to everything. In taking Carl's place, Curtin had found his own, and while he consciously tried not to take credit for any of his friend's ideas, he had been given the credit in a generous way, and he was old enough, and in certain ways impulsive and youthfully egotistic enough, to accept the admiration. Away from that introverted environment of the hospital, his exaggerated competitiveness disappeared. He felt himself standing shoulder to shoulder with his friend, the two of them launching, as it were, an idea upon the world. So comfortably he surveyed the room, comfortably sweating, and promised himself to find out what it was that was troubling his dearest friend.

401

So comfortably smiling, Curtin faced the big square room beneath the lighted chandelier which contended emptily with the late afternoon sky where all day the round sun burned ceaselessly over the hazed city. He saw the grouped doctors, and they smiled too, smiles flourishing on their contented faces, a sense of unity there and a good job well done, the fragrance of new ideas, a sense of fellowship, and even deeper than this, the first lilting wave of a cause.

The random tourists who had wandered into the room smiled, because everything had been so dull, not a real hearing at all, and now they would be able to leave without calling special attention to themselves. The professionals, attendants, stenographers, and the lone reporter smiled with genuine relief, winning with Curtin's last remark a few workless hours from the day.

On his raised platform, flanked by an empty chair to his left and Rep. Larrabee, immersed covertly in a Galveston daily, to the right, Chairman Vaughan smiled too, completing the general picture, and yet noticing that in the third row near the window, the dark man whom Dr. Bowman had pointed out to him did not smile, and did not seem, in fact, to know that the hearing was about over. With this exception there were general smiles everywhere.

The chairman inclined his colorless face across the shambles of his desk and murmured courteously, "Why thank you, Doctor." With this same politeness, with the same common smile affixed to his face, he now turned to his colleague and asked, "Any questions, Tom?"

"Why no, Joe," Rep. Larrabee drawled. "Not at all. The good doctor has been most co-operative, most co-operative I would say."

"Indeed, he has." All through the afternoon Vaughan's face had passed through the usual attitudes of attention, now a frown, now a nod, now assent and now doubt, but his hands, willful as wild boys, had never been still. The triple-decked blotting pad was torn through, ripped at its edges, and with his gold fountain pen the chairman had bled fuzzy ink blobs upon it and created fascinating Rorschach blots, blue creatures of the underworld

402

spawned automatically to represent his inner frenzy. The scratch pad was covered with hieroglyphs. On the calendar all the nines had been converted into eights, all the ones into fours, all the threes into B's, for this was forty-eight, the Beginning, he knew it was the beginning, this year now, at last after a political lifetime of waiting. Irritable, corrupted with the intense vision of success, his soul had played among these docile objects, these neat symbols of order, method, and record, and now the order was chaos, the method Freudian, and the record one of unbearable tension.

Vaughan picked up the gavel from his disordered desk and raised it as if to give the signal, a light tap, which would free the audience, when suddenly he paused, holding the mahogany instrument aloft, and asked, as if on impulse (and although planned, it was indeed impulsive, a driving shock of desire from his whole nature), "Just a question, Dr. Curtin, if you don't mind?"

"Not at all." Like the audience, already leaving, Curtin sat back heavily in his chair, recrossed his heavy thighs, and wiped his face with a handkerchief.

The chairman lowered his gavel, but continued to hold it, turning it again and again within his hot hands, holding to it tightly. He looked down to Dr. Bowman, sitting cheerfully in the front row, delicately pink, and then his glance roved again towards the dark man near the window who had finally slightly shifted his head to see what this delay meant. The smile on Vaughan's face which had been formal now filled with meaning and became his own, an anticipation.

"Why, you know, Dr. Curtin," Joe Vaughan said, "you know this subcommittee is a kind of watchdog of the people's money. You know we have the dirty job of seeing the money is well spent. It makes some people dislike us, but someone has to do the dirty jobs in a democracy."

Eagerly Curtin chimed in. "I realize that. But I'd like you to realize, sir, that the additional requests for funds that I've been making here are presented in all seriousness. We understand your problem, and yet, if we did not feel . . ."

"Naturally, naturally," Vaughan agreed. "I understand."

403

"We're trying to work out a method which will turn our patients into useful citizens again."

"I'm sure. And would you say your methods are generally successful, Doctor? Do they work?"

"Yes. That is," Curtin hastened to add, "within limits. I would say yes, within limits, within the limits of present-day knowledge. Our job at Sierra, we feel, is to push beyond the limits of present-day knowledge." He laughed good-humoredly. "Let's say our slogan is: everything is possible."

There was a good-natured murmur from the doctors in the audience. Everyone was finding this little tag to the hearing more human and more interesting. Once again Vaughan darted a glance to the dark man with the thin mustache and this time he found him smiling, listening and smiling, but with a distant smile, amused by the chitchat but not interested in it. "I presume," Vaughan asked more strongly now, leaning a little forward and bringing up his gavel above the desk, holding it quietly within both his hands, "I presume that these new methods are applied with the earnest hope that something new will cure these unfortunate victims of the war?"

"Why, yes. A question of exploration, of discovery."

"Naturally. And if the new method doesn't work out, why naturally you give it up and try something else?"

"Of course." Heavily pedagogical, Curtin went on, "We're empirical. Trial and error. After all, sir, all science advances through the method of trial and error, as you well know."

"And what happens," Vaughan spoke most slowly and most distinctly, "what happens if the trial happens to be an error? What happens if the experimentation on the patient results in the patient's death? Is this considered scientific too?"

The room had been quiet and attentive before, and yet not noiseless. The room had been quiet as the daily jungle is quiet, orchestrated with the ordinary lives, the common movements, the slow whispers of life within the sun-striped green, and then, as from nowhere, from the empty air, the unexpected roar of the lion launched violently on the air, magnetizing nature, fixing the heavy trees in place, converting shadows into traps, the yellow somber roar charging the whole jungle with a vacuum, fear coming, silence now, absolute. And like a heavily grazing animal caught suddenly within the open, Curtin turned a blind, uncomprehending face towards the chairman, and asked, "What do you mean?"

Again Vaughan's quick glance went to the window.

Thank you, Dr. Myers, he thought, thank you for your attention at last.

The chairman said crisply, "I simply mean, Dr. Curtin, if as a result of your experimentation on one of these poor insane boys, one of them dies, why then you reject that method and go on to something new."

Curtin exploded. His round face danced with blood, and he uncrossed his knees and half rose from his chair. "That's ridiculous."

Vaughan consulted the page before him where Dr. Bowman had written a few notes. "On the eighteenth of the last month," he read, "a patient at Sierra by the name of Edward Knox died under unusual circumstances. Are you familiar with this case, Dr. Curtin?"

Outside the sky thickened into amber but the windows stood in a blue shade from the massed bulk of the building. Inside, there was the cold hard shock of all the pleasantness dead, and here at last, so surprisingly that everyone saw it at once, this room revealed its secret shape, arranged for mortal combat, the high judge's chair and below the witness, the man on trial, the watchers before, behind, the great American flag. Attendants were, in fact, police. The stenographer at his tiny machine, silent, monkey-fingered, taking down the fatal question. Answer!

Alertly smiling, the reporter turned up an old news-wise face, scribbling notes with a practiced hand.

"I don't, that is, I can't, I mean," Curtin paused, fumbling, "that is, I don't understand you."

"Did a patient at Sierra by the name of Edward Knox die on the eighteenth of last month?"

405

In futile protest Curtin demanded, "What has that got to do with what we're talking about?"

Vaughan asked again, his voice dry and persistent, patient, expert, "Did he or did he not?"

"But yes. Still, I don't understand . . ."

Interrupting, Vaughan said smoothly, "Now, just a moment, Dr. Curtin, let's get the facts first. We'll talk about understanding them later on. We have time for your interpretation of the facts. First the bald, plain facts. He died then?"

"Yes." The affirmation came helplessly from Curtin. He waited dispossessed, caught alone out in the open, feeling his nakedness out there in the open, and he darted an appealing look towards Carl, in Carl's direction, yet not seeing him, for all his attention rested with Vaughan.

"He committed suicide?"

Again the roar, and Curtin couldn't answer. He could not settle himself within this new dangerous atmosphere, for wasn't this the same room, the very same safe place, and yet not the same? He raised a heavy hand and touched his dry, blubbery lips. He stirred there, too big for the chair, too big for the room, confined, and yet alone in the open.

"Did he?"

"It might have been suicide, or accident."

"It wasn't a natural death?"

Curtin's perverse imp popped up to his rescue and spoke ironically, "All deaths are natural."

For a long moment Vaughan surveyed the witness, and then with great dignity and oratorical solemnity read again from his notes, "It's a poor joke, Dr. Curtin, perhaps scientific, but to ordinary men a poor joke, to speak so of Edward Knox, three times wounded, holder of the Purple Heart, the Silver Star, the Distinguished Service Medal, a young man, a boy almost, given over to your care by the Federal Government."

But Curtin had found a role for himself, and his big hands gripped the arms of the chair, his big voice boomed, and satisfying anger dominated him. "I don't need any amateur lectures, Con-

406

gressman Vaughan, on the care of our patients. I can easily explain this unfortunate event, but I don't think you can explain your unfortunate attitude. I object to it. I demand an apology."

Precisely, slowly, Vaughan raised his gavel, let the whole audience see it, let it collect all the looks, all the feelings, the whole hush of the room upon its polished wooden surface, and then lightly, almost delicately tapped the desk. The gavel made a sharp, flat noise. "Shall we avoid personalities, Dr. Curtin? Shall we confine ourselves to the facts? He did not die in bed."

"The explanation is simple."

"The explanation can wait. The facts. He did not die in bed?"

"He did not, but that's because . . ."

The gavel came down again more sharply and stopped Curtin's sentence short, and Vaughan's voice took up the sound, continued, "Dr. Curtin. Will you please answer my questions? I listened quite patiently to your long statement and the statements of your colleagues. I didn't interrupt. Show this committee the same courtesy. You'll be permitted later to make any additional remarks you see fit, but meanwhile I have a few simple questions that demand simple answers of fact. I'd like to have them answered."

Curtin's anger disappeared again into confusion and he sat there silently, moving his massive head without purpose, passing a blind look about the room which had become oppressive and monstrous to him.

Ostentatiously, Vaughan laid his gavel down upon the desk and folded his hands piously before it. "Now, Dr. Curtin," he went on, "shall we continue? Did Knox die in bed?"

"No." Helplessly.

"In his room?"

"No." Passively.

"He escaped from his room and drowned himself in a pool, did he not?"

Protesting again, Curtin began, "The circumstances were such that he . . ."

And Vaughan grabbed the gavel and struck the rostrum with it, a loud, decisive blow that stopped Curtin dead. The whole room had become an object to be beaten into a single flat shape, and that shape the chairman's will, his need, his intent. He held the polished gavel aloft, held it ready and asked, "Did he or did he not, Dr. Curtin, escape from his room and drown himself in the pool?"

With a defeated sigh, Curtin replied, "He did."

"Good. We know that now. What time was it?"

"A little after midnight."

"Do you know the exact time at which he left his room?"

"After midnight."

"How do you know this?"

"That was the time when the attendants made their checkup."

"So sometime after midnight Knox escaped from his room?"

"Escape is the wrong word. He wasn't a prisoner there. We run a hospital, not a prison."

"Did Knox leave by the front door?"

"No."

"By a window?"

"We think so."

"The latch of which was broken?"

"Yes."

"So he was confined to the building, but not very well confined."

"It's a building," Curtin explained, "in which patients are not closely confined."

"We have evidence of that," Vaughan said ironically. A visitor tittered. In the rear the door opened and a few other people came in, their faces alive with excitement, a little pushing group, for word had gone down the halls that something juicy was happening before Vaughan's committee.

Vaughan consulted his papers again and then he asked softly, "Where were you at the time this tragic event occurred, Dr. Curtin?"

"In my house."

"Sleeping?"

"No."

"What were you doing, if the question isn't too personal?"

408

"I had some friends over."

In a rough, accusing voice, Vaughan cried out, "You were, in fact, having a party at your house, were you not, Dr. Curtin? A big party, were you not?"

As Curtin sat there utterly abandoned, not knowing how to answer this question, alarmed and overwhelmed by the attack and the implications, Vaughan saw that the dark man at the window was scribbling a note, and he could not help smiling. He leaned forward and pressed the question. "Was there a party at your house, Dr. Curtin?"

"Yes, there was. But you make it sound," Curtin complained, "as if . . ."

"I'm not making anything, Dr. Curtin, merely asking. You were having a party. Among the guests, were any of the staff present?"

"Most of them."

"Doctors who should have been on duty?"

"No." In a last rebellion, Curtin cried out, "No, no, no."

"Are you sure?" Out of the corner of his eye, Vaughan saw Dr. Myers hand the note to an attendant, who took it and nodded, and then slowly walked down the side of the room and approached the witness.

"One moment," Vaughan said to the attendant. "Were the usual doctors on duty that night?"

"No," Curtin said. "We had made special arrangements so that most of them could attend the party. It was an anniversary."

"I'm sure," Vaughan said, "the party was very important. Was it a gay party?"

"That's unfair. Very unfair."

"I'm sure," Vaughan said heavily, "it was quite unfair to Knox. Were there," he paused, isolated the word, placing it in neatly, ambiguously, with a smirk, "*ladies* present?"

Curtin nodded.

"Answer please."

"Naturally."

"And did anyone get drunk?"

"No."

"Are you sure?"

"How should I know?"

"It was your party. You were the host. Now, tell me the truth, Dr. Curtin, we know what happens at parties."

"Some people may have drunk a little too much."

"How many bottles of liquor were consumed?"

"I don't know."

"Ah!" Vaughan cried, false, incredulous, mocking. "That many?"

Quivering with rebellion, anger, humiliation, Curtin turned away from Vaughan and faced out towards the audience. Carl motioned to him and to the attendant, who half extended a little slip of paper.

"You may," Vaughan said, "give Dr. Curtin the note from his colleague, Dr. Myers."

There was no longer any possibility of a simple act, the simple handing over of Carl's note, and this is the point of all social ritual, to overweight with ultimate significance the general actions of life, somehow to convince the individual that in the presence of the state, he is face to face with a final destiny. As the white-shirted attendant accepted the permission and advanced a step, the moment became extraordinary and fateful; as he held out his hand and as Curtin extended his to take the note, the battery of eyes were fixed upon this event, and the action quivered there so ripe and forceful with meaning, so thirsty for significance, that Curtin taking the note was afraid to take it, and having taken it, afraid to open it, and lured towards Carl and grateful for the aid, afraid to accept any help.

But the note was in Curtin's hand. He held the little slip of folded white paper and heard Vaughan say sarcastically, "And if your colleague, Dr. Myers, is eager to help this inquiry, we can oblige him with a place in the witness chair." As Curtin started to open the note, the Chairman interrupted. "One minute, Dr. Curtin, a few more questions first, please." A light tap of the gavel emphasized the decision, this gavel which could not be answered, but

410

spoke each time with social finality, the whip of authority, the hangman's noose, the marshal's baton, the policeman's club, the excommunication of the church militant.

Curtin raised his bewildered eyes. It did not seem to him that he was there on trial, and yet he was on trial. He had nothing to be guilty of, yet he experienced a sense of guilt, for the nature of justice is to create guilt as well as to judge it, in a sense to create guilt in order to be able to judge it, just as there is no forgiveness and punishment unless first there is an idea of sin invented to sustain the forgiveness and the cruelty of a just punishment.

The chairman said, "While this party was going on, Dr. Curtin, and while Knox was going to his death there in the pool, would you please tell the committee what you were celebrating?"

The note in Curtin's hand had partly destroyed his state of isolation and he found the will to say, "The successful work we had accomplished at Sierra."

"I'm afraid," Vaughan said, "that poor Edward Knox would not be inclined to agree with you. Was this party paid for out of private or public funds?"

"Privately paid for, of course."

"The servants in your house, are they paid for out of your salary or borne as a general hospital expense?"

"They are part of my salary, the help, the house, and so forth."

"In a sense, then, they are part of the hospital."

"No more than I am, just as much."

"Was Knox considered to be a dangerous case?"

"No."

"Why not?"

"Because he was diagnosed by the staff as not being dangerous to himself or others. His illness was not of that nature."

"This diagnosis, Dr. Curtin, was made by whom?"

"Dr. Grant."

"Is he here?"

"No."

"Under whom does Dr. Grant work?"

411

"Under myself and Dr. Myers."

"Were you aware of the diagnosis?"

"What do you mean?"

"I mean did you concur in it?"

"Well . . . it's hard to answer that question. I was aware of it, but just generally. My job is the general direction of all the work of the hospital."

"Was Dr. Myers aware of it, the diagnosis, I mean?"

"I presume so."

"Do you know?"

"I'm not sure. It's hard to say."

"Who arranged the party?"

"I did."

"You handled it personally?"

"Yes."

"But not the diagnosis of Edward Knox's case."

"I just explained to you that . . ." Curtin gave up in disgust and without waiting for permission opened Carl's note. It read: "Don't let the son of a bitch badger you. Don't answer unless he lets you properly tell what happened. He's not interested in the scientific truth, only a scandal."

"May I see the note?" Vaughan asked.

"It's private," Curtin said.

"Does it have anything to do with your testimony here?"

"In part."

"I think then the chair is entitled to see it. Will you hand it up, please?"

"I don't think," Curtin began as he slipped the note into his pocket, "I don't think you're entitled to see what . . ."

In a sudden fury, his face as pale as if he were on the point of fainting, Vaughan began to slam at the desk with the gavel. He pounded without cessation, flailing away at it while he screamed, "I will see that note. Hand it up here. At once. At once. At once!"

The obscene and violent noise shattered the tension of the room, flung heads around, tossed the bodies, agitated and deranged the air, and Curtin got up from his seat and stood away from the

412

rostrum, looking incredulously out towards the audience. He did not know what to do, and he could not begin to do anything. A few of the doctors in the audience rose and began to talk to each other, their loud and distraught voices throwing the first confusion into a still more dissolute one, and with an almost childlike relief, Curtin found Carl at his side, found him taking the note and standing there in front of the chairman, calmly waiting for the racket to subside.

The chairman flung the gavel to the desk. "This is contemptuous of the committee," he shouted. He rose from his chair and bent over his colleague and they whispered together while the room grew quiet and the attendants circulated, motioning the audience back into their seats.

Ominously calm, Vaughan returned to his seat. "Will you take the witness chair, Dr. Myers?"

Carl walked to the chair and was sworn in by the clerk. He identified himself and then sat there waiting patiently, while Curtin took a seat in the front row, his hands shaking, unable to settle himself, unable to face anyone, looking only at the floor.

"May I see the note, Dr. Myers?" Vaughan was crouched over the rostrum, his lips still blue with rage.

"I'll read it if you like," Carl replied, and without waiting for permission, he read it.

A wind of indrawn breath touched the room, and someone laughed. The laugh expired even as it began, an inarticulate, strangled sound of hysteria.

"May I see it?" the chairman asked.

Carl handed the note to an attendant who in turn marched around to the rear of the rostrum and handed it to Vaughan, who studied it and then turned it over to his colleague. The two of them whispered together again, then Vaughan consulted his notes. "I am going to read a statement, Dr. Myers, which you made in New York." He lifted up a sheet of paper on which in red various sentences had been underlined, and he read in a loud and empha-sizing voice. "*We could accept the notion that society would have to be altered if we wanted to cure the patient, and the patient him-*

413

self would have to participate in the understanding and alteration of those societal influences which had damaged him. Did you say that, Dr. Myers?"

"I did."

"Were you aware of the diagnosis in Knox's case?"

"I was."

"Would you say that your diagnosis was based on the point of view of that statement?"

Carl said crisply, "It wasn't my diagnosis and it would be difficult at this moment to say what the diagnosis was based on."

"Would you say, Dr. Myers, that your theory is part of the thinking of the doctors at Sierra?"

"I hope so."

"Then it is your theory that is responsible for the death of Edward Knox?"

There was now a terrible pause in which Carl looked around the room and finally back to the intent, pallid face of the chairman. Carl waited a long time until Vaughan asked, "Is that true?"

"Why no," Carl said stiffly, "that's a damned lie."

Almost in a whisper Vaughan asked, "Are you accusing me of being a liar?"

"Are you making the statement?"

"I am."

Carl's abstracted face showed no delight in the exchange. "Draw your own conclusions. You're making the statement. The statement is not true."

Vaughan raised his gavel, his hand shaking, "The hearing," he announced in a low, quivering voice, "is adjourned until tomorrow morning at ten. Dr. Curtin and Dr. Myers are to be present then." He tapped the desk and the room opened into a roar of bodies and voices while the lone reporter raced for the door, crashing through the people, running like mad.

414

X

THE idea that shocked Curtin, the feeling he could not accommodate or even understand, was the notion of being banished, of having been pushed all at once beyond the security of his whole life, beyond the protection of society which he took for granted. He was outside, he felt himself outside, and he clung to Carl who was outside there with him. He raged against the shock. When he did not rage, he complained, and when he did not complain, he sat bitterly in the dumps, staring at his own face, golden in the dark mirrors of the closed windows where at the same time the city lights hung in the haze. There is nothing so painful to contemplate, as so many of the restlessly ill know, as the sense of alienation, the removal from the laws of the community, and no matter what Curtin's opinion of his community had been, it had been his, and now it was no longer his. He shuddered before the gross weight of the remembered afternoon, and like a tongue licking a broken tooth, again and again his sensitive mind touched the sharp surface until sensitivity disappeared, and nothing was left but numbness and disbelief.

Besieged by reporters, he and Carl had locked themselves away in the cold citadel of their hotel suite, and this added further to Curtin's desperate loneliness. Then the telephone had begun to ring without pause, and this other means of communication was now cut off. His only sense of contact with the outside world was the unseen but heard appearance of a bellboy who from time to time slipped curt messages beneath the hall door, names, numbers, requests. Although Carl told Curtin not to touch them, Curtin rose each time, read the message aloud, and added it to the pile on the table. The evening newspapers were scattered on the floor, on couches, on chairs, and each headline proclaimed another abrupt poem:

PSYCHIATRIST EXPERIMENTS ON INSANE VETS

SVENGALI DOOMS MAD SOLDIERS

PSYCHIC VIVISECTION IN VA

RED DOCTORS SUBVERT CRAZY GI'S

Carl offered what comfort he could. After a brief call to Sierra in order to warn the staff, he sat quietly trying to estimate the situation. In a peculiar way, Carl was relieved, the shock of the afternoon acting as a counterirritant to the anxiety which he had carried from New York. It was stimulating, almost refreshing, to be faced with a real attack and not the subtle exhaustion of memory, conscience and desire. It was an escape, and yet, escaping, he had the reminding sense that somehow it was all the same. He tried to think. He tried to force his will into the tiniest crevices of the day and his own history, but Curtin kept making too much noise.

"That Bowman!" Curtin protested. "I thought the son of a bitch was a friend of mine. Why I personally conducted him to a whorehouse during the war, introduced him around, opened up one of the most exclusive harems in Washington to him. He met the best people there, the cream of society." He hauled himself to his feet and stood there swaying, teetering back and forth on his heels, rocking with a soothing rhythm as great animals do in small cages. "You know what I'm going to do? I'm going to see that son of a bitch tonight and find out why. Why, that's what I want to know! Why?" Curtin's mind was just another muscle in his life, and he could not sit and plan. He had to act, to escape from the prison of the hotel and fling himself upon the world and do something, to be, to do. "I've got friends in Washington," he shouted, "hundreds of them, and if Vaughan is playing politics I can play them, too. I can get influential people on our side. I can. I will."

"I think you should then," Carl urged him. "I've called all the

416

important psychiatrists I know in New York to come down tomorrow if they could, or send wires if they couldn't, to start some kind of a backfire going, because this Knox business is no real problem if we can get enough real angry people into this farce."

"God damn it, then," Curtin said, "I'll do it. I'll show that cheap bastard how to play politics."

He bustled into the bedroom and changed into a clean shirt, he knotted his tie, he fought with the sleeves of his coat. This was action, action, opening and slamming drawers. Then all at once, he was standing almost pathetically in front of Carl, defeated again, remembering. "The way he treated me, like a criminal." He shook his heavy head helplessly.

"I think," Carl said as firmly as he could, "you should see all these people you know. It'll make a difference."

"We'll never be able to stop this thing. I know these people, Carl. I worked with them for years during the war. They'll keep this up until they've wrung the last bit of publicity and scandal out of it and ruined the hospital and all our work. They don't care about the truth. It's the noise. It's the Inquisition. That's what it is, and if they can, they'll burn us at the stake."

"Well," Carl dryly replied, "they'll discover we don't burn so easily."

"We'll smolder then." And Curtin roared into laughter, without pleasure, in terrible bitterness. "We'll smolder and stink, that's what. They'll smell us around the world and the name of Congress will stink on the smallest atoll in the Pacific. It will stink on the mountains of the moon. I could take that Vaughan and twist him into a pretzel," and he held out his hairy hands, grasped the invisible neck of Vaughan and wrung it. He started for the door and stopped. "What about you? Do you want to come with me?"

"I don't know these official friends of yours," Carl said. "You'll be able to speak more freely without me."

"That's right, that's right." But Curtin did not go. "What about the Seawithes? What about that call from the judge?" He moved to the table and sorted the slips. "There was a phone call from the judge, a number and an address. It's a Georgetown number. Why

417

don't you call them or see them? If we're going to fight, let's fight. Perhaps that old friend of yours can swing some influence? Isn't he a pretty big man?" By now Curtin wanted everyone in the world involved in his case. It was his case now. He was an event, no longer an exile. He felt the largeness of a cause. He had a call.

Carl wanted to refuse, but he was afraid to shift Curtin's attention back to self-pity, so he got up and said cheerfully, "Yes, of course. I'll put a call through as soon as you leave."

"No," Curtin objected. "I think you should see them. It's best to handle this thing personally."

"All right," Carl agreed. He got his coat and hat and prepared to leave with his friend.

But Curtin was complaining helplessly again, giving up again, "Those snoopers from the press'll be waiting in the lobby. They'll follow us like a pack of wolves, and no one'll want to help if it means getting involved in all this publicity." He shook his head and the energy drained from his voice. "I bet that not one of those twenty doctors you called shows up here tomorrow." He found new energy to attack Carl. "Why did you have to run off in a hurry and make that big speech in New York?" He found new lassitude. "It's a waste of time trying to do anything. We'll just have to sit it out. What am I going to say tomorrow when that son of a bitch starts on me again?"

Carl pushed him out into the hall and locked the door. "Your trouble is," he said lightly, "that you were brought up wrong. There's a poor man's exit to every rich man's building."

He led Curtin around a bend in the corridor to a red exit light, and they walked down the six flights to the basement while Curtin's combativeness revived, while he delighted in the trick and the sense of power he regained through fooling the reporters. There in the hot corridors, down among the concrete runways, they both wandered until they found the freight elevator and near it a flight of steps which led up to a back street. A watchman looked suspiciously at them, but here Curtin was in his element and he flourished a dollar bill and explained, "We're hiding from a couple of girls waiting for us in the lobby."

418

The watchman grinned. "What's their names? Maybe they'd like to see how the furnace works?"

In the thick heat of the street the two friends separated, and Curtin went off in a cab, muttering imprecations and disasters, agitated by a rediscovered energy and the light of battle, but as Carl walked on alone he had the feeling that Curtin still had no comprehension of the awful radiation of publicity and scandal which had been set into motion.

Carl himself, as yet, had no clear idea of what the whole affair meant, what it could mean and what he should feel towards it. He had aided Curtain because, suddenly precipitated into a struggle, his first impulse was to fight back. Everything in his experience, in the course he had set for himself in life, urged him, however, to withdraw from this battle of stupid men, and as he wandered without purpose in the slow, heat-exhausted streets, taking the lonelier ways, the ones with fewest lights, crossing circles, clinging to the darkness, the wet and humid swamp of this city, he had no intention of calling on the Seawithes at all. That would merely add another burden to the problems he faced within himself.

Gifted with quick reaction, he had so acted, setting into motion whatever machinery of connection he had to make the next day's hearing more bearable and less violent, but now, alone, escaped from Curtin's presence and the tight little rooms of the hotel, he found no passion within himself to make anything of tomorrow. Vaughan's vicious stupidity did not trouble him in his career. He could find no reality in the attack, neither the complaisance or opposition of Bowman, nor the electrical storm of newspaper headlines. Towards these he had, as towards the late war, a sense of fatality. The more he thought of it, the more indifferent he felt.

This indifference in the end was only superficial, serving to loosen the real anxieties which, like maggots, spawned within his heart.

It was difficult to breathe in this heavy night, in the oppression that shaped the air, drugging it with fragrance and the rot of some hidden swamp. The buildings clung to the earth and rich darkness to them, and when people appeared, they seemed to drift as in

419

water, a turgid current moving them, dragging them past, and he himself drifted in an opposite direction.

He was suffering, and within, transformed into one long conflict and possession, were Juley and his brother.

In his time Carl had seen many dead men and women, and as a doctor and a scientist explored the cold, springy, preserved flesh, searched out its secrets, cut the nerves and cells, sliced the tissue, stained and observed it. But these objects were merely as dead men to him. He had never known the presence of the dead as inhabitants of his own mind, spirits and powers who will not lie silently and dissolve into the waiting underworld of the inorganic, that dry region which cancels the sensual life with an abrupt, one-way equation. He could not exorcise his brother by projecting him above as a god, as he had in a way his father, so long dead, and now a creature of the heavenly host to be remembered with a careless inclination of the head.

Carl kept asking himself: Why do I feel guilty? What is the sin? Why do I mourn? Why do I fear?

Guilt and sin, sorrow and fear, hovered above Bill's head. Bill did not come to Carl as a single man or a single presence. He lived on as a host. There was a brother who was a child and a brother who was a man. These two appeared together. There was a brother who was a young man and there was a brother who was a dead man. Dead, Bill lived twice within Carl, twice dead, as the undiscovered Bill who could not be found in that stone cellar in Prummern, and Bill who had by magic stolen away and returned with a bloodied suffering face, wandering graveless within Carl's flesh.

The night panted in utter apathy, struggling to live on into the next day.

All the brothers of every time and every occasion were alive within Carl, and the most ominous was the brother who was Juley's husband. With all his will Carl plunged himself into this world of brotherhood and guilt. He did not shrink from it. He had to know, and beside it all events and all causes were pale and purposeless.

420

He was now in a region of public parks and buildings, on a stage where white temples stood shining within floodlights and the dark lawns like Euclidian lakes lay rippleless in their darkness, touched along their banks by regular lamps. Other strangers wandered here as he wandered, other faces, other silences. A winter evening returned to his memory. This was what Juley had done to him in New York. She had set in motion the rereading of his life, and expurgated experiences returned with a fresh novelty. An evening in Paris, winter, when he had wandered within the gardens of the Tuileries waiting for that call which would take him to the front and Bill. But Bill was already dead that night, or dying. He had been dying that night, caught out in that stone cellar.

The way Carl remembered it, he was on his way to see his brother. All those years of separation, parallel lives joined here and there from time to time in the strange geometry of the psychological world. At last, wanting to see his brother, feeling the necessity which had risen because of Juley, he had gone to see him. But he had felt the need when it was already too late to be fulfilled. *Because,* Carl thought, holding the thought, *because, because* it was too late. In coming to the decision, he had reached it *because* it was too late.

He could not have known that Bill was dead, and yet Bill at that moment (the long sleep-filled ride to the front) was dying. This was a coincidence, that he wanted to see Bill at the moment when it had become impossible for Bill to be seen any longer in this world. And the subtle unconscious that has no rationale but the logic of its antihistorical hungers, this demon, had called up a dream which he now remembered again, of Juley and himself *hand in hand,* going off *together.* All this, this dream, being in Paris and wanting to see Bill, Bill at the moment plunged into the well of death, these were coincidences which had come to take the form of an intention. Wanting to see Bill, Carl had not wanted to see him. Cain wandering, cursed and an outlaw, had in fact been searching for another Abel. And in memory Abel had never died, for men do not die within the souls of their survivors, until the need that they are doomed to fulfill is fulfilled, and only after that does

421

death come and the dead lie decently interred in their accomplished history.

What was it that he wanted from Bill? What did he want now? Did he want the brother's right to Juley, the easy command to succeed, the brother's right to love?

He had often imagined Bill's death. How many times had Bill died again and again in Carl's mind, held there, so to speak, in the arms of his mind, the two brothers, at last, alone and speaking to each other, exchanging the somber dialogues of the death scene.

Who do you think, Bill asked, will be remembered out of these times? The senators and congressmen, the flocks of businessmen and leeches, presidents, generals, the last, bloodless kings dying of syphilis and hemophilia? I live to be remembered, Bill cried, for I have made you into the future. I have made the future.

Carl answered soberly, arguing with him, A man does not live to be remembered. He lives to remember. That is all he can guarantee, that is, to find continuity in his acts. History belongs to natural law, memory to the artist and moralist.

If I am not remembered, Bill whispered (pale and bloodless the dead lips, the pallid head, the younger brother and yet the older, having the birthright and the gift of the father) it will be *because* (again because!) I have failed, and if I fail, the future will not come. In the. new barbarism who will be so wise as to be able to remember at all? It is absolutely necessary that the apple fall upon your head. It is nature that must precipitate the concrete causes and occasions which, entering one of its creature's souls, provides the ladder out of his ruminating mind.

But it was Carl all the time who was talking, and he knew it. He knew it!

He was standing still in the midst of the great lawns, on this stage of floodlighted temples, and he heard steps stop behind him. All the while he had heard these steps as he walked and now when he stopped, they continued a bit, and then they, too, stopped. He turned around.

Some twenty feet behind him a woman was standing, and when she saw him turn, she ambled up to him, swaying herself to provoke

422

him, for he was a man alone in the night and she was there waiting for such as he. He did not turn from her but let her come up until he could see her plump face, dedicated as the face of a priestess or nun, her face with the general expression addressed not to him, but to all men that might be abroad this hot night, lost in need. Her hair was heavy and coiled on her head, which was strange, and she wore a dark dress out of which, in the night, shone her white face and neck, her white arms, and her stockingless legs in their dark shoes. She did not have any expression for him, but she had a receptivity for one such as he might be.

The night was close, collapsed and sodden, and she seemed cool, plump, escaping from the darkness of her clothes into a whiteness of face and arms and neck, escaping from the dark tragic sense of night, as sensuality, the dream giver. She tended, as it were, the white temples of this stage, a priestess here as Vaughan was a priest.

"Hello," she said. There was warmth in her voice, but a general invitational warmth, for anyone, and therefore for him. When he did not reply, she thought he was shy, and she oozed a little closer and asked so thickly as to make the words physically extend like a tongue, "Would you like a little loving?"

"I'm like you," Carl said in that easy, trained way of his. "I'm looking around to give some." He tipped his hat. He said, "Good night."

He walked directly across the grass, heading for the distant circle where headlights whirled about before they were flung off into the roadways of the city, and as he walked, his body flooded with sensuality, the scattered limbs of Juley, the eyes of Juley, the smiles, the voices of Juley. She lived within his senses like a modern painting, but in motion, a leg here, a hand there, eyes as eyes, mouth as mouth, organized into his need and not in her person. She was there as the object itself, the place to touch, the breath to breathe, the lips to kiss, the eyes to close, a flood of Juleys at last loose for his desire, clasped in his arms, standing away from his rage, standing close to ask, tumbling, tumultuous, ever-present.

Carl took the first cab that came along and gave the driver Judge

423

Seawithe's address in Georgetown. He felt no stronger now than Curtin, and needed an external action to hold back, even for one night, the desire which had shaken itself free from the black prison of his will.

Desire, he thought, as he sat within the cab, his hands clasped on his lap, his head lowered, brooding within the isolation, waiting for the ride to the end and the world to appear again, why do I lie to myself? It is love, shameless love.

xi

AT first, Carl thought the house was in sleep. The street lamp flung a footlight across the Georgian façade, powdered the two trees and came to a dead stop upon the curtains. Down the quiet way a man in shirt sleeves walked with two boxer dogs, one on a leash and one roving, and the rover came dashing up with powerful grace and took a circle around Carl until a whistle recalled him. Carl stepped closer to the house, no longer planning to enter, advancing only because he was there, and once again the dog returned and stood a few feet away, watching him.

The red wet mouth in the black muzzle drooled with a heavy tongue. The wrestler's chest barred retreat, and yet as Carl looked back the dog retreated a few bounds and finally uttered a short, heavy bark and raced off.

Carl looked up at the house whose top-story windows rested on window boxes from which trailed a garland of vines, and by this time the shirt-sleeved man had come up with his two dogs and stopped nearby, the free dog looping in circles around Carl and the leashed dog straining in a straight line at him.

"May I help you, sir?" the man asked.

"Is this Judge Seawithe's house?"

"Yes, sir."

"Do you work here?"

"Yes, sir."

"I'm Dr. Myers, and I was about to call on the judge." He looked at the dead house and back to the man.

"If you ring the bell, sir?"

"I don't want to disturb them if they've retired."

"The judge is in the gardens, sir." And the man retrieved the length of the leash so that the dog would not slobber against Carl and rang the bell himself. "I believe I heard the judge mention your name, sir, that he hoped you would call."

Looking again at the house, Carl saw that there was a gleam of light caught in the folds of one downstairs window, but so small, so tangential as to be barely noticeable, and yet it was there to be seen.

A maid opened the door and the man said, "This is Dr. Myers come to call on the judge."

The maid stepped away from the doorway and Carl entered after thanking the guardian of the dogs.

There were two lighted lamps in the square foyer, a curving stairway with a landing, a mute thick smell of rugs and silence, the heaviness of the night congealed within. "Just ahead, please," the maid said, and she preceded Carl to each door, let him pass through and then took the lead again, each doorway becoming an obstruction for her until he had broken through. He caught gleams of polished furniture, doors and rooms that did not end, and there beyond were four French doors opening into a dark garden, hazed by closed screens, and a light that burned against a wall.

The maid opened one of the screen doors for Carl who could not advance by himself because he did not know where to go. The dark garden had no shape for Carl, seemed empty of everything but the descended night, seemed silent and empty of voices. Water ran, dribbled off, rang like minute bells, sucked softly in a basin.

Carl followed the maid over the uneven bricked path which took a turn around a large flowering bush that brushed a spiderweb of scent upon his face, and there in a little clearing, seated around a table, obscure in the darkness, were a man and woman. The man rose and Carl said, "David?"

"Dr. Myers is here, Judge," the maid said, waiting to one side.

"I'm glad you came, Carl," the judge said. He did not advance, nor did his voice, which spoke, but fell thinly and dried like a handful of blown dead leaves, and Carl went up to him and took

426

the hand and saw the face, and saw at the same time death and old age, but a remembered face smiling and pleasant in the webbed scents of the garden. The hand was bony and dry, but the grasp was firm, a real shake of the hand, and the judge urged Carl around and said, "You remember Aunt Corinne?"

The dark dress stirred and a face swam up as Carl approached, and he felt his hand dipped into an absorbing, receptive grasp, a fold of flesh that took his hand and caressed it and let it go, and a blurred voice which said, "It's nice of you to come." She was standing, her face close to his, plumper than he remembered it, yet not quite seen as yet, and she half turned him with her guiding hand, indicating generally a straw and pillowed chair, promising softly with her voice, "And sit down, please. The garden's the only cool place if you don't mind insects."

She seated herself and Carl creaked into the chair. The judge remained standing. "A cool drink, Carl?" he asked.

"That would be nice," Carl replied.

"Anything special, anything you prefer?"

"Some whiskey and ice, a little soda?"

The maid disappeared behind the large flowering bush, and the judge retreated into his chair, and after a small pause, as if to catch his breath, said, "This is a very long time. Very long. We read your name in the newspapers and I had a friend track you down."

Carl was sitting with his back to the house and little by little the garden retreated from its first darkness, remained obscure, but he could see the faces and the shapes of the judge and Aunt Corinne, he could see a foot-high statue standing above a basin and he caught the gleam of the sounding water. Some light came from the house behind and fell upon the wetness of the flower beds, the bushes, the vines against the boundary walls. Deep in the recesses where no light showed at all, only a darkness that kept retreating to unlighted one-story buildings, a garden spray was foaming thinly into the air and he heard the play of the drops on the leaves. There were these small motions like little ripples against the immovable, quiet rock of the people sitting in the garden.

427

Aunt Corinne said, "It sounds quite exciting, what we read in the newspapers."

"It's been exciting," Carl said. "It happened suddenly this afternoon, and a few obscure people like myself don't quite know what's happened to us."

"Congress," the judge murmured with infinite contempt. "If I did not know that democracy is the victim and not the cause of that duly elected gang, I'd prefer King Stork to King Log."

"But how have you been otherwise?" the aunt asked pleasantly. "Not that we haven't followed your career, we have. We've had a real interest in it."

The judge laughed lightly. "Fifteen hundred dollars' worth," he said. "At six per cent it's a decent sum."

"I sent you a money order years ago," Carl said, growing a little embarrassed.

"I know," the judge replied, "but I never cashed it. It seemed to me that you should not have to pay us for the mistake you made in accepting it." He said this with a certain irony and yet at the same time, affectionately, asking to be forgiven for not having understood something a long time ago, understanding it now.

"It's a gift to the post office department," Carl said.

"That's right. I just never thought of it again, having decided not to take it. We'll contribute it now to your defense."

"My defense?"

"Indeed. It'll take your whole life and all your money to defend yourself from a Congressional committee. They have the resources of the whole government and they use them."

"I don't intend to spend the rest of my life arguing with Representative Vaughan."

"But he intends." The judge laughed again. "He certainly intends."

A butler in a white coat came up with a tray of drinks, and it was the man of the street, now with a little black bow tie and a starched jacket.

"Thank you," Carl said, taking the drink.

"Thank you, sir," the butler said, and his white coat faded into the darkness again, out of sight behind Carl's back.

428

Carl wet his mouth with a sip. "Perhaps," he asked, "you have some professional advice for an amateur at this?"

"Run," the judge said. "Leave the country. Go to Europe, Africa or a tropical island. Or else get yourself a shotgun and shoot the man."

"That sounds like the way I feel," Carl objected. "I took my feelings to be amateur."

The judge sniffed. "Your only real hope is that something even more foolish and scandalous comes up elsewhere. For this is the way we govern today, by crisis and scandal. If ever America was a nation that lived by law, it has become material for scholars."

"We have your books here," Aunt Corinne said in a sociable way, "and David told us about you."

"What did he say?" Carl asked.

"Nice things," she said. "Nice things."

Her voice expired and no one spoke. Only the garden stirred, the water in the basin, the spray in the darkness, the insect hum and somewhere out of sight a bird with a hoarse mechanical voice like a tiny machine. The garden moved its small weight in the thick night. It moved its scent which was sweet and at the same time wry, wry from the green leaves and the grass, heavy from the wet earth, delicate from the blurred flowers which ringed Carl's head.

He saw Corinne looking past him to the house and he turned his head. Three windows on the second story were lighted, the bamboo blinds lowered with slits of light escaping, and a shadow kept passing back and forth before them, sometimes stopping to look out, yet all the while hidden and seen.

Aunt Corinne said, "That's David. I don't think they've told him you're here. Or he may have some work to finish before he comes down. He did say he wanted so to see you."

"I want you to see him," the judge said. "It's too bad you two haven't seen each other more often during these past years."

Carl apologized, feeling it was polite to do so. "I've been stuck in California."

"We are stuck everywhere," the judge replied. "How are you doing with your drink?"

"I've still got most of it." Carl raised his glass and sipped, and the cold ice knocked against his lips. "It doesn't seem possible that there should be a garden like this in Washington and that committee room, too."

"I don't like Washington," the judge explained. "But David has to be here and so we stay. I prefer my own native state."

"Have you retired from the bench?"

The judge chuckled. "Kicked out," he said. "I was called a reactionary because I found against the New Deal, and then I was called unpatriotic because I opposed the dictatorial legislation during the war, and just before they threw me out — at retirement age, of course, but I was thrown out, you can believe that — I found myself being called an addlehead because I thought the constitutional guarantees were guarantees and not illusory promises. I've been a failure in my own times. My only comment now is a profound silence."

The aunt protested fondly, "You're exaggerating."

"Only the unimportance," the judge said. "All my fears have become facts. A man can argue with his fears. He cannot argue with the facts. I give up. I sit here in a damned hot garden, in the hothouse territory of the District of Columbia, in a foreign land, an exile in the South, my enemy. Each day I die a little more and without pleasure."

The aunt repeated, "You're exaggerating."

"Well," he agreed, "I do not want to die. I want to live. I want to see the ruins myself. I'm hopeful it will happen in my time." He stopped and sighed. "An old man's revenge is always history, except when he is in command, and then it is his fate."

"Pooh," Corinne said. "You're trying to make Carl's hair stand on end." And she extended her hand and patted Carl's hand lightly, closed her hand upon his for a moment in reassurance, and then withdrew it again.

Carl looked around again and the windows were still lighted but empty of David's shape. "Is David still with the State Department?" Carl asked.

"In a way," Corinne replied. She spoke hurriedly and she spoke

430

as if she were about to continue but she did not continue. She arrested her voice, she almost arrested her mind.

A bird flew by into the flowering bush and stopped there. It sounded a few notes and then fluttered away. Carl heard the garden again. The garden did not seem to be a place. It was a creature and it was alive, always moving within itself, holding itself in place against the walls through heavy vines, its nerves flowering in the garden beds or on the bushes, and the wet sound of the spray was its cool breath, the fountain its voice, the night its home, the house its shell, as if later sometime it would withdraw there for the day. The garden was a creature of the night, having crawled out to feed, and everywhere it stirred, noticing the passing of the heat.

"Does David enjoy his work?" Carl asked.

"Do you?" the judge asked back.

"Sometimes."

"Well, I suppose he enjoys himself. I don't know." The judge sounded vague and uncomfortable, yet not as if he did not want Carl to ask, but simply because the fact was vague and uncomfortable.

"I'm sure he enjoys himself," Corinne said. She added suddenly, "I wish . . ." But she did not express her wish. It sprang into air, and there it remained and never descended. It hung there, a wish unformulated, and unexpressed, but nevertheless a wish.

When Carl looked at her, waiting for her to finish, she suddenly rose and said, "I'd better go and see him. I'd better tell him you're here." And she started off but after a few steps stopped and returned and said to the judge, "Would you like to call him?"

"If we wait," the judge said, "he will come."

"Yes, I'm sure." She waited and did not go, turning again and again to the lighted windows.

Carl remembered her from Furnace Dock, the strange and uneasy impression she had given him then, but she was an older woman now, and without strangeness any more. Her arms and legs were plump, and she no longer had the sensuality he recalled. She was an older woman, domestic, busy with the thoughts of her duties. At last she sat down again. "Why, yes," she said. "Of course. We'll wait."

"I don't want to disturb him," Carl said, "if he's very busy."

"You won't disturb him." The judge uttered these words without conviction. He brooded for a long moment within the soft, disturbed darkness and then asked, "Tell us about yourself, Carl."

"What shall I tell you?"

"About the mysteries of your profession."

"The most mysterious thing about it," Carl said slowly, "is what we think we're professing." And he began in a rather anecdotal way to describe some of the cases he knew of and their relation to the theory he had advanced at New York. He caught the attention of his listeners at once, and as he spoke on, he found himself telling the story almost mechanically, while out of the dreaming coolness of the garden the image of Juley began to emerge.

A viscous, hydraulic fluid seemed to flow thickly within his flesh, a dull, pressing sensuality. He remembered Juley. She began to form within his senses, taking on a fleshly shape, inhabiting his hands and eyes, and all the while this pressure grew within him, and under the pressure the fluid warmed, flowed more freely, palpable and imaginary like the world's ether. The dark garden moved more loudly. A new bird appeared as a voice, a sound that had no music in it, a clatter, a burr, a clatter.

Carl talked more loudly, and this sensuality was like drunkenness, freeing his tongue, urging it to speak, to shout, to be extravagant. He shifted uneasily in his chair. He looked around and found himself impaled upon the mouth of Aunt Corinne, that plump shapeless mouth, cut into her face, an opening healed into a soft scar, and he remembered David kissing her on the mouth on that winter day when they had both arrived at Furnace Dock. Carl's memory stumbled blindly into a storehouse of sexual experience, and without thinking to, he described a case he had known, a story of ambiguous homosexuality.

Quite suddenly he realized that the judge and the aunt were not listening but looking past him to the house. The screen door banged. Carl turned around.

432

The tall figure of a man was coming down the garden, disappearing behind the flowering bush, and reappearing within the little open space. He wore white trousers and a white shirt open at the collar, and his motions were rapid, sudden, a series of starts and pauses.

"Sorry," David's voice said, the same clear voice, "sorry to keep you waiting." He stopped in front of the judge, looking down at him. "It's terribly hot tonight, terribly. But I finished my work." He turned. "Corinne, you're sure there was no call for me today, you know, the one I was expecting?"

"No," Corinne said hastily. "No. The call didn't come."

"Someone might have taken it and forgotten." He raised his voice suddenly and called, "Robert, Robert."

The judge rose and said, "Don't you see Carl? That's Carl sitting there."

David made a vague gesture to Carl who had risen. "Hello, Carl," he said indifferently, casually, and he took two steps backward as the white-coated figure of the butler appeared. "Robert?"

"Yes, sir."

"Did you take any of the calls today?"

"Yes, sir. They're all marked down, sir."

"I know, I know. I saw those. You're sure you didn't forget one or two?"

"No, sir. Absolutely not, sir."

Carl moved a few steps forward to see David's face.

David asked, "You might have missed a call?"

"There was always somebody in the house, sir. There's always someone here in order not to miss any calls."

Carl was now only a few feet from David and could see his face more clearly, the same face, but much, much thinner, the fair hair thinner, the cheeks pale, the hands moving. David put his hands in his pocket as if to quiet them.

"I'm sure, David," Aunt Corinne said earnestly, "the call hasn't come."

"Thank you, Robert," David dismissed him with a nod, and without facing Carl, so turned as to look at his father again. "It

433

might be that the phone was out of order for a few hours. It's difficult to tell unless one is using it all the time. I've heard of such things happening."

Everything that Carl had been feeling up to this moment disappeared and he was left with an uneasy curiosity. He said in a lively way, "How have you been, David?"

At once, with a complete change, David took his hands out of his pockets and his face lighted with pleasure and affection. "Carl," he cried. "Carl. It's so good to see you again. So wonderful!" He extended his hands, both of them, and Carl took them, and they shook hands, both hands at once. The tense fingers gripped Carl's with passionate need. The hands were cold, damp, uneasy. But the face, closer now, vibrant, excited, grew young through its haggard, overworked lines. "How do I look?"

"Tired," Carl said. "You've been working too hard. I can see that."

The hands suddenly let go as if fainting into listlessness, and went back into David's pockets. The voice died, grew flat. "You don't know what it is," he complained. "No one knows." He looked around. His head darted this way and that. "Why doesn't everybody sit down? The important thing is to relax when you have a moment." And he flung himself into a chair, extended his legs, let his body grow limp, relaxing.

Very slowly Carl retired to his seat and sat down again. He was puzzled, and he looked at the aunt, to see on her face what this all might mean, but she was smiling, a small, fixed smile on her face, sitting down now, but leaning forward in her chair as if she could not for one moment release David from her attention, as if, Carl had the sense, she was supporting her nephew, holding him up against his weariness and nervousness.

"How did you find out where we were?" David asked Carl.

"I called him," the judge said. "I heard he was in Washington and I called him."

"We wanted him to come over and we're so glad he did come," Corinne agreed with herself. "It's like old times again, you and Carl sitting here, just like those days back at the farm."

434

David suddenly sat up. "Did anyone hear a phone ring?"

They all listened. The bird sounded its rough note, the soft spray hissed and continued to fall. In the basin beneath the little statue, the water rang again with its minute bells.

"Robert's in the house," the judge said. "If the phone rings, he'll take it."

Carl listened to the stiff, dry tone with astonishment. He found himself astonished and his uneasiness grew, and with it a sharpness began to focus in his mind. All the unclarity of the evening, of his own moods and self-examination, disappeared, and in its place came the old professional habit, that neutral penetration and attention which was his scientific attitude. He found himself outside the circle of these people. He was an observer.

"He might be asleep," David said. Worried, he rose again to his feet.

Carl said definitely, "The phone didn't ring, David. It's the water tinkling in that basin."

David stood there listening, and laughed. "Why yes, of course." He sat down again. Affable again, he stretched out in his chair and let his arms dangle over the sides, his fingers touching the ground. "You," he said to Carl, his tone amused, almost gay, "have certainly jumped into a hornet's nest."

"I certainly have," Carl agreed. "And I don't know how to get out. I don't even know why I'm in it."

"Jealousy," David said. "Sheer jealousy. You'll find that everywhere within the government. I'm sure it's that. I find the same thing in my own case. There are always an inferior mob of fools who do everything within their power to destroy men of talent and integrity. Although, of course," and his voice complained a little, "had you come to China with me, I think the whole situation would have been different now. But that's water under the bridge."

Corinne asked cheerfully, motherly, "Is anyone hungry? Are you hungry, David? Would you like something?"

He ignored her and looked around to his father, "Did you write that letter to your friend in New York the way we discussed it?"

435

"Yesterday," the judge replied. "We won't get an answer for several days."

"I have the feeling," David said, "that it'll do the trick." He swung around to Carl. "It's not easy. Not easy at all. In times like these when the very existence of our country is in danger, people insist on their personal feuds and turn mere dangers into disasters. At least, I'm doing everything I can." His voice finished hopelessly, ended, and no one spoke while the life of the garden began again.

Carl did not know what to say and no one helped. Corinne and the judge were looking at him, but as they saw his questioning head turn, they looked away. A pitiful suspicion emerged in Carl's understanding. It raised its shape, flowered, leaped into the garden and stood there wildly. He felt his heart begin to beat. He felt the pulse of his blood in his temples. He felt his hands grow wet. The horror was standing in the garden, and he tried to recall his mind to mere observation, but he could not do it. He sat there in empty astonishment. He sat there overwhelmed.

David was on his feet again. "Can I see you a moment, Carl?" he asked.

Carl did not reply at once.

The judge said, "It's quite all right. We don't mind if you two want to talk."

"Just a word," David said. "If you'll come back here for a moment, Carl."

Still hesitating, Carl got up and followed David's white-clothed figure to the rear of the garden. The spray was louder there, and now and then a drop fell upon him. David waited beneath a dwarf tree. They stood close to each other and for the first time Carl saw the deep lines on David's cheeks, the hollows of his eyes, and the bright flickering gaze, going this way and that, never resting on an object.

"I just wanted you to know," David said in an urgent, secretive whisper, "that this sudden attack on you isn't your fault at all. It's simply because you know me. I realize that you must be terribly disturbed, but I can assure you that nothing will come of it. I've

436

written a memorandum that clears you completely. On the other hand, it's partly your fault."

"In what way?" Carl asked. But he was shattered with the frightfulness of it all. He put out his hand and touched David's arm.

"You wouldn't listen to me in London," David said. "Believe me, Carl, I don't blame you. The two of us could have done everything. I was all alone there in China. However, despite the intense envy of the other officials, I have every hope that in the long run things will clear themselves up." He looked around. He plumbed the darkness and the secret scents of the garden. "Perhaps you could give me a little advice?"

"Anything," Carl murmured. He could not speak more loudly, for he felt the drain and bitterness, the sadness and the futility, the sorrow growing within him, this first friend and first enemy, this so recognizable and repeated tragedy of the times.

"It's sleep," David asked pitifully. "Sleep. I don't sleep. It seems to make no difference what I take. It's hard to live without sleep. I never realized how important sleep is."

"I believe," Carl said hopefully, putting all the hope he could into his voice, and taking David's arm at the same time, holding him, giving him the comfort of a hand, another presence, surrounding him at once with all his old friendship, "I believe I can help you with that."

"That's fine," David replied. "Just fine. Let's go back now. I don't want my father to think we're hiding anything from him. Everyone is so intensely suspicious."

They walked back to the little group but David was ready to leave. "I'm going up now. A little more work for tonight. A few things. You'll excuse me, won't you, Carl?"

"Of course," Carl said. "I'm going anyway."

"Well, good night everybody."

"Good night, son," the judge said.

"Won't you come in with me, Aunt Corinne?" David asked. "I'd like to talk with you a moment." Gallant, smiling, easy, a man of the world again, he flung a mocking bow towards Carl. "I don't want to steal her from you," he cried, "just borrow her."

437

He took his aunt's arm and they both went off around the flower-ing bush, and then they reappeared, going down the length of the path, coming clear where the wall light shone, opening the screen door while David stood politely back and held the door for his aunt. Inside, he took her arm again, and they disappeared into the house.

Carl watched them, waited, plunged into grief, and the judge was standing at his side. "What do you think?" the judge asked.

"He should be under treatment at once."

"I know, I know." That leaf-dry voice quivered for an instant, as if to break, but found some strength again. "But is there any hope?"

"I don't know," Carl replied. He was distracted, unable to offer anything concrete. Suddenly he cried, "It's a shame, a shame. Shameful."

"Why is it," the judge asked bitterly, of no one, of the garden, of the dark, of the heat being eaten away by the damp earth and the late hours, "why is it that men always die too soon or too late?"

ẍii

WHEN Carl got back to the hotel, Curtin had not yet returned. Contemptuous of reality as David's mind, the wild newspapers still lay scattered on the floor and chairs.

Carl slowly undressed.

He had no energy and was numb with the excesses of the day, his senses dissolute, emotions worn, meanings lethargic. He stood beneath a hot shower for a long time.

Afterwards, he turned off the lights and, propped up on two pillows, sat in the darkness, waiting for his friend's return. The washed air poured through the cooling system, softly hissing like water gliding before a ship's prow, and he seemed to be rocking gently on a sea voyage. His mind rocked, and as it rocked, he slept, and sleeping, he was awakened by a still more gentle rocking. He opened his eyes into daylight and there was Curtin's rosy face looking down upon him with a smile, and Curtin's heavy hand shaking him, and the big voice sounding like a drum. "Time to see the loved one, Vaughan, Vaughan, Vaughan."

The drum was actually a headache which throbbed at the back of Carl's head. "What time is it?" he asked thickly.

"The committee awaits. I've got breakfast ordered."

On the other side of the closed windows another hot day swelled within the sky, assaulting his weary eyes. Without another word Carl went back to the shower and stood there under icy water until Curtin came banging in, yelling, "We'll be late. The coffee is getting cold."

Shaved, dressed, unrefreshed, Carl sat at the breakfast table and drank some orange juice. He sipped the coffee. He asked tiredly, "How do we survive today?"

439

But Curtin was buoyant, extravagant again, hopeful. Neither the day whining with a summer's orgy nor the nights, soft, exhausted, passionless, could sap his boundless energy when his mood was manic. It was excited now. He announced loudly, "The barn doors are locked, the fences mended. Gentlemen, the fodder's in the shock. We have nothing to fear but fear itself." He snapped his fingers. "Man is a political animal and Washington is his stable."

"I can see," Carl said distastefully, "that I have nothing to worry about."

"You have not. How did you make out with the Seawithes?"

Carl looked into the black liquid that cost fifty cents a cup. He saw the greasy colors of his face without his features. "There's no hope there." And he stood up, his head shaking with the pain, with all the tensions of the days and weeks, and this final knowledge, this final emotional dead end that, in truth, there was no hope there.

"Fear not," Curtin laughed. "Fear not, old friend. My wartime services gave me that great American bureaucratic know-how which easily translates into know-who. I'll tell you all about it in the cab."

But in the elevator going down into the lobby, Curtin launched on a little anecdote which he told in a loud voice, still speaking as they marched across the lobby, disentangling reporters from their sides while flash bulbs shot off in their faces and Curtin roared, "Not my left side. I'm asymmetrical there."

"Did you know, Carl," he said with great gusto, "that there was once a congressman, duly elected and certified as sane, who was horrified to discover that since time immemorial men have been struggling with the awful burden of pi, an infinite irrational fraction? He decided to simplify matters, to aid progress, and encourage the race of mathematicians, to bring knowledge to the people. He devised the simple expedient of passing a law which declared pi equal to twenty-one divided by seven, which gives three, an easy number, according to the formula that two is company and three will please the crowd. The mystical number of three, the Holy Trinity, crap, three strikes you're out. Do you know

440

that such a bill was, in fact, passed in a Western state?" He shook himself with delight and mopped his brow with a handkerchief. "I saw Bowman last night and we talked till morning."

Each time the cab went around a corner Carl felt a twinge of nausea. He asked, "Do you have any headache pills?"

"What?" Curtin was surprised. "What did you say?"

"I've got a terrible headache."

"Naturally," Curtin said. He knocked on the back of the driver's seat. "Will you stop at a drugstore?"

Carl rested his head against the worn and dirty cushions of the car. The bright sun danced into his eyes from every shining point, danced through his closed lids, oppressive and monotonous, glaring as memory. He smelled gasoline, dust. He seemed to smell the hot sky. He sweated, and the hot wind coming through the open car windows evaporated the sweat and cooled his face, cooled his limp hands.

"I had a little difficulty," Curtin said, "bringing Bowman around to our point of view. But I finally did. It wasn't easy. His feelings are hurt."

"He started the mess."

"I didn't go into that. I just took it for granted. In any event, he agrees that the work of Sierra and the other hospitals should not be jeopardized by Vaughan. He's going to make it an issue with the Administration so that it becomes a Washington fight and not a junket into the wards."

"That's fine," Carl said. "Let's go back to California."

The taxi stopped at the curb near a drugstore. "What would you like?"

"Five grains of caffeine and five grains of aspirin."

Curtin lumbered out of the taxi into the sunshine, hurried across the hot walks and disappeared into the sun-reflecting chromium and glass. The driver lighted a cigarette and the smoke came back to make Carl feel sicker, but he said nothing, merely lying there, while the pressure built at the back of his neck and little ribbons of pain sewed up his lids.

There was no wind now. The heat stood in the cab. It stood in

441

the street. The traffic noises sounded like the machinery of civilization falling apart.

He forced himself to enter the throbbing of his pulse, mystically united with the suffering so that he did not contend with it, and oscillating there, being it, drowsiness touched him.

The taxicab lurched with Curtin's weight. "Here you are, Carl."

Carl sat up. He opened his eyes and took the waxed powder paper and the little paper cup of iced water which Curtin extended. Carl shook the bitter powder on his tongue, drank the water and dropped the cup out of the window. Curtin slammed the door. "Let's go," he said to the driver. "We have a date with His Majesty, the United States."

Now it became a question of waiting, and Carl waited for the drugs to take effect while Curtin began again with his news. "The fact is, Carl, that there's only one thing that bothers Bowman. It's not Knox, of course. He really is worried about the methods we might be using at Sierra."

"Why doesn't he come out and see what they are?"

"I asked him to. I pointed out to him that in general we follow the usual procedures of all the hospitals, and he said that he gathered from your talk in New York that we did not."

"Well, we do and we don't."

"For the sake of argument," Curtin went on smoothly, "I said we did. And then he wanted to know what the hell you were driving at in that speech you made. I said it was a theoretical approach, a suggestion for investigation."

Indifferent, conscious only of his aches, Carl said, "Who cares what he thinks. If he's calling this side show off, that's good enough for us."

Curtin was a little embarrassed. "Well, he wants some help from us."

"You help him then," Carl said ungraciously. "I'll sleep out in the audience."

"You might be involved."

"I'll worry about it when I am."

"But there's no doubt that Vaughan'll call you."

442

"If he calls me, I'll answer."

Curtin breathed out a long sigh. "That's just the point. I mean, Carl, the point is that Bowman feels . . ." He stopped short. "I wish you'd been there last night."

But Carl was all attention to his own pain at the moment for he felt a delicious, a delightful dreamy sense of numbness crawling into his nerves, stopping up his ears, loosening the pressure on the back of his head, and he started to relax. He let himself slide back within the seat. The heat no longer mattered because inside the cool numbness was growing, tiredness was growing, softness was creeping upon him.

More loudly, with a certain defiance, Curtin said, "Bowman wants us to tell Vaughan that the theory you advanced in New York was just an idea, that we have no intention of trying to apply it at the moment, and haven't. It's just something to consider. In other words," he said hurriedly, "the only way we can get off this thing is to give Bowman a chance to get off it, too."

"What's that?" Although Carl hardly was attentive, yet he sat up suddenly, felt another twinge of pain, but nevertheless sat up and looked at Curtin, who smiled a little loosely and sweated profusely and suddenly said, "It's hot! Damned hot."

"What does Bowman want us to say?" Carl asked.

"I might as well put it to you frankly," Curtin said. "We're almost there now and we have to decide what we want to do. You've got to remember that the hospital is at stake, all the patients there, all the work and sweat we've put into it. This Vaughan can blow us right out of the whole place. We've got to think of the work and not whether our feelings are hurt."

"Yes?" A sickness of the heart such as men feel before unbelievable death, touched Carl's body, the mortal death, the immoral defeat. There is always another degradation, he thought bitterly, beneath pain there is always more pain, beneath suffering more suffering, a bottomless well. He stared hard and long at his friend's face, at that molded, hard fat, the pale eyes, the fringe of red hair on the sunburnt scalp. He looked down at the hands clutching the damp handkerchief, the hands mottled with freckles and hairy

443

up along the fingers, and he said to himself, But this is my friend, Val. This is Curtin. Together we launched our lives. He asked softly, holding his voice to its smallest range, keeping the curtness out of it, the shock, "What are you talking about, Val?"

"It's for the sake of science. After all, a hundred years from now who'll know whether we lied or not, whether we made a fight over nothing or not? What counts, and you know it's the only thing that counts, Carl, is for the work to go on. That's all. Nothing else. I have Bowman's promise that this thing will stop right where it is if we give them the satisfaction of saying, not doing, mind you, just saying what they want us to."

"The lie," Carl said, "is the other side of the bribe."

"Christ," Curtin exclaimed angrily, "what do you want? Galileo lied, and we're no Galileos. And Bruno burned, and we're no Brunos. It's a simple thing. You've got a theory. Men always have theories."

"Why," Carl asked, "are you angry with me? I haven't done anything to you. Bowman has. Not me. Vaughan has. Not me."

"You're just thinking of your pride, not of the hospital." Curtin blurted this out. He spit it from his mouth. He spit it out, not believing it, and yet he could not resist.

Death jumped into Carl's hands. He locked his hands together in his lap. He saw the buildings running by. He saw the street swim past. He saw the cars, the sky, the day, the daily universe. The violence surged and beat within him. All the frustrations of these days, the years, the confusions, doubts, the paralyzing effects of unsolvable situations, rolled into one object, became Curtin, and Carl wanted to strike it all down at once, to kill it.

His hands shook in his lap. He held himself there. He said again and again to himself. This is Curtin. This is just Curtin. This is just Curtin. He heard Curtin ask, "What's the matter, Carl? Are you really ill?"

Curtin touched Carl's arm and the body next to Carl burned like the fiercest temptation, its fat living life crying to be destroyed. This is Curtin, he said to himself. This is Curtin.

Suddenly the taxicab stopped. They had arrived, and in a

moment the cab was surrounded by the press. There was a crowd, a crowd of people, and a hum.

"Christ!" Curtin cried out. "Look at it. We've joined the freaks."

Guards conducted them up the stone steps and the cameras clicked, the flash bulbs fired off their volleys, odds and ends of men and women asked questions. They were in the cool building, in an elevator. They were at the floor. The floor was empty.

"That room's just full," one of the guards said.

Carl took Curtin's arm. "Let's walk up and down out here a few minutes," and they both started off, while curious eyes watched. They walked on the marble floor. They walked within the marble halls as long ago discoursing philosophers walked within their temples, within their private walks, talking of life and death.

"I think we should be frank," Carl said. He spoke to Curtin as a man speaks to his pupil, to his beloved pupil, to his friend who is somehow not a friend, but friendly, as to a pupil. "You know that Bowman wants us to deny all the work we've done. He wants us to do it because he is afraid of the theory behind our work. You understand that. He doesn't care where science leads us, where truthfulness or honesty leads us. If it leads us where he is unhappy, to conclusions he refuses to accept because they conflict with his profoundest prejudices, then he says it isn't science. He wants us to say that we're dishonest, that we are foolish, that we are bad scientists. He says that if we say these things, then we can have our hospital."

"No," Curtin said.

"Yes," Carl replied. "You listen to me, Val!"

Carl looked around, a quick look, and saw a camera go off within the knot of reporters and a little man dart back, unscrewing a bulb as he ran. There was a break in the corridor, a defile with an office at the end of it. He led Curtin within the narrow little corridor. "You spoke of Galileo. The old man died a prisoner of the Pope, forced to lie and lie, to lie to the whole world, confined to his house. The Pope didn't let him see his physician. The Pope didn't let him be buried near Michelangelo. The Pope pursued him into his grave.

445

Without the courage of others the astronomical universe betrayed would have waited for others. It stays there waiting to be seen. Don't talk to me of Galileo. You're right. I'm no Galileo. You're no Galileo. We do not even know if we're right. We may be wrong. But we think we're right. And in the social sciences, to betray a thought is to betray an action."

Nervously Curtin drew back. "What are you talking about?"

"What's the point?" Carl asked. "After all, what's the point of all our work? We cannot solve this problem without the help of others. We can't have the help of others unless we advance our point of view. We're struggling for a point of view. That's our right. Our duty. Our only pleasure."

"But the hospital?"

"Listen to me, Val. Just listen." Carl felt cold as ice. When his hand touched his own hand, it felt numb. There was death in his hands. "Last night I saw my old friend, David, and his soul was dying of paranoia, the disease of our times. He lives there in a fine house and rules the world out of a delusion. It doesn't matter whether the men in that committee room are scientists, congressmen, or soldiers. It doesn't matter whether we pronounce them sane or insane, healthy or unhealthy. They all act in the same way. They act the way the times makes them act. I don't wish to die in that room as a martyr. I don't intend to. But we cannot get the help of the other scientists unless we advance our point of view, unless we advance the fundamental premise, unless we show them the point of the fight. Isn't that clear? We didn't choose this fight. We were drafted to it. Well, if we're drafted, let's elect ourselves to it."

A guard appeared at the head of the little corridor. "The committee's on its way in," he said. "Gentlemen, the hearing is about to start."

The two friends stood there waiting, looking at each other.

"I think," Curtin said in a very low voice, "that we can prove the theory without getting into a public scandal over it." He kept turning his head as if it were twisted on wrong, as if it pained him, as if his sweating collar were too tight. "It's one thing to argue with

446

other scientists. Why argue with idiots who don't even understand what we're saying?"

"If they don't understand," Carl asked, "why are they doing this to us?"

"They're confused."

"Shall we add to their confusion?" Carl sought out a final argument. "We've tried to influence other men in the field, Val. How can we influence them if we deny the validity of what we're trying to preach?"

"That's it! That's it!" Curtin cried out almost wildly, breaking away from Carl's glance. "We're only preaching. It's only a theory."

"Do you really believe so?"

"Yes, yes."

"There are indications of its validity."

"It's not proved."

Carl lashed out, letting his anger strike, "How can we prove it if we deny it?"

"It's my duty," Curtin answered solemnly, "to protect the hospital, the patients and the work there." He marched off, and after a moment Carl followed, and behind Curtin entered the committee room which suddenly burst into murmurs, the flash of cameras, and the smiling face of Congressman Vaughan, who raised his gavel and gave two sharp taps upon his desk, while off in the rear an attendant warned, "Quiet, please!"

447

xiii

FROM his vantage point in the front row, Carl heard Vaughan go through a few brief preliminaries, heard the questions and the quick answers through a screen of reporters crouched and busy around the press table. There were to be no secrets in this committee room. A little motion in a minor field of science had been turned into a wave, and everybody was prepared to pump and push and shove. An obscure question asked honestly within an obscure science was now an issue, and the scientific question like a struggling captive in the hand of torturers was being put to the public rack. Burdened by their authority which crumbled in their hands by the hour, the powers found enemies everywhere. A question was an enemy, an inquiring look a threat. Carl heard Vaughan ask, "Now, Dr. Curtin, could you tell us what methods of treatment and cure you use at the Sierra Hospital?"

It was bitter and it was absurd to hear this question.

It was bitter, indeed, for nowhere had such patient humanity been brought to the work with sick men and women as at Sierra, nowhere such care in the selection of even the most minor employee who came into contact with the patients, nowhere such devotion and strict scientific discipline in diagnosis, treatment, and the follow-up on discharged patients. There were no competitive drives for numerous cures at Sierra, no resistance to readmissions. And yet here this stupid question was being asked, not to learn, but to attack.

It was absurd. This small room which the day before had seemed so empty and so large, now breathed with anxious humanity, the bodies joined and packed, the heads leaning to one side or another

448

as irregular files of vision opened and closed, the air already stale, the tension acute, deliberately sensitized. Not far from Carl, Dr. Bowman glowed pinkly, cool in a thin linen suit, his look bland, his tiny hands joined upon his crossed knees. Scattered through the audience, the delegation of doctors who had come to demand funds were individually forlorn. Each was in his own place, the room a vise with its fulcrum on the small rostrum. And the crowd, the audience, this representative of the public? Carl could make nothing of them. They were one of the permanent characters in history and stood in the streets of Athens waiting for the sacred ship to return, or jammed the Piazza della Signoria for the rude priest, or sweaty in shirt sleeves sat out the hot Southern afternoons glowering at a schoolteacher who had heard of Darwin. It was absurd, and yet dream-ridden with meaning, and therefore absurd because the issue, whatever it was, could not be settled in this room.

Curtin replied, "At Sierra we use the approved methods of the Veterans Administration and current psychiatric practice."

"Do you believe, Dr. Curtin, that these methods represent the best modern theories in psychiatry?"

"Naturally."

"And you utilize them?"

"We do."

"Would you care to describe these methods to the committee?"

"I'd be glad to." Curtin's tone, his air, was almost pious as he plunged into a detailed report on the organization and structure of Sierra, how the various departments worked, the therapeutic practices, the spirit of helpfulness, kindness and devotion which greeted the entering sick veteran, and the audience listened with a rapt attention, peeping like children into the underworld of its own life.

It did not seem to Carl that this room and the usual world could coexist, just as during the war it was hard to realize that there was a Front, and a Home, too. He could not see over the high window ledges but he knew that down below the city baked, stifling in its

449

annual heat, and the vast ordinariness of existence went on, the cheating wars of lovers and celebrants, the salesmen on their rounds, the children dutiful in school, the parents dutiful at work, and in the sickbeds one out of five struck with cancer.

He observed his old friend with hostility, and yet watching him, anger vanished, and nothing remained but futility. For what did it matter after all?

Carl felt thirsty. It would be nice to have an iced drink.

Curtin's voice had taken on force and his spectacular vocabulary was in flower again, delighting and amusing everyone. It was a show, an exhibition; and a trial was, after all, nothing more than an exhibition of the known, an opportunity to dramatize what everyone knew. Vaughan had resigned himself to politeness, and, couched deeply within his high leather chair, his face supported by a hand, listened with the impartial polite air, the ritual politeness, of a hangman. Even Representative Larrabee had become fully aware of the significance of this hearing and had supplied himself with a silver mechanical pencil which indicated his readiness to take down anything pertinent and his ability to pick his teeth.

It was possible, Carl knew, to get up and walk out, and yet he did not leave. He sat with all the others and participated in the absurdity. His turn would come and he would rise to offer himself to these senseless blows that could not decide a single issue in the science to which he had devoted his life. He recalled that night in London at the restaurant when he had once before risen and offered himself for the first blow while David sat with the two girls and the brawl took shape, only to expire in conversation. He wondered what had happened to Alice. Together on V-E Day they had stood at a window overlooking Piccadilly Circus and watched the gay enjoyers. He did not then believe in the happiness of the celebrants for there had been no happiness in himself. And Alice had been sad, for her husband was alive and coming back to England, and while she no longer loved or thought of him, it was her duty, she felt, to waste the rest of her life with him because he had wasted so many years in a Japanese prison camp. Carl had not urged her either way, since he did not care, and not caring, they had parted.

The audience laughed at one of Curtin's fancies, and little by little the expectation of a prize fight was replaced by the good humor of a vaudeville act.

Carl settled himself within his chair, listening to the aftermath of his headache. He felt like a man, exposed too long to a storm of sunlight, now hidden away in a dark room, emptied of energy, decayed in the will, bored with thought and only wanting the coolness, the quietness, the peace. It occurred to him that perhaps Curtin was right. All that was needed were the few words to be uttered, an inclination of the head in the direction of senseless authority. A man could kiss the Pope's foot and still revolutionize a civilization of thought. What did it matter?

His mind droned with melancholy and he looked up and saw Curtin's mouth moving, heard the voice and did not hear it, saw the pale intent face of the chairman and thought of the feet beneath the desk. It did not seem pleasant to bow before those feet, and yet all day long and all life long, a man bowed before minute authorities and even offered up his life to them. What made everything bearable was the meaning of the acts, and the intent of Curtin's testimony was to save the hospital for the work at hand.

"Thank you, Dr. Curtin," the chairman said. "Thank you very much for the clear and unprejudiced way you explained the workings of the hospital." He paused, took in the room, held it suspended, opened the vacuum for its attention to rush in, let the attention swell to that exquisite moment when heads became uneasy and feet shifted, and then asked, "You recall your testimony on the case of Edward Knox?"

"Yes," Curtin said.

The room found a new level of silence.

"I didn't wish to give the impression yesterday," the chairman went on affably, "of having prejudged the situation, of having made certain accusations. This committee must make certain recommendations of a financial sort and we just want to be sure the money is being correctly and usefully spent."

451

"I understand," Curtin said, conspiratorial with smiles.

And Carl understood also. It seemed to him that he understood it all. Mutual apologies around, a sensation for a day, and the work could go on.

"I just wanted to be sure," Vaughan pointed out severely, "that no crackpot theories were being used at the hospital and no political influences being brought to bear on sick men."

"Absolutely not," Curtin said decisively. "I invite this committee to visit Sierra and observe the workings of the institution themselves."

"Are you," the chairman asked without emphasis, "familiar with the scientific point of view of Dr. Myers?"

As if a signal light had flashed above Carl's head all eyes focused on him, all but Curtin's. This joined impalpable pressure was physical enough for Carl, who held himself sturdily, feeling the radiance of all these eyes, the bright glare of attention, the sudden isolation and removal from the crowd, and although there was a witness on the stand, the center of the hearing nevertheless rested upon himself.

"I am," Curtin replied.

"Would you say that the point of view of Dr. Myers is identical with the best current modern notions, that is to say — " Vaughan was reading from a page in front of him and he was uneasy with the words and tried to rephrase — "Would you say, Dr. Curtin, that Dr. Myers agrees with what you said were the methods used at Sierra?"

"Why," Curtin said cheerfully, "Dr. Myers is the chief of the medical staff and directly responsible for the operation of these methods. I supervise the hospital in general."

"I see, I see." Vaughan looked down at his papers, studied them a moment and then asked again, "I'm afraid I haven't put it just right. Dr. Myers made a talk in New York in which he attacked most of the ways of doing things in our hospitals and . . ."

Boldly Curtin interrupted, "If I may correct you, sir?"

"Yes?"

"My colleague merely attacked the theories, or better, en-

452

deavored to correct their general orientation. I would say, sir, that this was his intention, to bring forth a point of view which would lead to discussion, with the earnest desire to aid the work which we are doing for our patients."

"Do you agree with this theory?"

Curtin made a tent of his fingers and judiciously looked at his shoes. "I do and I don't. But we have to be open-minded, especially when a man of Dr. Myers's capacity and reputation speaks up. There are so many tremendous unsolved problems in psychiatry that we must be open-minded. It's our duty."

"But it's our duty also," Vaughan insisted, "not to try out unproved theories on patients."

"Absolutely."

"It's also our duty," Vaughan said more sharply, "to realize when a theory is scientific and when it represents a man's personal political opinions."

"Naturally."

"You believe, I'm sure, that politics and science should not be mixed?"

"They should not. Science has its own laws, its own method."

"You would oppose the mixing of politics and science?"

"Absolutely."

"Do you think a man's political opinions could affect his attitudes in science?"

"Everything is possible. They don't affect mine."

"Would you say that if it should happen that a doctor permitted his political beliefs to affect his attitudes toward his science, that the science would suffer by it?"

"Absolutely. Science and politics are incompatible."

Vaughan smiled, shuffled his papers, and said generally to the room, "Thank you, Dr. Curtin. I may have a few more questions for you later on, but just now I think it would help if we heard directly from Dr. Myers himself."

Now, the short tumult of the intermission intervened as Curtin descended from the stand and took his place near Dr. Bowman, who leaned up, smiling and whispering, while Carl arose, dark, morose, distracted, and went through the preliminaries again, and Vaughan examined his papers and finally blew his nose. The little noises of the room went on and all the faces articulated in front of Carl, this face and that face, some known, most unknown, the sea of faces and forms in which life is spent, the statistics in which each personal history occurs as a violent joke of fate.

Carl folded his hands over his crossed knees, determining never to change his position, to remain as immobile as possible, not to yield by intonation, expression or gesture to any feeling whatsoever. Curtin had been a contemptible clown. It was his own turn to be contemptible, and yet in a certain respect, wise, to save the work and accept the role of such committees, headlines, and absurdities. Men jumped out of planes for less significant reasons. Others slaved all their lives to support families they didn't love. He would be contemptible.

The chairman looked up and signaled to Dr. Bowman, who rose and joined him and Representative Larrabee in a corner. They whispered between themselves, and the roomful of watchers observed.

Impassively Carl sat there and saw Curtin trying to catch his attention, holding his fingers up in an infantile gesture, fingers crossed. Carl did not smile. He made no response. He felt that his whole life had been a failure. It had to be a failure if now, at this moment, he found himself sitting here to participate in this idiocy.

Out of an old habit he removed himself from a physical scene which bored or displeased him, which had to be endured until it passed, and tried to think of something else.

He reflected that contrary to what was taught, it was not easy to be a failure.

It is not easy to be a failure because the real world continuously offers its creatures innumerable opportunities to fulfill themselves in happiness, power and security. Along with the others he had been present during his own times. He had lived and was now living in dangerous and fearful times. He had discovered and was continuing to discover that these dangers and fears were within

454

the souls of men, too, inside the men as well as outside of them, dangerous within them, fearful within them, dangerous outside them, carriers of fear outside them.

In a corner the conspirators whispered, agitating their dangers. This roomful of people had no guarantee that they would die of old age, or even of some wretched disease. A jaguar in a South American jungle had more chances than these pale faces. A hummingbird was safer. It had taken a geological epoch to extinguish the dinosaur. Like lovers, these attentive citizens had each other for their unhappiness, their misery, their fugitive joys, opportunities in each other for pleasure and murder. In Hiroshima three hundred thousand people had learned in one instant how to fulfill a Geiger counter. In Rome in the first year of the seventeenth century on the Campo di Fiori, the Servants of Justice had stripped Bruno naked and burned him alive to teach him that the universe was not infinite, that this sumptuous and important earth did not move, and that it was forbidden to have contrary opinions.

Vistas turned virtues to dust, Carl thought. Let the inquisitors return, and let me be contemptible rapidly.

A murmur of appetite trembled in the audience, and Carl looked up from under his half-lidded eyes and saw the hearing taking its hard shape again, the congressmen returning to their rostrum, the good Dr. Bowman to his seat beside Curtin. The nature of the conference was obvious. Had Curtin yielded enough? And it appeared that he had, for Bowman smiled to Curtin and touched the heavy arm.

Carl despised his old friend at this moment, and yet there sitting before him was the visible proof that his friend had been correct. Curtin had made it visible to him. It was humiliating, it was indecent, it was acceptable.

Vaughan picked up his mahogany gavel and tapped lightly upon the desk. He knocked on the door of Carl's attention. The knock was neutral, unemphatic. It merely demanded an entrance.

"Dr. Myers," Vaughan said softly, "you are the chief medical officer of Sierra?"

"I am."

455

"Louder please."

"I am."

"You are in charge of the work of the other doctors there?"

"I am."

"You supervise their medical practice?"

"I do."

"Their ideas of how psychiatry should be practiced?"

"I influence their ideas."

"You would not let them practice any form of psychiatry of which you did not approve?"

"I do not approve of everything they do."

"What does that mean?"

"There is a certain amount of free play in treatment, in judgments. Psychiatry is not an exact science. Diagnosis is often difficult, often guesswork, often impossible."

"I'm trying to find out, Dr. Myers, your relations to your staff."

Carl made no answer to this.

Vaughan asked again, "Didn't you hear my question?"

"I heard your observation."

Vaughan tapped on the desk with his gavel. "Let's not bandy words. Do you influence your staff?"

"I try to in every way possible." Carl looked at the gavel, at the hand that held it, and resented its very existence. He looked away.

"So you admit influencing the doctors on your staff?"

"It's my job to influence them and direct them."

"If a doctor disagreed with your point of view, would you ask for his dismissal?"

"The question never arose."

"Suppose it did arise?"

"It would depend on circumstances."

"What circumstances?"

"Whether, in my opinion, his point of view interfered with the treatment of the patients and the morale of the rest of the staff."

"So you would not keep on the staff a man who disagreed with your point of view?"

"I would under the circumstances I mentioned, if his view were

456

rationally held, sincere, and not harmful to the work of the institution."

"In whose opinion?"

"Mine and the staff."

Vaughan looked down at his notes and turned the gavel over within his hands. The room waited.

Vaughan raised his head and his voice together, speaking more loudly, riding a false note, not quite sure of what he was asking. "Do you try to keep your point of view hidden from the staff?"

"On the contrary."

"I mean do you tell them it's a different and strange theory? I mean do you try to influence them without their knowledge or directly?"

"Directly."

"Have they been influenced by your point of view?"

"Yes."

"How do you know?"

"By the evidence of their work in the hospital and the papers written for various scientific journals."

Vaughan leaned his head to one side and contemplated the walls. He pressed the handle of the gavel to his cheek, and after a few quiet moments looked gravely down upon Curtin.

Waiting for the next question, Carl noticed that it was not coming from Vaughan at all, but that by prearrangement, Dr. Bowman was on his feet, approaching the rostrum, and now stood just below the chairman who bent towards the stenographer and explained, "Dr. Bowman is going to ask a few questions for the subcommittee. You may proceed, Dr. Bowman."

"Thank you, sir."

The plump delicately colored man with his flashing glasses that hid the eyes stood innocuously there, hardly a great mind as Carl well knew, but easily an instrument. And this was the depth of the contemptibility, Carl thought, to be forced to bow, not to the temporal powers who had at least the force, the whips, the guns, the blows. He was being asked, and this unlike Curtin, to bow to the hierarchy of scientific opinion, to the intellectual authority

457

which he did not accept, to connive with this hierarchy against the freedom which was the very condition of his science, and this openly so that secretly the thought could be advanced.

Dr. Bowman had a sheet of paper in his hand and he read from it in a mild, inquiring voice. "Dr. Myers," he asked, "do you agree with Dr. Curtin's characterization of the psychiatric work at the Sierra hospital?"

"In general."

"What do you mean in general?"

"The description was incomplete."

Bowman glanced rapidly up at Vaughan and took a friendly step forward. "How do you mean, incomplete? You mean it lacks all the details?" And he emphasized this word *details*, he removed it from the rest of the sentence and filled it with an invitation, with an offer to join Curtin and let the gavel gently descend and call this hearing to an end.

Carl looked at his inquisitor, at this plump, hieratic man, vague and blushing with his pink blood, and, down below, Curtin was leaning forward, calling him, begging him to enter the security of Sierra, to return, to turn aside from the temptation of a ruinous struggle and postpone the fight for better days.

In his mind Carl said, why, yes, the details. And now he and Curtin were on the plane on their way to California. There would be explanations to be made to the staff, but who today did not understand the need of bending to the bureaucratic will? A generation of atomic scientists had shown the way. The final freedom lay undoubtedly in the mind itself, and if this were lonely and subjective, the times demanded the role. Yes, he would be in California, and Juley would be in New York.

Would avoiding the open fight, putting aside for the moment the question of dignity, prevent the development of the theory? To Curtin, Carl had said it would. But did it really? There was no time now to explore this problem, because there stood Bowman, and on the rostrum the impatient chairman waited.

"It's difficult to answer the question," Carl said.

Vaughan interrupted. "The committee is simply trying to find out, Dr. Myers, whether the influence you have at Sierra and your authority there is being used in the prescribed manner, in the manner described by Dr. Curtin?"

It was a question that permitted endless evasion, a kind of truthfulness, endless generality. An act of will was being demanded of him, this Carl fully realized, an act of truthfulness which went beyond what he believed or disbelieved. Ultimately it was a choice being offered, to bend to authority, to sway with it, or to contend.

He evaded again, "I find the question too general."

"Answer it as best you can," the chairman demanded.

But they did not want his best answer, Carl thought grimly. They wanted his worst answer.

He dawdled within the contradiction and he felt the pressure to answer opposed by the pressure of not answering. He mused there, impotent, desiring to follow Curtin and refusing to follow him, knowing all the while that no matter what his answer would be, and this feeling grew within him, taking shape and form, no matter what happened here in this committee room, he had parted with Curtin and Sierra. They were friends, which was to say, so much of their past was bound together in the common work. But this work was finished. He no longer would find it possible to share his ideas with Curtin, to find any basis for that old equality which had been decaying for months anyway.

There was a tap of the gavel and Carl heard it like a knock on the door. It came to him this way for the second time that morning, that flat wooden sound which could be many things, which came to him each time like a knock on a door.

Carl looked up and saw the chairman sitting there with the little gavel raised, and Carl waited to hear the sound again, to listen again to it, wondering why it sounded like a knock on the door to him.

With a little casual flick of the wrist, Chairman Vaughan hit the desk. It was the gavel. Yet it was a knock.

"Will you answer the question, Dr. Myers?"

Before Carl, Dr. Bowman stood waiting, smiling to him, and below Bowman, Carl's old friend leaned forward waiting, inviting

459

him, excusing himself yet nevertheless inviting him. And somehow on the rostrum that gavel sound, that knock on a door, spoke too, inviting Carl into another kind of life altogether, another room, another era, another time.

"In a programmatic sense," Carl said, "Dr. Curtin's description is accurate. But from the point of view of what we are striving for at Sierra, I would say his description is incomplete, necessarily so, because there would be hardly enough time to go into all the details, problems and ramifications."

This was true. It was also an evasion, and before him Bowman shifted back a step and wiped his mouth with a tiny smile, while Curtin relaxed in his chair, eased of the strain.

The strain in Carl, however, was enormous. He had not lied, and it did not occur to him to think of his answers as truths or untruths, since no one at this hearing was interested in the truth or untruth of any scientific propositions. They were interested in obedience or resistance to authority. He had not lied, but he had evaded.

"Thank you, Dr. Myers," Bowman said nicely. "And now, I would like to ask you another question. In the course of your career you have published a number of books and papers in which from time to time you've advanced certain theories. Would you say that all of them have equal validity?"

But the gavel came down. It struck the rostrum sharply, sharply as a knock on a door, as a door cracking open. And Vaughan's voice descended, flew in, demanded, "I'd like to have the first question answered first, Dr. Bowman."

"I believe," Dr. Bowman said, "that Dr. Myers answered it."

"Not to my satisfaction." Vaughan leaned forward, twisting his pale face towards Carl, and the gavel was held in his right hand, raised half a foot above the desk, held tensely there to strike the hearing into shape at any moment. "Now, Dr. Myers, it doesn't seem to me that we are asking you a very complicated or difficult question. I simply want to know, and I think you can answer it simply, whether you agree or disagree with Dr. Curtin, yes or no. That's all. Just answer yes or no. If you want to qualify your

460

answers, you will have the opportunity later on. At the moment, however, I want a yes or no answer."

A little nettled, Bowman intervened. "If it please the chair," he said, "I should like to point out that obviously Dr. Myers doesn't agree completely with Dr. Curtin. I'm afraid you wouldn't find two psychiatrists in the world who agreed that much with each other."

There was a snicker from the audience, and the gavel slammed down rudely, hard, beat suddenly into Carl's brain like a blow. He jerked his head up and looked at Vaughan, who had tensed and now held the gavel out, pointing to the audience. "I shall clear the hearing if there is any laughter," he cried. Then he wheeled on Carl and said harshly, "I'm asking you a simple question. You know it. I'm not asking whether you and Dr. Curtin see eye to eye on details. I'm asking, do you agree with the policy and methods of practice described by Dr. Curtin, which are the policies and methods of all hospitals, or do you have your own private theory which is encouraged at Sierra in opposition to what happens elsewhere? That's what I'm asking, and I'd like it answered, yes or no. That's all. Just a yes, or just a no." He struck the desk to emphasize his point. "Yes or no?"

It was difficult for Carl to listen to the questions, or even the tone of the chairman, because of the distraction of the gavel. That little wooden hammer struck him with an almost mysterious violence each time it hit the rostrum. It abstracted into memory and concretely plunged into feeling. It was a knock on a door, a beating of a pulse, pain and anger. Each time it fell, whether loudly or softly, it fell like a stone into his past, and motions started, vague, uncomfortable motions, and these, rising and touching him, obscured this hearing, hid the questions, shattered the shape of this room with the shape of other rooms, a locked door, a sense of helplessness. That was it, and it flushed within him in embarrassment and shame. It revived a sense of helplessness, a sense reappearing within this hearing room.

He was helpless before the choice, and yet all his life he had practiced to be ready.

461

The practice of life was in certain respects a practice in readiness, and he was now being asked whether or not he was ready.

A loud noise assaulted him. They were knocking again on the door, and Carl knew there were three, the three of them, all three. Like a dreamer he raised his half-drugged, memory-laden eyes and saw the gavel being raised again, coming down again on the rostrum, striking again. It struck him savagely. It seemed to strike his mouth. It struck brutally, staggering him back, and a voice cried over it, "Answer the question!"

He was in this hearing room, Carl knew this, but where did that door open, that dark, unlighted door, firelight shining on it, outside a rickety stairway, a knock. The door flies open. Three men stand there. A burly gray-suited figure wearing a felt hat, a man in a red sweater, a third man, dark-suited was he? What kind of suit did that man wear?

The gavel descended. "Answer the question!"

A blow on Carl's face. He staggered back and there between him and the enemy a blue slipper with a red pompom.

The wild night returned. Tarrytown. The room that was a cage of pain and fear. The old beating crawled back into his flesh, creeping up out of his nerves, out of his body cells, coming from its hiding places where parasitic and tormented it had passed the years, pent with horror, with terror, with the inexplicable and powerfully meaningful, waiting for this day, this morning, to be released, to show its meaning. The old beating crawled back, the beating that had been for Bill but which he had taken in Bill's place, not accepting it, not willing it, but taking it, forced to, because he was there. The old beating crawled back, coming not with actual pain, but tense and violent with memory. Fear besieged him. Rage caught at his muscles.

"Did you hear the question?"

I hear my brother's enemies, his soul cried, I hear their feet slipping across the floor.

The gavel burst upon the rostrum, struck and struck. "Answer the question! Do you refuse to answer the question?"

462

I feel the blows, the blows on Bill's dead flesh, his conscience cried, his soul cried, his whole life cried out at this.

In the silence of the committee room the wild fears contended.

Carl did not think to act. The demand was too intense, too immense, too central and basic. It was so far within his soul as to be it, indissoluble. It was his whole life that he was being asked to fling out here upon this floor, to present to this committee, to present to the world, and to himself. To expose it and to let it be beaten into a pulp of no resistance. But even on that night he had refused to die. He had survived.

The pulse of Carl's awakened blood throbbed in his eyes, and it was difficult, as he turned his head up to look, to see Vaughan. He saw the night and this morning superimposed. He saw Vaughan and he saw Tarrytown and the man with the red sweater and the club. The man raised the club and struck him and the rostrum resounded with the gavel. "Are you going to answer my question, Dr. Myers?"

Carl spoke. His voice issued without his control, but it spoke, and each word was as hard as the will to live. "Yes. I'm going to answer."

"Then do so."

"I'm going to answer."

Everyone waited. It was not enough to answer, Carl thought, not enough merely to enter this violent room of memory and be assaulted again, to welcome the blows again, and answering merely assert what everyone knew he believed. This was not enough. This was not the issue here. What was the issue?

Carl asked, "Are you, as the chairman of this Committee, Mr. Vaughan, setting yourself up to decide what kind of scientific theories may or may not be held by men like me, by my colleagues, by scientists everywhere? Is that what you conceive your role to be?"

The gavel rattled on the rostrum. "You're not here to ask questions, Dr. Myers, but to answer them."

So this was the issue. There was his own opinion at stake, and he

463

would tell them again what it was. This was easy. There was also the issue of this hearing. This was difficult.

"Are you going to answer the question, Dr. Myers?"

And it seemed, at last, to Carl that Bill was indeed dead and had taken his place with all the dead to make room for the living who had elected themselves into his place.

"If my scientific work leads me to criticize, or even condemn, a society which creates the illness which it is my duty to treat, then I shall devote my life to exposing this society, condemning it and changing it." Carl had to shout this above the pounding gavel. The gavel refusing to permit such answers. It demanded half answers. Carl asserted full ones. The flashbulbs went off, the room erupted into tumult, and all the while Curtin sat in silence, huddled so largely in his small chair, yet smaller than his chair, sliding down, going away, disappearing into the vacancy which he himself had opened.

Carl repeated the statements he had made in New York.

"You dare say they are true?" Vaughan shouted.

"Listen to yourself and you can be certain they are true," Carl replied.

"You are in contempt," Vaughan yelled, and he shook with fury and banged the rostrum.

"I would indeed be contemptible," Carl told him, "if I did not assert my rights against the gavel and the miseries of the time."

The tight room was exploding into the world.

"I am a scientist," Carl cried above the flaming violence of the gavel. "I cannot devote my life to the acceptable, only the inevitable. I recognize only the necessity of the truth."

And Bowman, livid too, flinging his questions in, an enemy too, demanded, "And suppose you are wrong? How do you know you are right?"

"He's wrong," the gavel reiterated. "He knows he's wrong."

"I'm right," Carl said, "and if I'm wrong I shall discover it through the methods of science and not the authority of this committee."

In the end the chairman shouted, "Leave the stand. Leave the stand! Take that man away from the witness chair." He adjourned the hearing *sine die,* "because we have indications here of the necessity for a long examination of the evidence."

The battle had exhausted itself, and by noon the newspapers were in the street.

xiv

AT the airport terminal in New York, Carl checked his luggage and walked out into a warm mild drizzle eddying through the soft fall of night. The rain fell upon the flowering lights, the red and blue and the green, upon the evening excitements of the city, the flood of people, the traffic roar. A sea mist had edged in upon these noisy stones jutting upon the ocean. The darting faces, the massed unfolding faces, shifted like schools of fish in the ocean of the darkness, and moment by moment the artificial lights grew more luminous, wavering in the mist and tender drizzle, until as Carl walked up Lexington Avenue he felt like a man wandering beneath a fragrant tropical sea, gliding in and out of the reflections of great ships whose lanterns shone down deep into the water.

He was glad to be hidden from the newspapers which on every stand proclaimed his name, advertised his face, and delivered his reputation, his words, his future, to the crowd, which, absorbing him, concealed him from itself.

The first strain was over, the first phase, and what the next would be he did not know. He felt emptied, empty of anger, empty of guilt, empty of tension. He could have thrown himself into the street, and careless of the fine spray of rain idled and smoked a cigarette and watched the flow of matter go by, sometimes a car, sometimes a man, sometimes a star. It would not be of any consequence to him now because he was resting from the frenzy of combat.

He wished for himself a particular place, a house, a street, rich with the presences of the living and the dead, a place to which he might return and there among familiar essences lose the sense of

466

mortality as a disaster and find mortality there as life continuing. But he had no such place, and so he wandered, possessing only his morality which even yet he did not fully understand.

After a very long time, his face damp and his clothes damper, he found himself before the tenement in which Juley lived, and without considering it, he entered and slowly climbed the old stairway, going up and up until he reached the top story, never hesitating. He had no particular intention in mind. He had only guided himself without meaning to, yet nevertheless meaning to, to the one familiar place in all the world for him.

There were voices within.

He did not expect to find silence.

He knocked on the door.

The voice of Juley said, "The door's open."

Carl turned the knob, and the door gave before his hand. It was both usual and unusual and this was his idea of the world at the moment, how usual it was and how terribly, strangely magical.

He caught full upon himself the five faces, Juley's, and those of two men and two women.

Juley stood up as Carl closed the door.

On the table which had been dragged into the center of the room, a table whose blue cloth supported in its mild blueness coffee cups and silverware and a big chocolate cake, he saw the remains of a domestic, friendly dinner, and he was happy to see this, to find this usualness here, and yet somehow the blueness of the cloth seemed like a piece of sky and the silver of the spoons very rich, and the people amazing.

In various places were editions of the different newspapers, and one big man with a dark face and dark hair, a very strong and healthy man, was sitting in his shirt sleeves and he had a newspaper opened to a page where obscurely Carl's white face was caught and held.

Juley was surprised and the others began to rise. He saw them standing up. Juley said to them, "This is Bill's brother. This is Carl."

The people became handshakes, welcoming smiles, welcoming

467

faces, a man named Sanchez and his wife, a man named Chamberlain and his wife.

Juley drew up a chair at the table for Carl and she helped him off with his damp coat. "You're wet," she said. That bewildering voice of hers almost escaped from her control. She hurried into the kitchen and returned with a cup and saucer and a pot of coffee. She poured the coffee out for him and he raised it to his mouth, drinking it.

When he put the cup down they were all looking at him, uneasily, wondering, but he smiled at them out of his idle tiredness and they all smiled back to him.

"We were reading the newspapers," Juley said, "and talking about you."

Sanchez spoke heavily, "Maybe we should go? We don't want to be in the way."

And Juley looked at Carl. He felt her face there most strongly. His weary eyes, his sleepy mind, were unusually sensitive at the same time and the vision of her face was rich with sensation, so that seeing her, he felt her face against his. "Why, no," Carl said. "Please don't."

"Did you come straight from Washington?" Juley asked. "Did you come straight here?"

"I walked from Forty-second Street," Carl replied. "I needed a good walk. But it's quite far." He drank again of the coffee. The warmth frayed like sleep within his body.

"I wanted to call you," Juley said. "I tried but I couldn't get you there."

The people around the table helped themselves to more coffee.

"Are you hungry?" Juley asked.

"No," Carl said.

"Do you want some cake?"

"No."

She cut off a piece of cake and put it on a plate. Carl started to eat it, and the sweetness was quite marvelous, the chocolate interesting, the texture crumbling and dissolving within his mouth, taking to his mouth.

468

The man called Chamberlain said, "They gave you quite a going-over there."

The woman near him who was his wife said, "He gave them the same."

Sanchez laughed. He hit his hand upon the table and made the cups jump and spoons rattle and the cake tremble. "What do you expect? They picked on one of the Myers boys."

"You look very tired," Juley said.

"I'm pretty tired," Carl replied. He was. He stretched his damp feet out beneath the table and listened but could not hear the rain.

The woman who was the wife of Sanchez, a very dark, middle-aged woman, with black shining hair and very black eyes, said, "I think we ought to go home. Maybe Dr. Myers wants to go to sleep."

"Oh, no," Carl said. "Stay here. Stay." He looked vaguely around. He was with these people in the room, but he did want to lie down. He looked around again.

Juley said, "Do you want to lie down?"

"If you people don't mind," Carl said very politely. "Please stay, but I think I'd like to lie down a little. Just for a few minutes."

Juley rose and went into the bedroom. Carl heard the light snap on there. He very distinctly heard the bed being made up, the weight and shift of the coverlet, a pillow plumped, the creak of the springs.

"We heard about you a long time before this," Sanchez said, striking the newspaper with the back of his opened hand. The page flapped. "I wanted to meet you a long time ago. You know I was a good friend of your brother's. All of us here. Old, old friends from a long time back."

Carl nodded. He wanted to say something nice and thought of it for a long time. Finally, he said, "It's nice to meet you."

Juley returned. "You can go in and go to sleep now."

"Excuse me," Carl said. He got up. "Don't get up, please. I just don't want to fall asleep in front of all of you." And he smiled and turned around and walked away from them into the bedroom. He

469

closed the door behind him and saw only the bed. He took off his clothes and put on a pair of pajamas. He wondered only for a moment whether they were Bill's or Halloran's, but it didn't seem of much consequence. He got into the bed and turned over on his back and lay there. The light remained on and so he stretched out his hand to the night table and pulled the little metal chain. The light clicked off.

First, the room was very dark, and then, slowly, it began to fill with light, the drawn shades glowing with the night that never was really night in this city.

Behind the door he heard the low murmur of voices, hushed for his sleep.

He was really exhausted, and exhaustion is sometimes like alcohol, a flutter and drone among the nerves, a rubbing gentleness upon the touching skin, a floating quietness.

Yet, he did not fall asleep. He lay there quietly and moveless, his eyes closed, but not sleeping.

Now when he listened for the rain he heard it and through its delicate fall the wonderful sweep of the cars in the streets, the cars sweeping through the streets like dancing skirts.

Without wanting to, he found himself on the stand again. Now that he was ready to sleep, he was awake and sitting again beneath the gavel. The whole scene began again, and laboriously he endured it, going through it until it ended. He still did not sleep.

He walked outside into the Washington sun and passed his friend, Curtin, standing there among the newspapermen, giving an interview, and Curtin's big voice was saying, "I want you to understand that I completely disagree with the tactics of this committee. On the other hand, we at Sierra are not responsible for the private opinions of our staff." There was more, but Carl passed by and did not even try to speak with his old friend.

A leap in history had separated them.

The door to the bedroom softly opened, but Carl did not open his eyes. He heard Juley's tiptoeing steps. She stood beside him and then he heard, he felt the motion of her body as she knelt down beside him.

470

Carl said, "Juley."

"Why aren't you sleeping?" she whispered.

"I am," he replied.

She put her face down against his, and her cheek was burning and his was so cool.

It was his right, he thought, to love and be loved.

"Go to sleep," Juley murmured.

"For a few hours," he said. "I've got a lot of things I want to talk to you about."

She made no answer to this, but suddenly stifled, he heard a concealed, an almost smothered laugh, soft and furry as the passage of a mouse.

"Go back to your friends," he said, "I want to sleep."

The mouse darted again, out of one corner into another. "They've been gone for hours."

He waited for her, tired, but not without curiosity, and instead of thinking of how much he loved her, he thought of the city, crowded and immense, leaning over the wave-tossed seas, just as the mind, shattered with light, leans into the dark future. He thought of the women he had known in his life, and how even with love, and, in truth, especially with love, as with the utmost convictions of the abstract mind, with truth, there was in every situation a practical moment when the future was seen to have begun because it had already happened — an action, that marvelous gift of nature to the desiring mind.